ONE FOR MY ENEMY

OLIVIE BLAKE

ONE FOR MY ENEMY

TOR PUBLISHING GROUP
NEW YORK

ONE FOR MY ENEMY

Copyright © 2019 by Alexene Farol Follmuth

A version of Acts I–III was originally published in 2018 by *Witch Way Magazine*.

Interior illustrations by Little Chmura
Endpaper illustrations by lasq.draws

A Tor Book
Published by Tom Doherty Associates / Tor Publishing Group
120 Broadway
New York, NY 10271

www.tor-forge.com

Tor® is a registered trademark of Macmillan Publishing Group, LLC.

The Library of Congress Cataloging-in-Publication Data is available upon request.

ISBN 978-1-250-89243-0 (hardcover)
ISBN 978-1-250-90288-7 (signed edition)
ISBN 978-1-250-88486-2 (ebook)

Our books may be purchased in bulk for promotional, educational, or business use. Please contact your local bookseller or the Macmillan Corporate and Premium Sales Department at 1-800-221-7945, extension 5442, or by email at MacmillanSpecialMarkets@macmillan.com.

First Tor Edition: 2023

Printed in the United States of America

0 9 8 7 6 5 4 3 2 1

for **LITTLE CHMURA**,
who spirits my daydreams to life,

in exchange for the rare gift you so readily share,
and for the magic you have given me:

Here, have this book.

ONE FOR MY ENEMY

CONTENTS

THE CHARACTERS

THE FEDOROVS

KOSCHEI *the* DEATHLESS, *sometimes called* Lazar, *the Fedorov family patriarch,*

DIMITRI, *called* Dima, *the eldest of the Fedorov brothers,*

ROMAN, *called* Roma *or* Romik, *the second of the Fedorov brothers,*

LEV, *sometimes called* Leva, Lyova, *or occasionally* Solnyshko, *the youngest of the Fedorov brothers.*

THE ANTONOVAS

BABA YAGA, *sometimes called* Marya, *the Antonova family matriarch,*

MARYA, *named for her mother and called* Masha *or sometimes* Mashenka, *the eldest of the Antonova sisters,*

EKATERINA, *called* Katya, *twin sister of Irina, together the second of the Antonova sisters,*

IRINA, *sometimes* Irka, *twin sister of Ekaterina, together the second of the Antonova sisters,*

YELENA, *called* Lena *or sometimes* Lenochka, *the fourth of the Antonova sisters,*

LILIYA, *sometimes called* Lilenka, *the fifth of the Antonova sisters,*

GALINA, *called* Galya *or sometimes* Galinka, *the sixth of the Antonova sisters,*

ALEXANDRA, *exclusively called* Sasha *or sometimes* Sashenka, *the youngest of the Antonova sisters.*

THE OTHERS

IVAN, *the bodyguard of Marya Antonova,*

ERIC TAYLOR, *a classmate of Sasha Antonova,*

LUKA, *the son of Katya Antonova,*

STAS MAKSIMOV, *the husband of Marya Antonova,*

the TAQRIAQSUIT, *shadow creatures controlled by Koschei,*

ANTONOV, *the deceased husband of Baba Yaga,*

BRYNMOR ATTAWAY, *often called* The Bridge, *the half-fae informant of Marya Antonova,*

ANNA FEDOROV, *the deceased wife of Koschei the Deathless,*

RAPHAEL SANTOS, *a property manager in Koschei's employ,*

JONATHAN MORONOE, *an influential Borough witch from Brooklyn,*

and THE WITCHES' BOROUGHS, *the governing body of magical New York.*

SCENE: New York City, New York; Now.

THE PROLOGUE

Many things are not what they appear to be. Some things, though, try harder.

Baba Yaga's Artisan Apothecary was a small store in Lower Manhattan that had excellent (mostly female) Yelp reviews and an appealing, enticing storefront. The sign, itself a bit of a marvel in that it was *not* an elegantly backlit sans serif, carried with it a fanciful sense of whimsy, not unlike the brightly colored bath bombs and luxury serums inside. The words "Baba Yaga" were written in sprawling script over the carved shape of a mortar and pestle, in an effort to mimic the Old World character herself.

In this case, to say the store was not what it appeared was an understatement.

I just love it here, one of the Yelp reviews exclaimed. *The products are all wonderful. The store itself is small and its products change regularly, but all of them are excellent. Duane Reade has more if you're looking for the typical drugstore products, but if you're looking for the perfect handmade scented candle or a unique gift for a friend or coworker, this would be the place to go.*

The hair and nails supplements made my pitiful strands twice as long in less than a year! one reviewer crooned. *I swear, this place is magic!*

Customer service is lovely, which is such a rarity in Manhattan, one reviewer contributed. *I've never met the owner but her daughters (one or two of which are usually around to answer questions) are just the most beautiful and helpful young women you'll ever meet.*

The store is never very full, one reviewer commented blithely, *which is odd, considering it seems to do fairly well . . .*

This store is an absolute gem, said another, *and a well-kept secret.*

And it was a secret.

A secret within a secret, in fact.

Elsewhere, southeast of Yaga's apothecary on Bowery, there was an antique furniture store called Koschei's. This store, unlike Baba Yaga's, was by appointment only.

The storefront always looks so cool, but the place is never open, one reviewer complained, giving the store three stars. *On a whim, I tried calling to arrange a time to see one of the items in the window but couldn't get in touch with anyone for weeks. Finally, a young guy (one of the owner's sons, I believe) brought me in for about twenty minutes, but almost everything in the store was already reserved for private clients. That's fine, obviously, but still, it would have been nice to know in advance. I fell in love with a small vintage chest but was told it wasn't for sale.*

REALLY EXPENSIVE, contributed another reviewer. *You're better off going to Ikea or CB2.*

This store is sort of creepy-looking, another reviewer added. *There always seem to be weirdos moving things in and out of it, too. All the stuff looks really cool, but the store itself could use a face-lift.*

It's almost like they don't want customers, groused a more recent review.

And they were right; Koschei did not want customers.

At least, not the kind of customer who was looking for him on Yelp.

ACT I

MADNESS MOST DISCREET

Love is a smoke made with the fume of sighs,
Being purg'd, a fire sparkling in lovers' eyes;
Being vex'd, a sea nourish'd with loving tears.
What is it else? A madness, most discreet,
A choking gall, and a preserving sweet.

Romeo to Benvolio,
Romeo and Juliet (Act I, Scene 1)

I. 1

(Enter the Fedorov Sons.)

The Fedorov sons had a habit of standing like the points of an isosceles triangle.

At the furthest point forward there was Dimitri, the eldest, who was the uncontested heir; the crown prince who'd spent a lifetime serving a dynasty of commerce and fortune. He typically stood with his chin raised, the weight of his invisible crown borne aloft, and had a habit of rolling his shoulders back and baring his chest, unthreatened. After all, who would threaten him? None who wished to live a long life, that was for certain. The line of Dimitri's neck was steady and unflinching, Dimitri himself having never possessed a reason to turn warily over his shoulder. Dimitri Fedorov fixed his gaze on the enemy and let the world carry on at his back.

Behind Dimitri, on his right: the second of the Fedorov brothers, Roman, called Roma. If Dimitri was the Fedorov sun, Roman was the moon in orbit, his dark eyes carving a perimeter of warning around his elder brother. It was enough to make a man step back in hesitation, in disquietude, in fear. Roman had a spine like lightning, footfall like thunder. He was the edge of a sharp, bloodied knife.

Next to Roman stood Lev, the youngest. If his brothers were planetary bodies, Lev was an ocean wave. He was in constant motion, a tide that pulsed and waned. Even now, as he stood behind Dimitri, his fingers curled and uncurled reflexively at his sides, his thumb beating percussively against his thigh. Lev had a keen sense of danger, and he perceived it now, sniffing it out in the air and letting it creep between the sharp blades of his shoulders. It got under his skin, under his bones, and gifted him a shiver.

Lev had a keen sense of danger, and he was certain it had just walked in the room.

"Dimitri Fedorov," the woman said, a name that, from her lips, might have been equally threatening aimed across enemy lines or whispered between silken sheets. "You still know who I am, don't you?"

Lev watched his brother fail to flinch, as always.

"Of course I know you, Marya," Dimitri said. "And you know me, don't you? Even now."

"I certainly thought I did," Marya said.

She was a year older than Dimitri, or so Lev foggily recalled, which would have placed her just over the age of thirty. Flatteringly put, she didn't remotely look it. Up close, Marya Antonova, whom none of the Fedorov brothers had seen since Lev was a child, had retained her set of youthful, pouty lips, as fitting to the Maybelline billboard outside their Tribeca loft as to her expression of measured interest, and the facial geography typically fallen victim to age— lines that might have begun expelling around her eyes or mouth, furrowed valleys that might have emerged along her forehead— had escaped even the subtlest indications of time. Every detail of Marya's appearance, from the tailored lines of her dress to the polished leather of her shoes, had been marked by intention, pressed and spotless and neat, and her dark hair fell in meticulous 1940s waves, landing just below the sharp line of her collarbone.

She removed her coat in yet another episode of deliberation, establishing her dominion over the room and its contents via the simple handing of the garment to the man beside her.

"Ivan," she said to him, "will you hold this while I visit with my old friend Dima?"

"Dima," Dimitri echoed, toying with the endearment as the large man beside Marya Antonova carefully folded her coat over his arm, as fastidious as his employer. "Is this a friendly visit, then, Masha?"

"Depends," Marya replied, unfazed by Dimitri's use of her

own diminutive and clearly in no hurry to elaborate. Instead, she indulged a lengthy, scrutinizing glance around the room, her attention skating dismissively over Roman before landing, with some degree of surprise, on Lev.

"My, my," she murmured. "Little Lev has grown, hasn't he?"

There was no doubt that the twist of her coquette's lips, however misleadingly soft, was meant to disparage him.

"I have," Lev warned, but Dimitri held up a hand, calling for silence.

"Sit, Masha." He beckoned, gesturing her to a chair, and she rewarded him with a smile, smoothing down her skirt before settling herself at the chair's edge. Dimitri, meanwhile, took the seat opposite her on the leather sofa, while Roman and Lev, after exchanging a wary glance, each stood behind it, leaving the two heirs to mediate the interests of their respective sides.

Dimitri spoke first. "Can I get you anything?"

"Nothing, thank you," from Marya.

"It's been a while," Dimitri noted.

The brief pause that passed between them was loaded with things neither expressed aloud nor requiring explanation. That time had passed was obvious, even to Lev.

There was a quiet exchange of cleared throats.

"How's Stas?" Dimitri asked casually, or with a tone that might have been casual to some other observer. To Lev, his brother's uneasy small talk was about as ill-fitting as the idea that Marya Antonova would waste her time with the pretense of saccharinity.

"Handsome and well hung, just as he was twelve years ago," Marya replied. She looked up and smiled pointedly at Roman, who slid Lev a discomfiting glance. Stas Maksimov, a Borough witch and apparent subject of discussion, seemed about as out of place in the conversation as the Borough witches ever were. Generally speaking, none of the three Fedorovs ever lent much thought to the Witches' Boroughs at all, considering their father's occupation meant most of them had already been in the family's pocket for decades.

Before Lev could make any sense of it, Marya asked, "How's business, Dima?"

"Ah, come on, Masha," Dimitri sighed, leaning back against the sofa cushions. If she was bothered by the continued use of her childhood name (or by anything at all, really) she didn't show it. "Surely you didn't come all the way here just to talk business, did you?"

She seemed to find the question pleasing, or at least inoffensive. "You're right," she said after a moment. "I didn't come exclusively to *talk* business, no. Ivan." She gestured over her shoulder to her associate. "The package I brought with me, if you would?"

Ivan stepped forward, handing her a slim, neatly packaged rectangle that wouldn't have struck Lev as suspicious in the slightest had it not been handled with such conspicuous care. Marya glanced over it once herself, ascertaining something unknowable, before turning back to Dimitri, extending her slender arm.

Roman twitched forward, about to stop her, but Dimitri held up a hand again, waving Roman away as he leaned forward to accept it.

Dimitri's thumb brushed briefly over Marya's fingers, then retracted.

"What's this?" he asked, eyeing the package, and her smile curled upward.

"A new product," Marya said, as Dimitri slid open the thick parchment to reveal a set of narrow tablets in plastic casing, each one like a vibrantly colored aspirin. "Intended for euphoria. Not unlike our other offerings, but this one is something a bit less delicate; a little sharper than pure delusion. Still, it's a hallucinogen with a hint of . . . *novelty,* if you will. Befitting the nature of our existing products, of course. Branding," she half explained with a shrug. "You know how it goes."

Dimitri eyed the tablet in his hand for a long moment before speaking.

"I don't, actually," he replied, and Lev watched a muscle jump near his brother's jaw; another uncharacteristic twitch of unease, along with the resignation in his tone. "You know Koschei doesn't involve himself in any magical intoxicants unless he's specifically commissioned to do so. This isn't our business."

"Interesting," Marya said softly, "very interesting."

"Is it?"

"Oh, yes, very. In fact, I'm relieved to hear you say that, Dima," Marya said. "You see, I'd heard some things, some very terrible rumors about your family's latest ventures"—Lev blinked, surprised, and glanced at Roman, who replied with a warning head shake—"but if you say this isn't your business, then I'm more than happy to believe you. After all, our two families have so wisely kept to our own lanes in the past, haven't we? Better for everyone that way, I think."

"Yes," Dimitri replied simply, setting the tablets down. "So, is that all, Masha? Just wanted to boast a bit about your mother's latest accomplishments, then?"

"Boast, Dima, really? Never," Marya said. "Though, while I'm here, I'd like you to be the first to try it, of course. Naturally. A show of good faith. I can share my products with you without fear, can't I? If you're to be believed, that is," she mused, daring him to contradict her. "After all, you and I are old friends. Aren't we?"

Dimitri's jaw tightened again; Roman and Lev exchanged another glance. "Masha—"

"*Aren't* we?" Marya repeated, sharper this time, and now, again, Lev saw the look in her eyes he remembered fearing as a young boy; that icy, distant look her gaze had sometimes held on the rare occasions when he'd seen her. She'd clearly learned to conceal her sharper edges with whatever mimicry of innocence she had at her disposal, but that look, unlike her falser faces, could never be disguised. For Lev, it had the same effect as a bird of prey circling overhead.

"Try it, Dima," Marya invited, in a voice that had no exit; no room to refuse. "I presume you know how to consume it?"

"Masha," Dimitri said again, lowering his voice to its most diplomatic iteration. "Masha, be reasonable. Listen to me—"

"Now, Dima," she cut in flatly, the pretense of blithe civility van-
ishing from the room.

It seemed that, for both of them, the playacting had finally
ceased, the consequences of something unsaid dragging the conversation to a sudden détente, and Lev waited impatiently for his
brother to refuse. Refusal seemed the preferable choice, and the ra-
tional one; Dimitri did not typically partake in intoxicants, after all,
and such a thing would have been easy to decline. *Should* have been
easy to decline, even, as there was no obvious reason to be afraid.

(No reason, Lev thought grimly, aside from the woman who sat
across from them, some invisible threat contained within each of
her stiffened hands.)

Eventually, though—to Lev's stifled dismay—Dimitri nodded
his assent, taking up a lilac-colored tablet and eyeing it for a moment between his fingers. Beside Lev, Roman twitched forward almost imperceptibly and then forced himself still, dark eyes falling
apprehensively on the line of their brother's neck.

"Do it," Marya said, and Dimitri's posture visibly stiffened.

"Masha, give me a chance to explain," he said, voice low with
what Lev might have called a plea had he believed his brother capable of pleading. "After everything, don't you owe me that much? I
understand you must be angry—"

"Angry? What's to be angry about? Just try it, Dima. What
would you possibly have to fear? You already assured me we were
friends, didn't you?"

The words, paired with a smile so false it was really more of
a grimace, rang with causticity from Marya's tongue. Dimitri's
mouth opened, hesitation catching in his throat, and Marya leaned
forward. "Didn't you?" she repeated, and this time, Dimitri openly
flinched.

"Perhaps you should go," Lev blurted thoughtlessly, stepping
forward from his position flanking his brother behind the sofa, and
at that, Marya looked up, her gaze falling curiously on him as she

proceeded to rapidly morph and change, resuming her sweeter dis-position as if just recalling Lev's presence in the room.

"You know, Dima," she said, eyes still inescapably on Lev, "if the Fedorov brothers are anything like the Antonova sisters, then it would be very wrong of me to not reward them equally for our *friendship*. Perhaps we should include Lev and Roma in this," she mused, slowly returning her gaze to Dimitri's, "don't you think?"

"No," Dimitri said, so firmly it halted Lev in place. "No, they have nothing to do with this. Stay back," he said to Lev, turning around to deliver the message clearly. "Stay where you are, Lev. Roma, keep him there," he commanded in his deepened crown-prince voice, and Roman nodded, cutting Lev a cautioning glare.

"Dima," Lev said, senses all but flaring with danger now. "Dima, really, you don't have to—"

"Quiet," Marya said, and then, save for her voice, the room fell absent of sound. "You assured me," she said, eyes locked on Dimi-tri's now. It was clear that, for her, no other person of consequence existed in the room. "Spare me the indignity of recounting the rea-sons we both know you'll do as I ask."

Dimitri looked at her, and she back at him.

And then, slowly, Dimitri resigned himself to parting his lips, placing the tablet on the center of his tongue, and tilting his head back to swallow as Lev let out a shout no one could hear.

"It's a new product, as I said," Marya informed the room, brush-ing off her skirt. "Nothing any different from what will eventually come to market. The interesting thing, though, about our intoxi-cants," she said, observing with quiet indifference as Dimitri shook himself slightly, dazed, "is that there are certain prerequisites for enjoyment. Obviously we have to build in some sort of precaution-ary measures to be certain who we're dealing with, so there are some possible side effects. Thieves, for example," she murmured softly, her eyes still on Dimitri's face, "will suffer some unsavory reactions. Liars, too. In fact, anyone who touches our products without the exchange of currency from an Antonova witch's hands will find them . . . slightly less pleasant to consume."

Dimitri raised a hand to his mouth, retching sharply into his palm for several seconds. After a moment spent collecting himself, he lifted his head with as much composure as he could muster, shakily dragging the back of his hand across his nose.

A bit of blood leaked out, smearing across the knuckle of his index finger.

"Understandably, our dealers wish to partake at times, so to protect them, we give them a charm they wear in secret. Of course, you likely wouldn't know that," Marya remarked, still narrating something with a relevance Lev failed to grasp. "Trade secret, isn't it? That it's quite dangerous to try to sell our products without our express permission, I mean. Wouldn't want someone to know that in advance, obviously, or our system would very well collapse."

Dimitri coughed again, the reverberation of it still silent. Steadily, blood began to pour freely from his nose, dripping into his hands and coating them in a viscous, muddied scarlet streaked with black. He sputtered without a sound, struggling to keep fluid from dripping into his throat while his chest wrenched with coughs.

"We have a number of informants, you know. They're very clever, and very well concealed. Unfortunately, according to one of them, *someone*," Marya murmured, "has been selling our intoxicants. Buying them from us, actually, and then turning around to sell them at nearly quadruple the price. Who would do that, I wonder, Dima?"

Dimitri choked out a word that might have been Marya's name, falling forward onto his hands and knees and colliding with the floor. He convulsed once, then twice, hitting his head on the corner of the table and stumbling, and Lev called out to his brother with dismay, the sound of it still lost to the effects of Marya's spell. She was the better witch by far—their father had always said so, speaking of Marya Antonova even from her youth as if she were some sort of Old World demon, the kind of villainess children were warned to look for in the dark. Still, Lev rushed forward, panicked, only to feel his brother Roman's iron grip at the back of his collar, pinning him in place as Dimitri struggled to rise and then collapsed forward again, blood pooling beneath his cheek where he'd fallen to the floor.

"This hurts me, Dima, it really does," Marya sighed, expressionless. "I really did think we were friends, you know. I certainly thought you could be trusted. You were always so upstanding when we were children—and yes, true, a lot can happen in a decade, but still, I really never thought we'd be . . . *here.*" She sighed again, shaking her head. "It pains me, truly, as much as it pains you. Though perhaps that's insensitive of me," she amended softly, watching Dimitri gasp for air; her gaze never dropped, not even when he began to jerk in violent tremors. "Since it does seem to be paining you a great deal."

Lev felt his brother's name tear from his lungs again, the pain of it raking at his throat until finally, finally, Dimitri fell rigidly still. By then, the whole scene was like a portrait, gruesomely Baroque; from the crumpled malformation of his torso, one of Dimitri's arms was left outstretched, his fingers unfurled toward Marya's feet.

"Well," exhaled Marya, rising from the chair. "I suppose that's that. Ivan, my coat, please?"

At last, with their brother's orders fulfilled, Roman released Lev, who in turn flung himself toward Dimitri. Roman looked on, helpless and tensed, as Lev checked for a pulse, frantically layering spells to keep what was left of his brother's blood unspilled, to compel his princely lungs to motion. Dimitri's breathing was shallow, the effort of his chest rapidly fading, and in a moment of hopelessness, Lev looked blearily up at Marya, who was pulling on a pair of black leather gloves.

"Why?" he choked out, abandoning the effort of forethought.

He hadn't even bothered with surprise that his voice had finally been granted to him, and she, similarly, spared none at the question, carefully removing a smudge from her oversized sunglasses before replacing them on her face.

"Tell Koschei that Baba Yaga sends her love," she said simply.

Translation: *Your move.*

Then Marya Antonova turned, beckoning Ivan along with her, and let the door slam in her wake.

I. 2

(What People Can See.)

"Alexandra Ant—ah, sorry, Anto-*no*-va?"

"Hi, that's me," Sasha said quickly, raising her hand in the air. "It's An-*ton*-ova. I go by Sasha."

"Ah, okay, cool," the TA said, obviously failing to commit it to memory. "You'll be with, um." He skimmed the list in his hand. "Eric Taylor, John Anderson, and Nirav, uh—"

"Vemulakonda," someone a row down from Sasha supplied coolly.

"Yes, that," the TA agreed. "Right, so, if you guys just want to circle up and sort it out, you've got about ten minutes left of class. I'll be here if you have any questions," he added, though by then his voice had been drowned out by the sounds of students shifting around in their seats, haphazardly rearranging themselves in the lecture hall.

"Hey," Sasha said, nodding as the other student with the unpronounceable name made his way toward her. He wore his black hair in a dramatic wave up from his forehead, the ends of it feathered like a raven's wing. "Nirav, right?"

"Right, and you're Sasha," Nirav replied. "I like it. *Sa*-sha," he repeated emphatically, baring his teeth a little as he lolled it around on his tongue. "Good name."

"Thanks. Solid branding," she offered wryly, and he chuckled, gesturing over her shoulder to nod as the two others from their group approached.

"Eric," said one, extending a hand. He had his blond hair parted cleanly, as impeccably polished as his dark blue V-neck sweater. "This is John," he added, gesturing beside him to the quiet, dark-skinned student who generally sat some rows behind her. "So, should we plan to meet up and go over the details?"

Perhaps unsurprisingly, Eric seemed to consider himself the leader. "I could do noon tomorrow at Bobst," Sasha suggested, naming the library. "Or, if you guys were up for coffee tomorrow afternoon, I only have class at two, and th—"

"How about a drink instead?" Eric interrupted, speaking almost exclusively to John and Nirav. "Tonight, at Misfit? We can go over the business plan and then work on splitting up the roles."

"A bar?" Sasha asked doubtfully, feeling her expression stiffen as Nirav and John made tentative noises of agreement. "Don't you think that's a little—"

"Brilliant?" Eric prompted, grinning at her. He might have been handsome, she thought, if he weren't so ruthlessly irritating; as it was, she had to stifle a general need to shove him down several rows of the theater-style chairs. "What do you guys think? Maybe around eight this evening?"

Sasha cleared her throat, willing herself not to voice aloud the untenable words *but it's a school night*. "Look, I really don't think—"

"Eight works for me," John interrupted, glancing down at his watch. "Sorry, have to run, got class—"

"Me too," contributed Nirav, shifting his backpack to both shoulders and giving Sasha an apologetic glance that only frustrated her further. "Cool, see you guys at eight, then—"

"Yeah, see you—"

Sasha watched, dismayed, as the other three proceeded to exit the classroom, Eric winking outrageously at her over his shoulder before catching up with the other two. She grimaced, clenching a fist (her mother would *not* care for it, and frankly, in twenty-two years Sasha had never really been the bar-going type), and slowly made her way out of the building, wrapping her scarf loosely around her neck before bracing herself for the late-winter chill.

"Sasha!"

She paused, catching the familiar sound of her eldest sister's voice, and turned to find Marya walking in her direction, their heftily bundled two-year-old nephew Luka's mittened hand clutched tightly in hers. Luka was their sister Katya's son, but as often seemed the case these days, Marya was stooped slightly to walk beside him, unwilling to release Luka's insistent fingers but equally unwilling to stop wearing her signature stiletto heels.

"Sasha," Marya called again, hoisting Luka up in her arms and breaking into a brisk trot to catch up with Sasha, sitting the toddler on one elegantly tailored hip. Immediately, Luka wrapped his chubby fingers around a clump of her hair and gave what appeared to be a painful tug, though Marya didn't seem to mind. "I thought I might find you here," Marya told Sasha, gently nudging Luka's hand away. "Heading back to the store?"

"Yes, of course," Sasha replied, shivering momentarily before giving little Luka an enthusiastic wave in greeting. "I know the deal, straight to work after class—"

"Are you cold?" Marya asked, frowning at the motion of Sasha's shiver. She shifted Luka to the left side of her hip, beckoning for Sasha's hand with her right. "Here, come here, give me your hand—"

"Don't do magic *here*, Masha, people can see," Sasha hissed, giving her sister an appropriately cautioning glare as Marya reached out, catlike, and snatched at her fingers. "No, Masha—Masha, *stop*—"

"People only see what they want to see, Sashenka," Marya said in her brusque, matter-of-fact way, shifting Sasha's recalcitrant hands in hers and blowing lightly across the tops of her knuckles, enchanting them with warmth. "There. Better?"

"Don't 'Sashenka' me, Marya Maksimov," Sasha sighed, though she did feel much better, as if she'd warmed her palms against a softly crackling fire. One of Marya's specialties—those little enchantments that seemed small at first, the way choosing the right silhouette for a dress or the appropriate table linens for a dinner seemed like a pointless bit of knowledge until it made all the difference. Marya seemed to know as much, giving her sister a smug, berry-tinted smile of victory.

"I'm an Antonova, same as you, *Sashenka*," Marya replied irreverently. "A Maryovna, in fact," she clarified, referencing their mother's name and Marya's own namesake, "though that sounds stupid."

True. And, "Fine." Marya had already resumed walking at her typical brisk pace, adjusting Luka's knitted hat and maneuvering all three of them in the direction of their mother's store. The sudden recollection of their shared destination was Sasha's timely reminder to pick her battles, as she'd certainly have one tonight. "Is Galya working now?" Sasha asked. "I'll need her to cover for me tonight. Just for an hour," she added hurriedly, though there was no mistaking the possibility of investigatory follow-up. As a rule, Sasha didn't go places. (Not Sasha's rule, obviously, but a rule nonetheless.)

"Oh?" Marya asked, curious as Sasha had known she would be. Marya had the same sharply inquisitive eyes that belonged to their mother, only they became softer, more sympathetic when she looked at Sasha, the baby of the seven Antonova daughters. "What's going on tonight?"

"Nothing. Just a stupid group project," Sasha muttered, as Marya arched a brow, unconvinced. "It's for school."

"Ah. Well, Galya won't be happy," Marya remarked. "She mentioned a date tonight, I believe, but you know our Galinka." No one was ever serious for Galya; the whole sequence of dating was more recreational, as far as Sasha could tell. Something Galya did to keep her reflexes sharp. "Lend her that sweater she likes and you'll be back in her good graces soon enough."

Sasha made a noncommittal noise of agreement, distracted with her own troubles. "Well, I guess I'll have to take whatever graces she's got on offer, seeing as I can't get out of it." Marya offered a questioning glance, and Sasha gladly ranted her frustration. "One of the guys in my class is one of those terrible douchebags that will happily shove my ideas out of the way rather than admit I have a brain, I can already tell."

"Ah, can't have that," Marya agreed, glancing down at their nephew, who was listening with rapt attention. "You won't be a card-carrying member of the patriarchy, will you?" she asked Luka. "I'd be frightfully disappointed."

In response, Luka merely babbled incoherently, placing his mittened fingers in his mouth.

"Luka's right, you know. You could use a spell," Marya suggested, nodding sagely at their nephew as if he'd contributed something helpful. "I'm sure Mama and I could make something to enhance this douchebag's listening skills. Or, you know, simply curse him into oblivion so that he's no longer a problem," she suggested as a plausible alternative.

"Well, that's very thoughtful of you, Masha," Sasha sighed, "but somehow, I think I should just get used to it. We can't curse all the men in the world, can we?"

"Not in a single day, at least," Marya replied, "much as I try." She glanced sideways at Sasha as they stopped at a light, observing her in silence as they waited for the many agitated taxis to pass. "I'll cover for you, Sashenka, don't worry. But don't tell Mama it's for school, okay?"

Sasha already knew better than to try—there was a reason Galya went on multiple dates a week while Sasha had to sacrifice a sweater just to complete a class assignment. (Galya would give it back, of course. Eventually.) Still, she felt a twinge of guilt over her sister's generosity. "You've already done your time at the shop, Masha, it's fine. If Galya can't stay, then I can just be a little late, and—"

"No, you can't," Marya corrected firmly, neatly sidestepping a man who'd paused to gawk at her. She gave no indication of having noticed his attention, instead prodding Sasha along at her usual expeditious pace. "You need to be there to make a fool of him, Sasha, or I'll never forgive you. Besides, school or no school, it doesn't hurt to know how to deal with men like him. Heaven knows Mama and I encounter them often."

"Well, I suppose not all men are Stas," Sasha agreed wryly, referencing Marya's husband Stanislav, who accounted for one of the myriad reasons Marya never took interest in anyone pausing to admire her looks. "But thank you, Masha."

"What are sisters for?" Marya replied, shrugging. "Poor Luka," she added, shifting him in her arms so that he stared, wide-eyed, at Sasha, flapping a hand toward her. "He'll never know what it is to have six sisters trying to borrow his clothes."

"Well, maybe he will," Sasha teased. "Katya always says she wants more babies, and maybe one day you'll have seven daughters of your own."

"Please, don't curse me today, Sashenka," Marya said. "I've had a very trying morning, and I simply cannot bring myself to imagine such a dystopian future right now."

It was obviously a joke, but Sasha still caught the sound of her sister's exhaustion. Abruptly, she registered its source. "You met with the Fedorovs today, didn't you?"

Sasha knew little of her sister's day-to-day activities (a consequence of Marya's sheltering more than any lack of interest by Sasha), but there was no forgetting even the smallest mention of their family's primary rivals. Any meeting with the Fedorovs had to spell trouble—theirs was a name rarely spoken in the Antonova house except with undertones of cursing. Sasha had never met any of the Fedorov sons, but she imagined them to be old and cruel-eyed and fierce, like the Koschei the Deathless she only knew from her mother's stories.

"Hm?" Marya replied reflexively, looking lost in thought. "Oh, it was fine, Sashenka, I took care of it."

"I know you took care of it," Sasha said, rolling her eyes. "You take care of *everything*, Masha, you're worse than Mama. But was it okay? I thought you used to know one of the brothers," she suddenly recalled, frowning. "Dima, you said?"

"Dimitri," Marya corrected. "I knew him once, a long time ago, before Koschei and Mama had their little disagreement. We were teenagers, then. Practically children. You were still little then, too." She grew quiet for a moment, resurrecting from her thoughts only once Luka tugged viciously at her hair. "In any case, it's really nothing to worry about, Sasha. The Fedorov brothers won't be bothering us again."

"But what exactly happened?" The night before, Sasha's skin had pebbled with unease at the low tones of argument between her mother and sister from behind closed doors. The Fedorovs were always a touchy subject, but even so, the wrath of Baba Yaga was rarely so acute. "Mama seemed really furious—"

"It's nothing, Sashenka, nothing. Okay?" Marya cut in, and grudgingly, Sasha relented. Marya would not use that tone for anything shy of dismissal. "But let me be the one to bring up your absence this evening," Marya added carefully, "as I don't think Mama will want to hear it."

By that, Sasha understood that the meeting hadn't gone well, and that she very firmly should not press for any details.

"Okay," she agreed. "But are you okay?"

"Me?" Marya seemed surprised. "It's nothing, I promise, just business. Even if you're the one at the fancy school," she added teasingly, "I can handle the occasional disagreement."

That was an understatement. Even with a baby on her hip, Marya Antonova cut an imposing figure. Her magic didn't stop at household enchantments and neither did her methodology for conflict resolution. Though she took great care to obscure the details of her work, it wasn't difficult to know its nature. Still, for Sasha, Marya Antonova was always Masha—the woman playfully biting their nephew's cheek—and never the witch whose name was only ever spoken in whispers.

From the time Sasha was little, she'd known two things with utter certainty: There were monsters, and then there was Masha, who kept them safe.

"Okay," Sasha said again and reached out fondly for Luka's outstretched wave, allowing his chubby hand to close around her magically enchanted fingers.

I. 3

(Life among the Deathless.)

"He's alive, at least," Roman said, glancing over Dimitri's unconscious body where they'd placed it on a cot, crafting a makeshift bedroom within their father's warehouse. "Only a coma." He rubbed his dark brow, shaking his head. "We're lucky. It could have been much worse."

"There has to be more we can do," Lev protested, frustrated with his middle brother's apparent acceptance of the utterly unacceptable. "*Only* a coma? He should be in a hospital, Roma! Not *here*," he grumbled, gesturing around the warehouse, "hidden away like one of Papa's artifacts, practically already in a *box*—"

"He's safest here." Roman's expression was stone-carved with certainty. "Papa's enchantments will hold better here than they would in any hospital room. If Marya Antonova or even Yaga herself comes back to finish the job—"

"Finish the job?" Lev echoed, dismayed. "Why?"

"You heard Marya. Dima was cheating them, taking their drugs and reselling them at a higher cost. Still," Roman muttered, "this was barbaric. This was *savage*, just like those Antonova bitches. I suppose we should be flattered they sent Marya herself and not one of the younger ones to do Yaga's dirty work."

"I still don't understand. Did Dima need money?" Lev asked, barely listening to Roman's bitter rant as he stared at his oldest brother's placidly sleeping face. "I just don't see why he'd do this, it isn't like him at all. Business has been slow for Papa lately, sure, but *this*—"

"We'll have to fix it," Roman cut in firmly, dark gaze cutting sideways to Lev. "We can't let Baba Yaga and her daughters get away with this. We have to strike back, Lev, where it hurts. We have to do to them precisely what they've done to us."

"Right, an eye for an eye, famously the best thing to do in these circumstances," Lev deadpanned, realizing only after he said it that Roman had apparently been serious. "What, really? You want to go after Marya?" Lev asked, stunned. At Roman's silence, he wondered whether to laugh or check for head wounds. "But—Roma, she's a powerful witch, and she's constantly protected—"

"No, not their heir. We're not monsters like them. We'll go after their *money*," Roman clarified—a little too belatedly for Lev's taste, but at least there was a modicum of rationality to the conversation. "You said it yourself—Papa's business has been slow. The more Yaga and her bitches add to their vaults, the more they are a threat to Papa. To *us*. The more they feel they can come for our family, our territory. Leva," Roman said gravely, resting a hand on Lev's shoulder, "we have to do something. We have to make Yaga pay for what she's cost us."

"Roma," Lev attempted uneasily. "I don't know about this. I don't know. More bloodshed? Are you *sure*—"

But there was no denying it when the shadows fell in Roman's eyes.

"Fine." Lev exhaled, abandoning his hesitation once he was certain that his brother would hear nothing of what he had to say. "Then let's go talk to Papa."

I. 4

(First Rounds.)

"All right," Eric said, beckoning for Sasha to sit beside him. "What are you drinking?"

"Uh," said Sasha.

What do you mean Sasha's going out?

Sasha heard her mother's voice echo in her head, the silver streak in Baba Yaga's dark hair seeming to glimmer in the light as Sasha silently paced outside her mother's bedroom, awaiting her permission like a misbehaving child.

Where is she going?

Mama, Sasha's a grown woman, Marya had protested. *If she wants to go out, she can go out. She works hard, you know.*

I know that, Masha. I know my own daughter, don't you think?

"Drink?" Eric prompted Sasha expectantly. "Beer, wine, vodka tonic with a twist of lime, what?"

"Um. Beer's fine," Sasha replied, though she'd probably only had one or two in her entire life. Neither Baba Yaga nor her daughters were given to intoxication. "I'll get it, th—"

"Nah, first round's on me," Eric said, rising to his feet and slipping past her as Nirav sat down, John at his heels.

"*First* round?" Sasha echoed with a groan in Eric's absence, and Nirav chuckled, clapping a hand on her shoulder.

"Come on, we've got to practice this sort of thing if we're ever going to be successful in business school," he said. "I'm told networking is a skill worth developing."

Please. "This isn't networking. It's just a group project."

"Yeah, well, it's also Thursday night," John informed her, "and it's been a long week already." He leaned back in the booth, rubbing his eyes and adding, "Anyway, drinking is definitely a skill."

"Not one we need for entrepreneurial finance," Sasha grumbled under her breath, but she could see she was well past defeated once Eric arrived, beers in hand.

"You two can Venmo me," he said to John and Nirav. "Not you," he told Sasha with a wink, handing her a frothy, golden-colored beverage. "I'm a gentleman."

"I can pay for my own drinks, thanks," Sasha replied drily, accepting the glass. "How much was it?"

"Not telling," Eric said, holding his glass up for a toast. "Cheers, team. To the best group project Professor Steinert's ever seen," he added, and Sasha grudgingly raised her glass in the air, certain it was going to be a long, unpleasant evening.

I. 5

(Shadow Creatures.)

More often than not, the man called Koschei was, unlike the death belonging to the Slavic character whose name he bore, relatively easy to find, though not especially easy to speak with. That depended more on the mood of whoever was guarding the door, or who was doing the seeking.

Koschei wore a number of occupational hats—most notoriously the one belonging to the procurer of rare and sometimes dangerous magical objects—but also those of landlord, moneylender, smuggler, and tightfisted consoler of the unfortunate. If you were a witch in need of someone to appease a powerful enemy on your behalf, you came to Koschei. If you found yourself saddled with the threats of a dangerous bully, you came to Koschei. It was true that the rise of online marketplaces had not been kind to Koschei's empire—easier now to simply hire someone for a task than to owe a valuable favor to a man no Borough witch had ever been able to apprehend—but even so, his was an impenetrable network of debts for good reason.

If you needed something illegal, immoral, or even simply impolite, you would know to come to Koschei, and you could rest assured you need not answer any questions. It would cost you, of course, but if the problem were difficult enough, you would almost certainly come to Koschei—and you would typically find him underground, sitting in his usual chair amid the other creatures belonging to the Deathless.

For most, a visit to Koschei's underground was a rarefied privilege. For the Fedorov sons, it was merely one privilege among many.

The basement that so many would die to enter boasted little of architectural significance. A boxing ring had recently been erected at the center, around which were the usual scattered boxes and the grunting presence of Koschei's inner circle. A single table sat directly beneath one of the narrow windows, streetlight from the sidewalk above obscured by a makeshift curtain.

"Papa," Roman said, taking the seat at the table on Koschei's right as Lev stood silently behind them, waiting. "We need to talk about Yaga."

Koschei, a hardened man in his sixties who had long since ceased being called Lazar Fedorov, lifted his hand silently, calling for pause. He looked out over the boxing ring, narrowing his eyes.

"You see this?" he asked his second son in his quiet voice, gesturing to what looked, in Lev's opinion, like a blurred motion of shadows in the ring. The suggestion of light was glowing dimly from one of the slim upper windows opposite them, and a ray of moonlight, obscured by something no more substantial than a storm cloud, formed the silhouette of a man every time it slipped into the right light.

"Shadow creatures," Koschei explained as Lev squinted into the basement's darkness. "The Inuit call them Taqriaqsuit. Shadow people, who live in a world parallel to ours. They say when you hear footsteps and there are none to be found, it's one of these creatures." Koschei didn't turn toward his sons, nor look away from the ring. "It's very interesting, isn't it?"

Lev didn't ask who had purchased them, or how Koschei had found them, or whether they, like the other creatures Koschei had uncovered, now wished to fight for his amusement. As Lev had understood from boyhood, some things were simply better not to know.

"Anyway, you were saying, Romik." Koschei beckoned, and Roman nodded, turning away from the ring to face their father.

"Retribution," Roman said simply, and Koschei nodded; Lev had always thought his father spoke a language only the elder two sons understood, and vice versa. As far as Lev could tell, Koschei required no further explanation, but Roman went on, "I've heard that Yaga is looking to expand her drugs beyond witches."

That was news to Lev, though he knew Yaga's business had thrived where Koschei's had stumbled. Nothing Yaga did was any less dark—the Borough witches forbade the sale of most intoxicants, classifying them as poisons—but she made better use of the light. Her storefront, the legitimate arm of her business, was immaculate. No one would ever know the assassination of Dimitri Fedorov had been ordered by the cherub-cheeked manufacturer of overpriced hand soaps.

"If I were to guess," Roman continued, "Yaga will target the most obvious group of non-magical consumers."

Koschei arched a brow, expectant. "For her hallucinogens, you mean?"

Roman nodded. "College students," he explained, and Koschei nodded, curling his lips in recognition. "I have a source who tells me she has a considerable deal on the table with a distributor. If we can intercede with the sale, perhaps even expose her to the Witches' Boroughs, then . . ."

He trailed off pointedly, waving a hand toward some presumed path of inevitable destruction.

"Your source?" Koschei asked.

"One of Yaga's own dealers."

Lev blinked, surprised, but Koschei nodded. "A witch?"

"Of course," Roman said, and Lev frowned. It felt like a lie, though he couldn't be sure.

"Good," Koschei said, drawing a hand thoughtfully to his clean-shaven mouth. "No mistakes, Roma. You'll send Lev?"

"Yes, Papa—"

"What?" Lev cut in, alarmed. "Send me to what?"

"Don't ask questions," Roman warned impatiently, but Koschei held up a hand again.

"Let him ask, Romik." Koschei turned his head slowly, the dark eyes that were so like Roman's falling on Lev's with a slow, practiced calculation. "There can be no errors, Lyovushka. Yaga is a wickedly clever woman, and she will no doubt set traps. You must be certain of the time and place; of the identity of her chosen partner. You'll be less conspicuous than Roma," he added, gesturing to his second son, who had never managed to be inconspicuous in his entire life. "You're the right age. You have a young look to you, nonthreatening. You'll blend."

"Blend," Lev said, frowning. "Blend into what?"

This, however, Koschei had no patience for. He turned, facing forward, and beckoned for Roman's attention again. "You think it will be soon?" Koschei asked quietly, and Roman nodded.

"I'm certain of it. We can finally take her down, Papa. Make her pay."

Koschei nodded. In the ring, the shadows blurred, one colliding with the other.

"Start tonight," Koschei said simply, and Roman rose to his feet, shoving Lev toward the door without another word.

I. 6

(Vigilance.)

"Masha," Stas said, his hand coming to rest gently on Marya's shoulder. "Are you feeling well?"

Marya tried again to blink away Dimitri's bloodied face, clearing her throat and returning her attention to the dishes.

"They'll come for us," she said, briskly scrutinizing a charmed saucepan, and then she sighed, abandoning the effort when her husband's grip tightened knowingly around her shoulder. "I don't know if I did the right thing, Stas," she murmured in acquiescence, giving him a reluctant glance.

He shrugged, ever supportive. "You did what you were told. Your mother is far too ruthless to let the insult stand," he assured her, as if that were any reassuring thought. "Besides, I'm sure she intends to do away with Koschei once and for all. This will all be over soon."

Marya turned to face him; she placed her wet hands on his hips, resting her forehead against his shoulder. "We shouldn't discuss things like this," she said quietly, burrowing into the familiarity of his form, the softness of his sweater, the comfort of his presence. "You know I hate putting you in a difficult position."

Stas nodded slowly, taking her fully in his arms. He was a Borough witch, a politician of sorts. Plausible deniability was crucial to his livelihood, particularly considering what the Boroughs knew of his connection to Marya. Secrets, at least in this marriage, were a form of respect.

The Witches' Boroughs were the governing body of magical New York and therefore ideologically sovereign. It was really very simple. Structure was divided along the same geographic lines as the non-magical municipal boroughs. Representation was proportional by population. Responsibilities were voting on public issues; mandates, judgments, forums; laws, and therefore crime and punishment as well. In theory, Stas's elevated status as a Borough witch should have been a pocket ace for the Antonova family. In practice it was less so, at least to Marya. All of it was painfully restricting.

Were there closed-door meetings? Yes, of course. It wasn't populism, not entirely. Not in actuality. Not for a body of mostly rich mostly men who controlled the workings of an entire community, and who could so easily levy a crippling magical tax or simply blacklist anyone who crossed them. Witches had been lawless before and it had nearly brought them to ruin, so the appearance of order was sacrosanct. A witch's magic was one thing—indiscriminate, impossible to quantify, and easy enough to be born with if the circumstances were right—but their power was quite another.

Stas was a Borough witch, but not an Elder. He could be involved in the conversation if he cared to be, but he wasn't a particularly ambitious man. More likely he would serve a lifetime among the other Borough witches, as his father had done, and he would do so quietly. Wealth, status, influence . . . those were things for other men to concern themselves with. Stas Maksimov had aims for a quiet life and a loving wife, and he already had both, as far as he knew. It was far more within Marya's obligations to protect Stas than the other way around.

It was Marya's job, in fact, to protect everyone.

"Have you told Sasha yet?" Stas asked her, his fingers burying themselves soothingly in her hair.

Marya closed her eyes.

"No," she confessed to his sweater, muffling the sound shamefully into cashmere.

"Masha—"

"I don't want this life for her, Stas." A redundant refrain, by then.

"I know you don't, Masha. I know. But she's your mother's daughter, as much as you are. She's not a baby any longer, and she has a family to protect, just as you do."

"I know, but I just—" Marya exhaled. "I want to spare her. She wants more, Stas. She wants so much more than this life, and I—"

"It's Sasha's turn. You made this choice once, however many years ago," Stas reminded her, and again, "You made your choice, and now she'll make hers."

Marya bit her tongue on the many things she couldn't bear to say, letting her husband draw her gaze upward instead.

"And who knows. Maybe," he ventured softly, "with Sasha's help, you won't have to do so much for your mother's business. Maybe then we can start our own family, hm?" He smiled at her, warm and comforting, and briefly, she ached. "Have a little Mashenka of our own, maybe? A little cousin for Luka?"

Stas was enraptured by the thought. Marya, however, was less so.

"I don't think that's wise, Stas." She paused, wondering how many times they could have this conversation in different forms. "We're not safe. I can never guarantee our safety, I never will. Even now, the Fedorovs will come for me, for my sisters, and when they do, how will I . . . how *could* I—?"

She faltered a little, biting down on the unimaginable.

"I couldn't bear the thought of putting our child in danger," she finished uneasily, and Stas nodded slowly, reluctantly, but with softness.

"I love you, Marya Antonova," Stas promised her. "When the time is right, together, I swear, we'll keep our family safe."

She nodded. It was their usual détente: *Someday.*

Not today, but someday.

"I love you," she said as Stas gathered her in his arms, though she didn't close her eyes this time. She forced them to remain open, guarded, sharp; watchful of her husband's back, and vigilant of her sister's future.

Marya Antonova forced herself to remain everything that she did not feel as she blinked away her mind's portrait of Dimitri Fedorov's face. Once with his chin tilted up in sunlight, speaking quietly in her ear, and then again, his face pressed to the bloodied floor as he called out to her, voiceless and pleading: *Masha, Masha, Masha.*

I. 7

(Not Your Business.)

"What exactly do you expect me to do?" Lev hissed at Roman from outside the nondescript pub. It was a typical university-adjacent establishment, nothing special. Busy for a Thursday night only because the bouncer was woefully lax on IDs. "You really want me to wander around trying to buy drugs from college students? I'm not exactly equipped for this task," he growled, realizing the bar's name—The Misfit—was almost painfully ironic at this point, "and just because I *happen* to be the right age—"

"Listen. Our brother is lying in a bed half dead because of Yaga and her daughters," Roman cut in angrily, rounding on Lev with a

glare as if he might have forgotten the circumstances of their out-
ing. "Is it really so much to ask that you make an effort on Dima's
behalf? Just so we can—" Roman broke off as someone stumbled
out of the bar and onto the sidewalk, nearly stepping on Lev's toes.
"So we can be *sure*?" Roman hissed, dropping his voice as two sorority sisters made their way into the pub, one glancing disapprovingly
at Roman while the other paused meaningfully near Lev.

"Roma, this is ridiculous," Lev muttered, avoiding the eye of
the one who'd lingered and aiming a look skyward with a sigh.
For Dimitri, yes, Lev would do anything, far worse and more
troubling than this, but it was hard to consider retributive justice a more effective cure for his brother's condition than modern
medicine—though, Dimitri's ailment was no ordinary one, and
Marya Antonova's placid cruelty *had* left a proverbial taste for blood,
even for Lev. He warred with his milder—weaker, Koschei would
say—nature, gritting out, "*Surely* there is a better way—"

"Well, there isn't," Roman interrupted, giving Lev a shove. "Try
her," he added, gesturing to the sorority sister who'd disappeared
inside the bar, earning himself a grimace from Lev. "My source
said to stick with this block, but be careful. Yaga's informants float
around here—don't draw attention to yourself, Leva. Just stick to
the shadows and keep your ears open."

"Great," Lev muttered. "Blend in, but uncover details. What a
delightfully unspecific task."

"Don't sass me, brother," Roman warned, giving Lev's shoulder
another shove. "Have a drink. Chat up some girls, or boys if you
like." A smirk. "I assume that's not too difficult a task."

"Fine," Lev growled, glaring over his shoulder as he wandered
in, finding the bar already unpleasantly noisy and crowded. It was
perhaps ten o'clock—late enough for a crowd, certainly, but early
enough that it wasn't too sloppy—yet—and he slid a gaze around
with loathing, hoping to keep the evidence of it from his face.

"Hey," he called to the bartender, concealing the motion of his
fingers as he cast a brief attention charm. "Two fingers of Maker's,

please," he requested, shifting beside a young-looking girl who was already stumbling as the bartender nodded, turning away. Lev exhaled, waiting, and then glanced around the room again, getting jostled slightly from an elbow on his left.

"Whoa, sorry dude—geez, you're all over the place—"

"Let go of me," came a clear, distinctly angry female voice. "Eric, I don't want another drink, *I'm fine*—"

Lev blinked, startled, as the ferociously distressed girl whipped around, her dark hair trailing in waves that fell nearly to her waist. Her grey-blue eyes narrowed as she glanced at Lev, clearly unapologetic, but she hadn't dragged her frustration away from the blond whose arm remained loosely around her waist.

"Sorry," the guy she'd called Eric offered to Lev, sparing him a conspiratorial shrug. "We're fine."

Blend, Lev thought as the bartender slid him his drink. How hard was it to blend? Lev glanced around for Roman, who'd thankfully vacated the sidewalk outside the bar, and reminded himself this was all for Dimitri just as the girl began to speak in earnest.

"Look, I've been trying to get you to focus on the project for the last *hour*," the girl spat at the blond, pulling free of his (Eric's) reach and rounding on him with something Lev considered categorical rejection. "I don't want another beer, I want to leave—*now*, if you don't mind—"

"Sasha, come on." Eric's voice, playful enough, was paired with an unmistakable grab of her hand, a motion Lev tried to unsee. "We're just getting started—"

Blend, Lev thought. *This is for Dimitri.*

Just blend.

Just—

"Hey," Lev cut in, unable to overlook the way Eric's fingers had tightened around the girl's (Sasha's) wrist. "She said she wants to leave, man. Let her leave." There, now he could sleep at night.

Immediately, though, both heads snapped toward him. So much for blending.

"Hey, look, bro, stay out of it—"

"I don't need *your help*." The girl, Sasha, was glaring at Lev. "I can take care of myself."

"I'm sure you can," Lev blandly assured her, opting to ignore Blond Eric's stilted protests altogether. "But I really don't know what kind of person that makes me if I just stand here and let you elbow me every couple of seconds."

"I'm fine," Sasha said impatiently. "Just take your drink and go," she advised, gesturing to the glass Lev still hadn't touched. "I've got this."

"Right, sure," Lev said, rolling his eyes as he took a sip of his whisky. "Clearly."

She gave him a final parting glare and spun, heading toward a booth in the corner as the blond, Eric, trailed after her, continuing to insist on something as he went.

"Not your problem," Lev muttered to himself, watching Eric's hand reach out for Sasha's arm again. "Not. Your. Problem." He exhaled grumpily, shifting to take a seat at one of the available bar-stools. Getting in a fight with a tipsy blond who clearly spent too much time on his hair was not an effective method of blending. Besides, the girl didn't want his help. So be it.

Lev took another sip, glancing around again.

The bar was packed with NYU students—unsurprising, as it wasn't far from campus. If Baba Yaga's target demographic was, in fact, college students, this was definitely the place. None of them looked like the type to buy magical drugs, but that didn't make it out of the question. Near his feet, subwoofers thundered with non-descript rap music, impossible to tell at this volume. Ice clinked in his glass and Lev waved a hand, dampening the vibration, before shifting his attention to two of the students standing near him at the bar.

"—not totally useless," one was saying. He was overdressed, wearing a blazer and slacks, while the other wore a NYU hoodie and sweats. "I got some Adderall from him earlier this year. Studying for the LSAT's a bitch, man." The future lawyer made a face, downing his glass as he signaled to the bartender for another. "Hate it."

"Adderall, for studying?" the one in the hoodie drolly replied. "Groundbreaking."

"Hey, we can't all write the next great American novel," the one in the blazer said with a roll of his eyes while the hoodie flashed back a grin. "Some of us need to look over your contracts. And for the record, I'd call you by your last name, only I don't know how the fuck to pronounce it. Hey," the blazer added, picking up the beer the bartender slid toward him, "do you think we should check on Eric? I mean, Sasha's right," he added. Lev's ears unwillingly pricked at the sound of the girl's name. "We need to come up with a little bit more for the business plan before we split up the roles."

"Meh, Eric's just being a drunk idiot," said the hoodie. "Besides, I think Sasha left."

"With him?" the blazer said into his beer as Lev shoved aside the small internal wave of a red flag.

"Maybe, I don't know. I don't see her, or Eric, either—"

"Not your business," Lev grumbled to himself again. The comment about the Adderall was probably (definitely) more relevant to his purposes. *Blend,* he thought, forcing himself not to react to whatever drama was playing out between two people he did not know. Their brothers, unlike his, weren't lying comatose uptown, and therefore they were not his problem. "Not your business, not your business, not your bus—"

"Oh, yeah, he's going for it," hoodie said with a laugh, gesturing to the window where a blond head was bending toward a girl with long dark hair. "What a tool. I mean, I'd say read the room, but who knows. Maybe she's into it."

"Think we should check on her?" asked the blazer. (*Yes,* Lev thought with palpable annoyance. *Yes, obviously you should check on her, come on—*) "She did have a couple drinks and, I don't know." The blazer shifted against the bar with obvious discomfort. "I don't think she's really the drinking type."

"Nah, it's fine," hoodie said, shrugging. "She's a big girl. She can handle it."

Lev waited for the other one to argue. (Dimitri, he reminded himself. This was for *Dimitri,* and anyway, surely the blazer had good instincts, he wouldn't just—)

"Yeah, you're probably right," said the apparently useless future lawyer.

"Goddamn it," Lev swore, slamming the glass down on the bar and startling both students before heading outside, groaning furiously as he went.

I. 8

(Precautionary Measures.)

"Let *go* of me," Sasha seethed again, turning her head away as Eric tried to coax her back. He was insisting (once again) on something like the importance of their project—or, less flatteringly, her alleged inability to be reasonable. "I said *let go*—"

"Hey." The word emerged from somewhere over Sasha's shoulder like a slap in the cold January air. Vaguely, Sasha recognized it as the voice of the guy from inside the bar, the one who'd been so needlessly heroic earlier. "She said to let go, asshole. Does she sound like she's joking?"

Sasha groaned internally, not bothering to face her would-be rescuer as Eric stiffened in baseless territorialism. "Ignore him," she advised, before winding up and punching Eric hard in the nose, remembering at the last second not to tuck her thumb into her palm (something Marya had taught her when she was twelve, just as a precautionary measure) as the bones of his face splintered beneath her knuckles.

"There," she said, shaking out her fist as Eric doubled over, howling with pain. "Well, I'm going home. Email me whatever it is you want me to do for the project, I don't care, I'm done with you. And as for *you*," she said, wobbling slightly in her pivot to face the dark-haired, lean-hipped, busybody so-and-so from the bar, "I said I could handle it."

The guy from the bar had frozen, thunderstruck, in the wake of Sasha's casual violence. "I suppose you can," he mused, as Eric let out another groan, straightening with his hand pressed to the bridge of his broken nose. Surprisingly, his hair hadn't held its shape despite the generous hand he took with pomade, which was a pity. Baba Yaga would have something for that—and the bruising, too—but it seemed poor form to follow a sucker punch with a humblebrag, so Sasha turned wordlessly away.

"Come on, Sasha," Eric grunted after her. From her periphery, the thin trail of blood creeping toward his bottom lip was a brief, measurable gratification as she teetered unsteadily down the block. "It's starting to snow, you're going to freeze out here. Let me get you a cab, at least," he was calling at her back, voice muffled into his palm, "or, I don't know, let me take you home—"

"Oh, shut up, you asshat," muttered the guy from the bar, his footsteps beating against the pavement as he hurried to catch up to her. "Hey, um, Sasha," he called out, uncertain. "Just—look, at least give me your hand—"

"What? *No*," Sasha snapped at him, pivoting to face him and then, as a swift gust of wind (or something) blew her off course, promptly swatting him away. "Look, I'm fine, okay? It's just a couple of blocks to the subway."

"Yeah, no," the guy said firmly. "I'm walking you there. Have you seen you? You practically fell in the street just now—though, that left hook *was* impressive," he added tangentially, with an air of being powerless to the admission. "I really did not see that coming. Well played, honestly—"

"While I'm *overjoyed* to receive approval from you, a total stranger," Sasha interrupted him stiffly, "I didn't want Eric touching me and I definitely don't want *you* touching me, so you can just go, thanks—"

"God, you're infuriating. Hold still," he instructed, and reached brusquely for her hands, blowing across the tops of her knuckles. "There," he said, abruptly releasing her as Sasha, who hadn't noticed until that precise moment that she'd forgotten her gloves at the bar, felt a rapid tingling in her fingers, warmth alighting magically through them.

Ah, she thought dizzily. *So, that's that, then.*

She wondered if she should have been surprised, or maybe would have been if she'd been a little less drunk. She remembered, too, that whoever this stranger was, he *had* gotten a drink impressively quickly. Based on that alone, the man was either a witch or a hell of a lay. (Upon closer inspection, Sasha couldn't rule it out. It was too dark to see him clearly now, but it was no wonder that Kappa sorority sister in the bar had been eyeing him the whole time. He was . . . tall. Pretty. Pretty tall. And beautifully man-shaped, which Sasha was given to understand as of this moment was a shape she quite enjoyed, purely as a matter of spectatorship.)

"There. Now you can walk as long and as thanklessly as you want," announced the witch from the bar, jarring her out of her thoughts. "Have a nice night, Sasha, it's been an absolute *joy*—"

"I can do that too, you know," Sasha informed him stubbornly, conjuring a flare of sparks in her palm. "See?" she prompted, watching his eyes widen. "I told you, I can take care of mys—"

"Jesus, what are you—*Come on*," he growled, ushering her around the corner and out of sight from the lingering patrons outside the bar's busy doorway. "Are you *trying* to get yourself a Borough citation? Or chased through the village with pitchforks? I can't tell if this is your average Thursday or if it's just a spicy night," he remarked, partly to himself.

"I'm just saying," Sasha said, shoving him away. "I would have taken care of Eric myself. Could have turned him into a goat, really, if I'd been so inclined."

"Right, so TBD on the pitchforks." The man (boy? he looked her age, but carried himself much more forcefully) shook his head and was something like half laughing, the corners of his mouth quirking upward seemingly against his will. "A goat, though, really? Something smaller, I would think. Something to crush underfoot, like a bug."

"Well, you took that to a dark place," Sasha informed him, swaying slightly. "Anything to sober up?" she asked hopefully, grimacing. "I've never had to use a spell like that before."

"Nothing I've got on me," he said in a mildly regretful tone, which she thought was sort of nice. Sympathetic, at least. "I'm Lev, by the way."

"Sasha," she supplied, giving him a bleary-eyed glance. With the moonlight behind him, Lev's face was partially obscured, and she tried to recall what she'd seen of it in the bar—the dark eyes, the cynical shape of his mouth. The motion of his brow and the hair she would have thought was black if not for having seen it change in the light, shifting with the shadows. Yes, the Kappa had definitely been onto something. In solidarity, Sasha quietly wished her well. "So. You're a witch, then?"

"Not quite as blatantly as you, but yes," Lev confirmed, and shivered. "Seriously, it's cold. Let me walk you home, or to the train. Whatever."

Men, honestly. "I already told you, I don't need you t—"

"I know you don't," Lev cut in, groaning. "You've made that very clear, you don't need me and I'm sure the suffragettes are all very proud, but I can't just let you stand out here. Call it chivalry." Right, so, the very thing she did not want or need. "Do you live far?"

"Yes," Sasha said simply, pivoting to walk away. "Bye, Lev," she called over her shoulder, squinting into the dark for a moment before propelling herself forward. She got halfway to the end of the block before she heard a loud growl rip through the night, followed by the sound of half-running footsteps.

"Listen, I don't know why, but I can't let you leave, okay?" Lev insisted, materializing breathlessly at her elbow. "Just . . . let me assuage my conscience and come with you for a bit, would you? Buddy system. I have shit to do back there anyway," he added, jerking his head over his shoulder to reference the bar they'd just left. "So it'll only be for a few blocks."

There wasn't much variation to the sort of shit anyone ever had to do at a bar on a Thursday night (Sasha obviously exempted). "Meeting someone?" Sasha asked, and Lev scoffed, his attention cutting askance.

"Is that your way of asking me if I have a girlfriend?"

"No." *Men,* honestly. "Gross."

"Gross?" Lev echoed. "That's—I don't know what that is," he remarked, half to himself. "Inaccurate, I hope, but certainly rude, at the very least."

"Oh, shut up. I'm just—" She shrugged. "Not interested."

"Not interested?" Lev replied doubtfully, and Sasha rolled her eyes.

"Are you really just going to repeat things I say all night?"

"I might have to," Lev retorted, "if they continue to be so hurtful."

"Why, are *you* interested?" She wondered what she wanted his answer to be.

"No, I'm not," Lev insisted, "but, you know." His eyes met hers with something she might have called sincerity. It was . . . disarming. Unsteadying, and she was plenty unsteady as it was. "I'd appreciate being given the time to decide."

Sasha couldn't determine if that was a very odd thing to say or not, but either way, she concluded that he seemed to mean it. Satisfied, she shrugged, offering up a tangent instead.

"So, what were you doing back there? Alone," she noted, sparing

him a telling glance, and his mouth quirked again, another smile
working its way out against his will.

"Is it so strange to be alone?"

"Bars," Sasha informed him, "are hardly the ideal locations for
solitude."

She glanced at him, waiting to see if she'd made him smile again.
She had, and now the snow was starting to fall more steadily, crest-
ing regally on his not-black hair.

"Well, it was nothing important," Lev assured her, sliding her
another glance as Sasha hastily averted her attention to the snow
falling on the ground, eyeing the sidewalk's newly powdered
sheen. "What were you doing?"

"Group project." Sasha made a face. "I should have known it was
going to be a disaster when Eric insisted we have it in a bar, but—" She
shrugged. "Was probably going to be a disaster either way, and now
I've punched him." She paused. "Wonder if that'll affect my grade."

"Only in a positive way, I'm sure. He deserved it," Lev said
briskly, and then frowned. "Why are you in college, anyway?
You're a witch," he reminded her, as if she'd somehow forgotten.
"It's not like you need it."

"Well, in a surprising turn of events, pursuing an education and
possessing magic aren't mutually exclusive," Sasha informed him,
stumbling over a crack in the sidewalk and careening briefly into
him, then shoving him away as he attempted to prop her upright.
"Can't you do something about this?" she demanded, gesturing
vaguely to her questionable equilibrium.

"I could, but obviously it seemed more fun to let you shove me
all over Manhattan."

"I don't get out much," Sasha admitted, pausing to press a hand
to her temple, hoping to somehow steady herself that way. "Not a
fan of drinking," she added at a grumble.

"Certainly not like that," Lev agreed, holding her back for a
second as a cab blitzed through the intersection. "Careful," he
warned, and this time, glancing down at where his fingers were

placed delicately on the inside of her elbow, Sasha didn't shove him away. She hesitantly—gingerly—permitted a nod, allowing him to steady her.

When imminent danger had passed, Lev brought his hand down. This time, instead of letting his thumb tap rhythmically against his thigh, he held it still, letting his hand float in the air between them. It seemed a precautionary measure; in case he might need to use it again. In case he might need to be close to her again.

Sasha coughed loudly, shaking herself back to reality.

"I've got it from here," she informed Lev once they'd crossed the street, gesturing ambiguously over her shoulder. "Subway's just a few streets over and I'm fine, I promise. Thanks for your, um. Help, or whatever—"

"My help 'or whatever'?" Lev echoed, scoffing, "Nice, Sasha. Real nice."

"Look," she sighed impatiently, "as I'm pretty sure I've mentioned, I'm *fine*—"

"Right, extremely fine," he muttered, "which is totally obvious, considering you were almost just run over by a taxi—"

"—and I really think you're overestimating the actual work you've put into the situation," Sasha continued. "I mean sure, it's nice and all, I guess, assuming you're not just trying to hit on me—"

"—I'm genuinely trying to save your life," Lev snapped, "but if that's not immediately obvious, then I really don't know what I'm supposed to do about it—"

"—and look, anyway, my sister would kill me if she saw you with me; or, I don't know, at least have eight thousand questions, so—"

"—should really just let you fall into the street, considering how badly you seem to want to do that—"

"—just too many questions, honestly, it's hardly worth it—"

"—don't know why I'm still here, I guess I should really just—"

"—you should really probably—"

"—*go*," they finished in unison, and Sasha made the mistake of looking up, catching Lev's gaze as it fell on hers in the same motion, with the same sharp intake of breath, the two of them shivering synchronistically in the cold. His hair was dusted in flakes of snow, his head still uncovered (had he ever been wearing a hat? Evidently not; what a gallant idiot) and despite her memory of his constant motion, the twitching of his shoulders and the shifting of his expression, he was standing still now.

He was *holding her* still, she realized, one of his hands carefully propped under her forearm from the motion of turning her toward him, and she blinked, registering the feeling of his fingers pressing into her winter coat.

"Are you cold?" she asked him, and he cleared his throat.

"Freezing," he assured her, and she nodded gravely, reaching up to brush her charmed fingers across his lips. She waited for a moment, drawing the tip of her index finger back and forth along the line of his mouth, until finally his lips parted, his breath warm and tinged with a smoky hint of whisky.

"This," he said, her fingers still hovering above his lips, "is what they call mixed messages, Sasha."

She blinked, startled, and drew her hand away. "Right." She exhaled. "Right, of course, sorry, I was just, I wasn't—"

"Oh, hell," Lev rumbled softly, and before Sasha could respond, he had pulled her into him, wrapping one arm around her waist to slide his free hand beneath her jaw, tilting her face up toward his. He leaned close, pausing a matter of breaths from her lips, and then he stayed there, his nose poised delicately alongside hers. She felt his swift exhalation like a breeze against her cheek, the pounding of his heart visible beneath the line of his throat.

The implication was clear; he'd come as close as he was going to. He'd come close enough to imagine her, to taste the proximity of her in the air between them, but no closer—that was up to her. She paused for a moment in the stillness, in the paralysis between motions, in the cliff edge between what was and what could be, and for a pulse or two of time she simply luxuriated there, feeling the warmth of his breath against her lips and thinking, foolishly, that she could be satisfied with the magnificence of waiting—until she felt sure, as steadily as his heart thudding beneath her hand, that she could no longer stand the distance.

She brushed her lips against the side of his mouth, hesitant, and then pushed up on her toes, colliding with him. He steadied her for a moment before helplessly falling back, yanking her closer as he reached blindly for the wall of the building behind him, content to let brick and stone do the work of keeping them upright. It felt like drama of the vastest heights, his kiss the overture of all the greatest operas—the summit of every landscape's peak, a rush of tides and fates and furies—and she melted in his arms, warmed by more than just the spell at the tips of her fingers.

Almost immediately (his back shoved against the wall, her fingers in his hair, his hands on her waist and then up-up-*up* to the line of her neck, hands fumbling under coats and *oh oh oh*) it was much, much too much. Sasha wasn't wholly inexperienced; she knew enough (and had certainly been warned by her older sisters six times over) to know that when a kiss felt like *this*—like intoxication itself, like madness, so terribly impious and yet so purely, completely divine—it had to be stopped, and quickly, or else it would set fire to her every thought.

"I have to go," she whispered, and felt Lev growl his opposition, his fingers tightening briefly in the moment before he released her, allowing her to step away. He sighed, one hand still stretched toward her, and raised the other to curl it around his mouth, filling it with the arguments he clearly understood she didn't want to have.

"Are you sure you can make it home by yourself?" he asked after a moment, with a gravity that made her want to laugh. He seemed very serious when he wanted to be, even as he twitched with the need to be closer to her—which seemed appropriate, really, considering that she ached with the need to be closer to him.

"Yes, I can, I promise. But I can, um. I can give you my number?" she suggested, and immediately winced, bothered by the eagerness in her own voice. "If you want, I mean. Or not, obviously—"

"Yes, please," Lev said, mortally serious again. He fumbled for his pocket, removing his cell phone, and placed it in her hand, attention never falling from her face while she clumsily typed in her name and phone number.

"Maybe I'll see you, then," she said, locking his phone screen and handing it back to him before stepping away, not wanting to make a fool of herself twice over by falling into his arms a second time. "Or, I don't know, maybe—"

"Sasha." He reached out, pulling her close, and kissed her one more time, both his hands curling around her face and drawing tender lines around the landscape of it; *nose, cheeks, lips,* as deliberately as if he planned to paint her later, and would need to remember the arrangement of what he'd seen.

"See you." He exhaled, forcing himself a step back.

Sasha felt anything she said in return would be a stupid, incoherent mess.

So she tucked her smile into her palm until she could covet it freely later, disappearing around the corner and compelling herself not to look back.

I. 9

(Diamonds.)

"Mama, are you sure?" Marya exhaled, pacing her mother's bedroom. "I mean—are you *very* sure, because I really don't know if she's ready. This expansion, it's not just dangerous, it's *illegal*—if the Borough witches were to find out who was behind it, or worse, if Koschei sends someone to intervene—" She pressed a hand to her forehead, suffering either dehydration or the pounding constancy of stress. "Not to mention The Bridge loves deals enough to make them with the devil himself," Marya muttered, "provided he were compensated well enough."

"I thought you approved of the plan, Masha," Yaga said, arching a brow. "You assured me your informant could be trusted, did you not?"

"Yes, of course." Of course, of course. "I know both his talents and his tricks, believe me, and this is precisely what we've been working toward, but given everything—" She broke off.

"You don't think Sasha can do it," Yaga supplied for her bluntly. "Is that it?"

Silence.

"Or," Yaga noted, "is it that you simply don't *want* her to?"

Marya let her gaze cut away. "There's just no going back, Mama. You know that."

"Yes, I know that. But I never went back, did I? And neither did you." Yaga took hold of Marya's face with one hand, holding it steady, and Marya thought again how Baba Yaga was such a perfectly incongruous misnomer; a clever reference to a witch who was haggard and old instead of sleekly refined, graceful, so that nobody would ever guess a woman this lovely and this shockingly young would choose so unflattering a moniker.

"You know she's the right person to do it, Masha," said Yaga. "She's a student, after all, isn't she? That finally plays to our advantage, and besides, she's older than you were when we started this. She'll have to decide eventually where she stands, just like you did. Just like each of my daughters has."

Yaga paused, and then ventured with curiosity, "I've never seen you falter like this before, Masha."

"Mama, it's Sasha—it's our Sashenka," Marya pleaded softly. "You and I've both protected her for so long, we've been so *careful,* and now is hardly the ideal time. What if something happens to her? Look at this trouble with Koschei, with our dealers . . ."

But Yaga said nothing, her expression did not change, and so Marya trailed off at an exhale, dispelling her anxieties into empty air and abandoning them, unfurling her tougher shell in their absence. She was often relieved that, in moments like that one, their mother could be counted on never to soften, or to permit even a breath or two of fear. Marya trusted that the woman called Baba Yaga possessed no knowledge of what it was to be soft, and so she drew from her namesake, from her mother, and conjured for herself the tireless reminder that fear had no place on an Antonova witch's lips.

"Nothing will happen to her, Masha, if you do not let it," Yaga said in Marya's silence. "Am I understood?"

Marya nodded.

"Yes, Mama," she agreed. "I won't let anyone touch Sasha."

Marya felt her mother step away as she closed her eyes, the familiar smell of Yaga's perfume filling her mind and her memories with the promise of roses even as she tasted blood on her tongue, viscous and coppery and awash in every direction she looked.

"I'm glad to hear it," Yaga said. "And Dima?"

Marya's eyes fluttered open. "What about Dima?"

Yaga watched her closely, and then, finding nothing to arouse suspicion, said, "Then Mashenka, I expect you to tell Sasha the news in the morning."

"Me?" Marya was less surprised than she was troubled. "You're sure?"

"Yes," Yaga said, turning slowly. "She listens to you," she added, half beckoning for the gracelessness of argument, which they both knew she wouldn't get. In response, Marya simply hardened the way she'd been taught; the way she'd been bred.

My daughters are diamonds, Yaga so often said. *Nothing is more beautiful. Nothing shines brighter. And most importantly, nothing will break them.*

"Yes, Mama," Marya promised, nodding once. "I'll tell Sasha what she has to do."

I. 10

(Disquietude.)

Lev rarely used his cell phone. He rarely needed it, seeing as one or both of his brothers was nearly always at his side, but for once, he was very glad to have one. He bit a smile into his palm again, tasting Sasha's kiss one more time, and then dug for the phone in his pocket, hoping to prove to himself she hadn't been a dream.

He wiped a few fallen flakes of precipitation from the screen, squinting as the bright white contact page illuminated itself against the dark, foggy night, materializing across the screen like magic.

Immediately, though, Lev felt a brush of concern that processed in stages. A blink of disbelief, then a shake of his head, then a chill of disquietude, followed by the sensation of utter disembowelment.

Sasha Antonova, the phone said. Clear as day, even as he suddenly hoped he *had* dreamt it.

"Oh, fuck," Lev Fedorov whispered, staring blankly at the screen.

THE STAGING

THE FEDOROVS

The WAREHOUSE of KOSCHEI the DEATHLESS: *A warehouse, unassuming from the outside, filled with treasures within. Warded and locked, always. Here, Koschei keeps his most precious belongings; for example, this is where Dimitri Fedorov sleeps at Marya Antonova's hands, above the little storefront that so few are privileged to enter.*

The APARTMENT of DIMITRI FEDOROV: *Sometimes Dimitri Fedorov is slightly less unconscious. When he is, he lives in a spacious loft, befitting his princely attributes. There is only one room for privacy: his bedroom. It is the only room with a door. Outside of that, the space is open. He prefers to see everything—to observe his kingdom with a single sweeping glance.*

The APARTMENT of ROMAN and LEV FEDOROV: *Roman and Dimitri, as unalike as night and day, were quick to part with one another upon reaching an age when they could do so. Lev, however, prefers time spent in the company of his brothers, and finds Roman easy to live with. Their apartment is split-level, permitting them to occupy different spheres within the same orbit. They cannot agree on a design theme, so there is none.*

The HOUSE of LAZAR FEDOROV: *Sometimes Koschei is not Koschei. When he is not, he comes to his house. It is the same house his wife once occupied, along with his now-grown sons. Not much has changed inside his house for decades, only it's empty now. Such is the case when time goes by: emptiness.*

THE ANTONOVAS

The HOUSE of BABA YAGA: *While her three eldest daughters have moved away, Baba Yaga's house is still home to her young ones. Alexandra, Yelena, Galina, and Liliya still live here under their mother's watchful eye, though the house is different than it was when they were children. Several doors within the house are so securely shut the daughters have rarely or never seen them opened. Baba Yaga's bedroom is one of these places; her daughters, outside of her eldest, have each been inside it less than three times during their lifetimes.*

The HOUSE of MARYA ANTONOVA: *Here, the woman called Marya Antonova lives with her husband, Stas Maksimov. They moved in when she was still quite young, only twenty. Stas dreams of little footsteps in the corridors, imagines laughter ringing from the high ceilings back down to his joyful ears. Marya merely hears threats pounding from the walls at night, creeping in from the violent streets. Marya Antonova doesn't sleep particularly well, either here or otherwise.*

BABA YAGA'S ARTISAN APOTHECARY: *The shop where the younger Antonovas work, and a front for their mother's less public business. The store, like the Antonovas themselves, wears a prettily clever face.*

NEW YORK UNIVERSITY: *As far as Sasha's concerned, this is her place. As for the others, they could be persuaded either way.*

ACT II

FACE OF HEAVEN

Take him and cut him out in little stars,
And he will make the face of heaven so fine
That all the world will be in love with night,
And pay no worship to the garish Sun.

Juliet,
Romeo and Juliet (Act III, Scene 2)

II. 1

(The Matriarch.)

The most important thing to know about Marya Antonova is that she is a single force to be reckoned with, even as she occupies the bodies of two women.

At least, that was how the elder Marya Antonova had always viewed her firstborn daughter.

"Name the baby Ekaterina, after my mother," Marya's husband had said when their eldest was born, but Marya refused.

"You can name the next one," Marya assured him, holding the infant close, and in her head, she had thought: *You can have the next one, and all the ones after that, but this baby is mine.*

Before she became Baba Yaga, Marya Antonova was given in marriage at eighteen years old to a man she only ever called by his surname, Antonov, because he had never really felt real to her. He was already advanced in age (somewhere just south of thirty, which certainly seemed ancient at the time) and though he wasn't unkind, he wasn't particularly soft, either. Antonov was a businessman and a Borough witch, the youngest ever to reach the title of Elder in the Manhattan Borough, but he spent most of his free time concealing his shadier business practices, most of which Marya only came to learn while fading obediently into the background. She brought him his meals, refilled his glasses, and fetched his effects while he met quietly with other witches, never realizing how intently his young wife was listening. He didn't even know she spoke English until well into four years of marriage.

Marya gave Antonov seven children, all daughters. There was Masha—her eldest, named for herself—who sat quietly at Marya's knee, learning everything. Masha's eyes were wide and keen and sharp, and she was every inch the beauty Marya had been; perhaps more beautiful, even, and from the time she was a child, a witch uniquely blessed with rare abilities. Two years after Masha, like clockwork, there were Ekaterina (as promised to Antonov) and Irina, the twins; two years later, Yelena; two years later, Liliya; eleven months later, unluckily, Galina; and then, finally, there was the baby Alexandra, called Sasha.

"I cannot have more," Marya had told Antonov after Sasha, feeling something inside her shift and go wrong during her final birth. She'd always been highly aware of her body, and the moment Sasha had left her womb, she'd felt the last of her fertility go out. "I am sorry, but I cannot give you a son."

"Fine. I'm getting old anyway," Antonov had said, and he was right. Within ten years he finally slipped away, passing unremarkably in the night—or so the story was told by Marya, who wasn't present for her husband's final breaths despite everything that led to them.

Unlike Antonov, Marya had not needed a son. Antonov had been quietly desperate for one, being dated and old-fashioned (and envious of his good friend Lazar Fedorov's boys, particularly the eldest, Dimitri), but Marya knew she had exactly the heir that she needed in her eldest daughter, Masha. The younger Marya Antonova was cunning and witty, careful and meticulous, and of such undeniable beauty that she wore it cleverly as a mask, just as Marya herself always had.

This is the important thing, after all: nobody fears a beautiful woman. They revere her, worship her, sing praises to her— but nobody *fears* her, even when they should. Antonov could not have known that his young wife, who dutifully spoke to him only when spoken to, had been watching all of his movements. She had seen the hazy promise of the business he could build designing intoxicants—had scoffed quietly to herself at the way he merely gave them away for free, mistaking their value. He'd told his friend Lazar (whose alternate identity as the infamous Koschei the Deathless both men had believed, foolishly, that Marya did not know) that together one day they would build an empire, a great enterprise of fanciful witchery. Lazar had nodded solemnly, agreeing, and what

Antonov had missed, Marya had seen: that Koschei would take it for himself if he could.

So, when Antonov's health first began to flag, Marya took it first.

"I need you to do something for me," she said to Masha, who at the time was in the bloom of her youth; as old as Marya had been when she was first married to Antonov. "You know your papa's potions?"

"Yes, Mama," Masha said dutifully.

"We need to sell them," Marya said, and gave Masha a list of names and ingredients. "Can you do this with Mama, Masha? Can you help me? Are you afraid?"

"I am not afraid," Masha had said, and Marya knew it to be true. She and her daughter were one soul in two bodies, and that was how she eventually built an empire.

There had been only one time that Marya ever feared Masha might fail her. Masha was a young girl then, subject to youth's indiscretions; when they took on the shape of a handsome, golden-haired, broad-shouldered boy, even Masha struggled to resist. Marya could see that every time Dimitri Fedorov walked into a room, her daughter's knees went weak, Masha's unbending spine softening instantly in his presence.

Antonov, who'd so long envied his friend Lazar for his eldest son, had encouraged the silly, coltish romance between Masha and Dima, having failed to see in his own daughter what Marya had known so clearly from the start. Marya knew Masha was an heir, a blessing. By contrast, Antonov only saw Masha as a fortunate means to offer the world to Dimitri, to little Dima—who was handsome and bright, yes, but not his biological son, and certainly nothing like Masha. Not at all deserving of Marya's Masha.

Marya waited patiently for her husband to die, watching her daughter fall more in love with Dimitri Fedorov each day, until she could no longer stand to wait.

"I know what you did," Lazar Fedorov said to her in a low voice at Antonov's funeral. "I know what you did, but I won't tell anyone.

In fact, I respect you for it. He was a fool," he added, gesturing discreetly to the coffin. "A fool who was not worthy of you."

"I don't know what you're talking about," Marya replied carefully, catching Masha's eye across the room. Masha stood with Dima, of course. Marya could see his fingers twitching toward her, half stroking the air for lack of holding her. He had enough sense to know that openly touching her was not an option, but still, Marya had seen his fingers brushing the small of Masha's back, or resting too long on her forearm. Small things, certainly, but Marya knew her daughter like she knew her own pulse. Not just anyone could touch Masha. She was full of sharp edges; always a pointy little thing, a rose lined with thorns. Nobody got close to Masha unless she had already let them.

"I could build his business for you," Lazar offered, and Marya glanced at him, wary. She knew that he could—while Lazar's identity as Koschei was artfully hidden to all but her and her family, it wasn't a very well-kept secret what his activities were. She also knew his own wife had died while giving birth to his youngest, Lev, and since then he had only grown more detached from the rest of the Manhattan witches.

"I don't need your help," Marya said firmly, watching Masha's cheeks flush as Dima leaned in, whispering something in her ear.

"Of course not," Lazar permitted, sparing her one of his slow, grim smiles.

Without Antonov there to express his disapproval of her entrepreneurship (something that got in the way, presumably, of cooking his meals and darning his socks), Marya finally rented a storefront. It was expensive, but she brought Masha with her, and between the two of them the landlord was successfully persuaded to lower his monthly rent. The products, too, were designed by Marya with Masha at her side, the two of them working late into the night and nudging each other sharply to keep from falling asleep.

Within months, the store and its elusive owner were a meager success. The more successful Baba Yaga's apothecary became, however, and the closer Marya and Masha came to staking a sizable claim amid New York's magical black markets, the keener Marya's sense that obstacles, whether in the form of dangerous rivals or disastrous repercussions, almost certainly loomed ahead.

That Marya's hand might ultimately be forced against her wishes became inevitable one night when Lazar invited her to dinner. Masha was newly nineteen, Marya herself long past counting. She warily accepted the invitation, wondering if Koschei planned to proposition her for her business.

Or, as it turned out, for other things.

"You're in need of a husband, and I'm in need of a wife," he told her, more Lazar Fedorov than Koschei the Deathless that evening. "We can be very useful to each other, don't you think?"

"I can't have any more children," Marya said, hoping that would dissuade him, and Lazar shrugged.

"I have three fine sons. I hardly need any more."

She hesitated, caught in a precarious position. *I have built this business on my own,* she didn't say. *I do not need you.*

"I'll think about it," she replied, and came home to find that Masha's bed was empty. She waited on the edge of it, staring blankly into the dark until her daughter crept in, tiptoeing quietly and stopping, the heel of her hand pressed to her heart, at the sight of Marya.

"Mama," Masha gasped, immediately remorseful. "I was only—"

"You were with Dima," Marya supplied, as Masha winced. "Yes, I know very well where you've been, Masha, but I'm not upset. Not about this." She paused, and then, "Did Dima tell you his father has proposed marriage to me?"

Masha blinked, frowning, and fell heavily beside Marya. "No," she said quietly, "but I think maybe he doesn't know. He would have told me," she added, her jaw set with certainty, and Marya reached out, touching her thumb to her daughter's cheek.

"Tell me, Masha," Marya ventured carefully. "Is Dima any less of a son to his father than you are a daughter to me?"

Masha hesitated, and then, with a reluctant sort of expectancy, murmured, "No. Dima is as loyal to Koschei as I am to you, Mama."

"So, what would you have me do, then, Masha?" Marya asked her daughter, preserving her own thoughts on the matter. "If I marry the man who is Koschei the Deathless, you and I will no longer have to work so hard. He will give us the money we need to grow the business. He will help conceal us from the Witches' Boroughs." He had kept his own business locked tight as a tomb for as long as Marya had been alive. "You and Dima would be equals—"

"We would never be equals," Masha cut in darkly, brow furrowing. "Not to Koschei. Koschei wouldn't surrender his empire to me or to you, and we'll have built all of this for nothing. He'll make the decisions for us—or worse, make them against us; he'll bury us. He'll take it all and when he's gone, he'll give it to Dima, and then none of it will be yours or mine."

Marya said nothing. She already knew as much.

"But if you refuse Koschei," Masha said slowly, weighing Marya's options for her, "he'll take offense. He'll try to ruin you, ruin us."

"Yes," Marya agreed.

Silence.

"Dima," Masha exhaled, "will feel the offense, too. He'll side with his father. And even if he doesn't—"

Either way, I will lose him, Masha wasn't saying, but Marya knew perfectly what was going through her daughter's mind.

"So, what would you like me to choose?" Marya asked neutrally, and in the pause that followed, she wondered which Masha would come out on the other side. Whether it would be *her* Masha, who had been at her side since birth, and quite literally a piece of her (*her* blood, *her* name, *her* heart), or whether it would be Dimitri Fedorov's Masha, who was all flushed cheeks and tender smiles, melting to a shallow pool of wonder at his touch.

"Whatever you wish for us, I will leave it in your hands," Marya promised her daughter, and waited as Masha contemplated it, her discerning eyes gazing sharply into the dark.

"Don't marry Koschei, Mama," Masha determined finally, her

expression stiff. "Don't accept his offer. We built this. It's ours. We'll see it through."

"And Dima?" Marya asked, half holding her breath.

Masha swallowed hard. "It's over with Dima," she said, turning away.

As a gesture of kindness, Marya had left her daughter alone to grieve. Even as a girl, Masha had always been too proud to cry where Marya could see.

Once Marya had refused Koschei, she'd known there was no going back. She could no longer live a quiet life, nor have any quiet success; she would need to be powerful, so powerful she could not be ignored, and so, with Masha at her side, she remade her reputation from that of Marya Antonova, the quiet, dutiful wife of the Borough witch Antonov, to simply that of Baba Yaga, shrugging on a new and undeniable skin. Everyone knew Yaga's intoxicants were the best, slicing out a piece of Koschei's profits when they turned to her instead, but what could he do? At best, he was only a very apt middleman. Koschei procured products; he didn't make them. He and his sons were strong and powerful and bold, but they were not Marya and her daughters, who were clever and capable creators. Masha and Marya had known this, just as they had known Koschei couldn't turn her over to the Borough witches without his own identity being revealed. They had suspected, too, that by refusing Koschei, they would one day come to overshadow him. They played their hand well enough to trap him, and then took a not-so-quiet comfort from his loss.

By then Marya was many things, but she was still also a mother, and so she understood that the true birth of her empire had not been in the gaining of a fortune but in the loss of Dimitri Fedorov—in the hardening of her daughter Masha's heart. Masha was just as ruthless as Marya, had always been, but now, not even a shadow of fragility remained. Better yet, Masha was as good a witch as Marya, perhaps even better after a time, and fiercely protective of her family. Every witch in the Boroughs knew it was the young Marya Antonova, Baba Yaga's lieutenant, who had made the Antonova sisters the finest

army any of them had ever seen—and it was only because Masha had
buried the girl she'd once been for Dima, leaving her old skin behind.

Marya knew Masha filled the holes in her heart with her sisters,
especially Sasha; the youngest, the baby, the ingenue who was permitted the luxuries of affection that Masha had sacrificed, excising
them from her life. Masha made her sisters her entire focus, so
much so that by the time she met and was shyly courted by Stas
Maksimov, a good-natured Borough witch about five years Masha's
senior, Marya was surprised to discover her daughter had even considered the prospect of marriage.

"Do you love him?" Marya had asked her privately, when Masha
had announced her intent to accept Stas's proposal.

"I love him exactly as much as I wish to," Masha replied. *And no
more than that,* she did not add.

Marya understood. There would never be another love for Masha like the one she'd had for Dima, and rightly so. That love had
made her soft, and like her mother, Masha endured no softness.
There was no version of Marya Antonova that did not detest weakness and so, in choosing Stas, Masha had made a promise to herself
that she would never be weak again. After a few months, Marya
Antonova married Stas Maksimov with her mother's blessing, and
did not concern herself with Dimitri Fedorov at all.

(Not until recently, that is, but that is a story still to come.)

What else is there to know about Marya Antonova, in the end?
Only that now, she is called Baba Yaga, and of all her many trinkets,
her daughter remains the greatest treasure of them all.

II. 2

(To Feign Devotion.)

Much as Lev had hoped the events of the evening would somehow
become untrue, nothing had changed upon his arrival back home.
Sasha Antonova, his phone still inexplicably said, and Lev waited as
Roman stared down at the screen, contemplating its implications.

ONE FOR MY ENEMY

"Well, you'll have to see her again, and soon," Roman determined eventually, and Lev blinked with surprise. He'd been expecting something much more volatile—anger, perhaps, or at the very least, a harsh indication of displeasure. Some inescapable *What have you done?*

"What? Roma, I—"

"This," Roman pronounced brusquely, holding up the screen, "is a highly useful blessing. A stroke of fortune." He handed the phone back to Lev, rising swiftly to his feet. "You have to get close to her, Lev. Get as close to her as you can, in fact. Make sure she turns to you before anyone else."

"But—"

"The Antonova daughters—*all* of them," Roman reminded him emphatically, "are powerful witches who keep to themselves. An opening like this doesn't come along often, Leva. This witch could be the key to besting Yaga, to accomplishing restitution for Dima—she could be the crack in the Antonova foundation. Think about it," he said, resting his dark gaze on Lev. "The mother is controlling, the sisters are ruthless. She must be desperate for love, for romance—right? So, easy. Romance her."

"Roma, I'm not a whore," Lev growled, and Roman shrugged.

"Not yet," he permitted, flashing Lev half a smile, "but I'm sure you could accomplish anything if you put your mind to it."

That, Lev determined, was hugely unhelpful. "You want me to *use* her," he objected. "Even if I wanted to, Roma, it would be difficult. If she's anything like her sister Marya—no, no, forget Marya," he amended frantically, waving a hand. "If she's usually anything like what I saw for myself tonight—"

"Then she'll probably kill you if you cross her, yes," Roman agreed. "So let it feel real, then. As real as you can fake it. Let her think you love her," he suggested blithely. "Let her think you adore her. Will that be difficult?"

Lev hesitated. *Is she ugly,* Roman probably meant, but that was hardly the issue. Sasha Antonova was beautiful. In fact, she was more than beautiful; she was lovely and spirited, infuriating and razor-sharp and *mean*—terrifying, even—and Lev was fairly sure it would be easy to feel devotion.

To *feign* devotion, though, was a completely separate matter.

"You're certain this is necessary, Roma?" Lev asked his brother, grimacing.

Roman gave him an impatient glance of *yes, I told you, haven't I made that clear?* and Lev sighed.

Could he harm Sasha? No, probably not.

But could he *rob* her? Almost certainly, so long as the two were distinct. After all, her sister had nearly cost him his brother. It was a fair payment, Lev thought. A reparation of sorts.

"You swear," Lev said slowly, "this is about the money, and nothing else?"

"Only the money," Roman promised. "She'll be fine."

Lev sighed. "Fine," he determined unhappily. "Fine. For Dima, then, I'll do it."

Roman nodded. "For Dima," he confirmed, and returned his attention to the quaking boxes in the shop's storage room, dutifully carrying on with their father's wishes despite the protests from the creatures inside.

II. 3

(Unacceptable Hours.)

(212) 555-0131: good morning

(212) 555-0131: I know I should wait—

(212) 555-0131: what's the rule? 3 days?

(212) 555-0131: anyway, doesn't matter, because I can't

(212) 555-0131: mostly because it's a stupid rule

(212) 555-0131: but also because I can't sleep

(212) 555-0131: not sure I'll be able to until I see you again but try not to hold that against me

Sasha yawned, blearily glancing at the texts on the screen before jumping at the sound of a knock at her door. She tucked her cell phone into her pillowcase, stowing it safely out of sight before launching herself upright. Too fast—retribution for her hubris was swift and ruthless. She pressed her fingers to her throbbing temples, stifling a groan.

"Come in," she called, and her sister Marya poked her head inside, hair already set in her usual polished waves.

"Did you sleep well?" Marya asked, entering the room to perch at the edge of Sasha's bed as Sasha pulled her hand free from her forehead, grimacing. "Mama says you came home late," Marya noted. "I hope that boy from class didn't give you any trouble last night."

"He did, unfortunately," Sasha said. "But then I punched him in the face."

That earned Sasha a smile. "Good girl. Like I showed you?"

"Of course," Sasha said, unintentionally reaching up for her head again.

For a moment, Marya's brow furrowed, and then she reached out, rubbing her thumb in a slow circle against the center of Sasha's forehead. At once, the tension eased below her temples, the morning light no longer so oppressive, casual birdsong from the window less a personal attack.

"Thank you." Sasha exhaled in relief, but Marya merely nodded, uncharacteristically distracted as she removed her hand. "Was Mama upset?" Sasha guessed, sensing a disruption in her sister's mood, but Marya quickly shook her head.

"No, no, she's not upset. Mama understands some things must be done." A pause, and then, "But she does have a job for you, Sashenka. We," Marya corrected, clearing her throat. "*We* have a job for you."

"Oh," Sasha said, registering the reason for the lack of warmth on Marya's face. "What is it?"

Don't be gentle, she considered saying, but she doubted Marya would be, even for Sasha's sake. There were many different versions of Marya, some more familiar than others, and at the moment, Sasha recognized Yaga's Marya in the room. This was Yaga's lieutenant, her right hand. *Sasha's* Marya—her favorite sister Masha— was waiting in the wings for another time that wasn't related to family business.

"We have new intoxicants," Marya said. "They're designed for non-witches, and so have been crafted with cruder elements to make them look and feel more like non-magical drugs. Like prescription medications, amphetamines, or SSRIs." She paused, and then pronounced with finality, "We'd like to sell them."

"To who?" Sasha asked, tensing apprehensively.

"College students," Marya said, and Sasha flinched, finding her suspicions confirmed. "We need you to be the one to meet with our contact, Sasha."

Sasha. Not Sashenka. This, then, was to be a rite of passage.

"There's already a dealer in place," Marya continued. "He hasn't bought from us before but he has an established clientele, and we'll need to prove we are the preferred supplier to whoever he sources from now. We'll be supplying him next weekend, at a concert." Marya turned her palm over twice, a postcard-shaped flyer for an upcoming show materializing within it. "You'll need to attend."

"Me?" Sasha asked, taking the flyer. "Will he need to know I'm—"

"A witch? No," Marya said, shaking her head. "Better that he doesn't, in fact. You'll take Ivan with you," she added, referring to her personal bodyguard. "The dealer will expect you to come with muscle. In fact, I doubt he would find you legitimate if you came alone. But he doesn't need to know that you're much, much more dangerous than Ivan." She permitted a dry, berry-colored smile. "Are you afraid, Sasha?"

Every Antonova daughter knew the answer to that question.

"No," Sasha said, and at last Marya relaxed, shifting on the bed to sit closer beside her.

"Good," Marya determined briskly, opening her arm for Sasha. "I knew you wouldn't be."

"You won't be there?" Sasha asked as she settled comfortably into the nook of Marya's embrace, and Marya shook her head.

"Too old," Marya explained, gesturing wryly to herself. "Me, Sashenka? I'm ancient."

A lie. Marya's face didn't have a single line or blemish to suggest her age—if not for having brown eyes to Sasha's grey she could easily pass for Sasha herself, in a pinch—and no one on earth would object to her figure. More likely people would recognize her, Sasha thought, and therefore tip off some of the other Borough witches (or worse, Koschei) that Yaga was expanding her market before the deal was finalized. Yaga's intoxicants were unrivaled, of course, but what non-witch would know that? Any magical drug would easily prove more euphoric than Ecstasy, more effective than whatever dose of Adderall or Lexapro the average university student used to cope, but it still had to be proven. Until the deal was settled and the new client list secured, secrecy would be paramount.

Sasha sighed, reconciling her resignation.

"I'd be expelled if I got caught," she grumbled. "Arrested, even."

"No bars could hold you," Marya reminded her. "Nor would I let them. But the easier option is to simply not get caught, isn't it?"

"Easy?" Sasha echoed grumpily, burrowing into her sister's side, and Marya chuckled.

"Oh, everything is easy for us, Sashenka," Marya said, and paused. "Well, not everything," she amended, softening a little. "I won't lie to you, not everything in this life is so straightforward. But we are Yaga's daughters. We earn our right to success by the sacrifices we make. This one, at least, is easy."

Sasha nodded, resting her head against her sister's shoulder, and abruptly, Marya jumped.

"What's that?" she asked, alarmed, and Sasha laughed.

"My phone," she offered apologetically, catching the vibration and pulling it free from the pillowcase. "Sorry."

"It's very early," Marya noted, frowning. "Don't tell me you fell in love with the boy from last night?"

"What?" Sasha asked, startled.

"The boy, the bully. From your class."

"Oh, right." Sasha exhaled, relieved her sister didn't somehow magically know about Lev. That, whatever it was, seemed like a secret she should keep to herself—at least for now. "No, definitely not. He's terrible."

"Well, better terrible," Marya assured her, rising to her feet. "It's the wonderful ones you have to watch out for." She leaned forward, lightly brushing her thumb across Sasha's cheek. "I'll have more instructions for you later."

Then she left, and Sasha quickly reached for her phone, reading the latest message.

(212) 555-0131: this is Lev, by the way

She rolled her eyes, changing his name in her phone.

SASHA: have you never used a phone before? there's a protocol. salutation, introduction, the decency to wait until an acceptable hour . . .

She watched him type a response. Clearly, he'd been waiting for her answer.

LEV: acceptable hour? it's nearly noon

She checked the clock.

SASHA: it's 7:45
LEV: look, I said nearly
LEV: I wasn't being specific
SASHA: are you normally this inexact?
LEV: no, actually. I'm usually lauded for my accuracy

"Sasha," her sister Galina interrupted, bursting into the room and startling Sasha into dropping her phone on the floor. "Do you have that red blouse?"

"What red blouse?"

"The red one," Galina repeated impatiently (and, true to form, unhelpfully). "You know, with the—" She gestured vaguely to her wrists. "The sleeves?"

"If you mean the bell sleeves, then it's not mine, it's Liliya's," Sasha said, leaning down to pick up her phone.

"But you wore it on Tuesday," Galina said.

"Yes," Sasha sighed, "but that doesn't make it mine, does it?"

"And Liliya hates red."

"She normally does," Sasha permitted disinterestedly, "but she said she liked th—Look, do you want it or not, Galya?" she demanded, and Galina gave a contemptuous sniff.

"Always so rude in the mornings," she said, and shut the door behind her, leaving Sasha to look back down at her texts.

SASHA: 37$&%^*802y
LEV: are you by chance having a stroke?
LEV: or have I already reduced you to incoherence
SASHA: I dropped my phone. and you're awfully cocky aren't you
LEV: I could be, if that's what you like
LEV: or I could be an intellectual, or at least try to be
LEV: what do you think is more vast, the universe or time?

Sasha sighed.

SASHA: stop
LEV: stop what? which part
LEV: be specific
SASHA: all of it. most of it
LEV: you and I need to have a talk about words. specifically specificity

"Sasha," her sister Liliya interrupted sleepily, sticking her face between the door and the frame. "Do you have my red blouse?"

"No," Sasha sighed, exasperated. "Galya just asked me for it."

"Right, she's looking for it," Liliya confirmed, stifling a yawn. "So, do you have it?"

"I—*No*," Sasha groaned. "I don't!"

"Well then who does?"

"Liliya, *I don't know*—"

"Who are you texting?" Liliya asked, suddenly awake enough to slip inside the room and look at Sasha's screen before earning herself a well-deserved shove. "Is it a boy? Are you texting a boy?"

"What boy?" Sasha heard from the hallway, just before Galina poked her head in. "I didn't know you had a boyfriend, Sashenka."

"I don't," Sasha insisted, glaring at both her sisters. "Can you both just go, please?"

"What boy? I heard 'boy,'" announced Irina, appearing in the room as she sipped loudly at her coffee. "Tell me about him."

"You don't even *live* here!" Sasha growled.

"Speaking of boys," Galina said to Irina, "have you broken up with that . . . What was his name?"

"Vanilla," Liliya supplied dreamily, and then frowned, noticing Irina's outfit. "Is that my red blouse?"

"No, it's Sasha's," Irina said. "And he's not vanilla. He's just . . . he's, you know. From Connecticut."

"Ugh," said Galina and Liliya in unison, making twin faces of disdain as Sasha let out a loud groan.

"Can you all get *out,* please? And Irka, that's not my blouse, it's Liliya's," she said. "Give it back to her so she can give it to Galya so they can both leave me alone."

"Always so grumpy in the mornings." Irina tutted disapprovingly as Galina nodded, the three of them finally exiting the room.

LEV: so when can I see you again?
LEV: we can have a summit about language

LEV: or not
LEV: totally up to you
SASHA: I'm working tonight
LEV: I didn't ask when I COULDN'T see you
LEV: honestly, is that school you go to even accredited?
SASHA: I'm just stating the relevant facts
SASHA: you dick
LEV: :(

Sasha groaned again.

SASHA: you can come by for fifteen minutes
SASHA: you'll have to buy something
SASHA: I mean it

She waited, watching him type.

LEV: :)

She sighed.

SASHA: do people ever tell you you're impossible?
LEV: from time to time
LEV: I take it as a compliment
LEV: don't you? it's so easy to be possible
LEV: seems silly to limit myself to that
SASHA: you're impossible
LEV: stop
LEV: I'm blushing
SASHA: we have a serum for that. It's $74.99
LEV: wow
LEV: you didn't tell me you were a thief
SASHA: we thieves don't usually open with our occupations. bad for business

LEV: I want to know
LEV: EVERYTHING about this
LEV: like, is there a club for thieves? can I join
LEV: what are the initiation rites
LEV: blood oaths? yes or no
LEV: is there a monthly fee
LEV: do you host networking events?
LEV: do you have an alter ego
LEV: oh, do you wear a mask?
LEV: blink once if you wear a mask
SASHA: stop talking immediately
LEV: you're right, I should save these winning conversation topics
for later
LEV: see you tonight

Sasha smiled, and then immediately frowned. It wasn't as if this was going to be anything. Who was he, after all? She didn't even know his last name. Not that she intended for such things to matter.

"SASHA," Galina yelled. "DO YOU HAVE THAT TEAL SKIRT?"

"It's going to look awful with the red blouse," Sasha yelled back.

"WHAT RED BLOUSE?" Galina shouted.

Sasha sighed again.

SASHA: see you then

II. 4

(Moral Ponderings.)

"Well?"

"Jesus." Lev exhaled sharply, jumping at the sound of Roman's voice. "Could you be less stealthy, please?"

"Listen, Casanova, if you're done wooing the Antonova girl for the moment, I need you to deliver this," Roman returned, dismissing Lev's opposition to his presence and passing him a thin rectangular package. "Word of advice, though—don't open it."

"Cursed, I suppose?" Lev guessed as he accepted it, and Roman gave him one of his muted, scorpion smiles. "Is it a gift or a threat?"

"Do you really want to know?"

Lev sighed. "Fine. Where's it going?"

"Upper East Side. Address is on the label."

Lev glanced at it. "Isn't this that witch who tried haggling with Papa's people last week?"

"I don't know," said Roman, in a way that suggested very much the opposite.

Lev grimaced again.

"Fine, have it your way." He slid the package into his bag, nestling it gingerly at the base. "Anything else I should know?"

"Yes. From ten to eleven only his daughter will be home," Roman said. "His *favorite* daughter," he clarified slowly, "and the daughter he would do anything not to lose. Are we clear?"

"This isn't subtle, Roma," Lev grunted, rolling his eyes. "You're cursing his daughter so he'll have to come to Papa for the antidote?"

"Listen, I'm just trying to provide comfort to *your* delicate sensibilities," Roman reminded him impatiently. "You realize that Dima normally has me to do these things, right? And I don't need to wrestle with my conscience first. But, today I'm busy," he sniffed, "so try to keep your moral ponderings to something of a reasonable level."

"Busy doing what?" Lev asked.

"None of your business. Now go, would you? And be sure she opens it personally," Roman said briskly. "No point delivering it otherwise."

Lev sighed, tucking his phone into his pocket.

"Fine," he conceded, nodding to his brother before he left.

II. 5

(Thoughts and Questions.)

LEV: how's the store?

SASHA: you again, huh?

LEV: yeah. I thought about waiting until I saw you tonight, but then I thought nah

LEV: that doesn't sound fun at all

SASHA: ah, I see

LEV: so? how is it?

SASHA: quiet. though to be clear, that's a good thing. I have roughly eight million roommates so now I finally have some time to think

LEV: interesting

LEV: what are you thinking about

SASHA: that's a weird question

LEV: no it isn't. watch

LEV: ask me what I'm thinking about

SASHA: fine. what are you thinking about

LEV: I'm thinking about how strange it is that people trust their doormen so implicitly. like, if I really wanted to carry out a long revenge plot, I think I'd become a doorman. obviously I'd build up some sort of false identity beforehand which might take a while, but if I were really serious about it I think I could put in the time. also, why do people ever open the door to anyone, honestly? even without magic modern technology makes it so you always know to expect something that's arriving, right? so if a stranger shows up that just HAS to be bad news

LEV: I'm also thinking about how much I want to see you

LEV: can I kiss you? actually no don't tell me

LEV: surprise me

SASHA: I honestly don't know what to say to any of this

LEV: good

LEV: personally I like the idea of rendering you speechless

II. 6

(Seeings.)

"Is everything arranged, Masha?" Yaga asked, and Marya nodded.

"All set, Mama. The dealer and I have agreed on a time and place, and I've arranged for Ivan to be with Sasha, so she'll be safe."

"And you, in the meantime?" Yaga asked, arching a brow.

"I thought I might keep an eye on the Fedorov brothers. See to it they're no longer cheating us out of our profits."

Yaga's glance sharpened, doubtful. The single silver streak in her black hair seemed especially bright, flashing in the light that slid in through the window.

"I thought the matter of the Fedorovs was dealt with for the time being," she remarked in a low voice, and in the same thread, "Perhaps I should have sent someone else."

"No, Mama," Marya said firmly. "The Bridge is my informant. Koschei and the Fedorovs are my problem."

"And are they still a problem?"

The correct answer was no, Marya knew, but she had always been too careful to traffic in absolutes. "If they are, whatever threat they present is limited. Dimitri is—" She cleared her throat. "My sources tell me Dimitri is unconscious. In a coma. He's the one who set off the thief's curse," she added, "so he's the traitor. The other two are probably not involved, but if they are . . ."

Yaga arched a brow, expectant.

"I'll kill them," Marya confirmed without hesitation, and Yaga nodded, unsurprised. "If they cross us again, I won't leave a body behind this time, Mama, I promise you."

"I know you wouldn't." Yaga rose to her feet, cupping Marya's cheek in her hand and taking a long, discerning look at her. "You are my daughter, my Marya, a piece of me. You don't make mistakes."

"Never," Marya promised, and Yaga nodded absently, still scrutinizing her face.

"You look tired, Masha," she murmured, and Marya shifted uneasily, hearing something strange and distant in her mother's voice. "Are you not sleeping well?"

"I'm fine, Mama," Marya assured her. "There's simply a lot of work to be done." She paused, adding, "The Bridge has proven himself loyal, at least in this respect." Though perhaps *conditionally reliable* would have been a better term for her informant. Either way, it didn't seem worth clarifying at the moment.

Yaga, however, remained unconvinced. "Why don't you let Stas have a night to himself, Masha? And let me have my daughter. Let me watch over you, Mashenka, just for a night. Okay?"

"Mama, I'm not a little girl any longer," Marya reminded her. "It's been a long time since I've slept in your house. Is something bothering you?" she asked, and hesitated before adding, "Have you seen something?"

Yaga paused for a moment, and then, carefully, she smiled.

"No, nothing, nothing," she assured Marya, abruptly releasing her. "Just consider giving an old woman some company, would you?"

At that, Marya laughed. "You're not even fifty, Mama. You're hardly old."

"Don't sass me, Masha. If I say I'm old, then I'm old."

"Okay, Mama," Marya permitted drily, turning to the door. "You're very, very old, then."

"That's better. I love you, Masha," Yaga called to her, catching her just before she left. "I love you, your sisters love you, your husband loves you—"

"I know this, Mama," Marya said, waving a hand without turning. "Yes, yes, I know—"

"Masha. You do not need Dima," Yaga warned, and at that, Marya's heart stuttered and skipped, convulsing in her chest as she paused in the doorway.

ONE FOR MY ENEMY

"Yes, Mama," she carefully agreed, and then she slipped out, shutting the door quietly behind her.

II. 7
(Games.)

LEV: *ok*
LEV: *that's it I'm done waiting*
SASHA: *waiting for what*
LEV: *the opportune moment*
SASHA: *ah yes of course, silly me*
LEV: *there's such a thing as too eager sasha*
LEV: *believe it or not*
SASHA: *hate to break it to you but you left "too eager" about two hours ago and now you're somewhere in the realm of "zealously available"*
LEV: *interesting theory*
LEV: *ok see you in five minutes*
SASHA: *okay*
LEV: *unless you don't want me to come?*
SASHA: *I already said you could lev*
SASHA: *don't make me change my mind*
LEV: *ok good I was trying to be polite*
LEV: *which was a real roll of the dice*
LEV: *but hopefully my good intentions are showing*
SASHA: *you play a very risky game*
LEV: *yeah I like to live dangerously*
LEV: *see you in 5*

II. 8
(Luxuries.)

It was the first time Lev had ever actually planned to enter Baba Yaga's shop despite existing in its orbit for what felt like his entire life.

He'd been careful to ask Sasha for details ("Where is it?" "Which intersection?" "Wait, what do you sell again?") but it was easy enough to find from the patterns of his own memory. He was half holding his breath when he pulled open the door, bracing for whatever he might find on the other side of the glass. He hadn't completely ruled out the possibility that he might trip some sort of Fedorov alarm and wind up dead on the floor, quicker than he could even say *This was Roma's stupid idea.*

While death remained a rationally consistent outcome, what Lev discovered upon entering the shop was the rich, warm scent of something that might have been honey and vanilla, like a caress to all his senses. The lighting of the store was soft and inviting (unlike Koschei's, which had scarcely any lighting to speak of), and the walls were swathed in some sort of soft fabric that made him want to curl up and take a nap . . . after he took a very long, very luxuriant soak in an oversized Jacuzzi.

So, maybe not quite a doomsday situation, then.

A sound to his left caught his attention and he turned his head, locating Sasha where she was perched on a stool behind the counter. "You're here," she noted without ceremony, and he angled himself in her direction, unable to prevent a smile. She was wearing a pair of worn skinny jeans and a white T-shirt, one leg crossed over the other so that one of her oh-*so*-very-dirty Jack Purcells was propped against the counter. A pencil was shoved into the thick mass of her hair, a paperback book propped up by a trident-grasp of three fingers. She wasn't wearing any makeup that he could see, and frankly, she looked very, very much as though she'd put no care whatsoever into dressing herself for his arrival.

Though, that being said, she also looked like she was fighting the need to propel herself toward him, so he counted that as a victory of some kind.

"Sasha," he acknowledged, and she set the book down. "Where's that serum you mentioned?"

She gestured with her chin. "Right there," she said, pointing to a series of tiny bottles with matte pastel labels, each one the color of a Parisian macaron. "Third from the left."

"Terrible customer service," Lev noted, pointedly giving her a look, and she arched a brow.

"Do you need me to hand it to you personally?"

"I'm just saying it'd be nice," he sniffed, and she gave a low, facetious sigh, rising to her feet and wandering around the counter to where he stood. She paused, purposefully clipping his shoulder as she passed him, and then tilted her head, gesturing for him to follow as she led him to a set of copper-wire baskets that each contained something that looked like a jewel-shaped pillbox.

"Here." Sasha offered one to him, and he reached out to take it, frowning a little with confusion. "Bath bombs. They make the water fizz and whatever," she explained with stunning ambiguity, waving a hand. "This one is Rosé."

He sniffed it, making a face. "You think I want to smell like this?" he asked, and to that, she spared half a smile.

"It's designed for relaxation," she told him. "Also gives you a little bit of a buzz."

"Okay, sure, but—"

"Just try it," she instructed, taking it back from him to place it in a small paper bag. "I'll let you sample the first one free, but the next one'll cost you. That's the trick," she added slyly, holding the bag out for him. "People always come back for more."

"I don't take baths," Lev said, though he warily accepted the offering. "Sort of a feminine thing, isn't it?"

"That's very heteronormative of you," Sasha remarked, slipping a loose lock of hair behind her ear. "And impractical. Are men exempt from self-care?"

"Well, I hate to be any sort of normative," Lev permitted, tucking it into his pocket. "Though, I thought you said I had to buy something," he commented, and she shrugged.

"I'm not totally heartless," she said, and at her nearly not-antagonistic tone, he leaned ever-so-deliberately into the radius of her space, resting his arm against the display of moisturizers behind her. She seemed to have noticed, her gaze quickly scanning the distance between them before settling on his, but she neither invited him closer nor pushed him away.

"So," she said, tucking her hair behind her ear again. "That's five minutes gone. Per our agreement, you have ten more."

"Tell me about your day," Lev suggested, and she made a face.

"*That's* what you want to talk about?"

"Well, we don't have to. You can tell me about anything," he assured her, watching with amusement as her attention slid unwillingly to the lean of his hips, then dragged back up. "Anything you want."

She seemed to find this unconvincing. "You came here just to talk to me about my day for fifteen minutes?" she asked, and Lev shrugged.

"You'd have done the same, I'm sure."

"I definitely wouldn't have."

"Ah," he said. "Well, that's too bad."

They paused, each shifting slightly.

"So," he beckoned. "Your day?"

She looked up, considering him. Or, alternatively, looking at him.

"Fine," she said eventually, seeming to have arrived at some unknown conclusion inside her head. "Spent most of it here. Emailed with my classmates for a bit about our group project."

"Ah, right, the group project," Lev said. "How's Eric's face?"

She fought a smile. "Oddly enough, he didn't say."

"Well." Lev leaned forward, waiting to see if she'd lean away. She didn't, though he thought he felt her breath quicken sharply. "That's very interesting."

That time, he could have sworn he felt her shiver. "How was your day?"

"Oh, not bad." He leaned down, his nose brushing hers, and felt her lashes against his cheek as she let them flutter shut, open. Shut, open. "Ran a few errands. Counted the hours until it was reasonably 'tonight' enough for me to show up here."

"God, have a little self-preservation," she told him, lifting her chin. "It's sad, Lev."

"Is it?" he demurred, brushing his lips against hers. Not a kiss, though. Not yet. "Seems to be going pretty well for me so far, don't you think?"

"Just shut up and kiss me," Sasha growled, and he laughed, lifting one of his hands to secure her hair behind her ear himself, holding it in place with his thumb.

"But what happens after I kiss you?" he prompted, as one of her fingers slipped incautiously around his belt loop, tugging him closer. "I only get what, five more minutes? I'm not going to waste them," he murmured, removing her hand from his jeans in favor of sliding his fingers carefully between hers, "by starting a kiss I don't plan to see through."

"Fine. You can stay, then," she said, toying with the collar of his shirt, "a *little* longer."

"How much longer?"

"I don't know. Twenty minutes," she said with an air of grave concession, and he laughed, pulling her against him.

"Well, that's all well and good, but if I kiss you now, Sasha, that's a short story. That's . . . what? A kiss, sure, and then, I don't know, maybe I go down on you behind that counter," he mused, feeling her grip on him tighten as he gestured over his shoulder, "or maybe we have sex in a storage room or a supply closet or something and then I go home, and okay, so in the moment it's great, it's fun, it's exciting, and sure, I'm not saying I wouldn't *want* to—but that's not the start of something big, is it? Nothing significant ever starts like that."

She tensed with surprise, unnerved.

"I'm not here for a one-night stand, Sasha," he told her. "The story we're writing? It has chapters. Installments. I don't want once."

With that, he pulled away, checking his watch. "Fifteen minutes on the dot," he announced, flashing the face of it at her, and she blinked, standing absurdly still as he disentangled himself from her grasp. "Maybe I'll see you again," he suggested. "Maybe soon, even, if you find yourself free."

He could feel her eyes tracking his path as he left. "You really are impossible."

"I'm actually extremely easy," he informed her regretfully, heading to the door. "I just want this more than you think I do."

He was nearly out of the shop by the time she called after him.

"Lev," she said, sounding resigned, and in response he gave a perfunctory pause, obliging her with an expectant glance over his shoulder.

She stood quite still for a moment, a spectacular furrow of uncertainty pressed between her brows as she gauged whatever impossible proposition she might have on offer, and briefly (unhelpfully) Lev wanted to run over and press his fingers to it. To soothe it beneath his touch.

Instead he waited, his fingers tapping impatiently against his thighs.

"You play a very risky game," Sasha remarked eventually.

You have no idea, Lev thought.

"I'll text you," he replied, and she rolled her eyes.

"You'd better," she said, and then, "Enjoy your bath."

He nodded, compelling himself to go.

Maybe it was his imagination, but he was certain her gaze had followed him out the door.

II. 9

(Crimes.)

LEV: this bath is criminally relaxing
LEV: you should be arrested
SASHA: told you
LEV: going to bed soon?
SASHA: yes
LEV: me too

SASHA: you don't have to keep me updated on every minute of your life
LEV: guess what I'm doing now
SASHA: no
LEV: I'm going to bed
SASHA: okay
LEV: goodnight sasha
SASHA: night lev
LEV: talk in the morning?
SASHA: do I have a choice?
LEV: yes
SASHA: well then I guess you'll find out in the morning
LEV: mysterious
LEV: I like it
LEV: sweet dreams
SASHA: you too

II. 10

(Analysis of Cost.)

"Holy shit, Eric," Nirav exclaimed, blinking at the sight of him. "What happened to your face?"

Sasha didn't look up, discreetly burying a smile as Eric sidled up to the rest of their group in the lecture hall. The impact was days old by now, but still—she'd hit him hard enough that it wasn't too surprising to see the bruising still looked fresh.

"Walked into a door," Eric replied evenly, falling into the open seat between Sasha and John. "So, what's left to do for Friday?"

"I can put the PowerPoint together," Nirav offered. "Sasha was just finishing the final cost analysis—"

"I thought I was doing the cost analysis," Eric interrupted, turning to glance at Sasha. "Weren't you supposed to mock up the design?"

"Seems like your eye is giving you some trouble," Sasha replied, pulling up the email and turning her computer screen toward him. "I'm on cost analysis. You were supposed to do exploratory research on the product."

Eric grimaced. "I *did* that, but—"

"Look, can we just do our work, please?" John interrupted, as Sasha's phone buzzed on the desk.

LEV: so how is eric's face
LEV: tell me immediately I must know
LEV: I've been waiting all day

"Something funny, Sasha?" Eric muttered, as she quickly flipped the screen over.

"Yes," she replied coolly, and got back to work, typing a few sentences out in their shared Google Doc before smoothly picking up her phone.

SASHA: he looks like a little bitch
LEV: omg
LEV: you are ice cold

"Sasha, did you look over this part already?" Nirav asked, and she glanced up, innocently suppressing a smile.

"No, sorry," she said. "Which part, again?"

"Might want to focus," Eric grumbled under his breath.

"Might want to stop walking into doors," Sasha suggested, tucking her phone away and resolving to tell Lev about it later.

II. 11

(Baby Viper.)

"How's it going with Yaga's daughter?" Roman asked, clipping Lev with his shoulder as he muscled his way through the labyrinthine towers of Koschei's warehouse.

Lev looked up from his phone, groaning. "Can you not?"

"Rumor is there's a meeting happening Friday," Roman told him, "and we need details. You need to get close to her fast, Lev, or you're just wasting our time."

"I barely know her," Lev informed his brother. "Are you really *that* unfamiliar with seduction, Roma? Because for reference, it tends to take longer than a few days for someone to reveal their family secrets," he clarified, "much less whether they are or aren't participating in a massive drug deal—"

"You're on that fucking phone all day," Roman scoffed, kicking the corner of the boxes Lev was supposed to be filing away in storage. (One was marked, disturbingly, DO NOT DISTURB.) "What are the two of you talking about if not her family or her job? Surely she's given *something* away—"

"She's very private," Lev said, irritated. "And anyway, I really don't think she's involved. Well, maybe her older sisters are doing something," he conceded with a grimace, "but I doubt she is. She's really serious about school and working at the shop. I don't think she's invested in the illegal arms of the family business."

That, it seemed, was precisely the wrong thing to say.

"Have you managed to forget what her sister did to our brother, Lev?" Roman demanded, and Lev flinched, picturing Dimitri's unmoving face again—the blood that had spilled from his mouth while Marya Antonova had looked on, unfeeling.

"This girl is an Antonova," Roman warned, as if he'd read Lev's thoughts. "It's in her family, in her blood. None of them can be trusted, Leva. Take care not to be fooled, or you're just spitting in our brother's face by carrying on with our enemy."

"But Sasha's not like Marya. She's, I don't know. Softer than that, I guess." He tried to think of a way to put Sasha into words. "She's closed off, sure, but she's not actively hiding things—"

"Sasha is a baby viper," Roman returned brusquely. "Marya's full grown. That's the only difference."

"Don't you think you're being a little dramatic, Roma? It's been fairly quiet since Dima—"

Lev cleared his throat, breaking off.

"Nothing's happened since Dima," he amended, which was only another mistake.

"Yes, and silence is the most dangerous thing of all," Roman snapped. "Don't you know that much?"

He did.

He'd sat at his brother's side that morning, in fact, and fidgeted in the silence.

"Fine," Lev conceded tightly. "I'll see what I can find out."

"Do that," Roman advised with a sniff, turning to exit the warehouse.

II. 12

(Offers.)

LEV: *I'm coming over today unless you stop me*

SASHA: *don't read into this but I'm not going to stop you*

SASHA: *that sounds like a lot of work*

SASHA: *what would I do with the body, etc etc*

LEV: *damn son*

SASHA: *my sister galya will be working with me but she has a date at 8*

SASHA: *she's always late though so maybe 8:27*

LEV: *precision, nice*

LEV: *8:27 it is*

LEV: *don't you close at 9?*

SASHA: *yeah but you'll be gone by then*

LEV: *ouch*

LEV: *sasha*

LEV: *words can hurt*

SASHA: *don't be a baby lev*

SASHA: *how many bath bombs do you want*

LEV: *at least four*

LEV: *no five*

SASHA: that's too many baths
LEV: you did this
LEV: this is your fault
SASHA: k
LEV: god you are a monster

II. 13

(Trifles.)

"Papa," Roman called, and Koschei turned vacantly, glancing up as Roman circumnavigated the basement's center ring.

"News, Romik?" Koschei prompted, and Roman nodded.

"Lev is seeing Yaga's daughter tonight. He'll find out from her who Yaga's new dealer is."

Immediately, Koschei frowned. This had not been the plan. "The Antonova witches are not very free with their secrets," he commented warily, but Roman merely shrugged.

"I have faith in Lev, and anyway, we already know most of what we need to. We only need to know when and where to be able to stop it, and then—"

"Yaga will not take kindly to that," Koschei warned. "Nor do you have much familiarity with her daughters. When I said to plant Lyova, I meant to do it among strangers. Yaga's witches are not to be trifled with."

Roman bristled, sensing disapproval. "I know what I'm doing, Papa."

"I hope so, Roman. I hope so." Koschei scraped a hand over his cheek, thoughtful. "But is this what Dima would do, do you think?"

The words turned his second son's expression cold. "Dima's lying half dead in his bed, Papa," Roman said, parsing the words between his teeth. "Dima's judgment is what got us here, isn't it? So now, we're doing what I would do."

"I'm not questioning you, Romik," Koschei told him carefully.

"I simply miss my son. It has been a long time since I've had to act without him."

"I'm your son," Roman replied stubbornly. "I am equally your son."

Koschei reached out with a sigh, gripping Roman's chin in his hand to look at him; at the very image of what Koschei himself had been as a young man. Roman was as dark as he was, as determined. Dimitri was both their opposites.

"Yaga has wronged me in many ways," Koschei said quietly, "but nothing she's ever done has been as spiteful as this. Yaga tried to take my Dima, and for that, I will never forgive her." He paused, and then, "Do whatever it takes to bring Marya Antonova to justice, Roman, and her mother, too. Whatever it takes. I trust you to see that Yaga suffers as fully as I have."

"Yes, Papa." At that, Roman's spirits seemed to return. He lifted his chin, freeing it from his father's hold. "I swear, Papa, I'll make Yaga and her daughters pay."

"Good." Koschei sat back wearily, feeling his age creak in his bones. "Do not fail me, Romik."

"I won't, Papa," Roman promised him. "I won't."

II. 14

(Little Talks.)

"You seem troubled, Marya Antonova," remarked The Bridge, pouring her a glass of his mother's whisky. "How may I be of service?"

Marya spirited the glass away from him, closing her long fingers around it as his gaze furtively followed its path. "You can answer some questions I have," she said, "which we both know you so dearly love to do."

"Not without payment," he corrected, watching her take a testing sip. "Though, perhaps if you ask me nicely," he mused, pouring a second glass for himself, "I might be more inclined."

"Well, then," said Marya, "I suppose we're at an impasse," and in response, The Bridge smiled broadly, toasting her as he fell into the seat opposite hers.

The man who was called The Bridge, known to his mortal clients and to Marya Antonova as Brynmor Attaway, had been given a moniker befitting his connection with all the various realms of Manhattan, magical and otherwise. The illegitimate son of a powerful (albeit human) state politician and a magicless species of fae, Brynmor, commonly called Bryn, worked various positions as a contract attorney for a Wall Street firm, as a particularly conniving dealer among the more discreet members of the Witches' Boroughs, and, most recently, as an informant for the Antonovas, with Marya as his handler. Bryn was mostly sought after for his knowledge (and proficiency with deals), as he lived among both primary currency-wielding species.

He was handsome, like all fae, and slippery, like all lawyers, but he could be informative when the circumstances were right. Marya, who had questions she needed answered, had planned, per usual, to make them so.

"I want to know what the Fedorovs have done with Dimitri," she said.

"What makes you think I know?" countered Bryn, shrugging. "I know what everyone knows: that the eldest Fedorov has been dispatched, and Baba Yaga is to blame."

"But he isn't dead," Marya said, and to that, Bryn chuckled.

"Do you find that disappointing?"

"I find it," Marya began, and eventually settled on, "curious."

"Well, then perhaps you should improve the quality of your murders. As far as I can tell, they don't seem to stick."

"If I wanted him dead, Bridge, he'd be dead."

"You say that, and yet . . ."

Bryn trailed off pointedly, swinging one leg over the other, and Marya flicked her fingers, sending his glass of whisky dribbling down his shirt.

"Oops," she murmured, and Bryn glared at her.

"All because I pointed out the obvious? Dimitri is alive, you're being unusually petty, and this is fucking silk," he informed her, gesturing brusquely to the garment. "Not to mention the whisky itself was a gift."

"Hand slipped," she said, taking a sip, but at his look of irritation, she sighed, waving another hand to smooth the spill from the fabric. "Such a fussy little fae you are."

"This," he said, "is hardly asking nicely."

"Please, Bridge. You have no interest in my niceties."

"Well, then perhaps you should leave."

"Without getting what I came for? Bridge, you underestimate me yet again."

They paused, warily sipping from their respective glasses as each considered their position.

"You came without your muscle," Bryn noted, gesturing less-than-politely to the lack of Ivan beside her. "I was really starting to warm to him."

"Were you?" She sipped her glass, biding her time. "Funny. He loathes you."

"Ah, so you left him behind so we could be alone? I knew it," Bryn said, tongue slipping blithely between his lips. "Say the word, Marya, and that husband of yours could be easily dispatched."

"I'm sure he could, but not by you." Marya leaned back against the sofa, shaking her head. "Sex would never satisfy you, Bridge. We both know it's power or nothing."

"Something we have in common, isn't it?" he asked, and then, more salaciously, "Try me and find out."

She eyed her glass, making a show of considering its illumination. "Would it get me answers?"

"About the Fedorovs, or about something else? The realms of the living and the dead, perhaps? Yes and yes, I'm afraid." Bryn sighed facetiously, dialing up his most treacherous charm. "Don't tell a soul, Marya Antonova, but I confess, I'm a glutton for pillow talk. You'd have all the answers you needed, and a few that you'd wish to take back."

He smiled at her, effortlessly serpentine, and she raised her glass to her lips.

"Tempting as that is," she said, after permitting the whisky to settle on her tongue, "I'm going to have to decline."

"Pesky wedding vows again, is it?"

"That," she said, setting down her glass, "and I know easier ways to make you talk."

She crooked a finger, yanking Bryn toward her with a lurch, and removed his glass from his hand, watching the brief shadow of frustration on his face as he was forced to acknowledge, yet again, which of the two of them possessed the more persuasive powers.

"You didn't want your muscle overhearing, did you?" Bryn asked her, cheeks reddening as he struggled to lean away from her clutches and couldn't. "That's what this is about. You have questions you didn't want anyone else to hear."

Marya didn't consider the remark worth addressing. "You're sure," she said instead. "You're sure it was Dimitri?"

When he didn't answer, she slid her thumb along his throat, sending a shudder of warning up his spine.

"I said it was the Fedorovs," Bryn gritted unwillingly, and she touched him again, soothingly this time. A reward for good behavior. "That's all the information I have to give."

He almost certainly knew more, but Marya could see it would cost her more than she was currently willing to pay to uncover it. "Always with the tricky wording," she sighed, releasing him to rise to her feet. "I suppose I'll have to find out for myself, won't I? If you won't be any help, that is."

Bryn leaned back with narrowed eyes, saying nothing, and privately, Marya lamented that their little talks so rarely ended in mutual satisfaction.

"What do you think you'll learn from them, pray tell?" Bryn

called after her, watching her carefully pick up her coat and turn toward the exit. "From what I hear, the Fedorovs want you dead. Your mother and sisters, too, but you most of all."

Marya shrugged. It was hardly a novel threat, and certainly nothing she hadn't expected to hear. "You're nothing until somebody wants you dead, Bridge, remember that," she informed him, pulling her coat over her shoulders. "Until then, you've done absolutely nothing worth a damn."

"Bleak," remarked Bryn, and Marya smoothed her hair, sparing him a parting glance.

"That's the world we live in, Bridge," she said, and drained what remained of her whisky.

Then she vanished in place, leaving only a berry-red imprint on the lip of her empty glass.

II. 15

(Closing Time.)

"So, Eric's still giving you a hard time, is he?"

"Yes," Sasha muttered, adjusting one of the displays. "Check that tester," she instructed Lev, gesturing to the copper-lidded bottle behind him, and obediently, he turned. "Does it need a refill?"

There was a croak of resistance from the pump when he squeezed a dollop of hand cream into his palm. "Yes," he determined, rubbing it in and sniffing it. "Smells like flowers," he remarked.

"Yes, that's sort of the idea," Sasha said, observing with amusement as Lev sneezed. "It's supposed to smell like spring. There's a summer one," she added, pointing to it, "and a winter one, obviously, and autumn."

"Clever," he said, pausing to rub the excess lotion into his knuckles. "And people buy these?"

Sasha lifted a brow. "You tell me," she said pointing to the near-empty display, and Lev gave her a sly, boyish grin.

"The store must make a lot of money, then."

Sasha shrugged, nudging him toward one of the boxes that had yet to be unloaded. "Sort of. I mean, it does well, but with all that goes into it, I think it could make more," she clarified, catching his look of curiosity at her ambiguous response. "I keep trying to convince my mother to set up some sort of online sales platform but she's not interested. I think she prefers having a brick-and-mortar business."

"Well, fair enough," Lev commented, and hesitated. Sasha straightened, adjusting her hair.

"What?" she prompted, and he chuckled.

"I guess I just wondered what makes a family of witches decide to start a skin care line," he said. "It's aiming a little small, isn't it? Considering the scope of your magic, which seems . . . not inconsiderable."

He seemed to be getting at something—something specific, in fact, and Sasha kept her response light and disinterested. "So?"

"So," he echoed, "I guess I just wondered if you did anything . . . else," he finished evasively, and she arched a brow.

"Are you asking if we do anything illegal?"

He shrugged. "Just seems like a possibility."

"Well," Sasha posed neutrally, turning back to the box of hand creams so she didn't have to face him, "if our skin care line was just a front for some sort of witchy black market, do you really think I'd be at NYU trying to *build* said skin care line?"

"I never said you made any sense," Lev reminded her, and Sasha stifled a laugh, glancing at her watch.

"All right, it's closing time," she told him, careful yet again to conceal her feelings on the matter. "Get gone, Lev."

He looked disappointed, and confusingly, she couldn't decide how she felt about that. Did she actually want him to leave? Yes, of course. Maybe.

Did she want him to *want* to leave? Certainly not.

"Well, what if," Lev posed, sliding closer to her, "I stayed? Just an idea."

Sasha suppressed a small, inadvisable lift of triumph in her chest. "I have inventory to do," she informed him, gesturing to the boxes and her checklist, "and besides, I have doubts about your retail prowess. You were already fairly unhelpful with the last customer."

"What? I told her the glittery stuff looked nice," Lev protested.

"Yes, but it clearly didn't," Sasha said, rolling her eyes. "Customers like compliments, but they don't love lies."

"Well, then give me another chance. Please," he added, leaning gratuitously toward her. Once again his lips were disturbingly present, the shape and promise of them resuming their starring role in what was increasingly becoming a nightmare for Sasha's peerless restraint. "It'll be fun."

She hesitated, opting to use her moment of (hopefully temporary) instability to wobble over to the sign, flipping it. The side that said CLOSED now faced the street, leaving the side that said OPEN to rest carefully against the glass like an unsubtle wink.

"I have to work, Lev," Sasha told him without turning around. He took a few quiet steps to come up behind her, resting his hands lightly on her hips. "I'm serious."

"I know you are," he agreed, his lips brushing her shoulder as his fingers tightened around her waist. "I'm serious, too. I'll help you with the inventory," he offered, the rumble of his voice against her spine resonating in her chest like a purr of satisfaction. "Make use of whatever time you save?"

He lifted one hand from her waist, brushing his thumb delicately over her throat. When she tipped her head back, letting it fall against his chest, he rested his hand gently around the base of her neck, holding her against him to brush his lips beside her ear.

"How long does it usually take you to finish closing?" he asked, and she swallowed hard; he probably felt the impact of it under his thumb.

"An hour," she managed.

"Perfect." Lev abruptly released her and she stumbled backward without his presence for a counterweight, steadying herself to find him already unloading one of the boxes. "So, we'll do this," he informed her, gesturing to the work at hand, "and then I get whatever's left of the hour. Sound fair?"

His hands were exuberantly full of spring-scented hand creams. Helplessly, Sasha sighed.

"Fine," she allowed, shifting to do her work.

She tried to be subtle about her own anticipation, keeping her progress stoically measured, but it was clear Lev was quickening his pace. He replaced a full box of hand creams, rapidly adjusting their placements on the shelf, and then glanced over at her, mouth quirking slightly.

"What next?" he prompted, at which point she realized it was a race.

Two restocked displays, eight refilled testers, and ten minutes of counting spare change later and they were finally done, leaving her to glance down at her watch.

"Look at that," Sasha remarked. "I have an extra half hour."

"That's so *convenient*," Lev said, grinning. "So, where are we going?"

She paused, considering it.

"Um," she began, and Lev answered for her.

"Let's get a drink," he suggested, and Sasha hesitated, but permitted a nod.

"Okay," she determined, and Lev slid her a slow smile, leading her out the door.

II. 16

(Reprisal.)

Twelve years had passed since Marya had last entered the warehouse of Koschei the Deathless.

It seemed to Marya part of an entirely different life, or perhaps simply a dream she'd once had, that it was ever a place she had once considered safe, even sacred. For obvious reasons, that was no longer true. Had Koschei known that Marya Antonova had *ever* breached his defenses there would have been no end to his fury. Unfortunately for him, there had once been nothing of higher consequence than the stolen moments two young lovers had carved out for themselves.

Marya had once been thoroughly apprised of how to sneak inside the warehouse. Which wards to slip and which alarms to avoid, information that was passed to her in whispers only shadows would hear. She thought maybe she would find it different now—that perhaps Dimitri had undergone the necessary precautions to keep her out—but she discovered almost immediately that everything was precisely as it had always been.

She slid into the warehouse like a ghost, tiptoeing quietly.

It was easy enough to find Dimitri. After all, he wasn't some trinket Koschei could hide away in the dark, and neither would he wish to. Marya knew Koschei would have done as much in the way of protective enchantments as he could manage, and she felt pulled to the security charms that were pulsing up the stairs, the old wood creaking beneath her feet.

If any spells had been specifically designed to keep her out, they would almost certainly fail to manage it—without Dimitri, the Fedorovs would be at a considerable loss. Even Dimitri was only powerful for having grown up with Marya; for having once been the beneficiary of her fragile, discriminating trust. Koschei, for all his many talents, was always more businessman than witch, while Marya had all her father's abilities and her mother's, too. That she'd been generous enough (read: foolish enough) to share it all with Dimitri had long been something she feared she'd one day come to regret, though she never pondered it for long. There was nothing to be done about the past. For better or worse, she had always shared everything with Dimitri—until the day she'd shared nothing at all.

She passed through the enchantments to find him sleeping, his face placid and still.

Her fault.

Her doing.

She swallowed hard, reaching out.

He'd always been so golden, like a storybook prince. His hair was swept across his forehead in his enchanted sleep and she brushed it back, tracing the shape of his nose, his cheeks, his lips. He had been hers, once. She had known every motion of his face and true, it was older now, but still it was the same, as perfectly preserved in half-life as it had been in her memories. She slid her hand down, passing it lightly over his throat, and tucked the heel of her hand into the base of his sternum, her thumb a straight line against his chest.

Then she pressed her free hand down flat, shoving pressure into the spell, and Dimitri sat up with a gasp, choking.

"Masha," he managed when he could speak, wetness glinting at the corners of his eyes from the impact of coughing the curse from his lungs. "Masha, Masha please—"

"It wasn't supposed to have been you," she told him flatly, and he swallowed, collapsing back against the pillows. "You were supposed to have been fine. You weren't supposed to have been the one who betrayed us." A pause; a clenching of her jaw. "The one who betrayed *me*."

"I didn't," Dimitri said hoarsely, reaching for her. "Masha, please, listen to me. I—I *touched* the potions, yes, but I didn't—I didn't steal from you, I swear, I would never—"

"I can't stay," she said, tearing herself from his grip and rising to her feet. "I couldn't leave you like this, but I can't stay. You know that."

"Masha, please." Dimitri stumbled after her, lurching out from beneath the covers to follow her out the door. "Masha, wait, you need t—"

He faltered immediately, too weak to stand, and quick as lightning she was there, easing him upright. She grimaced, hating herself for doubling back, but she really was an unnaturally good witch. It wasn't her fault she was quicker than he was.

It *was* her fault, however, that she couldn't make herself let go.

"Be careful," she snapped. "You've been drained of most of your life for over a week, Dimitri. You can't suddenly try to walk, you'll only collapse—"

"Masha," he cut in, struggling to reach behind him for balance as she shifted him back toward the bed, easing him down. "You have to know I would never do this to you. Think, Masha, what would I have to gain?" he demanded, and then Marya saw the Dimitri who was the son of Koschei: the proud, charismatic boy who'd been cleverer than all the children their age; who'd first caught her eye with the way he never deigned to bend his golden head to anyone else's will. "I have no need for your mother's business, and even if I did, do you really believe I would try to cross *you*, of all people? I'm not stupid, Masha," he said, dauntless even when he lay weakened in his bed. "After everything that passed between us, I know better than to underestimate you."

"Then how do you explain this?" Marya demanded, ambiguously waving a hand to their shared circumstance. "*Someone* was stealing from us—"

"Yes," Dimitri agreed, grimacing as he must have suffered a cramp somewhere in his abdomen, "but it wasn't me, Masha. I promise you, it wasn't me. Nor will it happen again under my watch," he added, mouth tightening when he looked at her. "I'd only just found out, Masha, the night before you arrived—"

"Tell me, then," she said. "Tell me who it was and I'll kill them myself."

She'd been gravely serious, as always, but to her surprise, Dimitri smiled.

He *smiled* at her, infuriatingly, and in her agitation she curled one hand to a fist, turning away. Dimitri, of course, reached out to catch her arm, coaxing her back until she was sitting beside him on the bed, unwillingly.

No, not unwillingly. And all the worse for that.

"I can't tell you who it was," Dimitri said, "*because* you will kill them, Masha. In fact," he murmured, the smile fading slowly from his face, "I really thought you would kill me."

She said nothing.

"I had *hoped*, of course," Dimitri continued softly, "that you wouldn't. That perhaps something between us would have stopped you. But still, it was a gamble nonetheless."

"Yes, it was. You might have died," Marya informed him, staring down at the threads of his bedding. "I might have let you."

"Yes," Dimitri agreed. "But you didn't." He reached out, cautiously, to take hold of her chin, tilting it gently upward to draw her gaze back to his. "Why didn't you just let me die, Masha?"

She willed herself to look away from him. When she couldn't, she shut her eyes.

"Dima," she whispered shamefully, and in one reflexive motion he shifted to take her face with both hands, lips brushing her forehead with the erstwhile devotion he had shown her so many times, so many ways.

"Is it really so terrible?" he asked, sighing it to her temple. "Masha, my Masha. Is it really such a failing that you couldn't find it in yourself to kill me? Many people in love have failed to kill each other before, you know."

"I don't love you," she forced out, as coldly as she could manage.

She felt him catch something in his throat, swallowing it down.

"No," he agreed after a moment. "No, of course not."

"I don't." She floated around in the silence, fidgeting before adding, "I can't."

He stroked her cheek. "Ah, Masha, those are two different things, aren't they?" he asked knowingly, and she grimaced.

"Don't make this about technicalities. We knew a long time ago we couldn't be together, Dima—we knew twelve years ago we didn't stand a chance. We chose our sides, and now—"

"No. You chose *your* side," Dimitri reminded her, stroking her hair as her eyes fluttered open, meeting his. "*You* chose. But you didn't let me choose, did you?"

She blinked. "What?"

"You married Stas." His voice was pained. "You shut me out. You gave your life to someone else."

"Of course I did. Because I know, above everything, that you are your father's son," she began, but Dimitri cut her off.

"No. No, Masha, I am my own man." He stroked a line down the back of her neck with his thumb, loosely cupping his hand around it. "Why didn't you let me choose you?" he asked hoarsely. "I would have gone to you, Masha, if you'd asked. You would've only had to ask, and I would have chosen you over everything."

"Don't," Marya warned, swallowing hard. "Dima, please don't—"

"Are you happy, Masha?"

The question stunned her, quite unwillingly, to silence.

"Are you? I don't mean with Stas," Dima said quietly, and despite her fervent wish to feel nothing, she was helpless not to flinch. "I remember how joy looked on you, Masha. I remember *life*, and I don't see it now. I certainly didn't see it when I saw you last, carrying out your mother's wrath—so tell me, are you happy? Being the great Marya Antonova," he murmured, securing her within the insufficiency of his fingertips. "Being Yaga's enforcer, her right hand—Masha, is it all you thought it would be?"

She couldn't answer. To answer would be to betray herself, her livelihood, her family. It was to confess far more than she was willing to give, whether to him or to herself or to anyone.

She did not answer, but her silence was answer enough.

"I love you," Dimitri reminded her, and reached up, touching her cheek as she stared at him; willing him, impossibly, to stop talking, or even less likely, compelling herself to go. "I will always love you, I will love you until the day I die—and if you're the one to kill me, then by all means, you should know without a trace of doubt that you will not have turned me away. I will have spent the final beat of my heart loving you, just as I always have. Only you, Masha," he said, and she bent in anguish, resting her forehead against the still-sluggish motion of his chest while he gathered her in his arms, eternally hers. Even now, eternally familiar. "Only you, forever, I promise."

"Stop." She buried her fingers in his clothes. "Dima, don't do this to me—"

"We could run," he whispered to her. "We could leave, we could leave all of this behind us. Your mother has six other daughters, Masha. Haven't you served long enough? Haven't I? Twelve years we've done this," he said, calibrating their loss with the tapping of his fingers along her vertebrae. "Twelve years I've been without you and done nothing but lose myself. In twelve years you built your mother an empire," he reminded her, "and still, will it ever be enough?"

"We could never run." She knew that much. No fantasy could make it true. "Not now, Dima, it's too late—"

"It doesn't have to be."

"It does."

"Why?"

She wanted to kill him, to kiss him, to love him with her hands around his neck. Even as a boy, he'd always thought he understood everything. He'd always believed, frustratingly, that all things could be so easily explained.

She shot to her feet, or tried to. He held tightly to her hand, two fingers, whatever pieces of her he could reach. "Because it *does*. Because of what we've done, Dima—what *I've* done—"

"Then we'll find a way to undo it."

He paused, and for lack of better weapons, she clung to him in the silence. "If this world isn't what you thought it would be, Masha, I won't let you down. I won't disappoint you."

"Dima, don't do this. Please."

Marya Antonova, enforcer of Baba Yaga, the girl who had not cried and the woman who did not beg, was pleading now—in hearing it, the repulsion of her own weakness, she could feel Dimitri soften in sympathy. She fell into his kindness, into his tenderness, letting herself be lured back into his arms as she had always hate-fully known she could be if he ever so much as tried. He stroked her hair, allowing her the relief of silence, and then he bent carefully over her, sheltering her in his arms as she sank lower, falling to her knees beside his bed. She sighed, sliding her arms around his waist, and he curled himself around her like the shield she'd never asked for, his heart beating steadily, thrumming with futile oaths beside her ear.

"Dima," she said again, and his grip on her tightened. "Dima, I swear," she confessed to his chest in a whisper, "this love I have for you will be the death of me."

For a moment, he froze—battling with himself, most likely—but then he pulled back, fumbling, to draw her into him, having given up the fight. His eyes were wild, filled with nothing but the sight of her, and she let out a terrible, desperate sigh, resigning her-self to ruination, to the ascendancy of devastation as he pressed his lips to hers, holding what little remained of her in his hands.

In nearly the same moment that he pulled her close, Marya felt a jolt, a blinding stab of pain, and wondered if that was what the ab-sence had done to her; if she had loved Dimitri Fedorov so fiercely she could feel it now in the vacancies of her spine, plunged into the caverns of her heart. She gasped into his mouth, crying out in anguish, and instantly he pulled away—but his eyes were different now, his fingers clinging to the wetness of her cheeks as she regis-tered slowly, too slowly, that the pain wasn't from his kiss.

Not at all.

"Dima," she whispered, struggling to see, and felt her breath stagger and fail.

"Masha!" he shouted, the sound of it buried beneath the dull roar in her ears, and she closed her eyes, still seeing him in her mind; once with his face pressed to the bloodied floor, voiceless and pleading, and then again with his chin tilted up in sunlight, spinning his golden promises in her ear:

Masha, Masha, Masha.

II. 17

(The Gentlemanly Thing.)

"So," Lev said as he led Sasha out of the bodega, holding up the two paper-bagged cans of beer for her perusal. "Which one are you thinking?"

Sasha sighed, shaking her head. "This isn't exactly what I had in mind when you said you wanted to get a drink," she informed him, grey eyes sublimely doubting, and he grinned.

"Well, I only have thirty minutes, per your rules, and I'm certainly not going to spend them being surrounded by a bunch of Erics. So," he repeated, weighing the two for her benefit, "do you want the cheap beer, or the cheaper beer?"

Grudgingly, she permitted a wary half smile. "Give me the cheapest beer you've got."

"Done," he announced, handing it to her, and led her out the door, slowing slightly to match her contemplative pace as they headed down the sidewalk. "Cold?" he asked, letting her interpret any subsequent courses of action, and she took a long, pointed sip from her can.

"Nope," she said, after a swallow. "I can handle, oh, twenty-five more minutes of this. Can you?" she prompted, challenging him with a glance. He passed her a smirk in return, then a nudge that only subpar balance ensured was more playful than lingering.

"So," he ventured, as they ambled leisurely down the sidewalk.

"So," she agreed. He gestured left and she nodded, crossing the street as he fell back to take a path behind hers, swapping sides with her on the sidewalk. "What are you doing?" she asked, bewildered, and he took another swig from his beer, shrugging.

"The gentlemanly thing, according to my father," he explained, and then recited, "In the old days" (as Koschei's voice rumbled in his ear), "the mud from the street would fly up and get on the lady's skirt, so men always walked on the street side."

"I'm not wearing a skirt," Sasha reminded him, gesturing to her jeans, and Lev shrugged again.

"Well, no, but still." He tossed her a sidelong glance. "Wouldn't want to risk it. Precious cargo," he informed her with a sip of his beer, beckoning her onward.

Instead, she paused for a moment.

Turned to him.

Frowned.

"Damn it, Lev," Sasha grumbled with a sigh, "you're such a noble idiot."

"Am I?" he mused. "Huh. Sounds right, but then ag—"

He broke off as she shoved him hard against the wall of a building, slamming him into it with a motion so flatteringly calculated he had to wonder how long she'd been planning it in her head.

"*Oof,* Sasha—"

She kissed him, her lips tasting like summer-flavored lip balm and cheap beer, and he let his own beer drop from his hand, merrily forgotten. There was a toppling thud as it hit the ground, a hiss of liquid spilling over the sidewalk as Sasha's arm snaked around his neck to pull him closer, to keep him close. Lev responded with enthusiasm, hastily dragging the zipper of her coat and shoving the panels aside to place his hands on that single bare inch of skin— the little sliver of torso he'd been trying all night not to eye too indiscreetly.

Her skin pebbled instantly at his touch. "Could have just said so," he muttered to her.

"Shut up," she advised, slipping her tongue in his mouth.

Her hands wandered to the zipper of his jeans, and he shifted as she toyed playfully with his top button, trading places to shove her against the wall. He slid his hands up first, spanning the width of her ribs and sloping briefly over her breasts before dragging them back down, his fingers lingering on the lip of her button-fly jeans.

He wanted to.

Fuck, he wanted to, and if that wasn't a fucking problem.

"Shit," he whispered into her mouth, "I want you."

"Well, you still have twenty minutes," she replied airily, and he grimaced.

Fuck, he really wanted to.

But something (something glaringly obvious, at that) wasn't quite right. He ran the scenarios, feverishly failed each one, and withered.

Right or wrong, he'd have to take the losing odds.

"Does it bother you," Lev exhaled resignedly, "that you don't know my last name?"

She stiffened, pulling back to frown at him.

"You haven't even asked me what it is," he pointed out, and she shrugged.

"Figured you'd tell me eventually," she said, and leaned forward to kiss him again, only he paused her with a groan.

"I can't do this," he said, already furious with himself and growing rapidly more so after he'd forced himself back a step. "I want it too much, it's too—*you're* too—"

"Fine," Sasha sighed, rolling her eyes. Her lips were swollen and full and pink and *fuck,* he longed to kiss them again—had been longing to all night, plus every night before that. Every night since he'd met her, in fact. "Tell me who you are, then, if it's so important."

God, and wasn't she so cavalier. She was a fucking nightmare and he was desperate to keep her, to have her for himself. "You won't like it," he cautioned, and she frowned, her dark brow furrowing. "It's not good, Sasha. It's really not good."

She blinked.

Blinked again. (Ran the scenarios, he guessed.)

Straightened. (There it was. Any second now.)

Stiffened. (Oh, yes. Yes, now she knew.)

Scowled.

"You're a Fedorov," she deduced eventually, addressing him now as if he were a stranger. "You're—you're Lev Fedorov."

For a second, they simply stared at each other.

"Don't tell me anything," Lev warned firmly. "If you and your sisters and your mother are up to something, don't tell me. Don't trust me."

"I already don't," she said warily.

"Good," he agreed. "And I can't afford to trust you."

"No," she said. "No, you shouldn't."

He stood silently, wondering what to say next.

"Sasha, listen, I—"

"Does it matter?" she asked him, posing the question with a neutrality that jolted his thoughts to a halt. "That I'm an Antonova, I mean. Are you telling me you're doing this because of my family? My name?"

"No," he said honestly. "No. No, I—Sasha, I like you, none of this was a lie. Well," he amended, "I couldn't even manage to lie, could I? Because I *like* you," he groaned, "like some kind of noble idiot—"

"Then why does it matter if you're a Fedorov?" she said, taking a step toward him. "Let whatever's between our families be between them. You certainly haven't done anything to me, and I can ignore your surname for—oh, I don't know," she murmured, checking her watch, "the next fifteen minutes, anyway."

Lev stared at her, somewhere between disbelief and acute, organ-failing distress. "But—"

"If you can check your secrets at the door," she suggested, forcibly returning his hands to her hips, "then I can do the same."

A total fucking nightmare. He shivered with craving, bending his head toward hers.

Somewhere, he knew, his brother was lying unconscious in a bed, and it was the fault of someone who bore the same name, the same loyalties, the same blood as the woman in his arms. Maybe someday he would learn that Sasha was just as ruthless as her sisters, just as hard-hearted and cold.

But for now, in his arms, she felt like *his*—and it wasn't something he could ignore.

"This will be complicated," he warned her, though it was meant to remind them both.

"Oh, definitely," she agreed.

"We really shouldn't do it," he said, as she tilted her head up, brushing her lips against his.

"No," she said, "we really shouldn't."

"Fuck," he sighed, feeling the last of his already highly compromised reservations give way. "But we're going to, aren't we?"

"Yes, Lev," she confirmed, reaching up to tangle her fingers in his hair. "Yes, we definitely are."

II. 18

(Rearview.)

Ivan had been Marya Antonova's bodyguard for a very long time; ever since the first time a witch had tried to kill her. She'd been only twenty then, before she'd married Stas Maksimov, and Ivan had been sitting in a popular witches' tavern with his back to most of the crowd when he'd seen the witch aim a curse at Marya's back. The young girl had been about to leave, most likely after distributing a punishment or a debt levied by her mother, and Ivan had stood without thinking, yanking her to the side. In the blink of an eye, he'd saved her life, and young Marya Antonova looked up with her dark bird-of-prey eyes and registered what he'd done.

"You saved me," she commented neutrally, after she'd dispatched the witch who'd attacked her with the most breathtaking of ease. "Why?"

"I don't know," Ivan said, though he did. It wasn't that he'd guessed she was weak; it was that he'd known she was strong. She was more than strong, her head held high like the finest of military generals', but still, she was a girl who hadn't learned to watch her back, so he had watched it for her.

"Would you like a job, soldier?" she'd asked him, and Ivan nodded. With Marya, he would learn that he never needed to speak much, which he liked. She only asked him questions if she required an answer; she didn't trap him into conversation, as other people were prone to do.

"Then you have one," she'd said.

Ivan had always been a soldier, with a soldier's loyalty, and he studied his view of Marya Antonova's back like it was a map of her behavior, each contour indicating some topographical feature of interest. He knew the stiffening of her shoulders when she was angry. He knew the weary roll of her neck when she hadn't slept well, which was often. He knew her pride from the tilt of her neck, the danger that lived in the angling of her spine. He'd sat just behind her for nearly twelve years and had seen every version of her, both public and private, to learn the little indicators of her state of mind.

Which was how Ivan knew, observing in silence while Dimitri Fedorov nearly bled out across his own living room floor, that something he'd never seen before was happening to Marya.

She'd kept her voice steady, hard, cold. Everything she did and said was edged with ice, always, and she did not fail now, only there was something else to her, too—something forlorn, and Ivan had watched her hold herself back, her knuckles glowing white as they dug into the tapestried arms of her chair.

Ivan had never seen Marya Antonova suffer someone else's pain before, but he saw it that day and knew, somehow, that everything else would now be different.

He also sensed that something would soon go wrong when she'd sent him home for the evening, as she had never done before.

"You'll have your work cut out for you with Sasha," she'd said wryly, reaching up to touch his shoulder with affection. "You might as well have a night off, Ivan. I won't be doing anything tonight."

"Are you sure?" he asked uncertainly, noting that she seemed distant and distracted. "Is Stas home to stay with you?"

"Hm? Yes, of course," Marya absently replied. "Stas is . . . Stas is here, Ivan. I'm fine."

He hesitated. He'd never had too many magical gifts; his intuition was always more refined from experience than supernaturally inclined. Still, if this sense of unease were some sort of half-formed foretelling, he felt he was obligated to warn her.

"Marya," he'd said, "I don't wish to leave you."

She'd given him a slow smile.

"You worry too much, Ivan," she said. "I won't need you to watch my back tonight."

"Promise," he said, and she blinked. "Promise me."

"I promise," she assured him, sighing it out and waving him impatiently to the door. "And anyway, Ivan, if anything happened to me, I have six other sisters. You'd have a job watching one of their pretty necks, or even my mother's—"

"Marya Antonova, I work for you," he told her, swearing it like fealty to a king.

Her smile had been as bright as it was fleeting.

"You serve one Antonova witch, Ivan," she'd replied, "and so you serve them all."

Now, though, having served one so loyally and so dutifully for such a very long time, he was certain something was wrong.

"Yaga," Ivan called softly, tapping lightly on her door. "Yaga, it's Ivan."

The door opened slowly, revealing Baba Yaga in the frame.

"There's only one reason you would be here at this time of night," she noted.

Ivan shuddered at the premonition.

"Marya isn't home," he said. "She's not with Stas, or with Katya or Irka. She's not here, in your house." He swallowed heavily. "I failed her, Yaga. I feel it. I can feel it in my bones."

Yaga stared into the space between them.

"Get my coat," she said eventually.

Ivan didn't work for her, but for Marya's sake he fetched it anyway, drawing it from the coat closet and holding it out for Yaga as she stepped into the garment, her thin arms sliding effortlessly through silken chasms of fabric.

"Come." Yaga beckoned him. "Let us find her, then."

II. 19

(Promises, Promises.)

Before that night, Dimitri Fedorov would have given his life to hold Marya Antonova again, even for one last time. Had he known that doing so would cost *her* life, though, he would have gladly sent her away.

Only a moment ago she'd been in his arms. Hadn't she? Hadn't she been real, been *here*, been wanting? Only now—

There was a cold flash of steel in the darkness, a suspension of Dimitri's own pulse, and like a sudden splicing of time and space, his realities cleaved in halves, in thirds, in infinite possibilities, into the many ways things had been different—the countless lives in which this kiss had begun twelve years ago and never ended at all. He could see the razor edge of a narrow sword, a blade that had burst from her heart, and before it was gruesome it was beautiful; surreal. As if she'd cracked open her own ribs just to give her heart to him, destroyed herself just to prove her love to him, and in the moment before he realized, before he understood what happened, he knew like all their lives unlived that no curse had ever been truer. That however certain their doom, they would have only said yes, yes, yes.

But time resumed and so did ugliness. Twelve years ago she had left him, and now she was torn from his arms once again.

"Masha!" Dimitri shouted, reaching out to stop her fall as she lurched backward, the tip of the sword that had burst free from her chest slicing into the bare skin of his. Either this or the extent of his prior injuries, Dimitri did not notice. He did not care. Frantic, he searched for reason, for explanation, and found only pulse after pulse of fear—until someone emerged from the shadows. A recognizable silhouette.

"Roma," Dimitri gasped in disbelief, staggering upright with Marya in his arms to find the shape of his second brother stretching over him from where Roman stood blocking the dim glow of the corridor. "Roma," Dimitri rasped, "what have you done?"

Roman said nothing, only giving the sword's handle a sharp tug. It was a spatha from their father's collection of cursed weaponry, a thin gladiator's weapon designed for killing for sport. It didn't come free at first; it had been lodged in Marya's spine after piercing her heart, emerging cleanly through the other side. She faltered back, collapsing at the waist as Roman yanked it, hard. One pull, and then another, testing the limits of Dimitri's compromised reach. It was a horrifying spectacle, but only once Roman had pulled the sword free did he finally let the pommel fall from his hand, tossing it to the floor with a clatter.

"Roma," Dimitri hurled at him, trying desperately to hold what still remained of Marya, pressing his hands to the wound and finding nothing, no magic, no miracles that could be conjured at his touch. Her blood mixed with his where the tip of the spatha had nicked his chest, her fate carved into his sternum like the writing on the wall. "Roma, what have you done? Masha, *please*—"

Marya's head fell heavily backward, blood staining his hands, the neat fabric of her dress. Dimitri, tasting bile, struggled to keep her upright until his body, too, betrayed them both, knees buckling beneath him. He slid helplessly to the floor as she collapsed against him, limp.

"Masha, stay with me," he said to her, trying to help her up— trying anything, trying everything. "Roma, help me, I can't—I can hardly move, I need you t—"

"No," Roman said, unflinching. "After what she's cost us? No, Dima. Believe me, I'm the one saving you."

That, more than anything, was unfathomable, incomprehensible.

"She brought me *back,* you idiot!" Dimitri yelled, because rage was softer, more endurable than grief. "What have you done, Roma? Yaga will have your fucking head for this—"

"Why?" Roman snapped, folding his arms over his chest. "Do you intend to turn me in this time, Dima? This was what was always going to happen." A threatening pause, and then, "I told you, there was always a plan."

"Roma." Dimitri stared at him. "Roma, you can't . . ." He strained to speak, the numbness of dread settling in his limbs. He had done this, he realized now. Not just his wanting. Not just the indecencies of his tired heart. He had missed something, something important, something he alone could have—*should have*—seen. Measurably and without exemption, this was his doing, and how would he live with that now? "Roma, how far does this go? I thought this was about *money*—you told me this was a simple matter of settling a *debt*—"

"Nothing's ever just money, Dima," Roman said blandly. "You wouldn't understand. You don't understand everything I've done for you, for us. You've always had things so easy, haven't you?" He laughed bitterly. "Everything was always handed to you, never earned. You don't know what it's like to fight for what's yours."

Dimitri tried and failed to make sense of it. The extent of Roman's scorn, his animosity. His venom.

"We're brothers," Dimitri said blankly, still holding Marya's head protectively to his chest, as if he could transfer whatever life remained from his heart to hers. "Everything mine is yours, Roma. Everything!"

But Roman only shook his head. "Power isn't given, Dima," he said. "Power is taken. The most dangerous of the Antonova witches is dead now, and who will Papa thank for that, hm? Certainly not you." He cracked a hardened smile, backing slowly away. "You would have ruined all of us for her sake, you would have thrown it all away, but I won't let you do it."

The weight of Dimitri's anger then was almost too much. Had

he even one ounce of magic left in his veins he'd have used it to kill his brother, he was sure of it. He could taste the impulsivity of violence on his tongue. "Roma," Dimitri raged, struggling fruitlessly after him. "ROMA!"

But Marya was heavy in his arms, too precious, and his brother had disappeared, the bloodied sword left abandoned in a black pool of carnage on the floor. Something ricocheted in the silence, some fanciful delusion or last hope of salvation that trickled away from Dimitri slowly, drop by calamitous drop. Only when the sound of blood rushing in his ears had faded did Dimitri register the sting of the cut across his chest; across his own heart, which for some reason had not stopped beating despite the stillness where Marya Antonova's should have been. He'd been so sure that it would, for having loved her. He'd been positive, once, that it would break, shatter, deliver itself to oblivion, all for love of her.

"Masha," he whispered to her, holding her close. Pain overrode fear, though he knew that would be real enough. Soon, he knew, fear would be all he could feel besides pain.

But for the moment, that would have to wait.

Dimitri had first told Marya Antonova he loved her when he was thirteen years old. She'd been shading her eyes from the sun, giving him her narrowed, impatient look (at fourteen she was older, worldlier, more experienced), but he hadn't dropped his gaze from hers, fearless, taking power from the sun's rays and tilting his chin up to say the words without hesitation:

Marya Antonova, I'm in love with you.

You don't know anything about love, Dimitri Fedorov, she'd told him, and it had made him love her that much more fiercely. He was a Fedorov, the son of Koschei. He was the son of a very great man, and someday he would be a great man himself, and only one woman would ever be fit to stand beside him. Only one woman was ever bigger and more alive than he was.

Masha, Masha, Masha, he had sighed, shaking his head. *Don't you know we belong together? It's inevitable. You might as well give in.*

She'd said nothing at first; only dropped her hand from her eyes and stepped toward him to beckon him for his. *If I ever decide to give my heart to you, Dima,* she'd said, holding his hand palm up, *then cut it out of my chest and keep it somewhere safe, where no one else can find it. Keep it locked somewhere,* she murmured, repeating the old stories as she brushed her lips across the lines of his palm: *Inside a needle, inside of an egg, which is inside of a duck, which is inside a hare, which is in an iron chest—and then bury it under our green oak tree, Dima, where no one will ever find it.*

Keep it safe for me, Dima, will you? she'd asked, and he'd blinked, dazzled by her, by them, by all of it as she'd closed his hand one finger at a time, burying her request in the hand that she'd kissed.

I will, he'd promised as if he could keep it.

She had not failed him, in the end. He'd been the one to fail her.

He bent his head over hers, pressing his cheek to her hair, and touched her fingers to his lips.

"I won't fail you again," he promised, and tucked her hand against the bloodied slash across his heart, swearing it much, much too late.

II. 20

(Long Games.)

"Time's up," Sasha said, holding up her watch, and Lev groaned, letting his forehead drop to her shoulder.

"You're ruining me."

She hid a smile, leaning over to nip lightly at the side of his jaw.

"I thought you said the wait was part of the book," she reminded him, giving him a shove. "What was it you said again, about us being a long story?"

"Biblical, at this rate," Lev lamented, but she rolled her eyes and he was helpless to smile, throwing an arm around her waist and pulling her close again. "One more," he said, and dropped another kiss to her lips, savoring it that time. "Okay, now go," he exhaled, eyes still closed, "before I completely lose all composure and fall prostrate at your feet."

"Composure? You've already lost it," Sasha assured him. "It's long gone."

"Maybe so," Lev agreed. "But I'd trade it for you any day."

She tried to glare at him but couldn't quite manage it.

"Good night, Lev Fedorov," she said, and his mouth quirked, one eye cracking to watch her go.

"Good night, Sasha Antonova," he replied as she turned away, hiding another stolen smile.

II. 21

(The Firstborn.)

When Marya did not come home, Yaga knew at once where she'd gone. Only one other time had her daughter gone missing. Despite the decade-and-more between occurrences, Yaga knew one of those episodes was not unlike the other.

"Dima," she said, and Dimitri Fedorov looked dizzily up from the floor, his cheeks streaked black with tears. "Give me my daughter back."

"Yaga," he rasped, not looking at her. He didn't sound surprised. He had a bloodied slash on his chest and was staring down at Marya, her Marya. "It wasn't me. It wasn't me."

"I know that," Yaga said, her voice harsher than she'd intended. Behind her, Ivan crept in to let out a low hiss at the sight of Marya, like a wounded animal. "I know you wouldn't have harmed her, Dima, but she is still my daughter." *She is still mine.* "Give her back to me."

Dimitri shuddered, his fingers tightening on Marya's body. "Please." A swallow. "Please don't take her."

"Dima." Harder now. She was numb, but that would fade. The shock would fade, and then the pain would be unbearable. "This wouldn't have happened if not for you, Dima."

A cruel thing to say, probably, and she wasn't even sure which part she meant.

This would never have happened if you'd never existed—
—if she'd never loved you—
—if you hadn't wronged her, wronged us, wronged me—

"Yaga, I—" Dimitri slowly held up his bloodied hand, his voice leaving him at a whisper. "I took something."

Yaga inhaled sharply. She glanced back at Ivan, whose face had paled.

"Have it, then," she said eventually. "It was always yours. But give me my daughter back."

Dimitri let out a low, incoherent sound of anguish, and Yaga gestured to Ivan.

"Take her," she said to him. "He won't fight you."

Ivan shifted with a grave nod, coming forward and bending to rest on one knee. When it was clear Dimitri could not do so of his own volition, Ivan removed Dimitri's fingers, prying them free one by one to gather Marya up in his arms. Then Ivan rose slowly, staggering to his feet as he stared down at her unmoving face, and Yaga rested one hand on his arm, steadying him.

"Who did this?" Yaga asked, and Dimitri didn't answer.

She waited, but he merely remained unmoving, his hands still covered in her daughter's blood.

"Fine, don't tell me, but know this: Whoever did this to my Masha will suffer for it themselves, tenfold," Yaga pronounced firmly, swearing it to all three of them. She let her curse hover in the air, binding itself to truth, and even then, Dimitri still said nothing.

But once Yaga had turned to leave, she heard his voice at her back.

"If you are even half the witch my father says you are, Baba Yaga," Dimitri Fedorov beseeched her hoarsely, "then bring her back. Even if you have to go through hell to do it, Yaga, do it. Bring her back."

She paused, stiffening. "We are only witches, Dima. Not gods."

And then she turned to walk out of the room, one hand on Ivan's shoulder as he carried her lifeless daughter back home.

II. 22

(Epics.)

LEV: this story we're writing sasha

LEV: it's going to be epic

LEV: that, or a disaster

LEV: tbd

SASHA: in fairness most epics are about disasters

LEV: true

LEV: not you and me though

LEV: definitely not us

SASHA: you sound awfully confident

LEV: hard not to be

LEV: I can still taste you

LEV: when can I see you again

SASHA: when can I see you again

SASHA: jinx

LEV: ! don't jinx us

SASHA: fine

LEV: soon, though?

SASHA: yes

SASHA: soon

AN INVENTORY LIST

KOSCHEI'S WAREHOUSE

a GLADIATOR'S SPATHA, *once used*

CURSED MANACLES, *two pairs*

a MAGIC CARPET, *really more of an entry rug, unregistered with the Witches' Boroughs (could be registered by request, though it will cost you)*

a SET of DIAMOND EARRINGS, *responsible for at least three (3) false confessions*

an APOTHECARY TABLE *(marked* DO NOT TOUCH *for good reason, only to be handled with gloves of a particular kind of Argentinian snakeskin)*

GLOVES *of a particular kind of* ARGENTINIAN SNAKESKIN, *sold separately*

a VINTAGE CHEST *(of little value, save for the letters inside that detail a moderately frowned-upon method of youth extraction)*

an EMERALD POISON RING *(poison sold only by special request)*

BABA YAGA'S ARTISAN APOTHECARY

"INTOXICATING!" BATH BOMBS *(Prosecco, Rosé, Champagne)*

MOISTURIZERS *(Spring, Summer, Autumn, Winter)*

SERUMS *(Bestseller: "IT'S MAGIC!," designed to limit redness and restore elasticity of skin)*

HAIR *and* NAIL SUPPLEMENTS

a small display of CRYSTALS *(mostly rose quartz for cleansing, and because it's pretty)*

"GLOW GET 'EM," *a whipped luminizing* BODY BUTTER *(available in* PEARL *for a faintly hollow sheen,* BRONZE *for self-tanning, and* MOONLIT, *a seasonal special for the paranormal romance crowd)*

Baba Yaga's HANGOVER CURE *(aspirin)*

ACT III

WOES SHALL SERVE

JULIET: *O think'st thou we shall ever meet again?*
ROMEO: *I doubt it not, and all these woes shall serve*
For sweet discourses in our times to come.
JULIET: *O God, I have an ill-divining soul,*
Methinks I see thee now, thou art so low,
As one dead in the bottom of a tomb,
Either my eyesight fails, or thou look'st pale.

Romeo and Juliet,
Romeo and Juliet (Act III, Scene 5)

Ask for me tomorrow, and you shall find me a grave man.

Mercutio,
Romeo and Juliet (Act III, Scene 1)

III. 1

(Succession.)

To believe in destiny, one must also believe in succession. If the world is ruled by predetermination, then it must also be ordered, measured, paced out from first to last:

If this, then this.

Roman Fedorov knew nothing of the stars at his birth, but if he'd been told they stood for loyalty, for duty, for immobility of faith, he would have easily believed it. For Roman, destiny was a vehicle for purpose. If this, then this. If he was born a Fedorov son, then he would know no other identity. If he was born the second son, then he would revere his brother Dimitri as the heir. If he saw his father and his brother wronged, then he would defend them without regard for cost. He would take a threat made against his brothers as surely as if it were his own body in harm's way.

This methodology of purpose was for love of family, but it was more than that, too. It was because if Roman Fedorov didn't believe in succession, then being second-born would surely drive him mad. How was it possible to feel such greatness in one's bones and yet be kept from it by some inconsequentiality of birth? To give in to such a feeling would be to submit, inevitably, to chaos.

So—if this, then this.

Roman was six years old the first time he had seen his indomitable father silenced, and by his seven-year-old brother, no less. Their brother Lev had just been born, their mother passing in the night shortly after, and Dimitri—golden Dima, with his princely smile and his quick wit and his sun-stroked hair—had been the only one brave enough to touch their father's shoulder, resting one small hand on Koschei's back.

"Go to bed, Dima," Koschei had said without turning around, "and take that baby with you."

That baby. Koschei had nearly spat it out, ruthless in his grief.

Dimitri, then, rather than answering, had turned from his father's side, gathering the infant in his arms from the cradle that still sat beside their mother's bed.

"This baby is named Lev," Dimitri reminded his father, holding the child out for Koschei as Roman looked on, rigid with apprehension, and their father kept his hard gaze turned away. "He is called Lev, as Mama asked for him to be. Lyova, like a lion. I'm this lion's brother. I will protect him with my life, Papa, but I am not his mother, and I am not his father. If you will only be his father for me," Dimitri pleaded, "then I will be his brother. If you will not fail him, Papa, then neither will I."

He held out the baby then, and Koschei didn't move. He didn't blink. He merely stared at his own hands, and then Dimitri, astoundingly, shifted as if to drop the infant. The movement was so unpredictable and sharp that both Koschei and Roman stumbled forward, panicked, and the baby Lev began to cry in earnest, wailing with his little hands curled into fists.

"Dima!" Koschei roared in anger, snatching Lev from his eldest son's hands and pressing him close to his own chest, protective at last over the fragility of his newest son. "You would have dropped him!"

"No," Dimitri corrected, laughing his clever warrior's laugh, "because you wouldn't have let me, Papa. Nor would Roma," he added, gesturing over his shoulder to where Roman had stumbled forward, nearly falling over himself in his effort to keep the baby aloft. "Because we are all brothers," Dimitri explained, and Roman blinked, watching Koschei's eyes widen with understanding.

"Because, Papa," Dimitri finished, reaching out to let the crying Lev reach for his fingers, soothing him gently, "we are all your sons."

It was the first time Roman had ever seen his father humbled. Koschei was a great man, a man whom others listened to, but never had Roman seen that sort of rapt attention given from his father unto others. Devotion, Roman had always thought, was an act reserved for lesser men. But Koschei had reached up then, pulling Dimitri's golden head to his, and pressed his lips gently to the forehead of his eldest.

"I will give you everything, my son," Koschei had whispered, the words buried in Dimitri's golden brow, and in that moment, Roman understood that the entire world had shifted.

(*If this, then this.*)

For years Roman had replayed that moment in his head, wondering what exactly Dimitri had done to earn their father's hardwon respect. He wondered, too, what *he* would have done, had Dimitri not been there to speak for both of them. Even in Roman's most earnest of imaginations, though, he finally had to admit to himself the divergence of his nature from his brother's—had to concede, grudgingly, that he would never have done as Dimitri had done. Roman would have followed his father's instructions without question. He would have abided by his father's wishes, as any dutiful son should do. He would have taken Lev and cared for the baby himself, or tried to, if only so that Koschei's wishes would not have been so impiously pushed aside. If it were Roman, he would have made certain a man like their father never had cause to doubt the loyalty of his sons.

But was that not admirable, too?

It wasn't that Roman hated his brother. He didn't, not at all. Dimitri was frustratingly easy to love, after all, and Roman loved him as everyone else loved him—with helpless reverence, and with genuine awe. Roman saw his brother for all his splendor and rightly offered him his due, and to Dimitri's credit, he wasn't undeserving in the slightest. Dimitri was a brilliant leader, wearing his inherited authority like a comfortable garment; like a crown, resting naturally atop his golden head. He was a talented witch, a clever negotiator, a loyal brother—and Roman loved him, fiercely, as he loved his younger brother Lev as well. They were the Fedorov brothers, the three sons of Koschei, which Roman had always considered the singular truth that mattered most of all. He'd thought, for much of his life, that the Fedorov brothers, so long as they stood together, would never stand to fall.

But Dimitri Fedorov, like all heroes, had one near-fatal flaw.

Roman, ever a keen and questioning observer, vividly remembered the first time he had caught his brother Dimitri with the witch Marya Antonova, the daughter of Koschei's friend Antonov. It was back when Dimitri had been only sixteen and Marya seventeen, and while the Antonova witches had not become their enemies quite yet, there had still been something unnervingly treasonous about a girl—especially *that* girl, with *those* eyes, which clearly saw too much—being among Roman's father's things, tangled up with his brother's limbs. Roman himself had been just fifteen then, interpreting less the transgression itself than the pink in Masha's defiant cheeks and the not-quite-sorry look on Dima's face. His brother had turned around, pressing his finger to his lips: *Don't tell Papa, Roma,* he'd warned, though at a glance, he'd been nothing more than smug and unconcerned. Happy, even. As ever, all of Dimitri's golden features had been ablaze, and Roman felt the slightest divide then; the gaping of loyalty between them.

(*If this, then this.*)

He'd told Koschei anyway.

"Leave Dima be, Romik" was all Koschei had said, waving it away. "Calf love, that's all."

But Roman knew Marya Antonova did nothing with innocence. He'd seen her spells, her magic; the way that, increasingly, she would reach out and adjust Dimitri's hands, his power surging instantly and incomprehensibly at her touch. Even as a witch himself, Roman was uncomfortably certain that whatever Marya Antonova possessed was no trifling amount of skill. Masha was not a calf. She wasn't capable of a calf's love.

She also didn't seem to like Roman in the slightest.

"He's always watching," she'd whispered to Dimitri, who'd

laughed, blithely ignorant as always of Roman's ever-present orbit, even after years had passed.

"He's protective," Dimitri told her. "He's my brother."

"Protective like a vulture over a corpse," Marya muttered, shuddering. "He's not like you, Dima. He's not a hunter; he has no honor at all. He's a scavenger, and he death in his eyes—"

"Why should he have to be like me?" Dimitri countered, royally unfazed. "There's more than enough of me already, I imagine."

"Well, I prefer to have only you," Marya said gruffly, though she was quieted for a moment by the sound of a kiss, all muffled touches and tender sighs. "Only you, Dima," she said, her voice softening around his name.

"I am only for you," Dimitri had sworn to her. (Out of sight, Roman had curled a fist.)

"And I am only ever for you," Marya agreed. "Which is why, Dima, I don't trust Roma. Not with you. You're much too valuable."

Roman waited, tensing at her admonition, but again, his brother only laughed.

"If you love me, Masha," Dimitri said, "you will learn to love my brother, too."

"Why should I?" she retorted fiercely. "I'm not a Fedorov."

No, she wasn't, Roman thought, slipping away. Nor would she be, if Roman had anything to do with it.

"I don't like her," he'd said to his father, gritting his teeth around resentment that tasted like rage. "She's manipulative, Papa. She wants to take Dima for herself and steal him from us. She would have him turn his back on his family."

"Nobody will ever take Dima from me," Koschei replied, impassive, "but if you are so very opposed to her—"

"I am," Roman replied staunchly.

"—you will have to change your mind quite soon, as she will shortly be your sister," Koschei finished, and despite the unpleasant news of his father's proposed marriage to Baba Yaga, Roman had struggled to stifle a victorious smile.

Even then, Roman had known that the elder Marya Antonova would never agree. Inevitably, the Antonova witches would choose each other, and Dimitri, like Roman, was a Fedorov son before anything else. Dimitri could never forgive the slight against their father's name—of that much Roman was certain, and he soon found himself proven correct.

"She has refused me," Koschei informed all three of his sons, though at eleven, Lev was much too young to understand the complexities of what may as well have been an open declaration of war between the families. "No longer will we consort with the Antonova witches or their allies. They are nothing to us, and nothing to the Boroughs. We will not speak of them, nor do business with them, nor bother ourselves with them. Am I understood?"

"Yes, Papa," said Roman. As did Lev, who knew next to nothing of their brother's ill-advised romance. Dimitri, by contrast, had hesitated for a moment, but only one.

"Is it perhaps unwise, Papa," Dimitri ventured slowly, "to burn bridges with witches so powerful? Couldn't the relationship be salvaged still?"

"Baba Yaga has insulted me," Koschei said firmly in return, "and therefore, she has insulted all of us. Kill whatever softness you have for her daughter, Dima, as there is no mistaking what she has chosen. There is no misinterpreting what she's done."

Ever the Fedorov son, Dimitri dutifully buried his affections when asked, or so Roman had assumed. True, at first Dimitri had not lost hope that something might still come from the feud between Koschei and Baba Yaga—had seemed to believe, silently, that circumstances might soften, or that perhaps Marya might be persuaded to change her mother's mind—but that hope was doused with quiet violence at the news that the eldest Antonova witch would be marrying Stas Maksimov, an unremarkable Borough witch several years their senior who was the son of another equally uninspiring Borough witch.

Roman had seen the lines around his brother's mouth that meant for the first time, possibly ever, Dimitri was angry, or anguished. Perhaps both. Either way, Dimitri Fedorov's sun had shone very little that day, and Roman had taken it as a sign. His father had been wronged by the Antonovas, and now his brother, too. It was up to Roman, who loved them both, to seek out restitution.

(*If this, then this.*)

The younger Marya Antonova had been right that Roman had a watchful eye, and as punishment for her accuracy, he had specifically never stopped watching her. He kept tabs on her movements, becoming keenly attuned to her dealings with other witches, which was not necessarily a difficult thing to do. Marya's role as Baba Yaga's right hand and enforcer meant she eschewed subtlety for power by necessity. She, like Dimitri, bore the blessing and the burden of a highly distinctive face, one that some found beautiful while others, like Roman, found it disquieting, and so she was easy enough to find and easier still to follow. It was hardly much work at all to notice that she kept visiting the same person at regular intervals, and if it wasn't an affair—which Roman highly doubted it was—then it was obviously business.

After nearly a decade's vendetta, Roman finally managed to uncover Marya Antonova's primary informant: the man called Brynmor Attaway, who was otherwise known as The Bridge.

Koschei would never have worked with The Bridge. He hardly needed him, firstly, considering his own network was so vast, and secondly, it was no secret that Roman's father cared little for non-witches. Marya Antonova, by contrast, having no obvious sense of pride and even less of scruples, paid The Bridge handsomely for his information. But it was Roman who offered him something even better than money—the one thing he knew The Bridge could not resist.

Power. Specifically, the only power The Bridge could not produce for himself.

A *witch's* power.

"One vial per week," Bryn had said, eyeing the magic hidden

inside Roman's blood, "on Saturdays." The seventh day, biblically, and a day of portent. Typical fae nonsense, Roman knew. They as a species were helplessly given to ritual. "Do that for me, Fedorov, and you have a deal. I'll tell you who Marya Antonova is selling to, but if you're even a day late—"

"I won't be," Roman assured him coolly, perhaps six months ago, before he'd come to realize that what he offered wasn't quite as renewable as he had hoped.

(*If this, then this.*)

Dimitri had been the first to notice that Roman was slowly draining himself of his magic.

"Your hands are shaking," Dimitri noted, circling Roman with his usual princely concern. "Your control is limited. Are you giving it away, Roma, or selling it?"

"Neither," Roman said through gritted teeth, though the answer, more aptly, was both.

"Tell me what's going on," Dimitri commanded, flashing golden once again.

"We're going to bring down the Antonovas," Roman replied, and while he'd said it with certainty—with *promise*—he'd only seen Dimitri's eyes go hard, tension deepening around his mouth.

"Show me," he'd said, so Roman had brought him the tablets he'd intercepted. *I want chaos for the Antonovas,* he'd said to Bryn, who smiled his sharp-eyed smile, flashing his pearly teeth and checking his expensive watch. *Easy enough,* replied The Bridge, and just as quickly, the scam had begun. Bryn told Roman when the Antonova witches were selling the tablets. Roman bought them, turned them around, and sold them for a profit through Bryn, who took his earnings in vials of blood in exchange for thick stacks of bills. The constant draining of Roman's magic was taxing, sometimes like a fever, and his magic was wildly inconsistent, even unpredictable— but it was worth it, he reasoned, to one day bring down Baba Yaga and her Marya.

The plan had always been to hit their rivals where it would hurt them most, which was almost certainly the money. The Antonovas, unlike the Fedorovs, lacked the dignity of witchcraft built by a history of honor. They were nouveau riche, whereas Roman had always felt the Fedorovs were aristocracy, and the Antonovas took their conceit from the value of what they bought and sold rather than who they were. They were selfish, they were ruthless, and most importantly, they were rich, the first two things being dependent on the latter. It was to be a simple matter of draining them where they would feel the sting—but unfortunately, things had not gone as planned.

(*If this, then this.*)

"You can't continue like this," Dimitri said, watching Roman suffer a spasm of magic that rattled the walls, manifesting like a tremor beneath their feet as they glanced over the tablets. "You could kill yourself, Roma, if you're not careful—"

"Don't tell Papa," Roman warned instantly. "Or Leva. Please, Dima—"

"This has to stop," Dimitri cut in, "*now*, Roma. Today. You won't be giving The Bridge any more of your magic, and that begins immediately."

"I have to," Roman gritted out, irritated. Was Dimitri not even listening? "It's Saturday, and if I don't—"

The consequences were, quite literally, life-threatening. The Antonovas would kill him if they found out, not to mention what Koschei would think if he learned who Roman had been consorting with.

"The Bridge sells to the highest bidder, Dima," Roman continued, skirting the details, "and if Yaga finds out what I've done now, before we're ready—"

"I'll do it, then." Dimitri exhaled, shaking his head. "I'll do it for you today, Roma, but then it has to stop. It *has* to stop."

Roman had not appreciated his elder brother's tone. Nor had he appreciated the way Dimitri had strutted back to the apartment, chin too high, when Roman had been waiting for promising news. For *any* news, at least, that his efforts had not been wasted.

"I told him it was done," Dimitri said, and Roman clenched a fist. "If Mash—if *Marya*," Dimitri corrected himself, "were to find out what you've done, she'd kill you, and Roma, you can hardly defend yourself now, not like this—"

"Did you at least keep to our deal?" Roman demanded, rising to his feet. "Dima, you arrogant fucking fool, did you give him a vial?"

But Dimitri Fedorov, who had always been too arrogant to feel shame, suffered none from Roman's urging. "I don't consider your deal worthy of my approval," Dimitri said plainly, and turned away, leaving Roman behind.

Roman, then, had run.

"Please," he said to The Bridge, his hands still shaking. Thirty minutes past midnight. Sunday, by all accounts, though Roman had hoped there was some reasonable window of time with which to bargain. "Take it, take whatever you need, my brother was—" He broke off. "I shouldn't have trusted my brother," Roman seethed, or perhaps realized. "He's too blinded by the softness of his past—"

"Actually, your brother made some excellent points," Bryn informed Roman, lazily crossing one long leg over the other. "Why *should* I settle for your blood, Roman? It only gives me a fraction of what you possess, doesn't it? And you're getting weaker by the day. It's hardly enough for me to accomplish much at all, and certainly nothing I can produce on my own. No, I think he made a rather compelling statement," Bryn mused affirmatively, eyeing his glass, "and now I would prefer something a bit better, if you'd like to re-negotiate our contract."

"Better?" Roman echoed, disbelieving. "Look at me! How much more do you want? I'm not here to renegotiate."

At that, Bryn rose to his feet, striding forward to pause beside Roman. "A bit of free legal advice, Roman Fedorov? Our previous contract was violated earlier this evening by your own failure to meet the terms of our deal. Perhaps it slipped your notice, but renegotiation is all you've got."

Roman stiffened. "I didn't fail. My brother failed me."

"Technicalities," replied The Bridge, unfazed. "If you wish to renew our agreement and save yourself, Roman, then my demands are very simple: I want Dimitri Fedorov's magic instead," he said, and Roman felt the blood drain from his face.

"Why?" he demanded. "Why Dima?"

"Oh, I don't know, Roma," Bryn remarked, turning abruptly to pour himself more whisky. "Perhaps because yours is too easy. Perhaps by now it's too weak. Perhaps I simply enjoy raising the stakes for my own amusement. Or perhaps I'm a fucking fairy," Bryn suggested, taking a testing sip before nodding his approval, "and I've spotted the opportunity for a better deal than the one I have now."

"What about someone else, then?" Roman cut in, desperate. "Not Dima. Someone his equal."

"Who is possibly Dimitri Fedorov's equal?" Bryn scoffed. "Certainly not you."

Roman grimaced. "What if I gave you—" He paused, blinking. "What if I gave you Marya Antonova's magic instead?"

At that, Bryn paused; a dead giveaway. Something valuable had been placed on the table, and not even The Bridge himself could conceal his interest. "And how would you do that?" Bryn asked, though Roman could see the deal was as good as done.

"Not easily," Roman admitted aloud, "and it may take me some time. But yes, it could certainly be done."

It wasn't a total impossibility. Played correctly, Marya Antonova and Dimitri Fedorov had always been a match set to burn, perennially mere breaths from disaster—two people born as much to oppose each other as to be made for one another. There had been no question in Roman's mind that reuniting them would be precisely the explosion he needed. Marya would not be able to kill Dimitri; Dimitri, too, would be unable to oppose Marya. At best, Dimitri Fedorov was Marya Antonova's greatest weakness. At worst, she was his.

Of course, a voice whispered temptingly in Roman's mind, in what might very well be an inevitable stalemate between the

Antonova heir and the Fedorov heir, Roman himself might finally be permitted room to rise. Roman could surface as the loyal son, his fidelity unwavering—and in so doing, he would both spare his brother and gain the honor of finally destroying the Antonova family's most powerful witch.

(*If this, then this.*)

"So, do we have a deal, then?" Roman prompted, holding out a hand. "I'll give you Marya Antonova's magic, and in exchange, our deal continues. You help me bring her down, and I'll give you what you want."

"And if you fail?" Bryn prompted.

"And if I fail," Roman said, and swallowed. "I'll give you Dima."

He wouldn't, of course. He was certain he wouldn't have to.

Bryn eyed his outstretched hand, considering it. "Deal," he said eventually, clasping Roma's hand with his long, narrow fingers and binding him to his word with the only gift the fae possessed, the contract of their engagement tingling against Roman's palm. "Though, I should tell you, of course, that Marya already knows," Bryn murmured as an afterthought, and Roman blinked.

"Knows what?"

"She knows that someone cheated her," Bryn replied, releasing Roman's hand, "and now, I believe, she suspects a member of your family. Did I not mention this?" To Roman's gaping silence, The Bridge continued, "Sadly, it seems that one of Marya Antonova's *very reliable* informants saw fit to share his suspicions sometime around midnight on the eve of a broken deal—and now," he lamented, taking a laughing sip of his whisky, "it appears she's mildly displeased with what she's heard."

For a moment, Roman was frozen with disbelief. Once the words had processed, though, he lunged, seizing a threatening handful of Bryn's lapel. "Why didn't you tell me this before we made the deal?"

"Well, it seemed largely a family matter," Bryn replied, nudging Roman away and taking another restrained sip. "Besides, I hadn't really thought you capable of offering me anything I wanted. Seems I was wrong, so good on you for that."

It was terrible news. The *most* terrible, as far as Roman was concerned, and he felt well and rightly tricked, knowing now why The Bridge had been so willing to secure another deal in place of the old one. "But she will come for me, *and* for Dima," Roman said urgently, fidgeting, "and we're not ready—*I'm* not ready—"

"Sounds like a you problem," Bryn remarked, dismissive. "But I'm sure you'll think of something. After all," he said, the single slab of ice tinkling in his glass, "I'm sure you wouldn't want me any further dissatisfied, seeing as now your brother's life is on the line."

At that, Roman suffered a sickening wave of disbelief, glaring at him. "What can you do to me, to any of us?" he demanded. "You're not a witch, Bridge—"

"No, I'm not," Bryn confirmed, "which is perhaps the most compelling part. After all, would Koschei the Deathless be pleased to hear his son is in my debt?" he asked, and as Roman's expression stiffened at the acknowledgment of his father's private identity, The Bridge merely shrugged, shadows on the wall dancing in the space between them. "Didn't think so. It's common knowledge what Koschei thinks of creatures—and now, after everything, your debt is even weightier." Bryn's mouth was a tormenting smile. "Your clock is ticking, Roman Fedorov. Don't keep me waiting."

Roman's return home after his meeting with The Bridge had been a blur, Dimitri's angered voice echoing dully between his ears.

Roma, what were you thinking—I cannot let you do this—I can't possibly do anything now but hope Marya will listen, that perhaps she can forgive me—

(If this, then this—)

"Leave my brothers out of it," Dimitri had said to Marya Antonova just before she killed him—*tried* to kill him. Roman suffered his secret for days, waiting impatiently for the inevitable. Waiting for Marya to remember her love of Dimitri and repent, to seek him out, to be at last unable to resist the lure she'd always felt for him and to be caught in the meantime, with nobody but herself to blame. But when Marya had brought Dimitri back, just as Roman had suspected she would, that had been far worse, because then Roman heard the truth about his brother's loyalty from Dimitri's own lips.

I would have gone to you, Masha, if you'd asked. You would have only had to ask, and I would have chosen you over everything.

Over *everything*, Dimitri had said, the words numbing Roman's heart from afar. Over his father; over his brothers; over being a Fedorov son; over Roman himself, even while Roman was struggling to save him. Roman had always known Marya Antonova would come for his brother—had known quite a bit about her, after so many years of enmity—but suddenly, he understood that he was the fool who hadn't realized the depths of his own brother's love; his obsession, and the reckless way Dimitri still loved a woman who'd turned on him, who'd defied him, who'd pledged her life to another man. For a moment, Roman hadn't even known his brother at all, and though he hadn't originally planned to kill Marya (he only needed her magic, only a piece of her, an organ of hers at most) it had been easy, the most obvious of choices, to pierce through the woman in Dimitri's arms, tugging the sword free and leaving her to collapse against the floor.

But for all that Roman hadn't anticipated the rage he'd felt over knowing the truth of his brother's loyalty, nor could he stand the remorse. He'd killed before, where necessary, but he'd never struck at his own brother's heart. He'd never seen Dimitri in pain at his own hands. He hadn't known it would be so terrible, like cutting out a piece of himself.

(*If this, then*—?)

So, in anger, Roman had left his brother behind to grieve, and when he returned, mouth full of apologies, he found he'd made a terrible mistake.

"Where is she?" Roman demanded, eyeing the pool of blood on the floor and the vacancy of Marya Antonova's body that his brother had curled around, suddenly small and dimmed and draped in shadow. "What have you done with her?"

Dimitri wouldn't look at him. "Gone" was all he said, his voice hollowed and dull, and Roman's heart thudded in agitation. In warning.

In ever-present doom.

"No, Dima, no, we need her," Roman hissed, shaking Dimitri's shoulder and hoping that somehow, miraculously, the brother he'd known for a lifetime would suddenly reappear. "Where is she, Dima? I need her body—I need it *now,* before the magic drains out of it—"

"For what?" Dimitri asked, his haunted gaze sliding slowly to Roman's. "I ended your deal with The Bridge. You owe him nothing."

"Dima." Roman heard himself pleading. "Listen to me. You can't possibly—"

"What's this?" came a voice behind them, paired with the familiar sound of Lev's lengthy stride. "Dima," Lev gasped, catching sight of the blood and lurching forward, "are you hurt? What happened? What are y—Is this *blood,* Dima?"

Dimitri looked up slowly, the unfocused haze in his eyes gradually finding a place to land as he reached out, running two crimson-stained fingers along their youngest brother's cheek.

"Marya Antonova is dead," Dimitri said, the name sounding foreign on his tongue. For years he'd spoken nothing of her and now there was an echo of something very close to nothing, as if he were naming a stranger. "Roma killed her himself." He rose to his feet, gripping Lev's shoulder, and let his gaze travel slowly to Roman's, landing with the dull thud of a blow. "I hope it doesn't pain you too terribly, brother," he said softly, his fingers tensed and white around Lev's shoulder, "whatever this brings upon your head."

"You killed her?" Lev asked, his young face aghast when it met Roman's. "Why? How? But Sasha—"

"Sasha?" Dimitri cut in, still staring at Roman, who didn't look away. "Sasha Antonova? What have you done?"

Lev closed his mouth at once, glancing uncertainly between his brothers.

"Nothing," Roman insisted, lifting his chin in a way that meant *everything*. "I did what had to be done while you were being drained of your life in this bed. While you were dying, Dima, I was trying to save us. You."

"To *save* us?" Dimitri spat, and Lev glanced uneasily between them.

"What's going on?" Lev asked, frowning. "What are you saying?"

Please, Roman mouthed to Dimitri, who stiffened.

Don't tell Papa, don't tell Lev—

"Nothing," Dimitri said eventually, hardening again as he turned away from Roman. "It's nothing, Lyova. You came to see me," he added, touching their youngest brother's forehead in recognition. "I heard you speaking to me."

Lev nodded, leaning gratefully into Dimitri's touch.

"What's this about Sasha?" Dimitri asked him gently, but Lev, always caught between the wishes of his brothers, glanced at Roman first.

"Nothing," Lev said, hasty in his response. "I met her, that's all. She's—" He swallowed, glancing from Roman to Dimitri. "Up to something. The Antonova witches. They're planning something."

"Then let them," Dimitri said, resting both hands on Lev's shoulders. "Leave them be, Lyova, I mean it—"

"You're not Koschei," Roman cut in sharply, glaring at Dimitri from across the room. "You don't make orders, Dima."

Roman still had a debt. He needed Lev's loyalty if he couldn't have Dimitri's.

"True," Dimitri acknowledged slowly. "I'm not Koschei—*yet*."

It was a promise and a threat, a declaration of hierarchy, and it tore at the ties between brothers. Roman felt a shattering of something in his chest, the pieces settling to ash in his mouth and coating the length of his tongue in a chalky taste of fear and loathing. Worse, he didn't know which one he felt more.

"Leave us," Dimitri murmured to Lev, who hesitated.

"Dima—"

"Go," Dimitri said, and Lev obeyed, slowly turning to leave. In their younger brother's absence, Roman's blood turned to ice in his veins, subjecting him to a chill.

"Dima," he began, "I need you to listen to me. I need Marya's body, and I need it *now*—"

"I don't want to listen to you, Roma," Dimitri cut in coldly, his prince's voice tainted with rage. "I don't want to think about you, I don't want to see you, I don't want to hear your fucking voice, I don't want to know about your needs or requests or your *secrets*—"

"Dima. The Antonovas, you know that they . . . that they'll come for me." Roman swallowed. "As payment. For Masha." At her name, Dimitri flinched. "Dima, they'll kill me, you know they'll kill me, but I can stop it—I can *stop* it, and Papa will never have to know, if you'll just tell me where Masha's body is—"

"Why, so you can sell it for parts?" Dimitri demanded, snarling at him. "So you can sell off what made her what she was, just like you sold what made you what *you* are? You'd kill her and defile her too, Roman, honestly?"

"I—" Roman gritted his teeth, fighting a surge of irritation. "She's already dead, Dima. Hate me if you want, but nothing worse can come to a corpse—"

"No." Dimitri's voice was audibly final. "You can't have her, Roma. You won't take her from me twice."

"So you'd let me die instead?" *Or cost me you,* Roman didn't say, though he heard the undercurrent of fear in his voice, the longing, and wondered if Dimitri could hear it too. "Dima, please—"

He didn't register Dimitri stepping closer until after his brother had shoved him against the wall, glaring down at him. "Don't you dare beg me, Roma," Dimitri said darkly. "Don't beg me now, not after I begged you to help me save her life and you refused. You killed her—you *slaughtered* her—and now you think you deserve better than what she got?"

"Do you really love her more than me?" Roman slid through

his teeth. "More than this family, Dima, is that what you're saying? You'd turn your back on me, leave me to die, all because of her?"

For a brief moment, Dimitri's jaw went slack.

"Don't you see?" Dimitri said, not quite looking at Roman. "You took her from me, and still I would never give you up. You took her from me, and because of you, I'll never be whole—but would I let you die, brother?" He looked up then, pained and wearied. "Never. I would never let them touch you, no matter how badly I wish I could be rid of you. You're my brother." He exhaled into the palm of his hand, helpless. "You're my brother, and that's the worst part."

"Dima," Roman said, thinking he saw a white flag and reaching desperately for it. "Dima, please—"

"Whatever happens to our family is on your conscience, Roma," Dimitri warned, preparing to leave the room and pausing only briefly; only to glance askance at Roman. "Whatever comes of this, it will either be your doing, or your undoing. Whatever happens, you will live with the consequences, but it will not be on my hands."

Roman froze, swallowing heavily.

"I won't give you up, Romik, but that's it," Dimitri said. "I'm keeping you from death, not letting you live. There's a difference."

(*If this, then what? If this is the truth of my brother's heart, then what am I?*)

In the end, when Dimitri was gone, Roman was no longer much of a believer in destiny after all.

III. 2

(Promises.)

SASHA: *lev*
LEV: *i'm here*
SASHA: *my sister is dead*

Are you ok, he typed out, and then deleted it. Of course she wasn't. *Do you need anyth*

Stupid.

I know

Guilty.

Sasha I swear to fucking god nobody will ever hurt you, I will never, ever, let anyone hurt you, I won't let them touch you, I'll burn the world down myself before anyone ever lays a hand on you

He sighed, deleting the words, and shook his head.

LEV: *i'm coming*

Then he tucked his phone into his pocket, shivering as he stepped back out into the night.

III. 3

(Watch Me Burn.)

She waited for him outside, hair loose, eyes dry.

"You will carry on as planned," Yaga had informed Sasha, as if nothing had changed. The Fedorovs had tried to destroy them, Yaga explained, and therefore there was only one avenue. Business as usual.

Somehow, Sasha had come to reason internally that it was for the best. It wasn't enough to cry for Marya, who wouldn't want tears. If Marya were here, Sasha knew, she would merely stroke one finger down Sasha's cheek and whisper, *Sasha, my Sashenka, we are Antonova witches and we do not weep for loss.*

Sasha raised her chin, swallowing sorrow. It would be rage soon enough. Until then, she wanted comfort. She wanted warmth, devotion, distraction. Touch. She wanted Lev Fedorov, and the moment his face appeared, cheeks pink with cold, Sasha felt something monstrous untwist its hold on her heart, if only for an instant. The wind had whipped the dark strands of his hair into his eyes and he blinked them away, not taking his gaze from hers.

"Sasha," he said, her name mournful on his tongue, and she pulled him into her and kissed him, her hands tightly grasping the collar of his coat. Could he really taste so sweet, being her enemy? There was no doubt that he was, now and always, and maybe the scathing cosmic joke of it all was that instinctively, like muscle memory, she'd known it all along. Maybe the hilarity had always been in ever thinking she could have him, and now it curdled in her throat, the acidity of a mirthless laugh. Marya would disapprove, surely, but where was she to do so now? The thought struck at Sasha with the savagery of loss and she flinched, tugging Lev close, her icy fingers clutching the line of his jaw until he pulled away, breathless.

"Sasha," he exhaled, his hands shifting mindlessly to warm her arms, "is now really the time to—"

"Lev," she murmured in curt retort, not letting go. "Can you honestly promise me there will be another time?"

They both knew better. The irony was mutual, but so was the wanting. "Where do you want to go?" he asked eventually, eyes fluttering shut with resignation.

"Anywhere." A different life, a different world, somewhere under different stars. Any place but here and now. "Nowhere."

His grip on her tightened. "Sasha—"

"Lev." She slid her hands down from his face to settle her thumbs in the dip of his collarbone, resting them there. He wasn't wearing a scarf. Neither of them was ever prepared for weathering anything. "Don't be a gentleman right now." She pronounced the word *gentleman* like *idiot*. "We might not have time for an entire book."

"Don't say that," he managed, mouth dry. "Please don't say that."

Sasha leaned forward, lips against his cheek. "Write me a tragedy, Lev Fedorov," she whispered to him. "Write me a litany of sins. Write me a plague of devastation. Write me lonely, write me wanting, write me shattered and fearful and lost. Then write me finding myself in your arms, if only for a night, and then write it again. Write it over and over, Lev, until we both know the pages by heart. Isn't that a story, too?" she asked him softly.

He hesitated. "This isn't the story I wanted for us."

"It never is," replied Sasha, who knew better.

Lev shuddered, reaching behind him; with a rip, they tore through space, spiraling out of the grips of physicality and re-appearing in the cool air of a room, empty of sound, all the lights extinguished. Sasha looked around, identifying landmarks as they came into focus: Bookcase. Dresser. Nightstand. Bed. A single open window, with an airy white curtain blowing out into the night.

"It's winter, Lev," she said. "You're going to get pneumonia."

"I was listening for you," he said, confirming her suspicions: this was his bedroom, then.

His space. His place.

She took a step away from him, heading to the window. They were somewhere downtown still, the sights and sounds familiar. How often had she stood somewhere down below, wandering on the ground while he'd been above, gazing over the steps of her life without either of them knowing it? How many times had she shaded her eyes from the sun, not knowing that Lev stood above, looking on overhead?

She slid a hand into the night, testing the wind. It felt different now, living in a world where Marya was gone. All the space of it, and the city below, felt empty.

She thought to close the window and then thought better of it, turning to Lev. He stood still, waiting, feet planted, all his motion ceased for her. His world had stopped for her, and hers for him.

At least for now. Until the sun rose, and everything changed.

She could see his indecision. "If you'd prefer me to leave," she offered blandly, pointedly, and his mouth twitched, a helpless step drawing him closer.

"I brought you here, didn't I?"

She nodded. "It's nice," she said, running her hands over his dresser and inspecting her fingertips. No dust. Marya would appreciate his sense of cleanliness, Sasha thought, and felt a sudden surge of brutality. Of violence.

She turned to him sharply. "My sister is dead, Lev. My favorite sister. My best one."

He said nothing.

"My family will come for her killer."

Again, Lev didn't speak.

"Would you deny us that?" she prompted, unsure whether she was lashing out or genuinely asking. "You and your brothers, are you any different from us?"

He swallowed, shaking his head. "No."

"I didn't think so," Sasha murmured. "So, this may be the only night we'll ever have, Lev Fedorov." She paused, leaning back against his dresser, indiscreetly eyeing the motions he had yet to take between them and the distance he hadn't yet closed. "Do you want to spend it discussing the weather," she asked, "or do you have something more satisfying in mind?"

She waited for a cinematic abandonment of reluctance. A surge of ardency to ignite them both. Now that they were here, now that they'd both confessed the obvious, it should have been easy, should have been simple, straightforward—me, you, us.

It wasn't.

"You're hurting," Lev said neutrally. "You think I can fix it?" He shook his head. "I can't."

It was surprisingly dismissive, at least for him. "Fine." Sasha stiffened, turning away. "Take me back, then."

"No," he retorted, all stubborn angles and wild glances, and she glared at him. "Only if you want to leave," he amended with a grimace, "and I know you don't."

Sasha bristled. "Suddenly you're an expert in what I want?"

"Not an expert. Only a fairly good observer."

The assertion pricked at her, set her on edge. "Show me, then," Sasha snarled, rounding on him. "Show me how good you are," she suggested, drawing him close enough to slide her hand down his torso, but he caught her fingers, holding them still.

"I don't want your anger," he said. She recoiled, irritated, though he didn't release her hand.

"What do you want, then?" she said. "My grief? Is that it?"

"If it's real, yes," Lev permitted, shrugging. His hand was firm against hers, his breath shifting underneath it, and she hated that he was always so cavalier with his demands. She didn't want him on his knees, true, but she would have preferred a marginal softening of his chin. Even a single degree of humility might have set her rattled nerves at ease. "If that's what you feel, then it's what I want."

"You want me to cry on your shoulder, Lev Fedorov? You want me to be your damsel in distress? It won't happen. I'm an Antonova," she warned him, "and you're about to find out exactly what that means."

If it struck him as prophetic, he merely shivered without a word.

"Sasha," he said, his hand tightening on hers, "don't be stupid."

Strangely, she breathed a little easier at that—at the brief window of normalcy.

"I want you," he murmured, twining her fingers with his, "and you have me so easily, without lifting a finger. But don't use me."

"Then use me instead," she flung at him, trying to pull her hand away again and failing, rooted in place by his touch. "Weren't you supposed to be easy?" she said with a mirthless laugh.

"Sasha." He pulled her in close, holding her tighter as she resisted. "Sasha, if your heart is broken, sex isn't going to fix it—"

"Then why did you bring me here?" It sparked again, the violence. The rage that circled something darker, something into which she might fall and never return. "Why am I here, Lev? Just let me—just let me *go*—"

She beat a fist against his chest, furious and frustrated and faltering, the pain in her chest a slow bleed from a rotting incision, but he didn't relent. He turned his head, flinching slightly as she glared at him, but didn't ease his hold.

"If I lost my brother, I would chase his soul to the end of the world," Lev said quietly, and Sasha stopped fighting for a moment, paused by the weary timbre of his voice. "If it were me, Sasha, I'd want to strike down everything in my path, just like this, so believe me, I understand—but if I can only have you as a fire, Sasha, as a flame of what you are, then I want you to burn for me. Do you understand? I'll hold you if you want me to," he whispered, his voice a crook of a finger to the tired tendrils of her heart. "Want me to keep you close, Sasha, keep you safe? I'll do it. But if I'm going to know things—intimate things, like how you prefer to be touched," he said, firmly, in a man's voice—a *lover's* voice—"things I know I'll never be able to rid from my mind—then do me a favor and let me be selfish. Let me imagine you might have come to my bed for *me*, even if I can never h—"

He broke off when she kissed him again, restless fingers tugging at his coat. "Take this off," she said gruffly, and he stared down at her, indignant.

"Haven't you been listening?" he demanded, but she only stepped out of his arms, pulling her sweater over her head and watching his gaze drop. "I—Sasha, *Sasha,* I just said—"

"You want me to burn for you?" she asked. "Then watch me burn." She slid his jacket from his shoulders, tossing it to the floor, and shifted to wrestle with the buttons of his shirt, her fingers scratching the skin beneath each one with every inelegant fumble. She felt each pulse in his chest like a congratulatory thud of progress at her touch, her hands at once impossibly sure and helplessly unsteady.

He watched her, barely moving, until she finished to wrench his arms back, the sleeves caught around his shoulders. "Now would be the time, Lev," she said impatiently, and he blinked, suddenly leaping to help her, one arm snaking out to wrap around her waist the moment it had been freed.

The kiss between them then was brutally communicative, the rest of the conversation transmuted to touch. He asked permission and she gave it, her hips aligned with his; she begged him and he relented, tugging her backward to fall against him. She remembered his first kiss, how easy it had been, how difficult, how untamed and how helplessly delicate, and this was all of that and more, a thousand tiny earthquakes. When his hands slid to the curve of her hips she sighed between his lips, a moment of tender softness that could so easily have been a lie.

He leaned his head back, meeting her eye.

"I'm your enemy in the morning," he whispered. Fair warning.

His hand traced the shape of her scapula, fingers brushing the length of her spine and then curling upward, possessive.

"I'm your enemy tonight," she said, and kissed him again.

III. 4

(Blame.)

There were certain things from which Stas Maksimov had always turned his head, unseeing; a necessity at times, being the husband of Marya Antonova and therefore beholden to Baba Yaga's labyrinth of secrets despite his vocation as a Borough witch. Stas knew his wife routinely kept a vast number of things from him, replying to many of his questions with a smiling *Do you really want to know, Stanislav?* and he would no doubt demur, opting not to interfere. Borough witch or not, betraying his wife was never an option.

From time to time, though, there were things he couldn't ignore, being not entirely blind.

"Whatever you're doing, Yaga," Stas said quietly, resting his hand on his mother-in-law's shoulder as she busied herself among her herbs, "I beg you, do not."

Yaga didn't answer. She was a proud woman, and while she'd seemed to think well enough of Stas throughout his relationship with Marya, she'd certainly lent him no favors. He was merely the man who had married her favorite daughter, he knew, and nothing more than that.

In this, as in most things, he had no place in her regard—but still, he hoped she would listen.

"I love my wife," Stas reminded her, feeling a cruel, savage pain at the thought of it: *loved.* "I loved my wife well, and I will mourn her just as fully as I loved her in life, but nothing good will come of this. Don't make her life a cause for vengeance, and certainly don't make a monster of her, Yaga, please—"

"She didn't love you," Yaga replied coldly, a blow as crippling as any. "Not as she loved me, Stas, or her sisters." She was silent for a moment before adding, "Not as she loved Dima."

Stas flinched. He'd heard enough in his time about Dimitri Fedorov, a man he barely knew and tried desperately not to hate, which was a feat he only scarcely managed. Dimitri's was a name only used as a weapon, and was certainly nothing Stas wished to hear now, while he was mourning his wife.

I promise you I'll never see him again, Marya had said to Stas about Dimitri once while still early in their courting, *and you may trust my word on that without fail, if only because if I do, I may never come back to you at all.*

"She loved me," Stas corrected Yaga carefully. He and Marya had shared a life together, after all, and during that time, his wife had never spoken Dimitri Fedorov's name aloud. For close to twelve years she had been Stas Maksimov's partner, his companion and his friend and his lover, and whatever shape her past had taken before him, not once had she failed him. Not once.

"She loved me," he said again, "and I know you wouldn't cheapen our life together simply because you are suffering, Yaga. Maybe she never loved me like she loved Dimitri Fedorov, but there are other loves. There are better loves," he informed her, defensive, "loves that enrich us, that don't cost us our lives and our sanity—"

"This is not your business, Stas," Yaga told him, cutting him off just as Marya's bodyguard Ivan materialized in the doorway.

Stas turned, glancing up briefly at Ivan's entrance, and then instinctively looked away; his stomach twisted in agony to witness the look of anguish on the other man's face.

Clearly there had been many men who'd loved Stas's wife. Hard enough coming second to Dimitri Fedorov, but to imagine a hopelessness like Ivan's . . . impossible. If it had been Stas in Ivan's place, could he have brought himself to love her still, knowing perfectly well there was not one man before him in her esteem, but two?

Yes, Stas knew silently, and could not bear to see it written so plainly on Ivan's face.

Stas Maksimov, who had always been aware of his luck in being Marya Antonova's choice, suffered once again the blow of knowing she was gone. No other man could claim his pain; the meager suffering of others was built only on imagination, on delusion. Only Stas had possessed the fortune of loving the woman herself, of knowing her as she truly was, and thus only Stas could know what torment it was to lose her. It clawed at his chest to watch Ivan martyr himself, as if only his devotion had mattered in the end.

"Do you need me, Yaga?" Ivan asked her solemnly, and she shook her head.

"Your duty is to Sasha," Yaga reminded him. "That was Masha's request of you, wasn't it? See to it Masha's wishes are met. That's what you can do for me, and for her, and nothing else."

Ivan nodded. "Yes, Baba Yaga," he said, and stepped away, sparing a brief look of contempt for Stas. The intention was clear enough: *You let her go,* Ivan's expression accused. *You couldn't keep her. You didn't protect her.*

Stas lifted his chin. *Neither did you,* he made sure his posture replied, and Ivan turned away without a word, disappearing into the corridor.

"Go home," Yaga said to Stas, moving to enter the locked door of her bedroom again with a final glance at him over her shoulder. "You are right, Stanislav, that she loved you well."

Yaga paused, toying with something. For a woman who famously felt no remorse, Stas thought perhaps he saw a glimpse of it.

"If your love is dead along with my daughter, Stas, then bury it," Yaga suggested. "I will ask nothing more from you."

Stas's skin pebbled, reverberations of a threat. "And if I don't?"

Yaga's cool expression hardened. "Then you will not like what you see," she replied simply, and slid through the doorway, closing the door behind her.

III. 5

(It Is the Nightingale.)

The twinkling sound of his phone alarm woke Lev with a jolt, his arms tightening reflexively around Sasha's waist. She shifted, leg still slid between his in the tangled mess of sheets, and reached across his chest, turning the alarm off.

"I should go," she said, moving to sit up, and Lev vigorously shook his head, pressing his lips to her shoulder and holding her in place.

"Not morning yet," he murmured into her skin. "Look," he added, gesturing to the window. "Still dark."

"That's just winter, Lev," Sasha sighed. "It's morning. Your alarm? Remember? You set it yourself, and you know I can't stay here—"

"Stop." He kissed her shoulder, luring her back into his arms, and she let out a falsely irritated sigh, letting him draw her against his chest. "Stay."

"I can't stay," she reminded him with a shake of her head. "You know I can't."

"But if you leave now—" He shivered. "Sasha. I have the worst feeling."

"It's called seasonal affective disorder," she advised, moving to pull away again and reaching for her clothes. "And anyway, if anyone were to catch me here, I imagine that feeling would become much worse."

She slid her sweater over her head and paused, glancing over her shoulder as he pressed his lips to her spine.

"You're being dramatic, Lev," she informed him, her hair cascading down her back, soft and lush and leaving. "Normally it's endearing, but at the moment it's very unhelpful—"

"I'm not trying to help," Lev assured her, pulling her back into his arms and rolling the both of them over, pinning her shoulders against the sheets to drop his lips once more to hers. "Unless I'm doing it very badly," he murmured, smiling with satisfaction as she drew her legs up around his hips, "I'm trying to keep you in my bed."

"LEV!" came a shout from downstairs. "Lev, are you home?"

He slid a hand quickly over Sasha's mouth as she gasped aloud, the sound muffled into his palm.

"Quiet," he warned, and she glared at him. "You're right, you should go—"

"Weren't you just the one being unhelpful? See how it feels, then," she muttered, swatting his hand away. She teased her fingers down his stomach with positively villainous delight, forcing him to swallow what might have been an ill-advised moan. "It's barely morning," she purred, kissing his neck. "Just tell him you're asleep—"

"Leva," Roman's voice came again, somewhere on the other side of the door. "Are you sleeping? Wake up. Lev, I—"

He turned the knob, and Lev thrust out a frantic hand, spelling the door shut.

"What the *fuck*, Lev—"

"Siblings," Sasha whispered, shaking her head in mock disapproval as Lev gave her a scolding glance.

"You have to go," he hissed, trying not to groan aloud when her hips shifted against his. "Believe me, I don't want you to, but if he catches you in here—"

"Lev," Roman growled, "open the door. We need to talk, *now*. Has Dima been here?"

"Dima?" Sasha echoed, suddenly sitting up as Lev leapt to his feet, gathering the remainder of her clothes and tossing them to her. "But I thought he was—"

She stopped herself with a grimace, possibly having realized that *dispatched* was not a word Lev would take kindly to.

"No, he hasn't," Lev shouted to Roman, sparing Sasha a pleading glance. "What's so important it can't wait until I'm dressed, Roma?"

"Is that all this is?" Roman asked through the door, unimpressed. "I've seen your dick before, Lev, and as usual I have no interest in

it. We need to discuss the plan for tonight now, before Dima tries
to interfere—"

"Why would he interfere?" Lev and Sasha asked in unison, and
he glared at her again.

"*Go*," he hissed, "seriously—"

"The game is changing, Lev," Roman said, and then slammed a
hand against the door, startling Lev and Sasha both as she yanked
her jeans over her hips. "And you and I need to—" He let out a
growl of impatience. "Will you just *let me in,* for fuck's sake—"

Go, Lev mouthed urgently, as Sasha pressed her lips to his, kissing
his apprehension away. She rested her hand on his still-bare chest,
digging her nails in briefly, and then stepped back, swallowing. She
tilted her head—giving him one final, searching look, memorizing
him where she stood—and rippled in the air, disappearing at precisely the moment that an impatient Roman blasted the door open,
shoving through the remnants of Lev's flimsy ward.

"Jesus," Roman said, eyeing the disarray that had been Lev's
blissful night with Sasha. "What happened here?"

"What's the problem with Dima?" Lev asked without reply,
reaching for a T-shirt and pulling it gruffly over his head. "I don't
understand. What is it you want taken care of?"

"Marya's dead, Lev," Roman said, his gaze distinctly wild. "But
we—I—still need an Antonova witch. The deal won't be canceled,
I'm sure it won't, which means Yaga will send someone else in her
place. Someone Marya's equal," he said emphatically, eyes shining
with the frenzy of a man who hadn't slept, "which is precisely what
we need."

"For what?" Lev demanded. "Can't we just . . . can't we let this
go," he growled, pleading with his brother in a way he knew to be
hopeless and yet supremely paramount. "I understand your anger,
Roma, but Dima's alive—Dima's *alive,* Marya's dead, and isn't that
enough? Can't we just—" He faltered. "Roma, can't we—"

"Lev." Roman leapt toward him, mouth stiff. "You're my brother.

You know I wouldn't ask you for anything unless it were dire. Tell me you know that."

Lev blinked at Roman's uncharacteristic sincerity. "I do know that, Roma, but—"

"Lev. Please."

"I just want to know *why*, Roma—"

"I've cared for you, Leva. I've protected you, your entire life. I've never wronged you," Roman insisted, "have I?"

He seemed to be genuinely asking. Lev stared, breathless, as *dire* clearly began to personify in Roman. "You haven't," he conceded, and Roman nodded, visibly relieved.

"So you'll help me, then?" Roman asked, his grip tight on Lev's arm. "Are you with me?"

Lev felt the precipice of the moment like a chasm yawning beneath his feet.

"Of course," he said, knowing it was true and wondering how soon he might come to regret it.

III. 6

(Transference.)

Is it too soon to love you, Sasha? Lev had asked her the night before, holding her in his arms between episodes of reprehensible choices; between moments of passion equally inadvisable and undeniable, all of which would surely haunt her for the rest of her life.

Absolutely too soon, she murmured back. She'd felt him smile into her hair and then she'd buried her face in his chest, opting not to add the truth: that for better or worse, he had brought her down with him.

Still, her feelings aside, it was difficult not to think about what she'd overheard while Lev's brother had been breaking down his bedroom door. She'd known it was a Fedorov who killed her sister, but she'd wanted to believe, somehow, that it had been Koschei himself—that the villain she'd grown up fearing had spirited her sister away like the demon he was, rather than letting the blame fall to Lev or his brothers. Surely it wouldn't be someone so close to her own age, or to her own circumstance; surely not someone who barged into Lev's bedroom like one of her own sisters would do to her.

If I lost my brother, Lev had told her, *I would chase his soul to the end of the world.*

At the memory, Sasha felt foolish. She felt chilled by humiliation at the reminder that when Lev had found her—when her life had collided with his—he had already lost his brother, or narrowly escaped losing him by fortuity alone. He must have been seeking revenge then, just as she was now. The Fedorovs had acted against her family once, and he'd specifically said not to trust him, hadn't he?

Lev himself had said it: *I'm your enemy in the morning.*

Sasha had insisted they could both check their secrets at the door, but was that actually possible? *Not Lev,* she'd thought the moment she heard where her sister had died, *never Lev,* but wasn't he somehow complicit? Wasn't *she* complicit, too, when it came to the actions of her mother? Of her sisters? Of what would become her own crime, soon enough?

The thoughts pounded into Sasha's head as she returned home, finding a stranger in her bedroom.

Not a stranger, she amended, stepping close enough to see more clearly who was gazing out over the street below.

"Ivan," she said softly, reaching a hand out to touch his shoulder, and he jumped, looking as if he'd drifted off while staring blankly out her window.

"Sasha," he said, and cleared his throat. They'd never spoken privately before and it was a bit strange to hear his voice, she thought. She'd imagined it gruff and full of sharpness, a weapon as threatening as his size and his fists, but it was deeper than that, more soothing. Syrupy in a way, and it poured out like honey. "Apologies. I didn't mean to disturb you."

She paused, hesitating. "Does my mother know that I was—"

"No, no," Ivan assured her. "Though I don't recommend you being alone. Particularly not now."

He gestured for her to sit, shifting awkwardly himself to occupy the smallest corner of the bed she so clearly hadn't slept in. Sasha nodded, taking the proffered seat, then stared down at the threading on her quilt, running the pads of her fingers over the stitches. It had only been a matter of days since Marya had last sat there with her, alleviating her headache. Curing her ills.

"Do you know what happened?" Sasha asked, and Ivan shook his head. Clearly it pained him, and she resolved not to press for any further details. "I just keep asking myself what she'd want me to do," Sasha admitted, drawing her legs up to rest her chin on her knees. "I don't think I've ever woken up to a morning without the answer."

Ivan shifted again atop her bed, plainly uncomfortable.

"I'm sorry," he said, after a moment. Then, as if he couldn't rectify the moment or the crease he had formed on her quilt, he rose to his feet.

"It's not your fault." Sasha spared Ivan a glance that was at once admonishing and, she hoped, comforting. "Nobody on earth could have stopped my sister from doing anything she wanted to. I just . . . I don't understand—"

She broke off, grimacing.

"I don't understand what happened," she confessed. "Mama hasn't given us much information. Is it true that—" She caught the smallest sign of tension, a hint of a muscle straining near his jaw. "Was Masha really killed in Koschei's warehouse?"

Ivan either couldn't look at her or wouldn't.

"Yes," he said.

"What was she doing there?"

Sasha waited, but no answer. She hadn't really expected him to tell her even if he knew. Her sister was—had always been—very private. Somewhere, in a place in her mind that Sasha had always felt but never wanted to acknowledge, she knew there was more to Marya than had ever been shared with her. Good or bad, there were many parts of Marya that she had never wanted Sasha to see.

"Do you think it was Koschei himself," Sasha pressed quietly, "or—"

"I don't know," Ivan said, shaking his head, and then dropped his chin. "Though I blame him all the same. And myself." He swallowed hard. "I blame everyone, but I blame the Fedorov sons most of all."

"You do?" Sasha asked, and though Ivan didn't spare her an answer, she abruptly recalled what she had heard Lev's brother say that morning: *The game is changing.*

She heard herself, too, and an echo of her thoughts: *Not Lev, never Lev—*

—but possibly, maybe, could it be?

He was the one, after all, who sought her out. Who knew her name, her blood, her loyalties. Their meeting had been a potent one, but was it enough to overwrite their families' histories? If she had been in his place, would one kiss, one collision, have been enough to rearrange her stars?

Of course, if it hadn't been Lev, then he had nothing to worry about. If he had never intended to harm Sasha or her family before, then he certainly wouldn't now.

And if it *had* been him, then . . .

Sasha stiffened, shoving her feelings aside.

"What if we could find out who was really behind this," she posed carefully to Ivan, running her fingers thoughtfully over her lip. "Is there someone who would know what the Fedorovs were up to? The reason Masha went to see them in the first place?"

She glanced again at Ivan, who still said nothing. Marya had chosen her bodyguard well—even now, beyond the grave, he kept her secrets.

"Just tell me one thing," Sasha urged him, and he bristled with something—apprehension, she guessed. He no longer knew which

Antonova witch to serve. "How did my sister know the Fedorov brothers had crossed her?"

Ivan paused, weighing the value of the information, or perhaps his position in the room. Understandable that his loyalty would outlive Marya, but even he seemed to realize that there was only one way to serve her now.

"Ivan," Sasha cautioned in a tone she had learned from her sister, who had learned it from their mother.

With a sigh, Ivan inclined his head, relenting.

"Marya had an informant," he admitted. "A man. Fae."

"We should find him, then," Sasha said, rising to her feet. "Talk to him. See what he knows."

Ivan's reaction was lightning-quick, one strong hand gripping her arm and pulling her back. "No, Sasha," he said flatly, not releasing her until he was sure she was listening. "I won't take you to him. He's dangerous," he clarified in a low voice, "and your sister would never allow it. She'd never forgive me."

"My sister is dead, Ivan," Sasha reminded him, the pain of it curling up around her heart again, wringing it dry. "Masha is gone, but if she trusted him enough to use him, then so can I. I'm an Antonova witch as much as my sister," she added, lifting her chin. For once, it sounded like something Marya would want her to say. "I'm an Antonova, and we fear nothing—so if you still intend to serve my sister's wishes, Ivan, then you'll help me now. Is that clear?"

Ivan blinked with surprise, staring at Sasha as if he were seeing her for the first time.

It occurred to her that maybe he was.

"You're the most like her," Ivan remarked after a moment. It was no trifling statement—Sasha knew very few things about Ivan, but among them was that he'd served her sister with devotion, rarely willing to leave her side.

"I know," Sasha said, though perhaps a truer answer might have been *I hope you're right.*

Grudgingly, Ivan gave a nod of concession. "Fine. I'll take you to Masha's informant and watch over you," he exhaled, resigned, "but you'll have to be careful. He'll threaten you in ways I can't protect you from. The Bridge is no trifling dealer," he warned, "and no ordinary criminal. He'll withhold information where it pleases him; he'll betray you if it serves his interests well."

"Will he tell me what I want to know?" Sasha asked plainly, and Ivan grimaced.

"Yes," he said, and she nodded.

"Then take me to The Bridge."

At that, Ivan rose to his feet, inclining his head in a solemn bow as he had done so often for her sister.

"As you wish," he said.

III. 7

(Between Us.)

"If the deal is still going forward," Roman said, continuing to pace Lev's bedroom, "then we have to intervene. I'll need your help," he added, glancing up at Lev. "I can't do this without you—and I need you to tell me if Sasha's said anything, Leva. Anything at all."

"Why do you need *my* help?" Lev asked warily. Dimitri was the obvious choice, considering how worried Roman looked. Lev was rarely relegated to anything more than simple errands. "And why does Dima oppose you? I thought you said—"

"Dima's useless to us at the moment," Roman snapped, glancing again at his watch. Clearly he was waiting for something, though Lev seemed unlikely to find out what. "I have a source who may be able to give me some of the details of their meeting, but without Marya, I'll need someone to find out who gets sent in her place. Someone," he clarified, glancing pointedly at Lev, "who would know what the Antonovas are up to."

"What makes you think they'd go ahead with a drug deal after Marya's death?" Lev insisted, balking at the idea that he could betray Sasha now, after the night he'd spent with her. "They're surely devastated by the loss, Roma. Heartbroken. I know Sasha will be—"

He broke off, startled, as recognition seemed to dawn in Roman's eyes at the mention of Sasha's name. His brother's gaze traveled swiftly around the room, piecing things together, and when it landed again on Lev's, there was no mistaking the look in his eyes. The silent recollection of every omission, every lie.

Lev knew his brother well enough to see behind his mask of condemnation. Beneath the features so like Koschei's were all the things Koschei did not accept: humiliation, disappointment. Misery and loss.

"First Dima, now you?" asked Roman, his voice a dangerous quiet.

Lev opened his mouth to say he didn't understand, which he didn't. But he closed it again, knowing that what he did understand was far more relevant, and far worse.

"Choose, brother, where you stand," Roman warned, "and choose carefully, unless you want to spend the rest of your life pushed aside by Baba Yaga's bitches."

Lev sighed. "Roma, I'm only—"

"I have to go," Roman said flatly, spinning to leave the room. "I'll let you know if I hear from my source, but in the meantime, I hope you reconsider your loyalties."

Then he went, furious, and Lev was left behind, staring at the place his brother had been.

III. 8

(The Bridge and Those Who Cross It.)

Brynmor Attaway had been sitting in his office, carelessly poring over a contract up until the moment there came a knock at the door. It was followed, much to his displeasure, by the immediate click of the latch as it came unlocked.

Easy to tell, then, what sort of visitor it was.

"Hello, witch," he said without looking up, tapping his pen against his mouth. "I'll be with you in just one m—"

"You'll be with me now, actually," said a feminine voice, and Bryn looked up with surprise.

"Ivan," he said, acknowledging the quiet presence of the bodyguard, "and . . . *not*-Marya," he noted, his gaze flicking swiftly over the young woman who normally stood in her place. "Interesting," he said, sweeping his attention over the youthful ponytail, the casual clothing, and the very obvious indicators that this was someone very *like* Marya Antonova, but without the necessary battle-hardened armor she'd always worn. "A sister, I take it? I've never seen another Antonova in the wild before."

"This is hardly the wild," remarked the Antonova, whose eyes were grey—a slightly softer and more rounded version of Marya's sharpened gaze. "Are you The Bridge?"

"I am," said Bryn, letting the contract fall from his hand as he gestured to the vacant chairs across from his desk. "I take it you're in need of my services?"

She took a seat, warily. "I want to know how you knew about the Fedorovs."

A common request these days, it seemed.

"Declined," replied Bryn. "Anything else?"

Her expression stiffened. "Declined?"

"Yes, declined. Overruled, if you prefer. I don't part with my information for free," Bryn told her. "Neither as a fairy nor as an attorney. It's what makes me so darn effective at my job," he added, raising his WORLD'S BEST LAWYER mug with his pinky aloft for emphasis, "and which leaves me free to say things like 'no' when presented with unreasonable requests. Call it attorney-client privilege."

To his surprise, the witch smiled, satisfied. "So you do know what the Fedorovs are up to, then," she judged, and Bryn paused.

"Huh," he said, impressed against his will. "Well, you're younger than Marya, but well trained, I take it."

The witch flinched, but barely. He wondered what that was about.

"Do you know what business my sister had with the Fedorovs?"

"That's between your sister and me," Bryn told her.

"Not anymore," the witch replied. "My sister's dead."

Bryn blinked, genuinely startled. "What?"

"Marya was murdered last night," the witch clarified, "and it was a Fedorov witch who killed her."

Bryn cleared his throat, moderately discomfited. Strange to think he'd seen Marya just the previous evening; stranger still that he hadn't yet heard the news from Roman. Had it been, in fact, *Roman's* doing? If it had, then perhaps he'd come through on their deal. If it hadn't . . .

There was still room for negotiation.

"What do you want from me?" Bryn asked, biding his time, and the witch leaned forward.

"I want you to help me kill a Fedorov," she said.

Surprising, Bryn thought. Not too many women, witch or otherwise, had Marya Antonova's stomach for things like that. He rested his chin on his hand, staring at the woman who sat across from him and compiling a series of deductions. What was, in vocational terms, a case.

"You're Marya's successor," he guessed, and she shrugged.

"Maybe," the witch replied. "Or maybe I'm just really pissed off."

Ah, he liked her. He tried not to show it; instead brushed his thumb over his lip, thinking.

"I operate in deals, you know," he pointed out. "If you want my help, you can't have it for nothing."

"I didn't say I'd offer you nothing," she replied, and though Ivan was busy giving her a series of darting glances, she didn't acknowledge his concern. "I do have some relevant business acumen, though, if a deal is what you want."

"Have you?"

She smiled thinly. "Enough to know that everything is a matter of leverage."

"Is there something you think I lack?" He waved a hand around the ample square footage of his office, which was tastefully outfitted with all the usual markers of success. No gauche trinkets, of course. This was no witch's cottage of cauldrons and brooms. Bryn's was the kind of power you could feel rather than point to, some atmospheric sixth sense tipped off by the buttery richness of his leather furnishings or the first editions lining his shelves. "You'd be hard-pressed to offer me something compelling."

She seemed to disagree. "You're fae, right?" she prompted, at which Bryn fastened his unwavering smile more securely in place, reserving his apprehension for a less critical moment. "So, I take it you don't have magic in this realm."

"No, I don't," Bryn confirmed neutrally, shooting a glance at Ivan. It was no surprise that Marya Antonova's bodyguard would give that little tidbit away to her successor, but all the same, Bryn found it tasteless, like tucking an ace into his sleeve before storming in to rob the house. "Are you offering me yours?" Bryn asked the younger Antonova, pleased to see Ivan bristle with displeasure.

"Of course not," the witch replied. "I'm not an idiot, and besides, I could hardly offer you much of it while I'm alive. I'm offering you the Fedorov who dies as restitution for my sister," she explained, and Bryn, much to his displeasure, found himself leaning forward. Occasionally a very poor negotiator, Bryn, on account of an erotic sort of craving. Like all fae, when he wanted, he wanted powerfully. When Bryn's interest was piqued, it was like sensuality itself, mouth wetting for another taste, another hit.

"There's magic in a witch's organs," the witch continued. "The heart, the liver. The kidneys, especially," she said, and though Ivan flinched beside her, she notably did not. There was nothing gruesome to her about the conversation, which was, in Bryn's mind, the sign of a certain old school proficiency. Ironically, an Antonova and a Fedorov were more like each other than other witches were like them—in Bryn's observation, the difference lived somewhere in the generational inheritance. The actualization of the new age witch proved somewhat tamer than the hunger of the immigrant who'd carried nothing but stories on their back. "Anywhere blood is processed would hold several years' worth of magic, preserved well enough," the witch told him, "and I could help you preserve it."

Bryn considered it. "You're that good?"

"I'm that good," she confirmed, and added, "My sister taught me."

Interesting. Increasingly so.

"This conflicts with another deal," Bryn said, drumming his fingers on the desk as he weighed his options. Just kidding. There was no loss to him here—she'd be bound to her word, no loopholes, and the heat of incomparable satisfaction was on the line. Roman's displeasure would be an inconvenience, perhaps, or perhaps Roman would be dead and everything would be fine. Neither Roman Fedorov nor the Antonova witch sitting across from Bryn now had ever asked for loyalty or scruples.

Well—*Roman* expected it, most likely, but as with all contracts, such things required specificity. If Roman wanted honor, he should have looked more carefully at the name of the law firm on the door. "It will be a matter of who can pay me first," Bryn said, deciding that was fair. It was the equivalent of going to auction.

"Fine," the witch said, shrugging. "I can pay you tonight, if that helps."

Ah, Bryn thought, remembering. "The intoxicants are moving forward?"

"Deal closes tonight," the witch unwisely confirmed, and Bryn, usually more than willing to play by the (lack of) rules, tilted his head, tutting quietly before he could stop himself. She caught it, arching a brow in tacit prompting.

A pithy demurral was already loaded on his tongue, but at the last second he tossed it aside, favoring the game over the player. He may not have cared if she won, but he also didn't want her to lose like this, barely five minutes into the first round. "You shouldn't give away such sensitive information," Bryn warned her.

To his surprise, though, her mouth only quirked in reply.

"No?" she asked drolly. "I suppose I shouldn't tell you the place and the time, then, either. Heaven forbid you tell your Fedorov source," she murmured. "After all, one of them might *show up* there, and be completely vulnerable, at that—"

Oh. Oh, she was good.

"And which Fedorov would that be?" Bryn asked casually, testing her resolve.

"The dead one," she replied, unfazed.

He smiled. She was very, very good. He was beginning to think he wanted her to succeed, though as a rule he didn't choose favorites. He had betrayed Marya Antonova despite the minor possibility that he had loved her. He could admire the witch sitting before him and still cut her off at the knees if it meant he would win.

So Bryn held out a hand for hers, reaching gamely across the desk. "Miss Antonova," he said, "I believe we've come to a fruitful conclusion. I'll bring my Fedorov source right to your door, and in exchange, you'll give me his magic. Do we have a deal?"

The witch glanced at Ivan, who tilted his head; *Go ahead,* he seemed to say grimly, conceding for lack of a better option, and she nodded, shifting forward to perch delicately at the edge of her seat.

"Deal," she confirmed, closing her hand around Bryn's and binding his word to hers.

III. 9

(Counsel.)

"Dima," Lev said, finding his brother alone in the corner of his loft that served as his study. "Are you busy?"

Dimitri looked up, traveling a long distance through his thoughts to let his gaze fall on Lev's before softening then, slightly. The eldest and youngest Fedorovs had been close, always, even with how untouchable Dimitri had always been; how out of reach and, in Lev's view, godlike. It was a different relationship than the one between Lev and Roman, and certainly between Roman and Dimitri.

"Lev," Dimitri said, and rose to his feet, the collar of his shirt gaping slightly as Lev paused, spotting the outline of a bandage. A flash of yesterday's carnage resurfaced in Lev's memory, the blood on the floor and his brother's chest delivering him to a sudden chill.

"Is it bad?" Lev managed to ask, and Dimitri looked down, running a hand absently over his chest.

"It's nothing," Dimitri said. "I'll be fine." He cleared his throat, gesturing for Lev to join him in one of the leather chairs. "You need something, Lyova?"

"Sort of. I—" Lev hesitated, battling his instincts. "I wanted to talk to you about Roma. Well, about the Antonovas," he amended. "About both, I suppose."

Dimitri carefully lowered himself into the chair, concealing a wince. It appeared his previous suffering at the hands of Marya Antonova hadn't quite faded. "About Roma's aversion to them, you mean?"

"I just—" Lev swallowed. "I just wonder whether all this hatred is worth it, Dima." It was momentarily unbearable, the insecurity in his own voice. His father, Roman; Lev could hear them both now in his head, a dull refrain of disappointment. He shook it away, pressing on. "I know Roma's afraid of something," he said. "I know something's made him . . . not himself, and I know Papa has his own opposition to Baba Yaga, but—"

"But you don't have a place in it," Dimitri guessed. "Is that it?"

No. No, Lev knew his place, and that was exactly the problem.

"Ah. You don't *want* to have a place in it," Dimitri amended, and Lev looked down at his hands; confirmation enough. "Well," Dimitri exhaled, "I don't blame you. There are very few winners when witches have wars, and yours is inherited. It must make you feel rather . . ." He trailed off. "Unimportant, I suppose, in the scheme of things."

"Yes," Lev said, looking up. "It doesn't feel like my war, Dima. And yes, I know Roma is our brother, and I love Papa—Dima, you *know* I'd do anything for him, for both of them—"

"I do know that," Dimitri confirmed, gesturing again for Lev to sit. "I know the measure of your worth, Lyova. I take pride in it every day."

Lev slowly sank into the chair beside Dimitri's.

"Do you think I'm failing our family?" he asked, voice low. "With my . . . with my hesitation, I mean. I know it's not—" He grimaced. "It's not Papa's favorite trait."

"No, it isn't, but this isn't hesitation, Lev. Not the way Papa means it. You have convictions." Dimitri's glance slid over Lev's face, scrutinizing him. "You've met an Antonova witch," Dimitri recalled at a murmur, and Lev sat forcefully still, lest a single inadvisable fidget give him away. "They're very beautiful," Dimitri remarked, musing it to empty air. "Intelligent. Powerful. Any one of Yaga's daughters would be enough to change any man's mind, I'd guess—"

"It's not that," Lev blurted, a pained expression on his face, and Dimitri laughed his royal laugh, holding his hand to the bandage at his chest until gradually he quieted, shaking his head.

"I can't tell you who to side with," Dimitri said, "but I can tell you a bit of what I know. Roma is—" He toyed with his words, scraping a hand warily over the fine blond hairs he hadn't yet shaved from his cheeks. "Roma is weakened," Dimitri finally determined, and to Lev's frown of concern, Dimitri shook his head. "It's not my information to tell. But he's making desperate choices," Dimitri clarified. "He's facing life like a desperate man, and reason is far, far gone from him."

Lev felt a weight in his shoulders, like a mantle draped across his back. "So I should protect him, then?"

Dimitri shook his head. "You should do what you believe is right," he said. "If your instincts tell you this bad blood between our family and Yaga's isn't worthy of the costs—and be warned, Lyova, our lives, or yours, may very well be the price," he added, sobering slightly, "then you are responsible for honoring your own convictions. You're beholden to them first."

"I thought we were Fedorov sons first," Lev said, and again, Dimitri shook his head.

"What does it mean to be a Fedorov son if we destroy ourselves in the process?" Dimitri asked, and his expression was nothing Lev had ever seen on his face before. "What does it mean to be this family or that, if loss is the only thing that comes from it?"

Lev chewed his lip. "But Dima—"

"If an Antonova witch challenges Roma, he'll die," Dimitri said flatly, coming to the heart of it at last. "He can't defend himself, and even if he could, he still might not survive it. Roma knows it," he added, glancing at Lev again, "and now you do, too."

He rose to his feet, turning away as if he'd already said too much, and Lev leapt after him.

"But Dima—"

"I love my brother," Dimitri said in a low, blistering tone, rounding on Lev as if he'd tried to contradict him. "I love him. All his life I've protected him, I've fought for him—since the day he was born I have stood by him *without fail*—"

Lev flinched, recalling the words Roman had said to him only a matter of hours ago. *First Dima, now you.* "Dima, is everything—"

"I hope you never have to know what bearing our name has cost me," Dimitri said, his voice hunted and sharp. "Whatever choices you make, Lev, just be sure you can live with them."

It seemed Dimitri's mind was full of secrets, and the door to the vault was rapidly falling shut. Lev let him go, watching his brother slip back into the sanctity of his thoughts.

"I'm sorry," Lev said, though he didn't know why he said it.

By then, Dimitri was no longer listening.

III. 10

(The Deal Is On.)

"Tell me you have something," Roman said, barging into Bryn's office. "Bridge, if you want me to hold up my end of the deal, then I need this."

Bryn held up one finger from where he sat reading on his leather sofa, calling wordlessly for a pause. His eyes tracked the page for another few seconds before he finally reached to mark his place, subsequently glancing up at Roman with glacial deliberation. "Hm? Oh, that. Right," Bryn confirmed, "I do have something, yes. As it turns out, Baba Yaga's little entrepreneurial venture is still going on as scheduled."

Roman scowled. "And it didn't occur to you to contact me?"

"Oddly, no. And neither, apparently, did it occur to *you*," Bryn said with leisurely displeasure, "to mention that you killed Marya Antonova, who as you might recall was my source up until today."

So Baba Yaga had replaced her favorite general, then. Roman felt a shiver of portent mixed with repulsion at the thought that his enemies were still out there, just as they'd always been, only now they were faceless, unseen. "Who is it now?" he demanded.

"Does it matter? So Marya Antonova has a successor, so what. So does your brother Dimitri," Bryn noted, gesturing unflatteringly to where Roman stood before him. "When a witch dies, it isn't as if time stops, Roman."

As if Bryn knew the first thing about witches. "Are you going to tell me where the deal is happening, Bridge, or do I have to jump through hoops to get it from you?"

"You know, I hate to point out the obvious," Bryn replied in a way that suggested very much the opposite, "but none of this would be necessary if you had just given me Marya Antonova's magic before you killed her—as you *very specifically* promised to do."

"I obviously tried—I was *going to*, but Dima—" Roman let out a growl of frustration. "I can't now," he muttered to Bryn's look of bored expectancy. "I don't know what he did with her body."

"Well, I only need an organ, don't I?" Bryn remarked. "A liver? A kidney?" He paused, reaching over to take a loud slurp through the straw of some repellant green juice. "A heart?" he asked, after he'd taken an indulgent sip.

Roman grimaced, the pulse in his chest faltering at the thought. "I could use your help, you know. I can still get it to you, I know I can, but not if you—" His mouth tightened. "Not if one of the Antonovas kills me first."

Bryn shrugged. "Well, then you have until one of them kills you—or until you give up your brother," he offered with no apparent preference, "to hold up your end of the deal. Perhaps when you're no longer in my debt, I might feel more inclined to take your side."

No honor among thieves, no sympathy among fae. Was it any wonder Koschei hated creatures? "Bridge, for fuck's sake—"

Bryn sighed loudly, picking up his book. "Oh, relax," he murmured, tossing a piece of paper toward Roman that listed an address and a time. "I eventually come through, don't I?"

To that, Roman merely turned on his heel, doubting The Bridge deserved an answer.

III. 11

(A Cup of Tea.)

The tiredness of magic was unlike any tiredness Baba Yaga had ever known, even after years of raising seven children and running a household for a man who'd never once felt moved to lift a finger. Magic was not unlike any other flex of muscle; it was a grueling task, physically and mentally. It didn't come from nothing, and it had a price, a cost, a strain. To use it was to drain oneself, though she tried not to let it be too obvious as she wearily joined her youngest daughter in the kitchen.

"How are you feeling, Sashenka?" Yaga asked, seating herself across from Sasha at the table. Marya had not wanted Sasha to do this, Yaga knew, and now she felt a moment of disconcerting unease, wondering if her daughter would disapprove—or worse. If, perhaps, Yaga might not have lost Marya at all, had she not been so insistent on this expansion to begin with.

Sasha blinked, dragging her attention from wherever it had been. "Ah, fine, Mama. I'm not anticipating any problems," she said, with a faint grimness that Yaga assumed she had gotten from her older sister. Marya had always had a fitting sense of certainty, the unceremonious pragmatism of a person accustomed to doing what must be done, and clearly Sasha had learned it well.

"There is one thing, though, Mama," Sasha ventured slowly, clearing her throat. "I think it must have been one of the Fedorov brothers who killed Masha." She paused, biding her time before she added, "I think it was Roman, the middle one."

The vulture, Masha had called him. Eyes of death.

"Oh?" Yaga posed carefully, waiting.

"Yes," Sasha said, adding after a moment, "I set a trap for him."

That Yaga had not expected. "You did what, Sashenka?"

"Just leave it to me, Mama," Sasha told her, not answering right away. "I know I may have . . . disappointed you, in the past. But in this, I will not fail you." She paused for another pulse of silence before adding, "The Bridge knows who killed Masha, Mama, I'm sure of it. And I trust that he'll lead them to me."

Of that, Yaga was less certain—she had never trusted The Bridge herself. He'd always felt like a piece of the Old World that she was most eager to leave behind, only Marya had liked him. She'd found the blur of his morality amusing. *He's not so complicated,* Marya had always said, *and he's useful. Like an instrument that plays sweetly in the right hands.*

"I see," Yaga said slowly.

"It has to stop, Mama," Sasha continued. "This hatred between our families, one way or another, it has to end. Better this way. Better it ends on our terms." She looked up slowly, challengingly, her grey eyes rising beneath the framing of her lashes. "My terms," she clarified.

Yaga paused, considering this, and rose to her feet.

"I'm going to make us some tea," she said, and Sasha sighed.

"Mama, did you hear me? I just said—"

"I know what you said, Sashenka," Yaga said. "I heard you. I understand you. You wish to take vengeance on your sister's killer, and if I were a wiser woman, perhaps I would stop you. Perhaps I would remind you that an eye for an eye will satisfy no one, or tell you how a journey of revenge threatens two graves in the end. But seeing as I am grieving, and angry—seeing how I would gladly sink to death if it meant taking Koschei and his sons down with me— I'm simply going to make us some tea and remind you how best to kill a witch," she murmured, "because at the moment, I feel quite certain blood will satisfy me very well."

"But this will be the end, won't it?" Sasha pressed, eyes harder, less bright without the innocence Marya had been desperate for her to keep a few more years.

If only, Mashenka, Yaga thought. *If only any of us could stay so young.*

"Promise me, Mama," Sasha said. "Once I find Masha's murderer, our troubles with Koschei and his sons are over. It ends there." Another beat of pause. "Promise."

"I promise," Yaga swore to her youngest, and reached out, cupping her hand around Sasha's cheek.

This, her baby, was her most hesitant child; the only one whose heart Yaga felt she didn't truly know. She wondered if it might have been a mistake not to try to know it sooner.

"I would hate to lose you, Sashenka," Yaga murmured, and drew her thumb over her daughter's lips, tracing the shape of them. "Are you afraid?"

"I'm not afraid," Sasha said, and as with all her daughters, Yaga believed her.

"Good," she said, and lit a spark with the snap of her fingers, putting the kettle on for tea.

III. 12

(Underground.)

Lev found his father in his usual spot underground, staring contemplatively into nothing. A popular activity for the Fedorov men that day, Lev thought, though at the moment it was hard to find much humor in such things.

"You needed something, Papa?" he asked, and Koschei turned to look at him.

"Come," Koschei beckoned, and Lev nodded, taking a seat beside his father. It was rare that they were alone together; Koschei had always been relatively distant, preferring to call for Dimitri if he had any need for company, or Roman if he wanted something done. Still, it wasn't as if Lev didn't admire his father as much as the other two. "Are you well, Lyovushka?"

"I'm—" Lev hesitated. "A bit conflicted, I suppose."

On the walls, the shadows flickered slightly. Strange, Lev thought, considering there was only one source of light in the room, and it had not made any motion.

"Life can be very full of difficult choices," Koschei remarked. "Many things in life are a sacrifice, I'm afraid. Very rarely is it easy or straightforward."

Lev nodded. "I think I understand that."

"Good, good." Koschei cleared his throat. "You know, all my sons are very different from each other," he mused, and Lev waited, still unsure what his father had called him there to say. "Dima is something very rare, something very bold, something that catches in the light. Romik is like me, a man of duty. A watchful man. But you are very honorable." He turned, glancing at Lev. "You are the most loyal of them all, I suspect."

Lev blinked, surprised. "Me, Papa?"

"You have the purest heart. A lion's heart." Koschei smiled thinly. "Your convictions spur you, like Dima, but not one bone in you is selfish, Lev. You are mine in a way the others are not, because unlike them, you are their brother first before you are my son. You seek their approval before mine." He paused. "Isn't that true?"

"I—" Lev stumbled, uncertain. "Papa, no, that's—No, of course I'm your son—"

"Don't be ashamed of it, Lyova," Koschei assured him. "Your brothers raised you more than I did. Dima cared for you, he taught you, and Roma—oh," he sighed, "Roma loves you, perhaps more than anyone on earth. And they are right in their affection for you, just as you are right to revere them first." Koschei paused, glancing briefly at the shadows on the wall. "You are probably aware, then, that they are both rather troubled at the moment. Weakened."

"Yes," Lev said after a moment.

"Dima's heart is . . . not what it usually is," Koschei said. "And Romik, too, is compromised."

Lev nodded, remembering Dimitri's vacant gaze, Roman's twitching unease. "Dima mentioned it to me."

"What they need is their brother," Koschei said. "Do you understand me, Lyovushka?"

Again, the answer was no; it seemed to Lev that his father was speaking in riddles, saying things that Dimitri or Roman would understand, but not him. "Papa, I don't—"

"I will not ask you for anything," Koschei said. "I cannot ask you to choose one way or another. I can only hope," he exhaled, "that you will not abandon your brothers now, when they need you most."

Though he remained unsure of his father's intentions, Lev slowly nodded. "I won't, Papa. I won't fail them, or you."

To that, Koschei smiled slowly. "I know you won't, Lev," he said, with a little flickering of sadness. "Of all my sons, I know you won't."

A strange thing to say, Lev thought, but a moderately uplifting one. It wasn't often that he was on the receiving end of his father's praise, and he took the basement steps with a sense that something significant had passed between them. Something very oddly like hello, or possibly goodbye.

It was only when Lev had left the building that he regained his cell phone service, a quick series of vibrations going off in his pocket. Two of them were messages from Roman, listing a time and a place for them to meet; the others, though, were something else.

SASHA: I need to see you
SASHA: please
SASHA: it's important

Lev hesitated, trying to form words for refusal and finding himself empty-handed.

LEV: where and when?

III. 13

(The Deal, Done.)

When Yaga told her the identity of their mortal dealer, Sasha supposed she shouldn't have been surprised.

"Your face healed up nicely," she remarked, sidling up to Eric Taylor where he stood at the back of the concert, beer in hand. It was some sort of underground hip-hop duo—enough to draw a sizable crowd, but not enough for rowdy spectators. A wise choice, and therefore likely Marya's choice. A final message from her sister, like being visited by a ghost. "Too bad. With the bruises, you almost looked tough enough to be the kind of guy who can actually get a girl while she's still sober."

Eric's gaze slid to hers. "You missed class today," he commented.

"I did," Sasha confirmed. "Had a few other things to take care of. You're a drug dealer," she said without much room for pause—a statement, not a question. He glanced at her, disinterested.

"NYU's expensive," he replied simply. "X-rays notwithstanding."

"Ah," Sasha said. "I just assumed Daddy's firm covered the medical bills."

He grimaced. "I'm busy," he said. "If you want to finally stop playing hard to get and fuck, Sasha, all you have to do is say—"

"I presume you have the money?"

He blinked.

"You?" seemed to be all he could conjure, balking as he pieced together the significance of her presence there with her purpose at his side.

"Me," she confirmed. "I take it you dealt with my sister before?"

"I—" He stopped, staring vacantly at her. "But you—you're—"

"Doesn't matter which sister you deal with," she informed him. "We're all the same. We're all Baba Yaga's daughters—and if you fear one of us," she warned, leaning in to speak in his ear, "you fear us all."

He took a sip from his beer. "I'm hardly afraid of you, Sasha."

Right. Tell that to the sudden stiffness in his spine or the goose bumps creeping up his neck.

"Your loss," Sasha informed him briskly, "seeing as you have no idea who or what I am. If I were you, I wouldn't underestimate me." She leaned away and glanced over at him, expectant. "Do you have the money or not?"

"I have it." He seemed to be buying time, trying to control the pace of the encounter and, by extension, her. "Naturally, my purchasing the product is contingent on its quality. And on whatever else you're able to offer me," he added, letting it hang in the air between them.

What would it be like, Sasha wondered, to live in a world where no meant no?

"Naturally," she demurred, and reached into the pocket of her coat.

It was armor borrowed from her sister Marya, a favorite garment of hers, and Sasha discreetly removed a tablet from the pocket in the lining. "Well," she said, stepping close to Eric until she could feel the way his breath halted with a mix of terror and interest, "if you'd like to sample the product—"

Eric shifted his stance into a mirror of her motions, matching his hips to hers and settling his hands with a laughable eagerness on her waist. "All you have to do," Sasha murmured, drawing up on her toes and gently coaxing his lips toward hers, "is—"

"*Fuck*," Eric spat at once, choking on the tablet she'd practically forced down his throat. "Jesus, Sasha, what the *fuck*—"

"Enjoy it," she advised, passing a hand over his forehead. He calmed instantly, the dilation of his pupils serving to indicate the potion had already begun its effects. Soon, she knew, he would be well in the midst of hallucinogens designed specifically for him, which were probably disgusting. She hated him—hated the deal itself—but even that was only the very surface of her anger.

Soon, the Fedorov son who killed her sister would be waiting for her; waiting, like a sitting duck, at her convenience. She stifled the need to punch Eric once more for irony and watched him fall into a trance instead, sliding her hand into his jacket pocket and deftly pulling out the envelope inside.

"One more thing," she said, as she pressed the small case full of tablets into Eric's chest, shoving him back with a groan. "Baba Yaga sends her love."

Then she turned and walked away, the envelope with his payment tucked into the pocket of her dead sister's favorite coat.

III. 14

(What Divides Us.)

"Sasha," Lev said when he saw her, frowning with bemusement at her approach. She'd asked him to meet her outside some concert venue, which was already strange enough, and he noticed now that she was wearing a familiar garment—the same coat that her sister Marya had worn right before she'd nearly killed his brother Dimitri. It was a jarring reminder of everything the two of them could never be, which should have made this easier.

It didn't. "Look—" Lev forced a swallow. "I'm sorry. I wanted to see you, but I really don't have a lot of time t—"

"Did your brother ask you to meet him somewhere tonight?" Sasha asked him, and he blinked.

"What? Sasha, I really can't—"

"Your brother," Sasha repeated. "Roman. Did he ask you to meet him somewhere? A warehouse," she suggested, unsmiling. "Near the river?"

"I . . ." No. "Sasha, I don't—"

How could she possibly have known?

How else could she have known, unless . . .

"Sasha." *No, Sasha, please.* "What are you saying?"

"I need you to stay here, Lev," she said, taking his face in her hands. "I need you to stay *away*, okay? Can you do that for me? I don't want to hurt you," she whispered, and he wished he could have fought it when her lips touched his—he wished, fervently, that his hands had not slid so easily to her waist, the answer to a question he'd been trying not to ask himself since he saw her last. "I don't want to hurt you, Lev, and I don't want to lose you—"

"Then don't," he pleaded, tightening his grip on her. "Sasha, we don't have to be like this, it doesn't have to be this way for us. I like that we're already settling into our relationship problems," he added with a bitter laugh. "You know, you're messy, I'm neat, our families insist on bloodshed, I chew with my mouth open sometimes—"

"Don't do this," Sasha said, her nails digging into the notches of his vertebrae. "Don't pretend it can be easy. Wasn't this what we were born to? They won't let us out unless it stops, and it won't stop until the debt is paid. Your brother killed my sister, Lev," she reminded him acidly, the words burning on his lips, "and there's no hope of peace between us until the scales between our families are even."

"But does it have to be you?" Lev asked her, pained. "I don't know if I could forgive you, Sasha—I don't know if I could . . . if *we* could—"

"Then don't forgive me," she said with the venom he'd been drawn to from the moment her story collided with his, her gravity filling up the life he hadn't known was empty. Sasha Antonova, his nightmare, who kissed him again as he slid his hands under her coat, clinging desperately to her waist. "Don't forgive me, Lev, if you can't, and certainly don't love me. You'll only make fools of us both."

She pulled away and he held her back, fingers catching her arm.

I can only hope, Koschei's voice said in Lev's ear, *that you will not abandon your brothers now, when they need you most.*

"Sasha," he exhaled, reaching for her chin to drag her gaze back to his, "I do love you. I will love you." He laughed again, hoarsely this time. "I will love you even when I wrong you, and for that—for everything—I'm so fucking sorry."

She went rigid, hearing the change in his voice. "Sorry for what?"

"For this," he said, and forced her wrists against the chain-link fence. Twin threads of metal broke free at his command, winding themselves tightly around her arms, the sound of iron like the gnashing of teeth over her guttural hiss of betrayal, an augury to forever stain them both. "I can't let you do this, Sasha, I'm sorry—"

"This won't hold me, Lev," she snarled as he took a step back, already dazed by what he'd done. "You know it won't, Lev!"

"No, but it'll give me some time," he said, and then kissed her swiftly, brutally. "It'll give me the time I need to make sure I get to Roman before you."

"He's not *alone.*" Her eyes said *you fucking traitor* and Lev breathed back *I know, I love you, I know.* "I'm not that stupid, Lev—"

"Fine. Fine, Sasha, then maybe my brother will die tonight, but at least it won't be you who does it," he said, and tore himself from her side, allowing himself a single glance to look back at her face—to burn the outline of her rage into his memory, in case it was the last thing he saw of her. In case his punishment would be to live with the outcome of his choice. "At least it won't be you who kills my brother, Sasha. That'll be enough for me."

"Lev," she spat after him. "Lev, you're heading for a fucking trap!"

"I fell in love with you, didn't I, Sasha Antonova?" His laugh, the set of her jaw, they both said *I love you, it's over, we're doomed.* "I was always going to be trapped."

She let out a scream that broke halfway through, a shattering of grief and rage as Lev forced himself on from the wreckage, tumbling through a thin sliver of night.

III. 15

(The Sanctity of Tombs.)

Proximity to the Hudson always made everything seem more like a tomb. Everything was darker, more damp, sepulchral. Cloaked in shadow and contained. The warehouse Sasha had told The Bridge to report back to the Fedorov brothers was strikingly unlike anything Marya would have chosen, and anyone more familiar with the Antonova witches would have known. This location was more than private—it was dangerously secluded, in fact—and a place where people went to die, not to make deals. The actual location, the concert venue, was safe because it was in plain sight, clever because it was far easier to control. Marya would never choose something like this, with so many access points bottlenecked down to one escape: the river. Apart from the night of her death, Marya Antonova had always been a woman who watched her back. Ivan had made sure of it.

If the Fedorov had known Marya Antonova a little better, Ivan thought, perhaps he wouldn't have been so easily fooled. Perhaps all of this could have been avoided. Strangely, Ivan felt an intriguing sense of calm as he stepped out from behind one of the recently constructed beams, catching the silhouette that appeared from the shadows ahead.

Sasha was late, it seemed, but Marya's killer was right on time.

"So, you're the Fedorov rat," Ivan noted impassively. Nothing but the man's eyes and teeth glittered in the dark as he turned, making the comparison oddly poetic.

"Ah," the Fedorov murmured, recognizing danger only after it appeared. All the better for Sasha. All the worse for him. "So. This is a trap, then."

Ivan was almost certain Sasha's instincts had been correct—this was Roman, the middle brother. Dimitri was famously golden-haired, while the youngest, Lev, was slighter, younger-looking. This one had the body of a second-in-command, his posture stiff from looking over his shoulder.

The Fedorov pulled a gun from his waistband with ease at the first sign of trouble, but Ivan was quicker. He disarmed him with a motion from his thumb, quick as a trigger pull, and then shook his head, tutting softly to himself.

"Your magic is compromised," Ivan observed aloud, and slammed the Fedorov back against one of the concrete pillars. "Perhaps you should have thought of that before making an enemy of the Antonovas."

"You're not one of them," the Fedorov spat, looking sick with rage and fear.

Perhaps more of the latter, Ivan thought, stepping closer. He sniffed the air slightly, like a dog, and let his gaze fall coldly on the man before him. (Theatricalities, Marya had always said, were Ivan's most ferocious form of muscle.)

"You *work* for them," the Fedorov said, abruptly switching tactics, "and if you can be paid, then you can be bought."

"You underestimate Marya Antonova," Ivan noted. "Worse, you underestimate me."

The Fedorov scowled. "If you're planning to kill me," he said bluntly, "just get it over with."

"Is that the kindness you gave Marya?" Ivan asked him. The Fedorov flinched at the mention of her, but only barely. "She would be ashamed, I think, to find her killer begging for his own death. You make a mockery of her by doing it."

"Who says I killed her?" the Fedorov said. *His* theatricalities, Ivan thought, were far less threatening. They were like a child's shield; something to hide behind. They did nothing to mask his shame, or anything else that had crept into his dark eyes.

"Do you know what happens," Ivan posed softly, "when you kill something someone else loves?"

The Fedorov said nothing.

"Do you really believe people are so isolated that when they're gone, nothing grows in their place? To really kill something, you have to kill everything. You have to raze it to the ground." Ivan lifted the Fedorov's chin, eyeing him. "Do you have the stomach for that?"

"How many did Marya Antonova kill while you watched?" the Fedorov demanded, defensive. "Are you really telling me she felt remorse each time?"

"I'm telling you nothing," Ivan replied, shrugging. "I'm not here to teach you."

"You're here to kill me," the Fedorov sneered in reply, and again, Ivan shrugged.

"Blood for blood is not uncommon practice," Ivan said. "Why shouldn't it be yours next?"

"Do it, then," the Fedorov spat. "If you're trying to scare me, there's no need." He grimaced, suddenly relenting in his restraints. "Living would be worse," he muttered under his breath, and Ivan, to his dismay, felt himself hesitate, pausing briefly to regard the man before him.

"An unhealthy attitude," Ivan said, and again the Fedorov scowled up at him.

"Just kill me," the Fedorov said. Roman, Ivan thought suddenly. Roma, probably. Surely his brothers and his father called him Roma. "Just do it."

"Why should I," Ivan noted, "when you appear to be killing yourself just fine? I'm not a weapon at your disposal."

"You're Marya Antonova's weapon." He seemed very young, then. Younger than Marya. Not much older than Sasha. "That's all you are. The knuckles of her fist. The blade of her knife. You don't even wield yourself, do you?"

"Do you?" Ivan countered.

To his surprise, Roman let his head fall, a breath escaping him in anguish.

"I thought I did," Roman said, more to himself than to Ivan

before lifting his head, hollow-eyed. "But if you let me live now, my brothers are in danger. I owe a debt I can't possibly pay except with my life. I promise not to haunt you." He looked up, something close to mirth in the contours of his grimace. "I promise my death will not haunt you, Ivan of the Antonovas. You would only deliver me. Have peace from it."

Ivan stepped closer, near enough to let his hand linger over Roman's chest. He had killed any number of ways, either with magic or without. There were so many ways to drain a life, some easier than others; some more intimate than others. He could empty Roman's veins, let them drain onto the floor below. He could whisper something, a few words, and cause a clot in Roman's brain. He could slam Roman's head backward into concrete, into smithereens. He could stop Roman's heart, stop Roman's breath, stop everything and watch as vacancy inevitably set itself in Roman's eyes, like the deadness in Marya's. In Masha's. And then Roman would be like Masha, and would be nothing, and gone from Ivan's sight.

Gone, like Masha, and what possible justice was that?

"Peace doesn't come from death," Ivan said eventually, and Roman let out a shaky breath, equally tormented and relieved. Ivan took a hard step back, releasing his hold, only to hear a threatening growl behind him.

"Apologies, Ivan," said Stas Maksimov, "but I respectfully disagree."

III. 16

(Elementary Principles.)

Stas hadn't meant to follow Ivan. He'd considered himself uninterested in the ongoing nature of his wife's family's feud, but then his limbs had taken over—had unwisely taken him here, in fact. His feet, first, and then some sense of hunger, of pain, once he'd realized what Ivan was doing. What Ivan *could* do: a balancing of the scales.

Blood for blood. The most elementary of principles. The most ancient of reparations.

The Fedorov whose spine was pressed into the concrete pillar looked nothing like Dimitri and yet, somehow, the likeness was unmistakable. The too-proud chin, the too-keen stare, the hair that—while dark where Dimitri was fair—flowed like a crown around his head. It meant that *this* man, like all the Fedorov men, was responsible for Marya's death. Worse, he was the one who'd done it. He'd held the blade himself, bloodied his hands with it.

And now Ivan was letting him go.

The anger Stas had not permitted himself to feel about the loss of his wife flooded through him in a rush, draining him of his cooler senses and igniting his pain like a burst, a throb of grief. It was sharp and unopening, knives that tore up from his limbs, and he shoved Ivan aside to bring himself face-to-face with Marya's murderer, gritting his teeth in anguish. In loss.

"What did she look like?" Stas asked coldly, staring at the man who could only be Roman Fedorov. "When you killed her. Did you see her face?"

Roman said nothing, only grimacing, and Stas hit him hard in the solar plexus, knuckles driving out the air in Roman's lungs and leaving him coughing, gasping for breath beneath the impact of Stas's rage.

"Tell me," Stas growled, shaking Ivan off as the other man moved toward him. "Tell me, you fucking child, whether you faced her like a man or if you stabbed her in the back like a *traitor*, like a fucking *rat*—"

But the look on Roman's face wasn't fear. It wasn't humility. He spat out the side of his mouth, lifting his chin in defiance.

"When your wife died," Roman gritted out, "she was confessing her love to my brother."

His lips curled up slightly, taunting, and Stas aimed another hard blow, crushing Roman's ribs and sending a shooting, stabbing pain up the knuckle of his ring finger. Irony, to pair with a poorly aimed throw.

"She," Roman choked out, coughing again and sputtering, "she never loved you—she *never* loved you—"

She didn't love you, not as she loved Dima—

"No," Stas said hoarsely, trapping a hand around Roman's throat. "No, you're lying—"

"Stas, don't listen to him," Ivan said, reaching again for Stas's arm and dragging him away. "Stas—*Stas*—"

Stas yanked his arm free and gave Ivan a hard shove, a blow, the impact of both sending Ivan to the floor, rubbing his mouth in weary concession. "You're a liar," Stas raged over his shoulder, ready to turn on Roman, and in rapid succession—so quick he almost didn't see it, nearly blinked and missed it all—Stas spun, throwing out a hand, and felt the curse that left his palm aim true.

True enough, or would have been, had nothing gotten in the way.

"No!" Stas heard behind him, a scream that ricocheted around the half-filled walls, and for a moment he thought it was his wife, his Masha; thought he saw her there, in her favorite coat, a blur of familiarity in a sea of ache and fury.

But it wasn't Masha.

And it wasn't Roman his curse had hit.

III. 17

(The Lion and His Gifts.)

Dimitri had once told Lev he had the gift of timing. *Always perfect,* Dimitri had joked, ruffling the hair atop Lev's head, *right at the sweet spot, when one moment after would be too late, and one moment earlier would be too soon.* When Dimitri had first said it, he'd been referring to the way Lev would pull him to the sidewalk just as the ice cream truck went by or, as they got older, how Lev could always find a taxi, one going by with its lights on just at the moment he raised his hand in the air. *One of your little magics,* Dimitri had said, smiling as he'd said it, and it was what went through Lev's mind the moment he saw Stas Maksimov turning, his fingers extending slowly, as if time itself had been stretched.

He thought of it again as the curse struck him square in the chest, the spell finding its target perfectly. One moment earlier, or perhaps later, and it would have been Roman who'd taken the impact in his abdomen, unable to move. But Lev had the gift of timing, and so, in that moment, he thought of how it had served him; of how it had brought him Sasha, who had been there that night in that bar, of all places, at that time out of all possible times; and then, the moment he heard her voice, he thought of it again.

"Lev," she shouted, leaping over Ivan and shoving a stunned Stas aside to stumble to the ground beside him, taking his hand as she watched the curse bubble up in his lungs and take hold of his throat, his voice, his breath. "Lev, you idiot, stay with me." She pressed a hand down, easing it, soothing her thumb over his neck. "Stay with me, I'll fix it—"

"Sasha." He coughed it up, the impact of the curse restricting the beat of his heart. "Sasha, I'm sorry that I—I'm sorry about—"

"Don't you dare die, Lev Fedorov," she snarled, her voice as nightmarish as always. "Don't you dare. Not yet, Lev, not yet. We were supposed to have more time," she gasped, pressing her forehead to his. "We were supposed to have a *book*, Lev, you promised me a long story—and for fuck's sake, you idiot, *you owe me,* you can't die while I'm furious with you—while I—" She choked slightly, anguished. "You can't die while I haven't told you how I—how I *feel,* Lev, fuck!"

"It's my job to say crazy things, Sasha," he reminded her, forcing the words out with difficulty. She'd eased the impact of the pain, but only in places at a time; she couldn't hold it forever, not for much longer, so he pressed her frantic hands to his lips, helping him to speak to her. "For example," he coughed up, "how we might have had a very dull life together—"

"Don't say that." She was crying now, the salt of it bleeding onto his cheeks. "Lev, you stupid idiot, don't talk like that—"

"—mundane, you know? And probably wonderful." He gave an unromantic wheeze, gasping for a few more words, but held her still as she tried to pull away. "Don't let go," he said. "This is . . . peaceful, strangely. Don't let go, please."

Behind them, someone else was saying Sasha's name, but Lev couldn't tell who it was. His hearing seemed compromised; he only heard her voice, a solitary strand in the midst of his furious pulse, like a solemn whisper in the night.

"Lev." Sasha was pleading, no longer venomous at all, and it was that, her hand gently resting on his cheek, that made him sure it was the end. "Lev, please—"

Lev closed his eyes, pressing a kiss to the tips of her fingers.

"I'll find you, Sasha," he said, and felt himself swallowed up by sightless, endless volumes of nothing, of everything, as if he'd merely drifted off to sleep.

III. 18

(Not For You.)

Stas stared down at them, at the curse of circumstance that was Sasha Antonova and Lev Fedorov, as Ivan tried to coax her away. "Sasha," Ivan was saying, his voice low and urgent. "Sasha, come now, come with me—"

She was sobbing against Lev Fedorov's chest, refusing to move.

"Let go of me—*let go*—"

Stas blinked, his vision swimming, and all at once, again, the woman on the ground wasn't Sasha. It was Marya, as youthful as when he'd first laid eyes on her. When Stas Maksimov had first seen Marya Antonova she'd been smiling, her shoulders glowing and bronzed in a way that meant the sun had seen all parts of her; that she'd been carelessly cast beneath its rays, unconcerned with burning.

This one? Stas had thought morosely when he'd seen her, admonishing the artless tug of his heart. *Stas, you fool, this one is not for you.*

(*She burns for Dimitri Fedorov,* the whispered rumors said, then only charmed by the thought of it. *Young Dima, such a clever boy. He already has her heart, and by the looks of it, her body, too. She will never burn for you.*)

This one is not for you—

"Let go of him, Sasha," Stas croaked, trying to remember that this was not his wife; this was not Dimitri Fedorov, and not his Masha. This was someone else. This was someone else, and his own wife had loved him. He had been in love, and now she was gone. "Sasha, let him go—"

But the longer he looked at her, the more his vision swam with remnants of the past.

When Stas had seen Marya Antonova again, she was like a candle doused, a shadowed edge of what she'd been. It had been little more than months between occurrences but already she was close to unrecognizable; her dark hair, previously floating down to her waist, had been sliced to shoulder length, the ends of it sitting with careful precision along the line of her clavicle. She'd worn a sundress when he'd first seen her, the strap of it slipping from the curve of her shoulder, but that day she'd worn a plain grey dress, high heels, a meticulously tailored blazer. A few months before, she'd been a girl in love. When he saw her again, she was a woman.

Stas had walked toward her, half in a trance.

"Do you need something?" he'd asked her. He and his father were Borough witches, administrants of the banal. He must have looked stiff and boring to her. He must have looked plain, dark-haired and dull, compared to Dimitri Fedorov. Stas offered his assistance to a young Marya Antonova and winced at the eagerness in his voice, which he'd felt certain would turn her away. She'd fixed her dark eyes on his and blinked once, lashes fanning out against her pale cheeks, and considered the question in silence.

"Do I look like I need something?" she eventually asked in reply.

Stas wished he could have said he didn't love her right then, or that he hadn't felt a sense of urgency, some absurd need to hold her, to press her body close to his and murmur his devotion through the night. He wished he hadn't wanted to know her thoughts, to understand each tiny story of the freckles beneath her eyes, to learn to translate each spare degree of interest from her mouth. What did she look like when he made her laugh? When he held her hand, what would it sound like? How would her breath respond when he slid his hand between her legs and whispered, *Not yet, not just yet, not when I want so badly for this to last—?*

(*This one is not for you,* he knew, *but please, please, may I borrow her from someone else's fate? May I have her until her stars change, or mine? May I worship her until I die, and may I give her all of me, for better or worse, or worse, or surely worse?*)

"Stas Maksimov," she'd said—as if they were alone together; as if there were not several other men in the room watching his composure slide away to nothing on the floor—"would it be presumptuous to wonder if you might have a question for me?"

He asked her to have dinner. She accepted. Within weeks he had told her he loved her, having no other alternative but to confess. He'd watched her blink with surprise, taken aback; no doubt she'd heard the words before. Often, even. If Stas had been Dimitri Fedorov and free to say them, to hear them in return, he knew he would have told her every hour on the hour. A woman like Marya Antonova inspired a feverish sort of reverence; an affliction. Stas had spoken to Dimitri only once, perhaps twice, and yet he felt both a kinship he didn't understand and a hatred he couldn't smother.

"I understand," he'd said awkwardly to Marya upon confession of his feelings, "that perhaps you can't say those words to me yet."

She had reached up, brushing his hair from his forehead and considering him in a different light, shifting to see him from a different angle.

"You're a good man, Stas," she'd murmured. "Kind. Thoughtful."

He'd flinched, awaiting the inevitable *but.* "If you still have feelings for Dimitri Fedorov—"

"I promise you I'll never see him again," she said, cutting him off with the briefest, most subtle of motions from her hand, "because if I ever do, I may never come back to you at all." A pause, and then, "Knowing that, Stas Maksimov, can you love me still?"

This one is not for you.

Still, he'd bent his head to hers. "I'll never make you sad, Marya Antonova," Stas whispered to her. "I'll never take what is yours. I'll never demand anything from you. If you were mine, I'd take such care each day not to lose you. I'd give you my affection when you wanted it, my devotion when you needed it, and space to breathe when you did not. And you will always have my love, Marya Antonova," he'd sworn to her, "whether you wish to possess it or not."

That night he learned how her hair looked when it was fanned out like a raven's wing across his pillow. He'd learned what she felt like in his sheets, her skin soft as satin in his arms. He'd learned what a whisper of his name in his ear could do to the tension in his spine—and if it had been Dimitri Fedorov on her mind that night, Stas had told himself he would take it. He would accept the parts of Marya that she had to give him, however much they were, and eventually, when she told him she loved him in return—and he believed her, having seen a new and blessed fondness in her eyes—he didn't hesitate for a moment.

"Marry me," he'd said. Let fate be unsatisfied if it wished.

Those words, too—*marry me, Marya Antonova, be mine as I am yours*—Stas felt certain she'd heard some variant of before. He could almost see her thoughts dance fleetingly to Dimitri Fedorov, but even before Stas had said the words aloud, he had known there was no turning back. There was no denying the truth of his heart.

Fuck the stars. Let her choose him if she wished to choose him.

"Stas."

Stas blinked, looking down, and realized it was Ivan speaking to him.

"Stas," Ivan said, "don't do this. Please."

Stas looked down at his hands, realizing that he had power coiled inside them, the tips of his fingers glowing where his palm shook above Sasha, who hadn't left Lev Fedorov's side. She only looked up at him with blankness; with a hollow sense of apprehension.

"I wasn't," Stas began, and swallowed hard, curling his hand into a fist and taking two steps back. "I wasn't doing anything. I wasn't—this isn't—"

"Back up, Stas," Ivan warned, his eyes wide, and Stas hated him. Abruptly, he hated Ivan more than anyone in the world. More than Dimitri. More than Roman, more than Lev, more than anyone who bore the name Fedorov at all. Ivan was the one who'd failed, and countless times, too. Failed to keep Masha safe. Failed to keep Sasha away from Lev Fedorov. Failed, failed, failed again, in ways that Marya would never have forgiven had she been alive. Ivan had failed her, and failed Stas by extension, and now—*and now*—

"STAS!" Ivan shouted, throwing up a hand as Stas raised his own in anger, but for the second and final time that night, he failed to see until it was too late.

It was only after Stas heard a shot ring out in the night that he realized it was he who'd been the target. He looked down, watching a stain of crimson spread across his chest, and staggered to his knees.

"Masha," he whispered, reaching for the familiar fabric of her coat, and as his past caught up with him again, he let out a final breath of relief, his cheek colliding blissfully with the bloodied ground below.

III. 19

(Blood for Blood.)

"Hello, Koschei."

The old man turned slowly, tearing his attention from the empty ring to look over his shoulder at the visitor bathed in lamplight from the street above.

"Yaga," he said simply, easing himself back in his chair.

Wards, even the best of them, would not have kept her out. He had always guessed as much.

She tilted her head in wordless demurral, removing her gloves one finger at a time to reveal crimson-painted nails, each one a telling glimmer of perfection. How little she had aged compared to him. It seemed for the moment that the whole world was frozen, with only Koschei as proof that time went on.

"Perhaps on an occasion such as this one," Yaga suggested, "we might do away with pretense?"

Koschei arched a brow. "Mrs. Antonova," he said, and Yaga's mouth twitched, amused.

"Perhaps we might discard formality as well," she beckoned, "Lazar."

His grimace deepened. "Marya," he returned, and only then did she permit a smile. "And what occasion is this, then?"

"Ah. Death, of course." He said nothing, and she continued without any noticeable change in her expression. "It seems your sons have run amok, Lazar," she commented. "They've forced my daughters into murder, or else into inadvisable declarations of need."

Koschei permitted a grunt of something dispassionate. "Your daughters have always lured my sons to madness. Daughter, that is. And you." He glanced up swiftly. "You Antonova women are a curse."

"Well, that's very kind of you," Yaga permitted, "but flattery is hardly necessary, under the circumstances."

"Why are you here, Marya?" Koschei said, irritated. "Twelve years' worth of silence suited me well enough."

"My youngest daughter sought restitution for my Masha's death," Yaga said, and though Koschei was not a man to flinch, he almost couldn't breathe for hearing it. Her Masha. To lose his Dima would be to cut the lungs out of his chest and she knew it, must have known it. "One of your sons," she added as if she could read his thoughts, "owed it to her."

Koschei didn't want to give her the satisfaction of asking what she knew. "That's an Old World law," he said instead, and Yaga shrugged.

"It is," she agreed. "My daughters are well schooled, Lazar. They know their history, their origins, what makes them witches. Did you think I would teach them nothing of what they are?"

"Not everything ought to be taught," Koschei said warily.

"Agree to disagree," Yaga said. "And you cannot possibly tell me I am not owed something for my loss. One of you killed Masha," she reminded him, voice low, and Koschei's throat swelled with pain, with trepidation. "One of you killed her, and for that, I will accept no price less than blood for blood."

"You can't have Dima," Koschei said quickly, reflexively. "I know what Masha was to you, Marya, and I'm sorry for your loss, but if you touch Dimitri—"

"I wouldn't," Yaga assured him coolly. "I'm not the one who goes around killing when it suits me, Koschei. I'm generally too clever for brutality—or at least, I was," she murmured, "until tonight."

Koschei looked up, fixing his dark gaze on hers. "How do you know it was one of my sons who killed Masha?"

"Mother's intuition," Yaga said.

"And what is it you want from me?"

"A promise." Yaga didn't blink. "I want assurance you will not retaliate from your loss tonight."

"Impossible," Koschei scoffed. "If you kill one of my sons—"

"I should be clearer. You've already cost me my heir," Yaga said, slicing through the dark of the basement's wintry air, shadows falling still at the sound of her voice. "And you've as good as lost a son already." Koschei stared at her, apprehension gripping his chest like a vise, and she hardened beneath his scrutiny. "You cost me Masha's heart, first, and then her happiness, and now you've cost me her life. You should pay dearly, Lazar, and you should pay in kind— but I won't ask that of you. I only want to know an exchange has been willingly made, and therefore an agreement, too."

"It was Masha who started this," Koschei reminded her. "It was Masha who nearly killed Dima—"

"And it was also Masha who saved him," Yaga said, "so let that be

on his head. But aside from the loss of my daughter, I want something new from you." She stared at him, unbending. "I want assurance. I want an oath. I want to know that moving forward, you will
not come for me or my daughters again."

"So we're to put bad blood behind us, then?"

"Yes," Yaga said. "If you'll allow it."

His pulse beat quickly, double-time.

"Which of my sons?" he asked quietly.

"I don't care," Yaga said, shrugging. "What are they to me?"

"A trade, then?" Koschei asked. Around him, the shadows
danced. "Blood for blood, as you said."

"More blood?" Yaga glared at him. " How is that fair?"

"How is it not?" Koschei prompted. "If it will be blood for blood
to make a deal, Marya, then it will be one of yours for one of mine.
Your youngest for mine, to give us peace," he clarified, as her expression stiffened. "Masha was payment for Dima. This is another
deal, a new one for a higher price, and I will accept no less."

"Now *that*," Yaga remarked spitefully to Koschei, "is an Old
World law, indeed."

"I am a piece of the Old World," Koschei reminded her. "You
want to appeal to my fairness? Then be fair. Let's you and I grieve
equally tonight," he told her, unable to silence the drum in his
veins. "I have only three sons, after all. You have six remaining
daughters."

She flinched at the reminder of her seventh. "You're a hard man,
Lazar, and do not confuse that for flattery." She turned away, her
voice almost imperceptible in the silence. "I would have been a fool
to marry you."

"You were a fool not to," Koschei reminded her, and she spun,
rounding on him.

"What's to stop me from killing you now?" she asked him, her
voice a hard whisper as power surged to the tips of her fingers, a
pale glint that shone like moonlight in the stillness of the room.
"I could do it, Lazar. You wouldn't be the first witch to die at my

hands, and many others were killed for far less." From the glow of her power he could see what he hadn't before. The years. The anguish. The pain. "You, out of everyone, would deserve whatever death I chose to give you."

"Kill me and the witches will come for you," Koschei reminded her. "The entire council, Marya. All the Boroughs, and every witch who has ever been in my debt. Kill me and you'll paint a target on your back for generations, until each one of your daughters has bled for your enmity. Is that what you want?"

Yaga slowly let the tension in her shoulders ease, a gradual slip-slip-slipping with a shudder down her spine.

"You do not deserve my benevolence, Lazar," she said contemptuously, "but to honor my daughter's wishes, you'll have it." She held out her hand, and as he opened his mouth to speak, she cut him off. "You have no honor of your own," she told him, "so do not force me into pretense."

He took her hand, gripping it once. "So, this is peace, then."

Yaga yanked her hand away, repulsed. "This is not peace. This is a stalemate. This is sacrifice," she said, "yours and mine. We've both sacrificed, and this is the proof."

Then she turned away, disappearing with a rip into thin air, and Koschei let out a long breath, closing his eyes to suffer in solitude.

Or so he thought.

"Papa," a voice croaked, and Koschei looked up, startled again.

From the shadowed entryway at the top of the basement stairs was a gleam of gold, a halo of daylight so bright that Koschei felt the sudden need to squint, to seek shelter in darkness. Shame battered him anew as his eldest son stepped further into view, Dimitri's face leaving no question as he descended the stairs as to whether Koschei's deal with the devil had had an audience.

"Papa," Dimitri said, his voice breaking. "Did you just give up Lev?"

There could be no words now. Nothing to explain what had gone unsaid in order to remain undone.

"Dima." Koschei sighed. "Sometimes what is necess—"

"That is your *son*," Dimitri said, lurching back with repulsion. "My brother, Papa! How could you?"

"Dima, listen to me. It was bound to happen." Again left unsaid: *And it could have been worse.* "Restitution, Dima," Koschei said, in agitation he knew to be self-contempt. "And you heard Yaga. It was almost certainly going to be Lev—"

But his golden son was dark with fury, shadowed with pain.

"How has your hatred served you, Papa?" Dimitri asked him, gnashing the words between his teeth. "More than a decade ago a woman refused you—refused the offer of the great *Koschei the Deathless*," he said with bitter contempt, the voice of a boy who no longer believed in fairy tales, "and yet we have brought nothing but devastation to this family since then. The Antonovas built an empire, they built an enterprise, and what have we done?"

Koschei said nothing, and Dimitri shook his head. "What are we," he spat pridefully, "but hardened men and loyal sons who've destroyed each other and ourselves, all for the pittance of your approval?"

"Dima," Koschei sighed, reaching out for him. "Dima, please."

"I've lost enough today," Dimitri told him, shrinking back from his father's touch. "I've lost enough, and now my faith in you. I hope the taste of your peace is bitter with what you've done."

"Dima," Koschei begged, rising to his feet. "Dima—"

It could have been worse.

Dimitri would not want to hear it. He could never understand.

It could have been you.

But Dimitri, who had never turned his back on his father before, was already gone. Shame became rage like the snap of a finger, and in Dimitri's absence Koschei turned to the figures in the shadows, gritting his teeth.

"Be sure that Baba Yaga keeps to her end of the deal," Koschei hissed to the shadow creatures, who flickered in obedience.

Then the shadows crept out of the room, sliding eerily along the floor.

III. 20

(Peace.)

It was almost impossible for Ivan to tell what had happened first. Perhaps it had been Stas who'd raised a hand, aiming it somewhere between Ivan and Sasha, his target unknown; and then perhaps Roman, who had used a wild burst of magic to free himself from his restraints that nearly blasted aside the entire pillar, had recovered his gun, using it to shoot Stas in the chest. Perhaps it was the opposite. Perhaps the world itself had ended somehow and now Ivan stood dizzied among a sea of bodies, staring at the smoking barrel of Roman Fedorov's gun. Perhaps none of it was even real.

Ivan raised his hands slowly, glancing at Sasha, who stood with her hand over her mouth, white-faced. Roman, meanwhile, looked vacantly at Ivan, lips parted.

"Sometimes," Roman said, swallowing as he gestured to Stas's body on the ground, "death does bring peace."

Ivan blinked, and Roman carefully bent to place the gun on the ground, sliding it toward Sasha.

"So, will you kill me, then?" Roman asked her, rising to his feet. It was less a request this time than a question. *So, will you kill me?* as easily as if he'd asked, *So, will you be able to sleep tonight? Will you be able to live with all of this? Can you exist in this world as you once did? Will you ever be the same?*

"No," Sasha said, and Roman's dark brow twitched; surprised, or perhaps bemused. "Not that I don't want to," she said bitterly, letting her hand fall at her side. "I would think death no less than you deserved. But I couldn't—" She swallowed hard, lips pressed thin. "I can't."

Her gaze fell on the body of Lev Fedorov, who was only just beginning to lose the youthful flush in his cheeks.

"I can't," Sasha said again, her voice a well of brokenness. "He asked me not to."

Roman opened his mouth, about to speak, but Ivan stepped between them.

"Run," Ivan advised, gesturing, and for a moment, Roman merely froze.

Then he turned, not saying a word, and disappeared into a glimmer of nothing; as if he'd slipped and fallen out of time and space.

Ivan paused for a moment, uncertain what to do first—uncertain where to go, or who to move—when he heard footsteps behind him and turned, recognizing the sound of a familiar gait. The familiar tap of heels, which were unmistakable, and the lungful of rosewater he associated with only one person on earth.

The figure, which must have been a figment of Ivan's imagination—proof, then, that all of this must be a dream—strode slowly over to Sasha, who stared frozen with confusion, the paralyzing shock of utter disbelief.

"How is this—how are you—"

The figure tapped once against Sasha's temple, hard, a bright light bursting out from beneath the impact, and Sasha's knees buckled, collapsing beneath her. Then the figure reached down, slowly, and carefully lifted her, one hand slid under Sasha's knees while the other meticulously propped itself beneath her spine.

As Sasha rose in the air, carried in the arms of what could only be a mirage—or else a total stranger—the shadows swarmed around them and the figure itself turned to Ivan, expectant.

"Is she . . . *dead*?" Ivan asked in disbelief, staring at Sasha's glassy eyes. "Did you just—"

"Yes. For now. Are you coming?" the figure asked him softly, and Ivan blinked, stunned.

Perhaps the world *had* ended.

"Yes," he said eventually, because no other answer would come to his tongue. Figment of his imagination or not, that was always his answer when she asked him for anything.

"Yes, of course, Marya. As you wish."

At the sound of her name, Marya Antonova smiled, holding the limp body of her sister loosely in her arms as she waited for Ivan to place his hand lightly on her shoulder. "You're a good man, Ivan," she murmured, "though you have some room for improvement as a bodyguard."

As Ivan felt the cold evening air wrap around him—like an infant being swaddled, or a child in an embrace—he let out a laugh, half crying, the sound of it one more victim to be swallowed up by the night. And perhaps it was his imagination—perhaps not—but as they left the bodies behind, he could have sworn the shadows around them had flickered and danced, grotesquely satisfied.

III. 21

(The Heart.)

When Marya Antonova died, Dimitri Fedorov placed her heart in a box, carefully, and settled it in his desk, waiting for a time he might be willing to part with it. She'd already told him, some seventeen years ago, what she wished from him: she wanted it buried, protected, kept safe.

He wasn't—never would be—ready to say goodbye to her, but it felt wrong, somehow, to keep her like that, something to be mislaid among his things. To keep her frozen, as he was, and unable to prevent the sins committed by their families. Unable to salvage their vendettas, and therefore the atrocities that would invariably come next.

Dimitri carried the box mournfully in his hands, taking it out to the place he'd first told her he loved her. The ground there was hard beneath layers of greying snow, and digging wasn't easy work—he did it by hand—but eventually he'd made a hole in the earth, just near the base of the tree in the garden they'd played in as children. He had confessed to her here; kissed her here; loved her here; and now he would bury her here, as she'd once asked of him.

He paused, holding the box penitently in his hand, and then frowned, noticing something strange.

A *pulse,* he realized with alarm, and opened the box, his fingers shaking around the latch.

The moment he wrenched the lid open, there was no mistaking it. The heart inside was beating, throbbing, each motion syncopated and succinct. This was no error, no trick of a grieving mind. The marvel that was Marya Antonova's heart had started again, some-how, and Dimitri watched, breathless, as it sent him a sign; a calling; a declaration.

Keep it safe for me, Dima. Don't let anybody find it.

Slowly, Dimitri smiled, the arch of it glowing like the sun.

Marya Antonova's heart had started a war. Somehow, it would end one, too.

III. 22

(Vitality and Organs.)

There was a dull thud against Brynmor Attaway's custom coffee table just before he reared back with disgust, startled by the old man who'd materialized in his living room and the object that had been cast between them like a curse.

"What the—is that a—"

"Kidney? Yes." The old man sat across from Bryn with a wince, slowly lowering himself onto the cushions of the sofa. "Easy enough to live without," he muttered, "though not very enjoyable to remove."

"But—" Bryn blinked, resisting the urge to look closer. "How is this—what do you—"

"You think I don't know what happens behind my back, es-pecially when it comes to my children?" the old man asked, and several beats too late, Bryn realized the man before him could be none other than the reclusive Koschei the Deathless, Fedorov patriarch.

"I've lost one son tonight," Koschei said solemnly, "and I will not lose another. My son Roman's debt to you is paid."

Bryn sniffed at the kidney, his keen sense of equity getting the better of him.

"This is too much," he said gruffly, knowing that magic belonging to a witch like Koschei was worth far more than that of his son; even his eldest son. "The deal is uneven. I should offer you something else. Information, perhaps."

Koschei scoffed. "And what would I possibly want to know from a magicless fae?"

So the rumors of his bigotry were true, how lovely. "I'm not without my gifts," Bryn said. "In fact, I am called The Bridge for more than one reason, Lord Deathless."

"You can travel realms," Koschei said warily, and so it was a good day for rumors all around.

Bryn relaxed in his seat, pleased to have regained a foothold in the conversation. "Have to say hello to Mother from time to time," he explained, "though I spent the better part of the day doing something else. Behind the veil, that is," he clarified, and Koschei scowled.

"Why would that matter to me?" Koschei asked with a warning twitch of his fingers.

Suddenly, Bryn was far less concerned with the inequity of a deal than he was with teaching a witch, or perhaps several witches, a lesson about what—and *who*—could be easily dismissed.

"It matters," Bryn replied languidly, "because Marya Antonova isn't there."

Gratifyingly, Koschei froze for a beat—thrown. Weak. And obviously in pain.

"What?" A bad day to be Koschei the Deathless, thought Bryn with relish. "But how could that—how—?"

"Marya Antonova is not in the realm of the dead," Bryn repeated, "and therefore, reports of her death have been greatly exaggerated."

"But—Sasha, then," Koschei sputtered, shifting forward in agitation. The motion, unintended and terribly unwise given such a fresh wound, was met with visible strain. "What about Sasha? Is she there? Has Yaga kept to her deal, is Sasha truly dead?"

To that, Bryn permitted a smile, snatching up the kidney with his clever fae fingers. (Wouldst thou like to live deliciously *indeed*.)

"That, Koschei the Deathless," said The Bridge, "is outside the terms of our deal."

III. 23

(A Little Death.)

She remembered leaving Lev's side and standing, placing herself between Roman and Ivan. She remembered, too, that she had seen someone; her sister, of all people. Marya. Had it been a ghost? Was Sasha nothing but a ghost now, too?

Don't be silly. It is only a little death, Sashenka.

Very temporary.

Hardly enough to matter.

You won't even feel it when you wake up.

"Masha?" Sasha croaked, hearing her sister's voice again as a hand stretched out for hers, beckoning her gently. She forced her blurry vision to settle, recognizing the silhouette of her mother's face behind a veil; then Sasha reached out, taking hold of it with her fingers, and felt a wrench, her entire body drawn forth abruptly as if from drowning, with a cold, foreign air filling her lungs.

"Where am I?" She felt a seize of panic. "What's happening?"

"Hush, Sasha, be still," came her mother's voice, and in a blurry transfer of images, another figure leaned prominently into view. This one, too, was familiar, the dark 1940s waves falling around Sasha's face like a curtain, or a shroud.

"Mama," said the ghost, "I should think she deserves a minute to adjust, doesn't she?"

A very, very solid ghost. As Sasha's vision cleared, a jagged line was first to become starkly visible—a scar bisecting the chest beneath the thin silk of a woman's chemise. Then, just above, like the curve of a crescent moon, a familiar berry-red, and all around them a choking bloom of petrichor and roses.

"Masha," Sasha called out groggily, in awe and disbelief, and her eldest sister dimpled, pleased.

"Welcome back, Sashenka," said Marya, with a dazzling, radiant smile. "Come." She beckoned, taking Sasha's hand. "You and I have work to do."

THE ANTONOVA SISTERS, YESTERDAY

(Irina and Katya.)

Ekaterina Antonova, called Katya, and her twin Irina equally shared the misfortune of following their elder sister Marya in both geniture and affection. Neither was as clever or as beautiful as Marya—their accomplished sister Masha, beloved by mother and father and still, despite everything, by each of the sisters alike—and for a time, this succession plagued them hatefully. It wasn't until their mother Baba Yaga pulled them aside that they learned being second-born was powerful, too.

"Envy is a wasted emotion," Yaga said to her twin daughters when they were still very young. She'd held tight to both their little chins and searched them sternly, her dark eyes hard and intolerant of sulking. "You are born of my blood and your father's magic and you will not waste it; not even a drop. You are Antonova daughters, as equally as your sister, and you will find power in you no one else will ever dream of. You will have hunger no one else will ever feel, and it will drive you. It will push you to madness or else to greatness, and you have only to choose for yourselves what your futures will be.

"Do you believe I would have brought you into this world if I did not want you?" Yaga asked them, and the twins slowly shook their heads. "No, you're right, I would not. If I thought I only needed one daughter, I would have had only one. So, what would you have your lives be, Katya? Irka?" She gripped each of them tightly, her hands as firm as the steel of her will. "Would you have it be wasted in loathing? In pettiness and greed? Or will you prove to me and the world alike that the blood in your veins is as valuable as that of any witch who walks this earth?"

Katya looked at Irina, who looked back at Katya.

Then they both looked at their mother, a secret lingering on both their tongues.

"We can see things," Katya confessed, and paused, amending the statement. "I can see things," she corrected herself slowly. "Irka can hear them."

Yaga's expression remained still. "What things?"

"There's a veil," Irina explained, frowning. "A curtain, and sometimes, when Katya pulls it back for me, things fall out of it. Voices."

If their mother was frightened by this revelation, she didn't show it.

"All the time?" Yaga asked. "Is there a veil in the room with us now?"

Katya glanced around, shaking her head. "No. It isn't always there," she added solemnly. "Only sometimes."

"But when it is?" Yaga prompted.

"I call them out," Katya said, her gaze flicking to her twin.

"And I speak with them," Irina confirmed. "They tell me stories or ask me for favors."

For the first time, Yaga stiffened in apprehension. "And do you grant them these favors?"

"No," Katya said, and added hastily, "Masha says not to."

"Masha knows about this?" Yaga asked, surprised. She hadn't known her eldest kept any secrets from her. At the time, Marya was only eight years old, still with the rest of her life to keep many more. "She didn't tell me."

"She promised us she wouldn't," Irina said simply, which was answer enough. Honor, loyalty, fidelity, these were the hallmarks of an Antonova witch as they had been taught, and always, Marya was the best of them.

"Show me how it works, then," Yaga beckoned. "The next time Katya sees the veil, both of you fetch me, and only me. And Masha, if you wish," she amended quickly, as the twins exchanged another glance. "But no one else. Do you understand?"

"Yes, Mama," the twins agreed.

Within a week, Marya came running into Yaga's bedroom, her cheeks flushed with spots of concern. "It's happening," she said simply, and took her mother's hand, pulling her into the twins' bedroom.

Nothing looked out of the ordinary at first. Katya and Irina stood together in the center of the room, Katya's hand guiding her sister's upward as if to stroke the ray of sunlight coming in through the window of their bedroom. Irina, meanwhile, was murmuring something very quietly—translating, Yaga realized, so that Katya could hear.

"It's a man," Katya said aloud, squinting at something neither Yaga nor Marya could see. "He's very . . . upset." She looked up at her mother. "He's angry. Someone took his toys."

It hadn't made much sense until they'd seen the newspaper the next morning, Marya's small brow furrowed with contemplation as she slid the headline to her mother, out of sight from her father. QUEENS BREAK-IN RESULTS IN HOMICIDE, the article said, and Yaga had shown the picture of the victim to Katya, who nodded slowly.

"That's the angry man," she confirmed, and Yaga pulled both twins close to her, arms securely enfolding her daughters who could speak to the dead.

"Everyone will always ask you for something," she told them, "and ghosts are no exception. They are only people, same as living ones, who want only what they want. They do not hold more secrets or carry more wisdom simply because they have passed beyond this realm. But you must remember that their lives are ended, and though they will be drawn to you, you must take care of yourselves first. You must not let any spirits drain you of your own life; do not trade what is yours for what was theirs. Do you understand?"

They nodded.

"Why can't Masha see them?" Irina couldn't help asking. "Masha's the oldest—"

"Because Masha was born to live Masha's life," Yaga cut in firmly, "and you were each born to live yours. Some days this will be a blessing. Some days it will be a curse. But every day you are my daughters," she promised them, "and you are each other's sisters, and these will be the truths that will always come first."

It was a conversation they would not have to have again for many years. Occasionally Katya would excuse herself, nudging her sister, and Yaga would not ask why or where they were going. From time to time, Irina would request an unusual path home in order to speak to a stranger, murmuring something in their ear that would blossom to peace in their features. When Katya married Anthony, a social worker from the Bronx, she only said one thing to seal her mother's blessing: "He knows, and he doesn't mind it." For many years, the little they'd all shared had been more than enough.

Yaga never questioned her second-daughters about their gift, nor had she ever asked them to use their abilities. She never told a soul, not even her other children. In fact, she'd thought little at all about it until the night she watched Ivan carry her eldest daughter's body home from Koschei's warehouse.

That night, for the first time in many years, she thought at length about the gifts of her twins, and her first instinct was to summon her second-born daughters back to their mother's house. It did not surprise Baba Yaga, though, that her daughters were already there, having seen fit to come to her.

"Have you seen the veil?" Yaga asked Katya, who nodded as she crept into her mother's bedroom, pale cheeks streaked with tears.

"Yes, Mama," Katya said in a low voice, and stepped aside, revealing Irina just behind her. Yaga had never understood if the bond between her daughters was magical or biological, but it didn't surprise her that one twin's need might have summoned the other.

"You've spoken to her already, Irka?" Yaga asked Irina, who nodded gravely.

"She's calling for you, Mama," Irina whispered. "I think she's trapped."

Yaga fought a shudder. "I'll fix it," she promised them, "but I'll need your help. I warned you once it was unnatural to commune with the dead," she reminded them quietly. "If that is the counsel you wish to abide by now, I understand. With Masha gone, you are the eldest now. You are my heirs. You have earned your right to what is hers by virtue of succession alone—even if you were not already worthy," she added, "though I know you both are. If you choose to leave your sister in the realms of the dead, I will understand."

The twins looked at each other for a moment, saying nothing; communing as twins do.

"There's a reason we were born in Masha's shadow, Mama," Katya said slowly. "Because what we do, we can't do in the light."

"You were right when you said we'd always be hungry," Irina added. "It's why the dead come to us. Because they know we won't turn them away."

"But we don't want what belongs to Masha," Katya finished solemnly, shaking her head.

"We have callings of our own," Irina agreed, and Yaga nodded gratefully, tucking her hands around both her daughters' cheeks.

"Take caution, then," she told them. "It won't be an easy road ahead."

They were Antonova witches. "We are not afraid," they replied reflexively, and settled themselves beside their mother.

(Lena.)

Yelena Antonova was not surprised by much. Such were the pitfalls of hearing things, reading things. The universe spoke a language, if you were paying close enough attention. Many languages, even. Stars, leaves, flowers, cards, dirt—the universe was constantly spelling things out, though people rarely listened.

Lena did. Lena listened to everything, and watched, too. She and her sisters, for all their same blood, saw very different things when they looked at the world. Marya saw opportunity. Katya and Irina saw . . . some other world besides this one. Liliya, when she could be bothered to open her eyes for much at all, usually preferred to close them, returning to her dreams. Galina mostly saw herself. It was only Lena who truly saw the world as it was, though of all her many views, she generally chose the stars.

Lena still lived at home with her mother, unlike her elder sisters. Irina and Katya had moved away, and Marya, too. Lena, on the other hand, didn't enjoy being alone. There was too much to get lost in when she was by herself.

"Masha is dead," Yaga said, her footsteps preceding an explanation for the dread Lena had been unable to place all day. "I presume you already know as much?"

No, actually. Lena had read the futures for all her sisters, but of all of them, Marya's and Sasha's were the most unclear. They had fits and starts, like stars themselves. They never died out, no matter how many ways Lena read it, or they always died. They flickered and faded and shone, but did not follow a path she could understand.

"Not this time, Mama," Lena said simply.

Yaga paused, considering this, and held out the cup in her hand.

"I brought us some tea," Yaga said, and Lena sighed, knowing very well what that meant. Marya's version of this particular request had been slightly different; it had been luring Lena up to the roof of their building to look at the stars. Marya knew Lena's fondness for open spaces, understood her longing to see what was written in the sky, and encouraged it.

Still. Tea would work, in a pinch.

"I foresee a difficult choice for you, Mama," Lena confessed, accepting the cup but not drinking from it, toying instead with the ceramic of the handle. "I know what you wish to do, and I know you'll go through hell to do it. I know you know what it requires: sacrifice." She looked up, eyeing her mother. "I also know you may not like what you dig up."

The words seemed to register in her mother's spine, flickering on her face with recognition. What Lena had told her, Yaga already understood.

"Is that magic, Lena," Yaga prompted, "or intuition?"

"It's nothing that will satisfy you," Lena replied wryly, "but it's something, nonetheless."

Yaga nodded. She missed nothing. Lena suspected she spoke the universe's language herself, or else the reverse; the universe bent to her wishes, informing her of everything.

"You're going to do it, aren't you?" Lena asked, and answered herself, "Of course you are."

Yaga quieted, something dawning in her gaze.

"You're a good girl, Lenochka," she murmured, and then she and Lena sipped at their tea, holding their futures between the palms of their hands.

(Galya.)

To non-magical people, Galina Antonova was like a lovely, charismatic mirror. For each man she met, he became a funnier, smarter, better version of himself in her presence; inevitably he (any nameless he) would love her for it, at least for as much time as she would give him. She would give him very little, though, because she wasn't a fool, and it was always very clear to her what he truly craved. He loved himself most of all—specifically, the version of him she made him—and so, eventually, pretty Galya would be gone almost as quickly as she came, disappearing into the night.

It didn't occur to non-magical people that Galina herself was magic.

Her sisters knew better, of course, and her mother, too. They knew their Galina was, for them, something like a battery; an amplifier. When Galina was present, their magic was more refined, more focused. When her sister Marya was especially weary, she would call for Galina—*Galya, pretty Galya, come hold my hand*—and Galina, second-youngest, would always relent, twining her fingers with her sister's and waiting patiently for sparks.

Sometimes it was a very late night, and Galina would be awake long past her bedtime, sometimes until the early mornings. Still, she wouldn't move, knowing this was her gift. This was her importance. She didn't know how Marya had ever figured it out—a lucky guess, perhaps? Possibly something more purposeful. Marya always did see the important things, after all, and perhaps it was because Galina was so grateful for the observation that she, forgettable second-youngest, would never complain. She merely sat with her shoulders stiff, a perfect copy of Marya, right down to the shape of their midnight smiles.

In the morning, a still-tired Marya (who was never too tired for breakfast) would take Galina's face in her hands and smile a different smile at her; a tender one, full of gratitude. She would say something like *What are you hungry for, Galya?* and they would make pancakes in their mother's kitchen, dusting themselves in powdered sugar and licking syrup from their fingers until the whole house was awake, plates piled high with more food than they could ever eat.

"Masha is dead," Galina's mother told her that morning, and at the words, strangely or not-so-strangely, Galina tasted pancakes, struggling to swallow it down. "But I'll tell you a secret," Yaga added quickly, and Galina looked up, surprised. She was no Sasha, the baby, nor Marya, the favorite; she was only one in a string of pretty sisters with prettier talents and therefore she was easily forgotten, and rarely permitted secrets. The twins, Katya and Irina, had plenty of them. So did Liliya, who dreamed of them, and Yelena, who seemed to know all of them. But Galina had never had secrets herself, at least until today.

"What is it?" Galina asked her mother, who smiled thinly.

"If you help us, Galinka," Yaga murmured, "perhaps there's something we can do about it."

Galya, pretty Galya, come hold my hand.

"Just tell me what you need," Galina said instantly, and her mother opened her bedroom door, inviting her to come inside.

ACT IV

BE BUT MINE

O Romeo, Romeo, wherefore art thou Romeo?
Deny thy father and refuse thy name.
Or if thou wilt not, be but sworn my love,
And I'll no longer be a Capulet.

Juliet,
Romeo and Juliet (Act II, Scene 2)

IV. 1

(In Darkness.)

Dimitri Fedorov was the sun, the moon, and the stars. His mother had whispered it to him when he was a boy: *Dima, you are the sun, the moon, and the stars*. She'd meant that he was her entire universe, and probably he was. Her world was very small.

Marya had said something similar to him when he was fifteen, only she'd been joking: *Dima, you are the sun, the moon, and the stars*, she'd said with her talent for indifference. Dima, you never look around to realize the world goes on around you, outside you, in spite of you.

Now, again, Dimitri Fedorov was the sun, the moon, and the stars.

Shiny, dead things in space.

Dimitri and Roman buried their brother Lev in darkness. The irony of new moons, of beginnings in general, is that they are always begun with total blindness. No orb of light for guidance. No promise of the future, good or bad. Roman had come to find Dimitri, told him what happened. They were dead, both of them. Lev and Alexandra—Sasha, the youngest Antonova witch—whose body was already taken. Probably by Ivan, Roman said.

Dimitri said nothing. He didn't ask what happened. He said nothing of the heart he'd enchanted and placed in a small vial, tied with a leather cord around his neck. He said nothing of Marya Antonova's heart or his own.

Dimitri and Roman buried Lev in darkness, in silence. Then Roman straightened, cleared his throat, and spoke.

"The Bridge told me our deal is ended," Roman said.

This is your fault, Dimitri didn't say.

"Good" was his only answer.

"You hate me," Roman guessed.

Yes, of course. Of course I do. Do you not see what you've cost me?

"No," he said. "I don't."

"I never wanted this to happen, Dima," Roman told him.

No one ever gets what they want, Roma. I know that more than anyone.

"I know," said Dimitri.

"Papa," Roman began tentatively, "he wants us to—"

Dimitri shut his eyes.

"It can wait," Roman rushed to say.

Yes, Dimitri thought, *Koschei's wishes can wait. They can wait forever. They can wait until the rage in my veins dies down, if it ever does. Koschei can wait until my enmity fades, if it ever will. Koschei can ask for me again tomorrow, and the tomorrow after that, and all of my tomorrows. He can pound on my door and beg for me and see if I will answer. Koschei is without a death, without a life, without a conscience. For once, Koschei can wait for me to decide when I am ready to be moved.*

"See to it," Dimitri said, "whatever it is. Whatever he wants."

Roman's brow furrowed. "Dima," he began.

Koschei dies, you know, Dimitri doesn't say. *Koschei is only immortal until he isn't.*

"I have to do something," Dimitri said instead, and Roman knew something was wrong, most likely. Roman was probably wondering how to get his brother the universe (the sun, moon, and stars) to speak, but perhaps Roman already understood he no longer reserved the right to Dimitri's thoughts. Roman let him go, and after burying his brother Lev in darkness, Dimitri went to the only person he could think of. The only person he could stand to face.

"Oh," said Brynmor Attaway, pulling the door open.

Dimitri took hold of The Bridge's throat, little cracklings of power sparking beneath his fingertips.

"Oh," repeated Brynmor Attaway, less coherently this time.

The lights of The Bridge's apartment were too dim for Dimitri, who had buried his brother in darkness. He released Bryn, half throwing him to the ground, and then turned to the door, giving it a shove. As the latch snapped into place, Dimitri waited. Perhaps the fae would kill him? Stab a blade through his heart from behind? Koschei had often spoken of the dangers of meeting fairies. The stories varied from place to place, but the general lesson was always the same: Show a fae your back and he will gladly place a knife between your shoulders, unless he has something to gain from you.

So, when Dimitri discovered he wasn't dead, he guessed The Bridge still had some interest in him.

"I told Roma our deal was settled," Bryn said casually, "so either you're here for the pleasure of my company, or—"

"Marya Antonova isn't dead," Dimitri said.

Bryn's brow rose, amused. "And how would you know that?"

Dimitri felt Marya's heart pulse against his own.

"I know," he said.

"Ah, you witchy, mystical folk. What exactly is your connection to Marya Antonova, Dimitri Fedorov?"

She is my entire soul, Dimitri didn't say.

"We knew each other once."

"What, intimately?" asked Bryn.

It seemed a question meant to cause him harm.

"She isn't dead," Dimitri said again.

"And?" Bryn prompted. The conversation seemed to be branching off in a web of thoughts, with The Bridge holding all the silken ends. "I don't really see what that has to do with me."

But Bryn had already made a number of observations, Dimitri knew. He knew Dimitri had come to him for something. He knew Dimitri's connection to Marya was something more than nothing. That alone was dangerous information to put in a fae's greedy hands.

"You know, they say something very interesting about Marya Antonova in the land of the dead," Bryn said, gesturing for Dimitri to sit, which he did, warily. "I try not to listen to gossip, of course, but sometimes that's much easier said than done. Can't always avoid it."

Dimitri said nothing.

"They say she's missing something," Bryn went on, unbothered by Dimitri's silence. "A piece of herself, in fact. Now, normally this wouldn't be worth remarking," he mused, pouring himself a glass of caramel-colored liquid. "Sorry, did you want one?" he asked, holding up a glass. Dimitri didn't move. "Right, have it your way." He poured a second glass, eyeing it in the light, and then carried it over, holding it out for Dimitri.

After a moment or two of silence, Dimitri accepted the beverage.

Offer and acceptance. It didn't take a lawyer or a fairy (or one who was both) to know what that meant. The Bridge smiled his sly smile, falling into the seat across from Dimitri.

"Marya Antonova is alive, but absent something," Bryn said.

"I want you to take me to the realm of the dead," Dimitri replied.

"Okay, not the response I was expecting," Bryn remarked, betraying only the tiniest degree of surprise, "but it's certainly an interesting proposal."

They each took a sip of their drink. Whisky, Dimitri realized, but not mortal whisky. It occurred to him for half a second that perhaps he was being poisoned or drugged; maybe not all fae worked with blades. But then Bryn sighed, shaking his head.

"I wouldn't drug you," Bryn said, correctly interpreting Dimitri's delayed sense of hesitation. "What, and let my curiosities go unsatisfied? Never. I love myself too much."

"Fine." Dimitri set the glass down. "Yes or no?"

"What business do you have with that realm?" Bryn replied, which was neither a yes nor a no.

"My brother is dead," Dimitri said.

"Not Roman."

"No," Dimitri said through gritted teeth, "not Roma," *although it should be.*

"Family drama," Bryn noted. "This seems like a you problem."

"The *problem* is I have a dead brother when I don't need to," Dimitri growled in retort. "If Marya Antonova is alive, then surely Lev can be returned. I need to know how Marya did it."

"What makes you so sure Marya did it?" Bryn asked.

Marya's heart thudded once, twice, three times against Dimitri's chest.

"Seems like," Bryn estimated slowly, "I'm not the one whose answers you really want."

"Maybe not. But you're the one who can help me," Dimitri said, "so name your price, Bridge."

"Well, much as I do love this sort of bargain, even I can tell this one is off," Bryn replied, crossing one leg over the other. "Don't you know the fun of bargaining is in the struggle, Fedorov? You'll have to offer me something. A blank check leaves too much room for creativity, and I'm really not the imaginative type."

"What do you want, then?" Dimitri asked.

"What is most precious to you, Dimitri Fedorov?" Bryn countered.

Marya. Lev. Roman, on a good day.

Dimitri's name. His reputation.

His magic, whatever was left of it.

None of which he could give.

"Nothing," Dimitri said eventually. "Nothing is precious to me."

Bryn smiled slowly, letting it tease across his face.

"I think we both know that's not true," he said. "And unfortunately I'm not in a position to bargain with a liar."

"Why not?" Dimitri asked. "You made a deal with my brother."

"Ouch," remarked Bryn, insincerely. "Sad Roman's not here to appreciate it."

Dimitri's mouth tightened.

Then he rose to his feet, shaking his head.

"I don't know why I came here," he said, turning to leave, and Bryn laughed.

"You came because you're angry, Fedorov prince," Bryn said.

"You're accustomed to life going your way, aren't you? Only now the easy choices don't seem so easy. You can't murder your brother because you love him," he guessed. "You can't murder me because you want my help. You want to put your golden hands to something and watch the life drain out of it, understandably, but you can't. I'd suggest therapy," he added drily, "only I suspect you're too far gone."

Dimitri spun, rounding on him. "What would you advise, then?"

"Me? Revenge, of course." Bryn sipped daintily at his glass. "Whose fault is this?"

"I—" Dimitri hesitated. Roman's. His face contorted in displeasure.

"Go back a step," Bryn advised.

Marya's. She was the one who started this.

No, she wasn't. It was her mother.

No, Dimitri thought again, it wasn't.

This began with Koschei.

"You have something against my father," Dimitri guessed blandly, glancing at The Bridge.

"Look how clever you are," Bryn confirmed, toasting him from where he remained seated. "Brava, little prince."

Dimitri thought his opinions about Koschei were, at the moment, more wisely kept to himself.

"I have nothing to gain by standing against my father," he warned.

"Not much to lose, either," Bryn remarked, setting aside his glass to fix his peering glance more squarely on Dimitri. "What's his is yours, isn't it? Marked out for you, the heir to the throne. All this duty and honor," he scoffed distastefully, rising to his feet to join Dimitri where he stood across the room, lingering unwisely beside the doorway. "It's just so . . . *tiresome*, isn't it? All this power," Bryn mused, "and what has it ever done for you?"

Dimitri pointedly did not confess to having asked himself the same question.

"Bold statement," he said instead, "seeing as you're currently addressing one of the most influential witches in the Borough. In all the Boroughs."

"And what has that cost you?" Bryn asked.

Marya. Lev. Roman, on a good day.

The majority of his sanity.

The entirety of his soul.

"Just a thought," Bryn suggested, clapping Dimitri on the back and leading him back into the living room, giving him a brief nudge down to the sofa. "I happen to know your father is in an ideal place to be taken down a peg."

"Fae rumors certainly run rampant," Dimitri muttered, resuming the seat beside his forgone glass as The Bridge's hand remained securely on his shoulder.

"Something like that," Bryn agreed, amused. "But after all, why shouldn't he be? He just lost his son. His other son's magic is compromised, and then there's . . . you." Bryn's smile twitched, then thinned. "Your family's rather vulnerable, isn't it? I'd hate to think you have any enemies who might find a gap in your armor."

With that, Bryn flicked the side of Dimitri's neck, and he flinched.

"I shouldn't have come here," Dimitri said, and Bryn shrugged.

"Well, that's debatable," he said. "I was never going to make it easy, was I? No fun in that. But I *could* conceivably help you, in some respect. You chose well, if not wisely."

"So you want my father dead," Dimitri registered, dazed. "That's your price for taking me to Lev?"

"What? No, don't be silly," Bryn scoffed. "I mean yes, I most certainly *do* want your father dead, but that's more of a constant, secondary whimsy. He despises me and my kind, doesn't he?" he prompted, falling into his seat and picking up his whisky as Dimitri didn't answer. "No need to confirm. I know as much. But no, his life is not my price."

"Then what is it?" Dimitri asked, bracing himself.

"No price," Bryn said.

Dimitri frowned. There was no way the fae would offer him anything for free.

"I'm not offering it for free," Bryn assured him. "What I'm saying is that I can't actually offer anything at all. I don't know how Marya Antonova came back. I could find out," he acknowledged, shrugging, "but I couldn't do it for you. I could also cross over to the realm of the dead, but similarly, I couldn't take you with me."

"These are crumbs, then," Dimitri said. "Meager offerings."

"Aren't they?" Bryn agreed with a laugh, gesturing to Dimitri's glass. "Might as well finish your drink."

Dimitri looked down at it. "What is it?"

"Whisky from my mother's house," Bryn said. "She told me I would have a visit from the sun, the moon, and the stars. She's something of a disastrous psychic, my mother. Painfully opaque."

"What is she?"

"Oh, you know. A humble fairy." Bryn took a sip. "An expert distiller of whisky, that's for sure."

Dimitri lifted the glass to his lips, taking another sip.

It was very good.

"I'm not totally selfless, of course," Bryn permitted. "It pleases me greatly that you came here, little prince; I'd love to have the ear of the next Koschei. I have something of a witch infestation these days, and I'd like a more privileged position." He shrugged, adding, "Easier to swat flies from on high."

Dimitri blinked.

"You're," he began, and faltered. "Collecting me?"

"I love trinkets," Bryn agreed. "The more useful, the better. And you're certainly pretty enough."

"But I'm not useful to you. Not if I stay loyal to my father."

"True, that did cross my mind. But then again, you can't have your brother back if you stay loyal to Koschei, either. So, what'll it be?" Bryn asked, and Dimitri stared down at the whisky in his hand.

He didn't know the answer.

But either way, this was not the place for truth.

"I'm a Fedorov," Dimitri said, setting the glass down on the table. "I was born a Fedorov. I will die a Fedorov."

"Like Lev?" asked Bryn.

Briefly, Dimitri wondered if he shouldn't simply kill the irreverent fae. Perhaps it would make him feel better, ease the tightness in his chest.

"How did Roman satisfy his deal with you?" Dimitri asked instead.

"Someone paid on his behalf," Bryn replied. "The debt is satisfied."

Quietly, Marya's heart pulsed, thudding warningly against his.

"Who do you work for?" Dimitri asked, rising again to his feet.

"The highest bidder," Bryn replied.

"And who is that, currently?"

The look on The Bridge's face suggested that Dimitri had finally asked the right question.

"Not you," Bryn replied into his glass, chuckling.

Dimitri paced the floor, thinking.

Who else would have paid Roman's debt?

Who would want ownership of The Bridge's loyalty?

Only one person came to mind, however unlikely.

"How can I find Marya Antonova?" Dimitri asked, abruptly falling to a halt.

"How does anyone find Marya Antonova?" Bryn replied, shrugging.

They don't, Dimitri thought. *She finds you.*

"Go home, little prince," Bryn suggested. "Come find me again when you've had a change of . . ."

He trailed off, eyes tracking a line to the center of Dimitri's chest.

"Heart," Bryn finished, tilting his head, and Dimitri didn't answer. He turned, heading for the door, and didn't look back.

IV. 2

(Strings.)

In Dimitri's absence, Marya flickered into being in The Bridge's living room. She strode forward, picking up Dimitri's glass and sniffing it.

"Glad to see you're capable of remaining true to our deal, for a change," Marya noted, not looking at Bryn. She seemed intent on the contents of Dimitri's glass, which Bryn could have easily told her was nothing particularly remarkable. Fairy whisky was sweeter than her tastes—lacked a certain bite. "Or true to anything, that is."

"You know I like you, Marya," Bryn reminded her, watching her take Dimitri's seat on the sofa. "And you chose well. I want Koschei brought down as badly as you do."

"Even after he gave you what you wanted?"

"He gave me something he could stand to part with," Bryn scoffed, "which isn't the same as what I wanted. What I want belongs to you."

"I don't have it," she reminded him, drawing the neckline of her dress aside. The slice at her chest was stark and jagged, morbidly lovely amid verdant green lace, and Bryn might have been aroused by the exposure to skin if not for the more pressing curiosity about what lay beneath her décolletage. "You already know it's gone."

He did, unfortunately. It was rather a disappointment, though it made for a very different Marya Antonova indeed, and he wasn't totally opposed to the change.

"What exactly is your goal in this, Marya?" Bryn asked her. "Most people who wander back to life don't usually waste time with elaborate vengeance plots. Certainly not when you could kill Roman now and be done with it. He's weaker than he's ever been, don't you think?"

Marya dismissed him with a wave of her hand. "Roma is the least of my concerns."

"And your mother?" Bryn asked. "Her hands are hardly clean. She made a duplicitous deal with Koschei, didn't she?"

"She made a sacrifice to save her child," Marya snapped. "A forgivable lie."

"A lie nonetheless," Bryn said.

"My mother would never lie to me," Marya said. "Be wiser with your battles, Bridge. Or at least bring sharper knives."

"Where's your sister now, then?"

"Busy," Marya said, "and more importantly, none of your business."

She drained the rest of Dimitri's glass, rising to her feet.

"So. You'll keep our secret?" she prompted.

This time, the terms of the deal were painfully simple. He would not betray Marya Antonova, and in return, he would not have her for an enemy.

"I will," Bryn said.

"You lied to me once before," Marya noted disapprovingly.

"I did," Bryn agreed, and then added, probably foolishly, "You weren't free then."

To that, she gave a delighted laugh that fizzed like crisp champagne, delicate and cold.

"What makes you think I'm free now?" she mused, and before Bryn could answer, she had her hand around his jaw, sliding her thumb over his lips. "You don't even know whether you prefer me or Dimitri, do you? It's power you love, Bridge. Power that excites you. It must destroy you, then, being so close."

It did.

But he suspected the words meant more to her than they did to him.

"How did you know Dimitri would come to me?" Bryn asked her.

The old Marya Antonova would have faltered. This one hardly breathed. "Because I know him."

"Perhaps you did once—"

She tightened her grip, shaking her head. "Better not to ask," she whispered.

To that, Bryn twitched his hands, drawing a bit of Koschei's magic to the pads of his itching fingers. It still felt new, vaguely out of touch; he still had to ask permission to use it, and even then, it was raw and misbehaved. Marya, on the other hand, breathed hers in like second nature, putting out the fire of his before the spark was even lit.

"That power was stolen, Bridge," she reminded him, "and it will never work for you as well as mine will work for me."

She closed off his breath with a smile.

He felt his heart bang once, twice. Three times, skittering out of reach.

"How long would it take to suffocate?" she asked him softly.

He felt his eyes droop, and she sighed, releasing him.

"Lucky for you, I still need you," she said as he fell to the floor, gasping for breath. "You're doing so well, Brynmor," she murmured, dropping to touch his cheek, and as he shrank away, she gave another bubbling laugh. "In fact, you're doing so well I almost trust you."

She slid the tips of her fingers over his lips, reducing him to a shiver.

"Almost?" he echoed.

"Almost," Marya confirmed, and then she straightened.

She was twice as lovely as she'd been in life, Bryn thought, and twice as still.

Dead things were always so perfect. So very, very difficult to move.

"Get some sleep, Bridge," she advised. "Perhaps I'll teach you how to use those stolen powers of yours tomorrow."

He nodded numbly, and she sighed.

"No snappy comebacks?" she asked. "Disappointing. And here my expectations were so high."

"Title of my memoir," he said.

"That's better," she ruled, nodding with approval.

In a blink, she was gone.

"Fucking witches," Bryn grumbled.

Then he reached for his glass and drained it before resting his head limply against the floor.

IV. 3

(Terms and Conditions.)

"Sasha?"

She blinked, dragging her mind back to the present.

"I'm almost done," she called through the bathroom door, staring at her reflection.

It was strange, really, how much her face no longer seemed to match her insides. Was it really not so long ago that Lev had touched her here, here, here? Her eyes were glassy now, too wide. They'd seen too much. They'd seen life and death and the passage between. Her skin was pale, vaguely translucent. She reached for a bottle of Galina's brightening serums, hoping for vanity. Hoping to fill the gaps in her heart with some useless vices; with some other, less painful sins.

"Sasha." A sigh. "Sashenka, open the door."

Sasha paused, and then obeyed. Largely because Marya could find her way in if she wanted to.

"I'll be ready in a minute," Sasha said over her shoulder, picking up Galina's moisturizer for show, and Marya sighed again, taking a step inside the bathroom and closing the door behind her.

"Sasha," she said. "You won't be going to the store today."

"I—" Sasha looked up, blinking. "What?"

"You won't be going to the store," Marya repeated. She was wearing an ivory collared blouse buttoned all the way up, prim and proper as always, the grey pencil skirt delicately nipping in at her waist. "We have another job for you now, Sashenka."

Oh. "We," Sasha echoed, hollowly.

Masha stepped forward, drawing Sasha's chin up with a finger. "You think Mama betrayed you?" Marya asked quietly, scrutinizing Sasha's face. "Is that it, Sashenka?"

Sasha refused to look up. "You said there was a deal, Masha. Blood for blood."

"Yes." Marya's grip tightened on her chin. "But I would never have left you for dead, Sasha. Never."

"So then we broke our side of the deal when you brought me back," Sasha said dully. "And Koschei didn't."

"Because Koschei is a monster willing to kill his own son," Marya said, and added in warning, "Do not mistake apathy for honor."

"But why bring me back at all?" Reluctantly, bitterly, Sasha glanced up to meet her sister's dark eyes. "I understand why Mama wanted you, Masha. No one can do what you do. Nobody can be Mama's lieutenant but you. But me, there's no reason for me to . . ." She exhaled shakily. "If Lev has to remain gone, then—"

"Sashenka. Who has ever loved you more than me?" Marya cut in. "Name one. Name anyone."

Sasha hesitated. "But Masha, I—"

"Forget Mama. Forget Koschei. You really think *I* would leave you for dead?"

"Masha—"

"You're an Antonova," Marya reminded her. "You and I, we're not just one of many. We are parts of an indivisible whole. If Lev and his brothers are not what we are, so be it. That's the difference between an Antonova and a Fedorov. That's the difference between us and everyone, and everything. We aren't finished, Sashenka," Marya said, and where she might have once softened, she stood firm, fiercely their mother's soldier. "Look what Mama faces, Sasha. We cannot possibly be dead and done."

"But what about—" Sasha swallowed with difficulty. "What about Stas?"

Without Lev, Sasha felt strangely empty-handed. Where she'd

once held a horizon, she now saw only a receding line. She imagined that her sister, in losing her husband of nearly twelve years, would have felt the same way—as if a piece of her were gone, launched impossibly far, sent blindly out to sea.

"Stas made his choice," Marya said.

He was not an Antonova, she might have said.

"Roman killed him," Sasha pointed out. "Just as he killed you."

"Roman will suffer in his own way," Marya said flatly. "I wouldn't worry about it."

She looked impossibly cold, and inhumanly beautiful, like a diamond cut to shimmer in the light. *My daughters are diamonds,* as Yaga so often said. *Nothing is more beautiful. Nothing shines brighter. And most importantly, nothing will break them.*

"Don't forget at whose bidding Roman did all of this," Marya warned Sasha, tucking her hair comfortingly behind her ear. "Roman Fedorov is only Koschei's blade. A knife doesn't wield itself."

But it was Roman who should have died, not Lev—

But it was Roman whose blood I wanted—

But it was Roman, all this time it was Roman, *and now—*

Sasha swallowed her doubts, forcing them down.

"He'll suffer in his own way," she agreed, and then stepped coolly from Marya's grip—not to create distance between them, but rather to stand on her own, without prompting. To exist on a plane of her own agency.

"So, what will I do, then," Sasha asked her sister, "if not work at the store?"

"Koschei has no reason to know you're alive," Marya reminded her, "and we won't give him one. He has no reason to know what else we have in store for him."

"But business will simply . . . continue?" Sasha asked, frowning.

"Business will *grow,*" Marya corrected. "You closed the deal yourself, didn't you? That was only one dealer, Sashenka. That was only one pawn, but there are more. There are always more."

"But how will selling drugs to magicless addicts bring down

Koschei's empire?" Sasha said, stomach roiling at the thought. For this the world lost Lev? Her hatred for Koschei reignited and again the course ahead seemed small and insignificant, the scales of justice too arduously tipped. She wanted devastation. She wanted carnage. She wanted, badly, blood. "That might bring us satisfaction, maybe. Money, sure, but—"

"The only way to win anything is to have it all," Marya reminded her. "To take every scrap of him; to rid him of his possessions and his authority and his influence until all he has is his pride, and then we'll rid him of that, too." Her dark eyes flashed with meaning. "We'll become so powerful, so vast, that Koschei will have to bow to us, and when he bends at the knee to everything we've built—"

"We'll see his empire fall," Sasha murmured.

If his business is his everything, she thought, *then I will raze it to the ground.*

"Can you do it?" Marya asked seriously. Her hand drifted to the scar Sasha knew remained on her chest, marked out over her heart. "Tell me the truth, Sasha, because it won't be easy. There is little wisdom in power. There is even less in vengeance."

"I don't want to be wise," Sasha said. Lev had been a fool, hadn't he? Lev was killed by his own father's negligence, by the brother he fought so blindly to save, and why should she be any different?

"I don't want to be wise," she repeated slowly. "I want to win."

Gradually, Marya's lips curled up in a slither of satisfaction that was not quite fitting for the Marya she had been.

But Sasha was not the person she had been, either.

"Where would you begin, then," Marya asked, "if you wanted to rid a man of everything?"

Easy. Sasha was—had been—a business major at one of the most competitive schools in the country. She understood the basic principles, the economics of survival.

"Destroy his resources," Sasha said. "Rid him of access to anything he needs to go on."

"Good," Marya said, nodding. "And?"

"Turn his allies against him," Sasha said. "His influence. Cut it off."

"Yes. And?"

She paused a moment.

"Wipe out his army," Sasha replied flatly. "The other two sons."

At that, Marya was glorious. The arch of her smile shone bright, brilliant, blinding.

"Sashenka, you were born for this."

Sasha glanced at her reflection. Perhaps now her eyes were too wide for having seen too much, but maybe she was wrong to think them vulnerable. Maybe they were wide enough now to miss nothing.

"We should get started then, Masha," Sasha said, turning to smile grimly at her sister. "We have quite a lot of work to do."

IV. 4

(For Every Myth, a Villain.)

Eric Taylor was not a villain—he was merely a man playing the cards he was dealt. Did those cards mostly consist of access to narcotics and pharmaceuticals in lieu of something more useful, like a trust fund? Yes. But better that than to play empty-handed, as he'd always thought.

Eric was white, upper middle class, conventionally attractive, something of a late bloomer—a cautionary tale for the modern era. Smart, sure, but never smart enough. Inattentive father, unsentimental WASP of a mother. A familiar story, though it's no longer fashionable to waste sympathy on those sorts of foundational moral vacancies anymore. Unrequited love? Oh, absolutely, for a lifetime. Always coming second to someone, usually his elder brother, who went to Harvard and then Columbia Law and was currently on the fast track to becoming . . . whatever. A Supreme Court justice. He was clerking for a judge in Chicago, and honestly, what difference did it make? Andrew Taylor was probably going to be a senator someday, and when he was, Andrew would likely thank his humble roots and pretend he hadn't once shoved Eric in a locker while he was football captain in prep school.

Maybe it was small of Eric to feel sorry for himself, but in fairness, nobody else was doing it for him. Sure, it was wine o'clock a little too often for his mother to notice Eric was alive, and yes, his father had called him a disappointment more times than he'd said "I love you" (the latter occurring infrequently enough to be counted on one hand, and one of those times had been during a magazine interview for their hometown farce of a newspaper), but nobody had really seemed to care whether that affected Eric's development. His own shrink cared from time to time, having been assigned to him after he had a fucking nervous breakdown in the tenth grade and threw himself down the stairs of his high school, but mostly the affection Eric received was in the form of a prescription pad and the kind of free rein that only comes from apathy. (Not to demean the profession, of course. Eric imagined there were psychiatrists out there who did good work. He just also knew he didn't have one of them.)

So yeah, Eric sold Adderall. And Lexapro. And Ritalin. And some other drugs construction workers took to stay awake on cranes, which he had received after he complained to his shrink that all the antidepressants were starting to make him drowsy. And yes, he'd given pills to his classmates—*given* being, of course, not at all accurate, but they could afford it. (He wasn't unreasonable. It was definitely market value, or close enough.)

Was it a secret? No. Did it eventually become something of an enterprise? Yes. Eric almost got in trouble once, actually, stepping on the toes of a pharmaceutical ring that had already been in operation on NYU's campus. Of course, once that doctor's license got taken away (anonymous tips; so strange how those calls were so rarely traced), Eric found himself with an entire network of people who badly needed drugs. And wasn't the American medical system fucked up anyway? Who was he really harming? Drug companies? He figured they could take the hit.

Then he met Baba Yaga. Well, not Baba Yaga, exactly—her associate of some kind, who simply went by Marya.

"Like the fairy tale?" Eric asked, because he wasn't stupid. He read books.

"Sure," said Marya. "Like the fairy tale."

In the stories, a princess named Marya Morevna defeated Koschei the Deathless. Sort of. Then her husband ruined things, but Marya won again in the end.

"Marya doesn't work for Baba Yaga," Eric pointed out, but Marya wasn't interested in the details.

"Do you want money or not?" she asked.

Eric liked people who got straight to the point.

"How'd you find me?" he asked.

She smiled. She had an unnerving smile.

"Magic" slipped from her berry-colored lips, and he liked her anyway, even if she didn't get to the point that time. He liked directness, but he could play coy, too. Or thought he could.

He found himself slipping into little daydreams about Marya. Not her specifically, of course (she wore a gold wedding band around her finger and seemed less than convinced by the appeal of his presence), but . . . the *concept* of her. The powerful woman, named for a myth, who controlled the helm of a vast narcotics enterprise. He liked it, liked the taste of it; the fantasy of power succumbing to *him*, who'd always been second-best.

Thus, finding that Sasha was part of what was clearly a major crime family was something of a rueful exhilaration.

"Eric," she said, standing expectantly in the hallway when he opened the door to his apartment. Nobody had buzzed her in.

"Sasha," he said, attempting to mask the broad spectrum of reactions he experienced at the sudden delirium of her presence. The last time he'd seen her he'd been face-first in a candy-colored hallucination, one that involved pink-flavored clouds and the curves of her thighs wrapped tightly around his head. "Missed class again."

"I'm starting to think school's not really for me," she replied, and added, "I actually came to see you about something else."

He arched a brow, threw out a little "Oh?" because again, he could play coy.

She rolled her eyes. "You're disgusting."

"Am I?" he asked. One of these days she was bound to give in.

As if she could read his mind, she gave a dainty sigh; stepped forward to rest a single finger on the hollow of his throat, eyeing his mouth.

"Eric," she murmured.

He leaned forward.

Then she dragged a nail down the front of his chest and he howled in pain, stumbling backward into the Ikea side table that had been artlessly shoved against the wall.

"*What* the—"

"You're going to help me with something," Sasha said, and it wasn't a question. She retracted her hand, eyeing her fingers. If he'd expected to see claws, it didn't happen. She wasn't some sort of creature, he reminded himself. She was just a beautiful girl capable of causing him terrible pain, not unlike all the others.

"What am I helping with?" he asked, which was mostly reflexive, because he didn't want to.

Or did he?

It was hard to tell what he wanted, really, knowing instinctively she could wrap her pretty hand around his throat and drag whatever answer she wanted directly from his tongue. Nobody ever expected the quiet ones, he thought, perversely delighted. Sometimes the element of surprise jarred him out of his waxy dullness better than a drug. Better than the kinds of drugs he sold, anyway. That's why he never really felt bad about it—pills didn't do shit for the people who really needed them, truth be told. Brain chemistry was hugely unhelpful that way.

"You're going to be my eyes," Sasha informed him.

"What am I looking for?"

She smiled thinly. "Money."

"I can do that," he said.

"Of course you can," she said. "I'm telling you to."

He stared at her.

Fuck, did she own him?

(Did he *want* her to?)

"Got more of those drugs?" he asked. He didn't normally abuse his own products (outside of what was required for his own sanity, or something resembling sanity), but whatever Baba Yaga was making, he wanted it. He wanted to taste Sasha on his tongue again, even if it was only a dream.

Hell, better the dream. Reality left a bitter aftertaste. And occasionally a bruise.

"Right here," Sasha said, holding up a row of candy-colored tablets, "though you'll need this, too," she said, presenting him with a thin leather cuff.

"I'm not one for accessories," he said.

"You are now," she told him, and blithely, he figured he was.

Fuck, was it her?

Was it the drugs?

Maybe it *was* magic.

She slid the cuff around his wrist, running a thumb over the edges and locking it in place as it shrank down, fitting itself to his skin.

"Don't tell anyone," she said.

"Who would believe me?" he replied, staring down at it, and to that, she permitted a smile.

"Oh, you're well and truly fucked, Taylor," she said, and crushed a single tablet into powder between her fingers, holding it up to his nose.

Eric took a deep breath. Let it settle somewhere near the forefront of his mind. Let the vision of her swim into pretty waves of senseless oblivion.

He wasn't a villain. He was pretty sure of that.

But holy fuck, he was *weak*.

IV. 5

(Strings, Reprise.)

"You owe a favor to Koschei the Deathless," Dimitri said, "and therefore you owe me as well."

"You're not Koschei yet," snarled the witch.

His name was Raphael Santos, and he didn't technically owe Koschei a single favor.

He owed Koschei *several* favors.

Raphael was something of a jack-of-all-trades, though he was only marginally good at any of them. The only thing he was exceptional at was shrugging on a persona, which in this case was the unassuming demeanor of someone misusing his power out of sight. He was one of Koschei's property managers, mostly known for having a strong hand with tenants, which on its face was technically no worse a reputation than any other Manhattan landlord's. But that line was very fine.

Aside from skimming off the top like a usurious cleric, Raphael was a bully, with only minimal investigation by Dimitri proving he'd made a habit of smoking Koschei's tenants out with unlivable conditions whenever it struck his fancy. Unfortunately for Raphael, he wasn't the only man in the room with some experience with coercion, which was why Raphael was presently being dangled outside his own window with one of Dimitri's hands clamped tightly around his throat.

"Don't consider me Koschei, then," Dimitri suggested. "After all, I'm a different man. For example, I do not particularly care for people who don't answer my questions," he said, lifting a brow in warning. At Raphael's unwilling scowl of *I'm listening,* Dimitri continued, "I heard a rumor you worked with the Antonovas recently. They say Yaga's come to see you, and we both know what that means— though," he couldn't help adding, "I would have thought she had better taste. As far as I can tell, you're not much use to anyone."

"I told you already," Raphael managed in something of a wheeze, "Marya is *dead*." His eyes darted frantically to the street below. "Even if she were alive, I wouldn't know where to find her—She finds me, she always finds *me*—"

It had been the same answer from the previous Borough witch, and the same answer from the dealer before that.

Disheartening.

"Well," Dimitri said, dragging Raphael back inside, "if you see her, tell her I'm looking for her."

Raphael fell to the floor with a guttural retch, glaring up at Dimitri from his hands and knees. "You're—fucking—*insane*—"

"I prefer to think of it as highly motivated and pressed for time." Topically, Dimitri glanced at his watch, wondering if there was anything useful he could glean to salvage the visit. "Where can I find the Borough witch Stas Maksimov?"

The answer Raphael gave while he coughed up a lung was mostly incoherent, something like "You can't." Then he lifted his head, looking genuinely disturbed, and managed more clearly, "Stas Maksimov is dead."

Dimitri blinked. "What?"

"You haven't heard?" Raphael's voice, still a rasp, had finally regained some clarity. "He died right after Marya. They say it was your own brother who did it—though," he added with a bitter lilt of humor, "as with anything your family does, there's no proof."

Dimitri stared at him.

And stared.

And then said, brusquely, "You should remember that I'm not Koschei, Santos. Unlike him, I expect you to pay what you owe." Koschei may have looked the other way because Raphael, like many miscreants of his ilk, was well connected to other, more useful deviants, and a longtime acquaintance who routinely secured access to some of Koschei's more questionable collections.

Dimitri had no such hobbies. He was a collector of wills, not beings.

"Or else what?" Raphael grunted, dragging himself over to slump against the wall.

"Or else you'll spend your remaining days wondering 'or else what,'" Dimitri snapped. "Is that clear? But tell Marya Antonova I'm looking for her, and I'll cross one favor off your list."

"She's dead," Raphael said again, impatiently this time. Some inadvisable smuggery had returned since he'd left the zone of impending mortal peril. "Aren't you listening?"

"There are other realms through which to pass that message if you no longer care to exist in this one," Dimitri warned, and gratifyingly, Raphael flinched. "So. Are we understood?"

"Yes, Koschei," Raphael muttered under his breath, and Dimitri dipped his head in acknowledgment, turning to leave.

It had been said with venom, he knew, but still.

The title rather suited him.

IV. 6

(Playing Fetch.)

"Well?" Marya said, leaning against the door as Raphael looked up at her, glaring.

"He's looking for you," he said irritably.

"Yes, I gathered," Marya said, eyeing the marks dappling Raphael's neck, "but you know I'm not here about that."

Raphael scowled, apprehensive. "The money's in my desk drawer."

"Then go fetch," she advised, and Raphael struggled to his feet, snatching the bills from his desk and shoving it into her hands before collapsing back to the ground.

"There," he said. "Everything you asked for. *Plus* the secret."

"Good boy," Marya said, reaching down to pat his head. "Well, you can keep the money. I hardly need it."

"*What?*"

Uninterested in further conversation, Marya turned to leave.

Raphael, who'd been gaping at her back, managed to stumble forward, gripping her arm. "Why are you doing this, then?" he demanded, gritting it through his teeth.

She flicked his hand away like a fly.

"You're an important resource, Santos," she reminded him. "Take it as a compliment."

"I don't work for you," he spat, and she shrugged.

"We'll see," she replied. "What will you be giving Koschei this time?"

He hesitated, frowning. "I thought you weren't interested in creatures."

"You misjudge my interests," she informed him, and paused, considering it. "Keep a log," she suggested after a moment. "Everything in, everything out. I'll come back for it next week."

"Marya," he said, blinking. "That's—if Koschei knew I'd given it to you—if he even knew I *kept* one—"

"Yes?" she prompted, observing with amusement as his face went pale.

"He could ruin me," he choked out, and she tilted her head.

"Could he?" she mused, crouching down to meet his frantically evasive glance. "Hm. And here I thought I was the one who would be ruining you if you didn't do as I asked," she remarked in a quiet voice more suited to seduction, perhaps. Or to danger.

He flinched. "Marya—"

"Oh, don't worry," she assured him, patting his cheek roughly and rising to her feet. "You're useful to me, Santos. I have no reason to throw you to Koschei's mercy. By the way, how's your wife?" she asked. "Is the serum I gave her working?"

Raphael swallowed hard, and then nodded. "Yes. She's much better."

"Good, good," Marya said. "Next week, then."

Again she turned to leave, and again Raphael called after her, desperate.

"What about Dimitri Fedorov?"

Marya paused, glancing briefly over her shoulder.

"What about him?" she said, before disappearing from sight.

IV. 7

(Taking Inventory.)

Roman had been discussing a minor issue of flagging income with his father while waiting for Dimitri when the latter finally entered the room.

"Dima," Roman said, calling hesitantly to his brother. "Where've you been?"

Dimitri's gaze fell glassily on Roman's before turning away—dismissing Koschei, on whom they never turned their backs.

"Out," Dimitri said.

"Dima," Koschei sighed, beckoning for him with one hand still curved around a glass of whisky. "Sit with me, won't you?"

Dimitri paused, glancing over his shoulder. His eyes slid deliberately from Roman to their father.

"Why," he remarked flatly, "are you taking stock of inventory? Count your sons carefully, Papa." His mouth hardened. "You're still one short."

In that particular moment, Dimitri looked both more golden than usual, gleaming and sure, and also substantially less. He looked untouchable, in fact, in a way Roman had never seen him; hard and statuesque but lifeless, as if he'd been carved that way from stone. Dimitri was immovable and indestructible, and looked more like their father in that instant than Roman had ever seen him look.

For the first time, Roman felt the words *son of Koschei* rise up in his throat while looking at his eldest brother, and it gave him a sudden, portentous chill.

"Dima," Koschei said gently, "please. I understand you're angry with me—"

Dimitri turned and walked away, something Roman had seen their father do to other men many times. There was power in such dismissal, in judging one's time too valuable to waste. It was a tool by which to subjugate the other party, and now Dimitri employed it effortlessly, turning his back on both Koschei and Roman and slipping into his bedroom without a word. It wasn't a tantrum; there were no slamming doors, no stomping feet. Dimitri Fedorov had simply determined them not worth his attention and left them in his wake.

Koschei exhaled slowly.

"You should tell him," Roman advised his father in a low voice.

Koschei scarcely blinked. "He would only resent you more, Romik."

"Maybe he would," Roman agreed, "but still. It can't be easy on you to be at odds with him like this."

Koschei's dark gaze fell on Roman's. "It is no business of Dima's whose debts I choose to settle, or how. My arrangement with The Bridge is not for Dima to question. I only chose to tell you because it concerned you, and because if he's right—"

"Because if The Bridge told the truth and Masha is alive, then it's me she'll come for," Roman murmured to himself, and Koschei made a little disapproving scoff.

"You think too small, Romik. Always too small." Koschei reached out, brushing his fingers along the edge of a shadow on the wall as Roman stiffened, unexpectedly slighted. "Yaga and her daughters are not idle players," Koschei explained. "They do not take revenge when there is nothing to be gained aside from vengeance. The stakes, for them, will always be higher than that, and if The Bridge is right—or if they choose, ultimately, to defy the deal we made," he clarified grimly, "then it will not be a little fish that Baba Yaga aims to catch."

"You think she'll come for you instead?" Roman asked, brow furrowing.

"Me," Koschei agreed, "or Dima."

Roman blinked. "Why Dima?"

"He's my heir," Koschei said, shrugging. "He is the future of this family."

"You're saying—" Roman cleared his throat, something bitter rising up within it. "Papa. I am the one who killed Marya Antonova. I killed Stas Maksimov. I am the one who stole from Baba Yaga, who turned their source against them and deceived them. I am the one who played them all." Koschei said nothing, and the small lump in Roman's throat became a sudden blockage in his airway. "Are you really saying the Antonovas would still come for Dima over me because he's . . . more valuable than I am?"

Koschei's mouth tightened. "This is not a question of value," he said flatly, sipping from his glass before turning a hard look on Roman. "I saved your magic, didn't I? I saved your life. Do you still question whether I consider you worthy, Romik? Because I have a vacancy where my kidney should be that suggests you should put your childish insecurities aside."

Roman reeled, stung. "I was only saying—"

"If they ruin Dima, they as good as ruin me," Koschei said. "Dima is the one the Borough witches know. He's the one they trust. He's the one who represents me in my business, who handles conflicts on my behalf. If Dima falls, then it is a signal to the rest of the witches in all the Boroughs that this family is vulnerable. Weak."

"But even so, Masha's blood is on my hands." Roman's heart was a tribal drum, loud enough to fill the room. "Do you really think that means nothing to Yaga?"

"To Yaga? Yes, surely," Koschei said, shrugging. "And yes, maybe they have some sort of payment in mind for you, too. But your loss would only be personal to them, not strategic, and Yaga is too clever by half to waste her time on an emotional vendetta."

He sounded almost admiring of her. Roman shoved the observation aside, swallowing his frustration. And his pride.

"You could transfer some of Dima's power to me," he suggested instead. "Look at him," he added, gesturing to where Dimitri had disappeared. "He's secretive now, Papa, reclusive. He has other agendas." *Dimitri belongs to Marya Antonova in a way that he does not belong to us,* Roman didn't say, though he wished he had, because Koschei didn't seem to lend his input much consideration.

"Dima is a Fedorov son," Koschei insisted without pause, his hand tightening on the arm of his chair. "He is my son. He is angry with me, but he will never turn against me."

To Koschei it was a fleeting remark, to Roman a battle cry. It seemed quite a gamble, in Roman's view, to assume that Dimitri, who had already shown signs of being irrevocably altered, would make the same decisions he'd always made. Roman understood that the Dimitri who'd just walked in the door wasn't the same one who had existed before his reckoning at the hands of Marya Antonova.

And neither was Roman the same son who could so easily fall in line.

"Give me something, Papa," Roman implored his father, trying and failing to put aside the steady thunder of his pulse. "There must be something I can do for you in the meantime, without Dima."

Koschei rose to his feet, straining under the grimness of age.

"No," he said, and Roman's breath quickened.

"But Papa—"

"Had you not been so childish, Roman, Lyova would still be alive," Koschei reminded him, callously appeased when Roman flinched at the mention of Lev. "You say you killed, stole, deceived as if it was all an exercise of power. And yet if not for you, Dima would be my faithful son, as he's always been. Masha would be alive, fine, but her attention would be elsewhere. We had no reason to intervene and now—forever," Koschei hissed, "we will be the subjects of Yaga's enmity, held to the meager hope that she will keep to the terms of our deal."

Roman's heart, his rage, was amplifying. "But Papa, if I could have just—"

"No ifs," Koschei said, cutting him off. "The devil lounges in the word *if,* Roma. The circumstances of our conditions are not for us to ponder without slowly losing our minds."

He waited a moment, and then reached out, cupping his hand around Roman's cheek.

"You are my son, Romik, and I would deny you nothing," Koschei said quietly, "but for now, I beg you, be patient. Do nothing. Let the storm of Dima's anger pass, and when he is ready, you will be, too."

It seemed Koschei was unaware how much he asked.

"Dima is not your only son," Roman said bitterly.

With a slow, tender circle of his thumb on Roman's cheek, Koschei withdrew his hand.

"I do not forget I nearly lost two sons," Koschei said. "Forgive me, Romik, but even if you resent my decision, it will not change my mind. If I keep you in a vault, it is only because you're too precious to lose."

He turned away, preparing to leave, and paused just before he reached the doorframe.

"If Dima asks for me," Koschei began, and Roman nodded, voice thick with difficulty.

"Yes, Papa," Roman said.

"And do not tell him of my visit to The Bridge," Koschei warned. "Let that be between us. If he wishes to be angry with me, to forget what I would do for my sons, then so be it."

Roman nodded again, already spent.

"Yes, Papa."

IV. 8

(Aftertaste.)

"Damn," said the man, lifting his head from the marble countertop and brushing away the crushed tablet powder from his nose. "That's clean. Who's the supplier again?"

"New," Eric replied, leaning back against the cushions of his sofa. "And private. You interested?"

"Of course I'm fucking interested," the man replied. He was a banker of some sort, with a financier sort of name; Warner or Mark or Charles. Eric tossed his arm around Sasha's shoulders and she gritted her teeth in annoyance, doing what she could not to shove him away. It was better, she knew, to play it off as if she were nothing important. The mute, pretty girl on the arm of the showy asshole was never suspected of wrongdoing. She was only ever a pawn, and that was all Sasha wanted Greg or Andrew or Jonathan to think she was. Safer that way. Better.

Much as she loathed it.

"What's in this?" the man pressed. "PCP?"

"You ask a lot of questions, my man," Eric said, in a tone that Sasha (or any woman, for that matter) probably would have slapped him for. "Can't go giving away my supplier's secrets, can I?"

The man stared thoughtfully into the distance. The high was probably increasing in intensity now, though Sasha didn't have much patience to wait. She'd done as much as she needed to, anyway.

"Baby," she said to Eric, "are you done?"

She added a little whine to her voice. When she was gone, the buyer would remember her as pushy, entitled, demanding, or perhaps just an atmospheric pair of legs. He'd probably have a conversation with Eric about how women could be so exhausting. *Impossible to live with, right?* he'd say, and add something about how the head was barely even worth it.

And Eric would laugh, of course.

Because Eric was shitty.

"Not quite, babe," Eric told her, giving her nose a patronizing tap before nuzzling into the line of her neck with a chuckle. She wasn't even sure that was part of the pretense, or if it was something he'd recently convinced himself he could do. She'd have to prove him wrong later. "Want me to meet up with you in a bit?" he purred into her shoulder. "Dietrich and I have to finalize some things here."

Dietrich. Completely unguessable. She really needed to listen better, or care more.

"Fine," she said, rising stiffly to her feet from the sofa that was fashionably low, an elegant Japandi deathtrap. She felt the unwelcome presence of Dietrich's eyes on her as she went and fought the reflexive urge to gouge them out. "See you later, then."

She added a little sway to her walk and wandered into the foyer. Dietrich had the penthouse; the elevator opened straight to his suite. He was terrible and rich, just as a matter of objective fact, much like Eric was well connected and shitty. It was an unpleasant errand, and Sasha lamented that she could see her reflection in the metallic finish of the elevator doors as they shut, finally drowning out the sound of whatever trap album was now pulsing from the room where Dietrich and Eric remained.

The entire world looked different without Lev in it, with nothing more unrecognizable than Sasha herself. Every new adornment since he'd gone was unnatural and heavy—the false eyelashes, the glittering chandeliers that hung from her ears, the oversized pendants around her neck, all of it seemed to be dragging her to the floor. Her dress was several inches shorter than she would have wanted it to be and her shoes several inches higher. She was playing a character, she reminded herself; she was acting, filling a role.

Still. It was starting to be a little difficult to draw the line anymore.

The doors opened in the lobby and Ivan rose to his feet, offering her coat.

"How'd it go?" he asked.

"Well enough," Sasha said, letting him help her into it. "Did Masha call?"

"Yes," Ivan said. "I told her everything was fine."

"And is it?" Sasha asked bitterly. "Fine, I mean."

Ivan hesitated, correctly determining that she wasn't discussing this particular deal. "Lev deserved better than what happened to him," he said in his quiet voice. "And Sasha, if you need time to mourn—"

"I don't," Sasha said, her tone more biting than she'd intended. "And don't talk about him, Ivan," she added, removing her sunglasses from her purse and sliding them into place. "He's gone."

IV. 9

(Everything in Retrospect.)

"How is she?" Yaga asked in a low voice, and Marya angled her gaze toward the window, staring vacantly out of the frame.

"Not well," Marya admitted, folding her arms over her chest. She paused for less than a breath before adding, "It's not unlike when I lost Dima."

For twelve years, she hadn't dared speak his name aloud for fear it might crack open her ribs, puncturing her insides and bleeding her dry from the pain of it. Now, though, without the constant wrench in her chest to remind her what it had felt like to lose him, Marya could breathe a little easier. His grip on her was less anguished; her past was less constricting now that there was nothing left of her to hold.

If Yaga heard the difference in her daughter's voice, she said nothing. Instead, she asked, "Are we in danger of losing her?"

Marya turned stiffly. "Did you lose *me*, Mama?"

"Masha." Yaga's voice was low. "You know that you and Sasha are not the same."

True enough. Marya breathed out, grudgingly appeased.

"She's angry," Marya permitted after a moment. "But she has a purpose, as I did. We drag ourselves up, Mama, like always." She let her gaze fix on her mother's; on the dark eyes so similar to her own. "Like you."

Yaga hesitated a moment. "But you didn't lose Dima, Mashenka. You are not like Sasha." She reached out, curling the backs of her fingers along Marya's cheek. "You gave him up. You chose me."

Marya said nothing.

"You chose me over your love for him, and I do not forget it," Yaga promised her. "But now, as for Sasha—"

"It doesn't matter whether Lev Fedorov was taken or given up," Marya said firmly, perhaps too aggressively, in defense against some threat or weapon still unseen. "Sasha has no reason to stray from your side. Or from your vision."

Yaga nodded carefully, brushing Marya's hair back from her face.

"Sasha was always the most resistant of all my daughters," Yaga said. "You doubted that she was ready once yourself, didn't you, Mashenka?"

"I didn't doubt her," Marya said. "I just didn't want this life for her."

"And now?" Yaga prompted.

"And now I know this is the only life possible for any of us," Marya said, "and that anyone who promises otherwise is a fool or a liar," *or they are Dima,* she thought, which was particularly unhelpful.

It was impossible to tell whether this was an answer Yaga was pleased to hear. She was a hard woman, difficult to read, and even with a little brush of death to put things in perspective, Marya did not consider herself any wiser with regard to her mother's intentions.

Marya knew, though, that when it had mattered, she had not abandoned her mother. And when it mattered—when it was impossible to consider that such a thing could even be done—her mother had not abandoned her. After everything she'd already lost, Marya Antonova would not stray from her mother's side, and she wouldn't allow Sasha to do so, either.

"I'll talk to her," Marya said, and slipped out from her mother's room, padding quietly down the hall to Sasha's bedroom.

The door was ajar; Sasha, too, was staring out her window, eyeline cast among the stars. For a moment Marya only watched her, the shape of her sister's narrow shoulders and the tilt of her stubborn chin, and knew instinctively that Sasha could feel her there. Marya knew that now—whether Sasha knew it or not—the two of them were more similar than they had ever been. More alike than they would ever be.

They both knew the same grief, though Marya's was only a memory. Only an echo, rather than the too-sharp ache of it. Dimitri had remembered his promise to her, and now it was serving her well.

Still, she painted on a little softness, remembered as if from a past life. "Is it a pain that can be eased, Sashenka?" Marya asked gently, and Sasha turned to look at her, gaze still dark with contemplation.

"I don't think so," Sasha said. "Not yet. Not until . . ."

She trailed off, eyeing the stitching of her duvet.

"Not until I've made him pay," she murmured, drawing her fingers along the shape of the threading; tracing a line of inevitability, looping back and forth in an infinite wave.

"And until then," Marya said, stepping farther into the room. "What can be done until then?"

"Nothing," Sasha said, "unless you can make Eric Taylor less of an asshole." She paused the motion of her finger. "I know we need his network, Masha, but having to be near him is—it's horrible. It's *unbearable,* and all I can think is that L—"

She broke off.

She couldn't say his name.

I understand, Marya wanted to say—because truly, she understood few things better than the crippling taste of a lost name on her lips—but she didn't. She merely took a seat on Sasha's bed and reached for her hand, gently placing her fingers on top of Sasha's.

"Even good men will stand against you," Marya warned. That, too, she understood more than anything. "Even good men will let you down."

Sasha glanced at her hands. "Well, it's worse to have to deal with the awful ones."

Marya nodded. "Then don't," she said, and Sasha looked up, surprised.

"But—I thought the point was to expand our network, and then—"

"You don't need Eric Taylor to do that for you," Marya said. "You can forge your own way forward, Sashenka, if that's what you want."

"Only men are making deals this stupid," Sasha said, grimacing. "And none of them will ever listen to me."

Marya tightened her grip on Sasha's fingers.

"Then *make* them listen," she said quietly.

Sasha gave Marya a fleeting half smile. "You say that like it's so easy, Masha."

"Because it is," Marya said. "Because nobody will deny you anything the moment you stop denying yourself. Who could possibly have sovereignty greater than yours?" she asked, insistent. "Who on earth could have the right to refuse you, if you do not permit them to? If this isn't the way, Sasha, then find another one."

Sasha nodded ruefully, and Marya shifted to take her sister's face between both hands.

"Sashenka," Marya said, "you are not incomplete because a piece of your heart is gone. You are you, an entire whole, all on your own. If you have loved and been loved, then you can only be richer for it—you don't become a smaller version of yourself simply because what you once had is gone."

Sasha nodded slowly, taking it in.

"Is it strange, Masha," Sasha confessed in a hushed strain, "that I don't feel smaller at all? I feel bigger, actually. Vast." She swallowed again, fighting a lump in her throat. "But it's an empty kind of vastness."

Marya knew the feeling well. When she had told Dimitri they could no longer be together, she had seen the pain in his eyes, heard the undertones of pleading in his voice. She had felt herself swell up, luminous and cold, larger than she had been before and hollow somewhere, too. A piece of her had carved itself out and remained with him, even as the rest of her kept expanding, kept growing, kept stretching out until it was too large for its host.

She'd become a mutant of herself in her grief.

"Strength comes from struggle," Marya said. "Each time we bid farewell to a piece of ourselves we become different than we were. But each time we rise again in the morning, it's a victory," she said firmly. "Keep your memories. Keep your emotions. Keep your pain. Use them," she advised, taking Sasha's hands in hers again. "Happiness, contentment, they are dull but persuasive lures. A rosy disposition only means you miss what's lurking in the trees."

"Things aren't much sharper through a fog," Sasha said, setting her mouth. "I need a new direction."

"Then take it," Marya said. "I'll handle Eric. Consider it done. Do you need my help?"

Sasha stared into nothing for a moment, considering Marya's offer, then shook her head.

"No," she said. "Not yet. I'll do this myself."

Marya nodded. She didn't hide her approval from her sister, nor mask the victory she felt. She wasn't Baba Yaga. She was no mystery. She was Marya Antonova, and now more than ever, she was power personified.

"We'll ruin them, Sashenka," Marya promised her, "and they'll be so sorry they ever wronged you."

"Him," Sasha corrected, curling one hand to a fist. "They'll be sorry they wronged *him*."

That was new, Marya thought, but didn't argue.

"However you envision it, we'll make it happen," Marya assured her carefully, "only make sure you don't lose sight."

Sasha nodded.

"Then I know what to do," she said, and Marya smiled, satisfied.

IV. 10

(Idle Frets.)

"I thought I might see you soon," Ivan murmured, setting down his beer to glance up when Dimitri Fedorov made his entry. "So how will you threaten me, Dima? Gently, I hope," he mused, reclining against the pub's wooden barstool. "I'm sure you've noticed I'm getting on in years."

"Where is she?" Dimitri said without preamble, and Ivan shrugged.

"Dead," he replied. "As I'm sure you've heard by now."

"She's not dead," Dimitri said, hovering somewhere between exhaustion and exasperation.

"Hang me out a window, then," Ivan suggested, blithely lifting his glass for a sip, and Dimitri's mouth tightened. "You know perfectly well you won't find her, Dima," Ivan reminded him, watching Dimitri's eyes narrow at the familiar use of his name. "She finds you."

"Don't act like you know me," Dimitri said, though unexpectedly and perhaps a little absurdly, he took the vacant seat beside Ivan's, glancing briefly at him. "You have no idea what she is to me."

"No," Ivan agreed. "But I do know her, so believe me, you'll never find her. Not until she's ready." He rose to his feet, tossing a few bills on the counter. "Not even going to try?" he asked with a hint of disappointment, and Dimitri tossed him a dispassionate glare.

"The men I came to before you owed me something else," he said. "Something I don't expect to get from you."

"Loyalty," Ivan guessed, and Dimitri said nothing. "What are you playing at, Dimitri Fedorov?"

"Children play," Dimitri replied. "This is business."

"Maybe so, but people talk," Ivan advised him. "If you're collecting the men who owe Koschei in the hopes they'll serve you instead, assumptions will be made."

"I'm looking for Marya," Dimitri corrected him without a blink, "and I'm cleaning house. And seeing as you can help me with neither," he determined, signaling the bartender before arching a brow in Ivan's direction, "I don't think you're much use to me at all."

With a faint smile, Ivan raised his glass carefully to his lips, drained the tankard, and set it back down on the bar.

"Maybe not," Ivan agreed, and glanced down at Dimitri. "Though, for the record," he added, dropping his voice, "one piece of advice, Dimitri Fedorov, from me to you. When you spend enough time with someone, as I have, you begin to learn them like a muscle. You learn their little ticks, their eccentricities, their thoughts. You learn the signs and read them like stars, like lines in a book. And after a time," he murmured, tapping his fingers pointedly on the counter, "you learn them like a pulse. Like your own pulse."

He tapped his fingers again, rhythmically. *Duh-duhn.*

"Like a heartbeat," he clarified. *Duh-duhn.*

Duh-duhn.

"Do you understand what I'm saying, Dima?" Ivan asked.

Duh-duhn.

A muscle jumped beside Dimitri's jaw, tension strung taut between them.

Then the bartender appeared and Dimitri hastily cleared his throat, wetting his lips before signaling wordlessly for a pint.

"Tell her," Dimitri said to Ivan, dragging his regal gaze up from the wood of the bar, "that I'm looking for her."

Ivan stood straighter, smiling slightly.

"She knows," he said, and turned away, drumming the beat of Marya Antonova's heart against the side of his thigh as he went.

IV. 11

(Hauntings.)

Roman stared at Dimitri's closed door for nearly an hour, waiting, before he eventually rose to his feet, letting them carry him to the last place they'd put Lev to rest. The ground was mossy, covered in leaves and vines. It looked like a fold between universes; like a page in a book of worlds. It couldn't belong in this one, not here, but couldn't belong to another, either. It was foreign and still, a place that had never felt an echo. Roman wondered if it had been like this when they'd laid Lev to rest here, or if it had become that way for the benefit of the goodness buried in the soil.

"Lev," Roman said quietly, crouching down beside the place they'd marked. "Things aren't going so well without you."

Silence, of course. Consequences of Roman's mistakes.

"You know I'm sorry, don't you? You know that I . . . that I was the one who should have died instead of you." The thing in Roman's throat was still there, shape-shifting with his anguish. "I was always less than you, wasn't I? I worried so much about being less than Dima that I didn't even consider the finest man I'd ever know was looking to me for guidance."

He paused, struggling to swallow.

"How did you manage it?" he asked desperately, pressing his fingertips into the earth. "Becoming the kind of person you were, it couldn't have been easy. Maybe I'm the one who had it easy." He let his chin fall. "Maybe that's why I was so much less than you, in the end."

There was a breeze that rustled the trees around him, stirring the leaves, and Roman let out a matching sigh, letting it carry on the biting wind.

"Lyova," he began again, and then looked up, catching the sound of something coming from the motion of the trees.

Roman froze, straining his ears, and after a moment he tensed with apprehension, catching a blur of white from somewhere out of sight—a dress, he thought. Gradually it came into view, like fog lifting or the dissolution of a veil. A dress, long dark hair, a pair of grey-blue eyes, framed by darkened lashes—

"Sasha," Roman said, blinking as he looked into the trees. "Sasha, is . . . is that you?"

He shot to his feet, staggering toward her. "Sasha, forgive me," he said, scrambling in her direction as she took a step back, brow furrowing. "Please, forgive me," he begged, and stumbled in the tangles of weeds and vines, dropping artlessly to his knees. "Please."

Every few breaths, ragged and broken, his cheeks wetting with mud and frost, and salt. "Please, Sasha, please."

She only watched him, face eerily frozen, the ghost of her still and unmoved.

Was it a dream? A nightmare?

A haunting?

Eventually Roman struggled to his feet, regaining the presence of mind to flee, and turned only once to glance over his shoulder. The ghost of Sasha Antonova didn't follow—didn't take her eyes from his. She only watched him go, and in fear, in shame and remorse and some shattering form of heartbreak, Roman ran, faster and faster, until there was nowhere left to run.

IV. 12

(Ghosts.)

"You know, you do look quite a bit like Sasha," Katya remarked as the dark-haired man disappeared into the distance, and Irina rolled her eyes, turning toward her sister.

"I look like *you*," Irina corrected. "It's not my fault if the stupid Fedorov thinks we all look the same. Only two of us are twins."

"Yes, but you have Sasha's hair," Katya pointed out, gesturing to her own cropped cut. "And anyway, has he said anything else?"

"No, he ran away," Irina said, gesturing. "Didn't you see?"

"Oh, no, I saw that," Katya said, taking her sister's arm and redirecting her. "I meant *him*," she corrected, pointing to where the youngest Fedorov stood staring after his brother.

Irina couldn't see it, of course, but Katya could. She could see the look of longing on his face; it reminded Katya painfully of her son Luka when he was lamenting the loss of a toy.

"He brought us here for a reason," Katya said, returning her attention to her sister. "Has he told you what it is?"

"Yes," Irina replied. "But I'm not sure we should do it. Not this time."

"This time," Katya said, frowning. "What do you mean this time?"

Irina arched a brow that meant *You know what I mean.*

Katya sighed a sigh that said *But why would we even try that? He isn't one of us.*

"He's afraid of what will happen," Irina told her.

"What, to his father? To his brothers? That's on them," Katya said, hardly apologetic. "People always worry about the ones they leave behind when they pass on, Irka. We can't just help every dead person we meet, and besides, Mama made a deal with Koschei, remember?"

"It's not his brothers he's afraid for," Irina corrected, and then amended quickly, "I mean yes, he is, but that doesn't seem to be the primary thing."

"Then what's he worried about?" Katya demanded. "And why would you care?"

Irina hesitated before reaching out, her fingers twining with her twin's.

"Because it's about Sasha," Irina said quietly.

To that, Katya blinked.

"Well," she said with a burdensome sigh. "That certainly changes things."

IV. 13

(Connect the Dots.)

Kidneys did not come with instruction manuals; that much was obvious, and profoundly inconvenient. The Bridge sat with a glass of his mother's whisky and stared down at the bean-shaped organ, roughly the size of his own clenched fist. It was incredibly grotesque, and by the same token, grotesquely incredible. Magic had seemed a fanciful thing for so long—witches, after all, made it look so easy; made it appear theatrical in a way that seemed prettily accessible, the blink of an eye or flutter of a hand—that for Bryn to have the source of it sitting right in front of him was disrupting to the internal organs he already (less impressively) possessed.

It made sense in a strange, primitive sort of way that he should require something cut from the bowels of a witch in order to access the vaults of their power. Magic was in a witch's blood the same way realm-traveling was in Bryn's (genetic, as much as his slender build and meadow-green eyes), so of course the organ designed to filter it would necessarily contain traces of its power. To harness it, though, seemed to be entirely another matter. Despite his best efforts, it continued to feel borrowed rather than owned.

There was a sound at the door and Bryn jumped, hastily shoving the kidney back into his desk drawer just before Roman Fedorov burst in and slammed the office door shut behind him.

"Sasha," he croaked, and Bryn concealed the drum of his pulse with the arch of a brow.

"I think you could do better," he said, "if you're considering a drastic rebrand."

"No—*Sasha*," Roman repeated urgently. "Sasha Antonova. I just saw her—I just—she's—"

As Roman blubbered frantically on, Bryn had his own private suspicions. He also had an inclination not to share them. Instead, he nudged his foot out and shoved the spare desk chair out for Roman to collapse into, one hand drawn to the span of his forehead in obvious strain.

"I'm losing my mind," Roman said hoarsely, and Bryn shrugged.

"Certainly a possibility," he agreed. "Though, aren't we all? Day by day."

Roman wearily held up a hand. "Stop. Your constant barrage of whimsy exhausts me." He sat up, steepling his fingers at his mouth. "Bridge," he said, glancing up after a moment's torment, "just tell me one thing. Are ghosts real?"

"No," Bryn said. "And neither are witches. Or fairies."

"Not helpful," Roman muttered.

"Nor is this. You do realize I have a job, don't you?" Bryn said, gesturing pointedly around his office. "Not to mention that last I checked, you had one, too."

"Not at the moment," Roman said under his breath, an expression on his face hinting at something darker, but then he immediately rose to his feet, pacing the width of Bryn's desk. "There must be ways that people cross between realms. Aren't there?" He spun, facing Bryn. "You do it."

Despite knowing better than to expect a shred of dignity from Roman Fedorov, Bryn bristled. "Difficult as this is to believe, Roman, not everyone can do what I do. You are, after all, here for *my* advice, aren't you?"

Roman's mouth tightened. "My brother may as well be stone," he said flatly, "or I'd talk to him instead."

Bryn chose not to mention that poetically speaking, Dimitri was more like fraying rope than he was any sort of stone; it didn't feel particularly relevant.

"I certainly can't talk to him about—" Roman broke off. "About Lev, so—"

"Lev?" Bryn echoed. "I thought this was about Sasha."

"It's—" Roman grimaced, shaking his head. "You're right," he said after another moment's pause. "I shouldn't be here."

"You shouldn't," Bryn agreed, "but you are, aren't you? So, say what you have to say, then. Get it out of your system."

Roman considered it, obviously warring with his better judgment. Delicious, as far as Bryn was concerned.

"If Sasha is . . . angry," Roman said slowly, "could she come for me?"

"I'm sure anger supersedes death all the time," Bryn indulgently permitted. "But that doesn't mean everything that goes bump in the night is here to personally see to your demise."

"Have you heard of rusalkas?" Roman asked after another pulse of hesitation. "Old World tales. Women who die near rivers and come back as demons—"

"There isn't always truth behind every myth," advised Bryn, who'd heard enough literal fairy tales to know.

"But sometimes there is!"

"Sometimes, yes," Bryn allowed, though his interest was rapidly waning. "And what will you do if this Sasha-rusalka is hunting you, Roman?"

"Their purpose is to *kill men*," Roman croaked.

"Well, that sounds dreadfully misogynistic," Bryn remarked. "Have you considered that perhaps this delightful folktale is merely another arm of the patriarchy supreme?"

"You're mocking me." Roman's mouth tightened, though he fell back in his chair with some apparent relief. "Not helpful, Bridge."

"I'm not your friend," Bryn reminded him. "Ergo, my obligation to be helpful is highly dependent on my mood."

To his displeasure, Roman arched a knowing brow. "I take it my father's magic isn't serving you particularly well, then? I could help you, you know." He sat up in the chair, half smiling. "If I were so inclined, that is."

Tempting. Frustratingly so. Still, "I doubt Koschei would be pleased to find you here."

Roman bristled just perceptibly at that, an observation that Bryn carefully tucked away. "I'm not offering you anything."

"No," Bryn agreed, "which is wise, because I've offered *you* nothing. You're nearly as susceptible to deals as I am."

"Please," Roman scoffed, rising to his feet again. He was agitated this time; Bryn guessed he was finally leaving. "I'm nothing like you."

"No," Bryn confirmed, "which is unfortunate, I imagine, at this particular moment. Do let me know if you run into your rusalka again," he called after Roman, idly propping his feet on his desk. "Try not to die."

Roman's eyes narrowed at Bryn's sardonic tone. "You know, if you were even marginally less annoying, I might actually help you."

"And if I thought you could be any help to me at all, I might have asked," Bryn replied, though in truth, he wished he could have. Irritating enough that kidneys came without instructions; worse were Fedorov sons who came with entirely too much pride.

"You betrayed me," Roman reminded him.

"You broke a deal," Bryn corrected. "*Betrayal* is a soft term. I traffic in absolutes."

"Well, then I, *absolutely*," Roman said, "will not be helping you."

"Wonderful," Bryn said. "Again, and I mean this sincerely, don't drown."

"Don't waste that kidney," Roman retorted. "You don't actually think magic can last if it isn't preserved, do you, Bridge?"

Smiling came easily to Bryn, even in sharp pangs of distress. "And if I were to waste it?"

Roman's smirk was biting. "I know you won't. I know for a fact you'll come to me before you'd let that happen."

"And if I don't?"

"You will," Roman said, sounding certain. "You may not be my friend, Bridge, but you'd better hope that I'm yours, because you've got nobody else."

With that, he turned and walked out.

"Witches," Bryn grumbled under his breath. "Showy little assholes."

"I couldn't agree more," came a voice, and Bryn jumped, turning to find a young woman rippling into being behind him.

It was the same witch who'd come to him before, only she was different now. She had a familiar scent about her, a slightly overripe sweetness she hadn't had when she'd visited the first time.

"Though," she mused, "how much better are lawyers, really?"

"Rusalka," Bryn noted, and the young woman smiled. "You're Sasha Antonova."

"In the flesh," Sasha agreed, spiriting open the desk drawer to Bryn's right even as he tried hastily to shut it. "So, you managed to get a kidney after all?" Her voice sounded hard, disdainful. "You should know, you didn't get the one I meant for you to have."

"You wanted to give me Roman's," Bryn said, "but the one I have is more valuable."

"Yes," Sasha agreed, and for a moment, her features softened. "And I should never have promised you Lev."

Bryn opened his mouth to correct her—*This belonged to Koschei, not Lev, and by the way, how do you know Lev? Asking for a friend*—when it occurred to him that he wasn't an idiot. He knew perfectly well there were once three Fedorov sons, and now it seemed there was an Antonova who only played at heartlessness, unlike one of the others.

"Shouldn't gamble with things you're not willing to lose," Bryn said instead, tucking away his private observations once again, and Sasha hardened, suddenly repulsed.

"I'm not here about that." She slammed the drawer shut with the heel of her hand. "I came to make another deal with you. A financial one this time."

"I have money," Bryn said. "I also already have an Antonova deal in place."

If one could call it that.

"Which is?" Sasha asked, eyes narrowing.

"Hardly relevant to you, Rusalka," Bryn replied, but he considered the possibility of her offer anyway, observing her with renewed speculation as she leaned against his desk. "Give me your terms," he decided eventually, unable to resist his curiosity, "but I suggest you make them very, very interesting."

Sasha smiled grimly. "I'm tired of my mortal dealings. I want someone I can actually stand to do business with. Someone strong," she clarified, "who isn't a total idiot. Someone who can help me take down Koschei. Who wants him destroyed as badly as I do."

"Interesting." Bryn paused, folding his hands. "These are a lot of highly specific details, don't you think?"

"Many people want Koschei to pay for something," Sasha said, shrugging. "I doubt I'm the only one he's ever wronged."

"Oh? In what way has he wronged you?" Bryn asked, feigning impassivity.

She gave him a doubtful look that read, in no uncertain terms, that she had no interest in getting personal. "Try again, Bridge."

"Fine." He leaned back, considering it. "Why Koschei?"

"Think of it as trickle-down vengeance," Sasha advised. "When Koschei is brought down, his sons will go down with him." She paused. "*Son,*" she amended quietly, eyes flicking to where Roman had just been.

A chuckle leapt from Bryn's throat uninvited.

"Rusalka," he murmured to her, and she gave him a mirthless smile of acknowledgment.

"He isn't wrong about the suffering I want for him," she said, referencing Roman's vacancy with a contemptuous lift of her chin. "He's definitely losing his mind if he thinks I'm haunting him—which," she admitted, "is a very fun turn of events—but he isn't wrong."

"You wouldn't need much to destroy him, if that's really what you want," Bryn agreed. "He's falling apart at the seams. I imagine you could easily kill him now and have it done with."

"Death is no suitable punishment for him," Sasha said darkly. "I've done it myself, and I'm no worse for wear."

Oh, the *enticement.* "Aren't you?" Bryn couldn't help asking, though to her credit, she was much too proficient to flinch.

"Death," she said unwaveringly, "is not enough. I want him to have what he loves most ripped away from him, and I want him to know it was his own doing." She leveled her grey gaze at Bryn. "Don't you think that's justified?"

"I can't say I have any expertise in the matter of vengeance," Bryn said. "I keep to a very specific code of not getting personally involved in anything."

"Is that why you love things and not people?" Sasha asked.

"Ah, no, that's a separate matter. I'm hedonistic by nature," Bryn said. "Fae inclinations. You know how it is."

"I meant power," Sasha corrected. "Magic. You chase the things you don't have because, why? You deserve them?" she asked him, guessing. "You've never had a place in this world, and so you want all the places in all the worlds? Is that it?"

As usual, Bryn found it easy to keep a smile plastered to his face.

"You underestimate me," he lamented. "I'm hardly so superficial."

She watched him for a moment, all darkened eyes and lilted mouth.

"What does power look like to you, Bridge?" Sasha asked eventually. "When I was a girl, it looked like my mother. Like my sister Marya." Her gaze slid carefully over his face. "I remember creeping downstairs as a little girl to my mother's workshop and seeing the beautiful things my sister would create, but it took me years to understand that wasn't her power. It's magic, yes, and it's talent and ability, but *power* is knowing what you're capable of and choosing if and when you give it to the world. Power is knowing when to be delicate and soft, like my sister, and when to make foolish, small-minded people think beauty and goodness are the same. She has this look," Sasha said, lost to her reverie now, "where she makes you feel you are the only thing in the universe. She can make you feel like you are resilient; like you are enormous, and omnipotent, and that's where her power comes from. Her power comes from knowing she can make *you* feel powerful, and while you're sitting docile in her gaze, she can crush it, and crush you, and tear everything out from under you before you can even remember who and what you really are."

Sasha returned her attention to Bryn, fixing him with a smile. "My sister Marya is the most powerful person I've ever met," she said, and Bryn, much as he hated to say it, had to agree with her. He knew precisely what Sasha spoke of when it came to Marya, having long admired it himself—having *longed* for it, he amended internally, himself.

"It is not superficial," Sasha told him, "to want it. Whatever she has. Whatever she is."

Her attention shifted to the desk drawer again.

"I can help you come close," Sasha murmured. "I can help you use what you have, if you find me the connection I need."

Bryn considered it. Marya had already promised him the same.

Still, it would be interesting to watch.

"I think I have just the person," he mused aloud, and slowly, Sasha smiled.

IV. 14

(It Is the Nightingale, Reprise.)

"I hear you're looking for me," came a voice behind him, and Dimitri turned to find Marya Antonova waiting near the window of his bedroom. She looked unchanged, not at all like someone who'd unnaturally clawed her way back to the living. She appeared as she normally did.

Or, at least, as Dimitri *assumed* she normally did, though outside of the occasion of her death it had been some time since he had known her. He wasn't sure which version of Marya Antonova stood before him now, but he imagined he caught little echoes of the familiar.

Her hair was growing long again, he noted. Before she'd taken on her signature hairstyle—those meticulous 1940s waves—she'd worn her hair long and loose, and a prior version of him had fallen asleep with his nose buried in the waves of it, breathing in nothing but the petal-soft scent of her.

She wore a dress that was a muted shade of sage, and he wondered for a moment if she'd chosen it specifically for him; if she'd woken up that morning and put it on, thinking nothing of it, or if she'd reached into her closet and thought, *I wonder what Dima will want to see me in today.*

He wondered if she knew the dress perfectly matched his eyes.

"Masha," he said evenly. By now, he had been expecting to see her. "You're alive."

"Seems that way," Marya replied, leaning against the window frame and observing him as he sat at the foot of his bed, waiting. "What is it you want from me, Dima? You've been relentless," she noted. "It's beginning to irk my contacts, if I'm being honest, though Ivan didn't seem too bothered. Thoughtful of you not to press him too vigorously," she added, half smiling. "He's had a rough couple of months."

"I," Dimitri began, and paused, weighing how much to confess. "I had my suspicions you were back," he admitted. "And I wanted a favor."

"Mm," Marya said, unimpressed. "Do I owe you a favor?"

He watched her.

She knew, he determined.

She had chosen that dress on purpose.

"You owe me nothing," he said. "But I suppose I've always been too entitled not to try."

Her smile broadened slightly. "Did you do as I asked, at least?"

Dimitri paused, considering whether it was wise to tell her, and then decided that she must already know. With methodical effort he unbuttoned his shirt, stopping only once the vial around his neck was visible above the thin scar her death had left behind.

"Ah," Marya noted, observing it from across the room. "Well, you must realize your possession of it keeps me alive."

"I thought that might be the case," he admitted.

"Surely you know it's dangerous, then." Marya took a step toward him, her face coming gradually into view as she stepped in front of the moonlit window. "What will happen to your family, Dima, if none of them can kill me?" she mused, a glow of light from his nightstand catching in the familiar darkness of her hair. "If Roma cannot deny me, and Koschei can do nothing to stop me—"

"I won't be the cause of your death again, Masha," Dimitri told her as she took a step toward him. "Never again." Another step. "No matter what it costs me." Another. She came closer, close enough to reach, if not to touch, and he dropped his head with a heavy swallow, eyeing his hands. "But I was seeking you for another reason."

"Oh?" She fell beside him on the bed. "And what reason is that?"

He glanced at her.

Marya Antonova was meticulous, and she'd chosen the dress on purpose. She'd chosen this room, his bedroom, on purpose. Like the last time they'd been alone together, every inch between them now was a consequence of her choice.

"I want my brother back," Dimitri confessed, and watched the motion of her chest go still.

"Why would I help you?" Her voice was hard, indelicate.

"Because," he said, and paused. "Because, Masha." He turned to face her, reaching out, and gently twined one long curl around his finger. "Because it's you, Masha, and it's me. Because it's us." If he looked up he would have felt it like a blow, the impact of her eyes meeting his. He didn't. "Because you can, I know you can. And because," he finished, releasing her hair to run his fingers feather-light beneath her jaw, his gaze still carefully on the line of her shoulder, "I know you want to."

She sat perfectly still, not coming any closer.

"You know, I can hardly feel anything for you with nothing beating in my chest," she commented blandly. "If you're counting on my affections to persuade me, you may have miscalculated their effect."

"Masha," Dimitri said, shaking his head, luxuriating in the sound of her name, the feel of her quickened pulse against his. "Masha, even you know that is a lie," he murmured, letting his fingers hover over the scar where her heart had once been. "Every piece of you, body and soul, remembers what it is to love me, don't they? Whether your heart is in your chest or not. I know you do, because I do," he said softly, the two of them leaned so close the words brushed the fabric of her dress. "Sometimes, Masha, my eyes open and I know, somewhere in my bones, that I have formed myself to the shape of waking up beside you. Sometimes I smell your perfume on a breeze and wonder how it's possible that I still know the scent of you so well. Sometimes I wake up with the taste of you on my lips," he said, fingers stretching out to match the motion of her breath, "and I know, Masha, that the only reason you ever gave your heart to me to begin with was because it would never belong to anyone else, and neither of us could ever forget it."

Only then, when her lips parted, did he lift his eyes to hers.

"You gave me your heart, Marya Antonova, and I will keep it safe until my dying day," Dimitri promised, and took her free hand gently, placing it against his chest. If he only ever made her one vow, it would be this one. "I'll keep it safe," he swore, his pulse and hers in synchronicity, in truth beneath her palm, "and in return, you'll have my heart, forever, until someone cuts it out of my fucking chest."

She said nothing, only staring up at him. Considering him, and in return, he considered her.

"Your hair is getting long again," he murmured. "It's almost like it was when you loved me."

Only then did Marya move.

She exhaled, releasing him to turn away.

"Dima," she said, not looking at him. "I never stopped loving you."

He slid toward her, setting one hand gently on her waist. When she didn't push him away, he pulled her closer, aligning her hips with his.

"And?" he asked, and she shifted, her gaze rising to meet his.

"And I never will," she said.

It was no whispered confession. It was no gentle murmur in the dark. It was the truth, plain and bare, and she wasn't vulnerable for having said it. Instead, she wore her love like a shield, like armor, and he ached for her; for what she was to him; for what they might have been together.

She chose the dress. She chose this place. She chose to come here to him, knowing he would touch her, that inevitably they would spend part of this night together, and she wasn't afraid. She wasn't afraid, of him or of love or of anything, and for that he capitulated to her, kissed her. Bent his head and pressed his mouth to hers, to prove that he was strong for her, because he could be weak. Because she wanted him to love her, and because he would, without fear, for as long as he lived. For as long as his heart still beat beside hers, and for long after. For all of the afters, happily or not.

This time, he wasn't lying half dead in his bed. He pulled her against him with the intensity of every lost second, every spare craving of every night spent alone for the twelve years lost between them. His hands wrapped around her slender wrists like he could keep her there, like he could keep her. Her dark curls spread over his bedsheets and in agony, in bliss, Dimitri remembered—fuck, he remembered it all. Everything he had never had the self-preservation to forget.

"Is it true Stas is dead?" he asked her, a rasp of a question. So much for seduction. Now this would have to be more, so much more.

Marya nodded, not taking her eyes from his.

He considered how else to ask. "Do you still—"

"I loved him," Marya confirmed, toneless, and though he knew it, though he had expected it, Dimitri still flinched. "I won't pretend I didn't. But I loved him because that love made me stronger, not weaker."

"And this love?" Dimitri asked her, expectant; breathless. A coin flip between exultancy and grief. "Our love?"

She looked at him. Traced his cheek with her gaze.

"I would burn down the world for this love, Dima," she said, "so maybe I'll help you. Maybe I won't. Don't tell me what you're planning," she warned, "and let me have my secrets, too. Give me nothing. Deny me everything."

It pulsed between them, rapt as birdsong. Steady as a drum.

"Everything?" Dimitri echoed, one hand releasing her to slide under her dress, and she gave him a little brush of a smile.

"*This* is nothing," she told him, though she drew one leg up, tightening it around him. "Isn't it?"

He slid a hand through her hair to coax her head back, wrapping a fistful of the strands around his knuckles until she hissed a little through her teeth.

"Masha." His voice was hoarse with control. "We were never nothing."

"Maybe we weren't," she said, arching her hips up against his until his restraint slipped a little with a groan, "but still, this was the least of what we were, wasn't it?"

True.

He inched forward, lips parting over her neck. She made a breathy little sound, like a sigh, and then shoved him hard onto his back, forcing his shoulders deeper into the mattress as she leaned over him on the bed.

"I don't like being this close to you." She drew one fingernail down his throat until it rested just above the vial around his neck. "I can feel it beating. Like a phantom limb."

"Do you want it back?" Dimitri asked, exhaling as Marya slid both hands under his shirt.

"No," she said, and dropped lower, tracing her berry-red lips over his jaw, his neck, his chest. "You promised you wouldn't let anything happen to it, Dima. You're its keeper now."

He closed his eyes, every muscle finely wrought with misery and tension as her fingers brushed the clasp of his trousers.

"What else can you still feel, Masha?" he asked with sickening despondency, his breath consumptive from the pounding in his chest. When he opened his eyes again, she was smiling down at him, mean and victorious and cruelly beautiful, and she was everything, everything he had ever loved. She was the sun, the moon, and the stars.

She was fantasy incarnate, and she had chosen him.

"Let's find out, Dima, shall we?" Marya beckoned, and then she slid her hands under the fabric as her heart ran riot beside his own, reducing him perilously to a shiver.

IV. 15

(Old Souls, Old Soldiers.)

Ivan sipped slowly at his drink, contemplating things.

Marya and Dimitri.

Sasha and Lev.

Hate and love were really not so different, Ivan thought. He wondered if Koschei and Baba Yaga knew it just as well—that hate and love were so very similar. Both were intestinal, visceral. Both left scars, vestiges of pain. Hate could not be born from a place of indifference. Hate was only born from opposite sides of the same coin.

Ivan checked his watch, shaking his head; Marya wasn't back yet. *One hour,* she'd said, *and not a single minute more.*

He didn't ask questions; largely because he didn't want the answers.

He'd had a dream the night before. He was back at the spot by the river, hands raised in the air, looking at Roman Fedorov.

So, will you kill me, then?

And Sasha's answer: *He asked me not to.*

What tangled webs, Ivan lamented, shaking his head.

And from the light around him, he could have sworn he saw the shadows nod.

IV. 16

(Not the Lark.)

Marya Antonova stepped out into the night covered with Dimitri Fedorov's fingerprints. She was bathed in his touch, head to toe. He'd always had patient hands; they took their time. They were hands meant for mastery. His fingers were tireless, steady, certain. He had the hands of an artist, a craftsman. Hands like the rays of the afternoon sun: slow, but sure. Constant. Heated in every place they touched.

His mouth, by contrast, was restless. He had the lips of a vagabond, never resting too long in one place. A pilgrim's tongue, seeking holy ground. He would touch his lips to hers and it would be like home for a moment, for a breath, but then home would become the smooth stretch of her jaw, or the curve of her neck. Home would be the hollow of her throat. His mouth could make a home from the lines of her torso; buried in the twist of tension at her back. He could linger for a beat of time beside the bone of her ankle, his penitent fingers wrapped around her heel, and she would think, *That is your home, too, and mine.*

She shivered in the night, pulling her coat tighter around her, and looked for Ivan.

"Did you get what you needed?" Ivan asked, joining her on the sidewalk.

No.

Yes.

"I got what I came for," Marya said, which was less an answer than a truth. Ivan glanced at her, arching a brow, and gruffly, she clarified, "He wants his brother resurrected."

"And I presume you told him that only the holy rise again," Ivan said, half smiling, and in reply, Marya spared him half a laugh.

"I made no promises," she assured him. "I have my sister to worry about. I have my own problems without adding Dimitri Fedorov's to the list."

Which was a thing she could say, she knew, only because her heart pulsed somewhere out of sight; somewhere above her, where she'd only just been. Being without it wasn't faultless, of course—she still knew the motions of it, the decisions it might make, when she tried to summon it like a foregone muscle. The difference was that she was no longer pressed to rely on it. Her heart had been beyond her control, once. Now it was more like an elbow. It would bend only if she wished.

"How is she?" Marya asked, drawing her attention back to Ivan. "Sasha. Have you noticed anything?"

Ivan hesitated.

"She seems sad," he said. "Though I think if I hadn't come to know you through a decade of your own sadness, I may not have caught signs of hers."

Marya cut him an impatient glare. "You lessen me, Ivan."

"No, I don't," he assured her. "Why would I lessen you by humanizing you?"

"Because I'm an Antonova," Marya reminded him, lifting a brow. "I'm not some lovesick girl, Ivan, and neither is Sasha. She's a diamond. Nothing can break her. Nothing shines brighter."

Ivan gave a small shrug.

"Still," he said, a tacit protest, and Marya sighed, peeling back the fabric of reality and taking them back to her house.

It was quieter now without Stas; colder. Stas had been the house's warmth. He had been her warmth, Marya thought, so that she could remain cold. She hadn't forgotten that.

She hadn't forgotten him, but still.

Her heart beat elsewhere, and it was easily pushed aside.

"Will you need anything else?" Ivan asked, catching the look on her face, and Marya shook her head.

"No, Ivan." She paused, thinking, and reached out, touching his cheek. "You know I value you, don't you?"

He nodded, leaning into her hand. "And you know I would follow you anywhere."

She nodded. "I do."

That was enough for one evening. She had things to do, remnants of Dimitri Fedorov to be rid of before they scarred. She imagined the water she'd need to accomplish it and fought to keep from flinching. It would be scalding. She would burn, and then she would freeze. She would slather herself in rosewater and remorse, and then she would fall asleep to his words in her ear: *Come back to me, Masha. Whenever you're ready. When you've finished making heaven and earth your domain, come back.*

She swallowed hard and turned away, heading to her bedroom as Ivan slipped out into the corridor, heading home. She paused, though, noticing the flicker of light coming from inside the room, and considered calling him back before pausing, thinking better of it.

She was Marya Antonova; she only needed a bodyguard to watch her back. Her front she was more than capable of protecting.

She slid the door open and stopped, blinking at the unexpected scene.

"Don't panic," her sister Katya warned.

A ridiculous thing to say. Marya never panicked. Certainly not anymore.

"What is this?" Marya asked slowly, eyeing her sisters and cataloguing them, one by one.

Katya, who could see the dead.

Irina, who could hear them.

Galina, who could power a generator.

And behind them—

"Marya Antonova," said a corpse, and Marya heaved a burdensome sigh.

On the one hand, she could be angry. Her sisters had obviously done something stupid. On the other hand, at least they had gone directly to her. This, like all things, Marya could handle, and if it couldn't be handled, then it could certainly be put down.

She let out a breath, opting for patience, or something like it.

"You could have at least done something about the smell," she eventually told Katya, who shrugged.

"That's your arena," Katya reminded her. "Once upon a time, Masha, you were less an almighty drug lord than a girl with a fair hand at mending things."

"Diminish me, why don't you," Marya grumbled, and turned to the corpse. "What do you think to gain from me?"

"I have to save Sasha," it said. "I have to save her."

Marya looked up at the others. Galina gave a tiny, pretty shrug.

"Sasha is dead," Marya told the corpse. "It's too late to save her."

Irina and Katya exchanged a look.

The corpse, meanwhile, shook its head.

"I will save her," it said.

"From what?" Marya asked.

"The world," the corpse replied. "And if not this world, then all the others."

Marya frowned, glancing at her sisters for an explanation, and Irina hesitantly stepped forward.

"He's a bit . . . stuck," she supplied.

He. Marya already knew it was a he, but still.

"Stuck in what?" Marya asked, eyeing it. "The past?"

"His death," Irina clarified. "It's why we had to bring him back."

"He's been following me everywhere," Katya added. "Speaking to Irka. We had to do something."

Marya glanced at Galina, who shrugged. "I was just bored," she said, and Marya sighed.

"Fine. Galya, come here." She beckoned, and Galina nodded, resting her hand on Marya's shoulder. "And you," Marya said to the corpse, "have a seat."

The corpse sat. It was an obedient corpse.

"This may be a while," Marya warned, and then, because it was true, she added, "It'd be quicker just to kill you again."

"Funny thing about death," the corpse replied. "It does something odd to time."

Briefly, Marya felt the slow brush of Dimitri's fingers along her cheek.

Dead things never stayed dead for long. Things were always being resurrected.

"Yes," she said, laying her hands on the corpse's eyes and closing her own, breathing out. "Yes, it certainly does."

IV. 17

(Allies.)

To touch Marya Antonova was to grasp a strike of lightning. She was an electric shock, and Dimitri, paralyzed for having touched her, lay bare and alone in the twisted landscape of his sheets until the feeling returned to his limbs. Then he launched to his feet, taking briskly to the street and finding himself somewhere he'd been not so long before.

"Bridge," he called, "about that change of heart—"

"Ah, excellent," said Brynmor Attaway, turning from where he'd been obscuring Dimitri's view of his sofa. "We've been waiting for you, Dimitri Fedorov."

Dimitri paused. "We?"

Bryn stepped aside to reveal a young woman sipping quietly at a glass of something. More death whisky, Dimitri guessed, as she caught his eye and smiled.

"You must be Dimitri," she said.

The eyes were different. Outside of that, the resemblance was uncanny.

"You're Marya's sister," he said, and sifted through his knowledge of the Antonova witches. Not Ekaterina, not Irina, not Liliya, not Yelena. Someone younger. Galina?

No. He knew precisely who it was.

"You're Sasha," Dimitri realized, knowing what it must have meant that she was here. In reply, she smiled slowly.

"Pleasure's all mine," she said, and he grimaced.

"You're supposed to be dead."

"Death doesn't seem to stick in my family," she replied. "Have to assume it's genetic."

At that, Dimitri spun to face a smugly expectant Bryn. "What is this?"

"An alliance, if you want it," Bryn replied with a shrug. "More of an elaborate scheme, really, but alliance is a better word. You want my help," he explained to Dimitri, "and so does she. But, considering who I am—" *The Bridge*, Dimitri registered with an internal grumble. "—I always prefer outsourcing."

Dimitri took a moment to calculate.

"What did you offer her on my behalf?" he asked Bryn, who chuckled.

"Nothing," he said. "The offer is yours to make."

Dimitri turned to Sasha, who had risen to her feet, observing them like boxers in the ring. "Why should I not simply tell my father right now that Baba Yaga's broken her end of the deal?" he demanded. "We could come for you easily. Tell me why I shouldn't." To his dismay, it sounded more like a question than a command.

"Because we both want your father brought down," Sasha said plainly. "Because I want him to suffer, and so do you."

Dimitri stiffened.

"Bold claim to make to Koschei's heir," he said.

"It is, isn't it?" Sasha agreed. "But still—he *has* an heir, doesn't he? Which implies a kingdom of sorts to pass along. Rumor has it quite a valuable one, too. So," she offered slyly, "it seems a matter of convenience, doesn't it, to have your father out of the way?"

"What makes you think I'm in any rush to lose him?"

She gave him a lovely look of boredom she must have learned from Marya.

"The Bridge tells me you're troubled by dissatisfaction. Conveniently, I find myself in a similar situation. Our inheritance is not dissimilar, you know," she told him. "An empire. A rivalry. Loss. Guilt. Bloodied hands on both sides."

Dimitri glanced at Bryn, who shrugged, before turning back to Sasha.

"What do you want, exactly?" he asked. "Aside from the impossible."

"The Bridge already told you," Sasha said. "I need an ally. Someone I can trust. It's a business proposal."

"I don't like deals," Dimitri said.

"Well, you clearly came here to make one," Sasha pointed out. "Something changed your mind?"

Marya's heart pulsed once, twice against his chest.

"It's one thing to stand against my father on my own," Dimitri said stiffly. "Another to help my enemy bring him down."

"I'm your father's enemy, not yours," Sasha corrected him. "I want your father to pay. I want your brother to suffer. You I can take or leave." She gave a shrug to prove it. "I don't know what kind of man you are, Dimitri Fedorov, but I know what kind of man your brother thought you were. And I know there's a place, however narrow, where your interests and mine align. So," she said, stepping toward him, "all things considered, I'm your friend."

Those were not words of friendship, Dimitri thought.

But neither were they entirely wrong.

"Give me something," Sasha said. "Something to send Koschei reeling, to knock his empire out from underneath him. In return, I promise not to touch you."

Dimitri scoffed. As if he were so touchable. He was ethically compromised, not outright weak. "And if I don't agree?"

"I'll ruin you," she said without hesitation. "It may take me a little more time, but this isn't a negotiation. I'll bring down Koschei," Sasha said, unblinking. "Whether you help me or stand in my way, I'll look him in the eye and make sure he knows what he's cost me. But I'd be more efficient with a better partner, and I'm not in the practice of wasting my time."

She scrutinized him another moment. "And when I'm done with Koschei—" A pause. "When, not if. *When* he is no longer a threat, my sisters and I can bring Lev back."

That, Dimitri realized, was her real power. The true ace up her sleeve, as she must have understood all along. The fact that he hadn't yet turned away must have revealed more about him than he wished her to see, but it didn't matter now. Not anymore. Not after she'd said those words out loud.

"Without Koschei, the deal with my mother will be unimportant, null and void. My hands will no longer be tied. Think of me as if I'm not an Antonova, and you are not a Fedorov," Sasha suggested, her grey eyes fixed on his, "and we are merely two people who miss the same man."

There was very little Dimitri wouldn't do to have his brother back.

Still, he would have preferred something a little less . . . Antonova. *This* one, anyway.

"So." Sasha exhaled with a sense of finality. "Do we understand each other?"

Dimitri turned to Bryn.

"This wasn't what I wanted," he said. He needed to say at least that much out loud.

"No," The Bridge agreed. "But do you usually get what you want, Dimitri Fedorov?"

Almost never, he thought.

"Okay," he said slowly, turning back to Sasha Antonova. "What did you have in mind?"

IV. 18

(Only the Holy.)

"There," Marya said, leaning back to survey her handiwork. "How do you feel?"

The onetime corpse raised a hand to his cheek.

"You're very good at this," he noted. "A shame that my experience with your magic mostly involves my brother nearly dying at your hands."

"Well, only because you remember very little," she said, "Lev Fedorov."

Lev blinked, settling back into his bones; back into his life; back into his name.

"You can go now," Marya said to her sisters, placing her hand gently on Galina's. "Lev and I have things to discuss."

Irina hesitated. "But Masha, if Mama asks—"

"You'll say nothing," Marya told her firmly. "I'll tell Mama myself."

Katya and Irina looked as if they would argue for a moment, but then they nodded, resigning themselves to their exit. Galina, visibly exhausted, brushed her lips against Marya's cheek, following them out without a word.

"Now," Marya said, turning to Lev. "About why you kept pestering my sisters."

He was very like Dimitri had been when they were younger. This Fedorov had dark hair and eyes; he wasn't quite as golden, and his jaw was sharper, his cheekbones higher—but he had a familiar spark of youth to him. An earnestness that had long since left Dimitri.

"Well, nobody else could hear or see me," Lev explained. "Bit of a frustrating experience, death. Which," he added uncomfortably, "is apparently something you're familiar with."

"More or less," Marya agreed. "Still. What exactly is your fear for Sasha?"

"I thought maybe Roma would hurt her. Or worse, that she would lose herself."

Ivan's words—*She seems sad*—wandered in and quickly out of Marya's consciousness.

"You don't know our Sasha very well," Marya said, and Lev arched a brow.

"Don't I?" he countered.

Marya thought of the vacant look on Sasha's face and said nothing. She knew better than anyone the troubles with inadvisable love.

"Sasha's dead," she told Lev, adhering to falsity. She didn't know yet whether he might be compelled to tell his father, or his brothers, so she couldn't trust him—but that didn't make him useless. Not yet. "You can still help her," Marya told him, measuring out and changing the plan as she went. "After all, the man at fault is still at large."

Lev grimaced. "I take it you mean Roma?"

"In part." Marya was careful, tiptoeing around as her lies took shape. "But still, it's Koschei's fault that Sasha must remain dead, isn't it? No one can know you're alive," she warned him, "or the deal struck between Koschei and Baba Yaga will disintegrate. The damage would be catastrophic to both your family and mine."

"Koschei," Lev echoed, looking stunned. "My father made a deal?"

Marya nodded.

"But—" Lev swallowed hard. "But if he's responsible for her death, then you realize what you're saying."

Again, she nodded.

"You're asking me . . . not to be a Fedorov?"

"Yes." And she was. "But seeing as no Fedorov could have possibly brought you back, you owe your life to the Antonovas. Do you not?"

Lev hesitated. "But my brothers," he began, and stopped, clarity or something like it dawning on his face. "You didn't kill Dima," he recalled, frowning slightly as Marya kept her face perfectly still. "You saved him when you could have left him to die."

Marya said nothing.

"Marya Antonova," Lev said, blinking once. "Are you, by any chance . . . good?"

The laugh came bitterly, burning in her throat.

"No," she assured him. Had her heart been in her chest it might have stuttered with guilt, but it wasn't, so it didn't. "I'm just a woman with a dead sister. I'm just a weapon," she clarified, "aimed at the man who caused me pain."

Lev considered it.

"What would you have me do for you, then?" he asked, and she told him.

She told him, and he nodded.

After some discussion he extended his hand, and they agreed.

And then Marya Antonova slipped out in the night, heading straight for her mother.

She was about to knock on the door, waiting outside the frame, when she paused, hearing voices. It was a strange echo of what had happened just hours earlier; the unforeseen resurrection that had been waiting for her inside her bedroom. Marya waved a hand over herself, obscuring her own shadow, and slipped into the room, listening quietly.

"—so should we not, perhaps, bury our differences?" an older man was asking. "I remember you, Marya, as you once were. You thought I never saw you, or that I saw you as something to be owned, or to be used, but I saw you precisely. I saw a woman unloved and unvalued. I saw a witch capable of far more than her sycophantic husband ever was. I saw a partner, Marya. I knew you could be Baba Yaga before you did, and I was ready, and waiting—"

"Lazar," Yaga said softly. "Don't you think I would have been relieved to have you by my side?"

Marya swallowed hard, curling one hand to a fist. She hoped it was a trick. Or a lie.

But her mother, who had never revealed any softness for Marya, certainly looked soft now. Nostalgic, even.

"What fools we were," said Koschei, as Marya's nails bit into her palm. "Could we not bury our differences, now that we have both lost so much?"

"Make amends, you mean?" Yaga asked him, and sighed. "It would be easier, Lazar. Much easier, to work with you instead of against you."

Marya's throat burned.

The faint memory of her heart seared acidly in her chest.

"We have only suffered for our differences," Koschei said, reaching out to rest his hands on Yaga's knuckles, and Marya, who couldn't bear another moment, tore swiftly from the room, reaching through thin air to drag herself back home.

They believed they had suffered.

They believed *they* had suffered.

She wanted to scream.

She wanted to be sick.

In a rush, voices from memories flooded her mind.

Masha, don't do this—

Twelve years ago, her mother had asked her to choose.

Masha, please. Please!

Twelve years ago, she had looked her lover in the eye and told her most terrible lie; she told him she felt nothing.

You can't mean that, Masha. I know you don't mean that!

Twelve years ago, she had torn her own heart out, cast it aside, buried it somewhere deep.

Masha, you are the sun, the moon, and the stars—

Masha, if you go, you take my whole heart with you—

Marya Antonova, I will love you until the day I die—

"Dima," she let out in a whisper.

If you would only choose me, Masha, I would save you from this life.

She stared at the lines of her palms, waiting for clarity that didn't come. Even with Dimitri's voice fading from her thoughts, the sting of her mother's betrayal failed to ease.

I am just a weapon aimed at the man who caused me pain.

Just a weapon, she thought.

Just a weapon.

A knife doesn't wield itself.

Come back to me, Masha—

Just a weapon, aimed at a man.

And who, she wondered angrily, had aimed her?

Marya looked up coldly, curling her fingers around the edge of the blade that she was.

Baba Yaga was going soft.

But Marya Antonova could not be broken.

IV. 19

(Dirty Money, Bad Blood.)

Eric Taylor looked up from the tablets he'd been counting, eyes flaring with alarm before narrowing with indignation at the man standing in the threshold of his office. "How'd you get in here?" he demanded, and then frowned with recognition. "Wait a minute. Don't I know you?"

"You do, actually," Lev confirmed, leaning against the frame and gesturing over his shoulder. "Door was unlocked. Nice to see your face healed up," he added.

Eric's smile stiffened, then faltered.

"Well, I suppose I should have known," he muttered to himself, shaking his head and returning to his tablets. Lev glanced at the thin leather cuff around Eric's wrist, taking stock of it before redirecting his attention to Eric's regrettably unpunched face. "The noble ones are always hiding something, aren't they?"

"I suppose," Lev gamely replied.

After all, he wasn't wrong, though Lev doubted Eric Taylor knew much about nobility.

"So," Eric said, continuing to chat condescendingly to Lev as he worked. "I take it you're the new buyer, then? I understand your need for secrecy," he added, glancing up briefly. "I have a bit of a proclivity for it myself, but still, you might have mentioned it was you when we arranged the meeting."

Lev shrugged. "Can't be too careful."

"You're early, though." Eric gestured to his unfinished assortment of tablets. "Just as impolite as being late, in my opinion."

"Well, certainly can't have that," Lev said, and added, "So. Who's your supplier?"

"Ah," Eric said, not taking his eyes from the notes he was

scribbling; a code of sorts. Numbers and symbols, details about sales and inventory. "Can't tell you that, obviously. This is sort of a 'money talks' situation? As in, I don't."

"Right," Lev said, taking another step. "Not even to apologize, I imagine."

Eric laughed under his breath. "Apologize, to you? For what?"

"Well, you just don't have a particularly good track record, do you?" Lev said, and Eric's eyes narrowed, though he didn't look up. "You know," Lev continued, musing aloud, "before I came here, my employer specifically made a point to tell me that you were something of a . . . oh, what was the word she used," he mused, considering it. "I believe it was *chauvinist*. Or *narcissist*? Possibly *flaming trash pile of toxic masculinity*—I don't know, it all sort of blends together—"

"Excuse me?" Eric asked, glancing up. "Last I checked, I was the one who had something you wanted, asshole. If you're not interested in being civil, you obviously know where to find the door."

"I do, actually," Lev agreed, "and funnily enough, I'm not too interested in civility. Unfortunately, I do have to make one quick swap with you before I leave, so—"

"Swap?" Eric echoed, finally rising to his feet to face Lev. "That's not how this works, okay? I set the terms, and then you—"

Lev's hand shot out, circling Eric's throat.

"I," Lev clarified, "am taking over from here, Eric. I'd bother with apologies, but—" He shrugged. "Recently I've come to learn that time is a highly precious thing."

Eric opened his mouth, struggling to speak, and Lev sighed.

"Right," he reminded himself. "Time is being wasted."

A quick little shot of power to the base of Eric's throat was more than enough, and once he'd gone limp, Lev permitted him to fall to the ground, nudging him aside. He bent, checking Eric's requisite lack of pulse, and then removed the leather cuff from his wrist, rising to his feet to pick up one of the tablets.

Right on schedule, there was a knock at the apartment's front door. Lev gathered the tablets, eyeing them briefly, and then tucked them into his pocket, sealing the office shut behind him and crossing the expansive marble foyer to the door. It was locked, of course, but unguarded in any of the important ways. Eric, unsurprisingly, had been underprepared for dealing with witches.

"Yes?" Lev said, pulling the door open to find a man in a crisp grey suit.

"Eric?" he asked. "We spoke on the phone."

Lev nodded and pulled the door open, gesturing him inside.

"Shouldn't take long," he said. "Sort of a 'money talks' situation, isn't it? As in, we don't need to."

The man paused, considering Lev, and frowned slightly.

"I thought I was here to meet with Eric," he said, eyes beadily darting to the door, and Lev offered a smile, twisting his fingers to lock it from afar.

"Eric is otherwise occupied," he said. "I'll be taking it from here."

ACT V

KILL YOUR JOYS

See what a scourge is laid upon your hate!
That heaven finds means to kill your joys with love,
And I for winking at your discords too,
Have lost a brace of kinsmen: all are punish'd.

The Prince,
Romeo and Juliet (Act V, Scene III)

V. 1

(The Patriarch.)

People believe shadows represent darkness, but that isn't technically true. For one thing, a shadow can't exist without light. A shadow, which is itself a slice of darkness, can only be seen when light persists, which is to say it can only be seen in the context of something brighter.

To claim the man known as Koschei the Deathless spent most of his life as a shadow is not an unreasonable conclusion. Lazar Fedorov had certainly been a shadow when he was born. His father had been a working-class witch, a cog in the workings of the New York Witches' Boroughs, who had scraped together all of his hard-earned money (through favors, odd jobs, and loans, most of them by other pilgrims who'd sought Lady Liberty's torch) to buy a dilapidated apartment building, which he turned into a slightly less dilapidated building until the occasion of his death in Lazar's midteens. The year Lazar's father died was a particularly bad one, for him and Lazar both, as it turned out. Lazar's eldest brother, whose health had never been especially robust, died shortly after their father. It was an infection in his lungs; something as inconsequential as breathing. Lazar, who had adored his clever brother, found himself alone, now the inheritor of their father's only two possessions: his good name and his apartment building. His needy tenants, too, whose oppressive demands continued even after his death.

Lazar began as his father had, with favors for the lowly, and if karma was a game to be played, Lazar approached the table with a winning hand. At only fifteen years old, Lazar Fedorov commenced what would become a complex system of favors, all of which began with a genuine intent to do good. A patched roof here. A repaired wall there. Oh, Lazar, thank heavens you were here, can you lend an eye to this problem I am having? In exchange I can offer you little, but here, take this—a trinket from our home. From our family. From our past. Something meaningful, something precious. Something that is priceless to me.

Lazar would nod, accept the gift, and store it somewhere. In his mind, largely. He learned the value of these offerings came less with a dollar sign than with the expression of gratitude that meant, unequivocally, "I now owe you everything."

What could I do with this? he would think, and then someone else would need a favor. And then he would think: *Would this person not benefit from my offering? And would I not benefit from their loyalty in turn?*

Before long, Lazar Fedorov was eighteen years old and in possession of a great number of favors. He was meticulous about them. Some nights he went hungry, but still, better to starve than to call in a favor before he knew how it was most wisely spent. Later in life, he would eat some expensive meal and invariably recall how it could never compare to the extravagance of having nothing. In the early days of his business, food was tinny and metallic, something out of a can, but crucially, it would also come paired with a realization: *Aha—I know how so-and-so can procure me the thing that I need.*

The first thing Lazar cast off from his past was the apartment building. He kept the ownership, of course, but hired a manager. His business would not be rooted in the thankless happiness of others, he thought. If he wanted to prosper, he would have to invest in the *suffering* of others. He would find those who wanted more and offer them a means by which to get it. He learned many things in his teenage years—namely, how to recognize the face of desperation, which came in many different forms. It came hungry, tired, homeless. But it also came in the shapes of the wealthy, the privileged. Desperation was a well that never emptied. Even the powerful had pockets of it, and they had far more to offer Lazar, and thus, disastrously more to lose.

The second thing to go was his family name, at least when it came to business. The problem with names, Lazar thought, is that they were themselves a shadow. The wearer bore his father's name, and if his father was nothing worth remarking, then neither was he, by default. Lazar, on the other hand, would not be as inconsequential as his father.

The name *Koschei* had slipped out from one of the Borough witches; the first of the Borough witches to recognize Lazar's talent for usefulness, whose first big favor had been the price of a Borough election. "I know you carry quite a lot of influence with the witches in the Brooklyn Borough," the witch had said, "and I hear you are owed something by one of the union leaders."

The witch had not needed to tell Lazar that he knew he would lose without the unions. In return, Lazar had not needed to tell the witch what the favor was, or how he had procured it. All that mattered was at the end of the week, every witch in the Brooklyn Borough had committed their vote to the requesting candidate, and in retrospect, the election itself was unimportant. The Borough witch would be forgotten. The only important thing would be the story of how he had come to a thin young man who was in possession of a great amount of secrets—who could not be bought by traditional methods, and therefore could not be easily destroyed. *He is like Koschei,* they would say. *He is deathless and immortal, like Koschei, and you can only find him among the shadows.*

If anyone had asked Lazar how he did it, he would have laughed and said, *Have you not heard of a whisper campaign? Not everything is witchcraft*—but nobody asked. They feared him too much by then. After all, nobody trusts something they cannot see.

By the time Lazar had any interest in taking a wife, he was getting close to middle-aged. He'd already lived longer than his father, owning considerably more than a single crumbling building. Lazar owned *several* buildings, in fact, and collected rent from all of them, though that wasn't his primary occupation. He was a dealer in many things; in everything. If there was something to be had, Koschei had it, or he could get it. It was only when the Borough witches began to resent his success that Lazar knew he had finally come far enough. Once he owned a persuasive piece of every witch from every Borough, he finally determined he could allow himself to rest.

"A wife?" his friend Antonov had asked doubtfully, half laughing. Antonov was relatively young, a low-ranking Borough witch whom Lazar had approached (first as Koschei, and then, gradually, as himself) when it became obvious that Antonov was far more of a witch than a politician, and therefore more promising to Lazar than his more senior counterparts. Buying Antonov a beer paid off a hundredfold in terms of what he would offer Koschei by the end of the night—some bit of spellwork, some magic that came easily to him, which, as far as Lazar knew at the time, came easily to no one else.

"Somehow I doubt your bed is cold, Koschei the Deathless," judged Antonov.

"Just looking for my Princess Marya, I suppose," Lazar said, always happy to indulge a reference to the fairy tale for which he was named. Like usual, he sipped his beer quietly while Antonov drained his.

"I have a Marya, in fact." Antonov chuckled to himself. "Quiet little thing. Get yourself one of those."

In truth, Lazar had little interest in a wife. What he needed, however, was an heir. A good one. Someone to carry on his legacy. A strong boy; someone he could raise who would be stronger than his own father's heir, who had outlasted his father by only a handful of breaths. What Lazar needed was a son of Koschei. Someone to carry on a dynasty, to shoulder the blessing and the burden of an empire on his back.

"Quiet is fine," Lazar said. "Quiet I can work with."

So Antonov found him Anna, a pretty blonde slip of a thing who obviously found Lazar terrifying. Not like Antonov's wife, Lazar thought jealously. Unlike Anna, Antonov's Marya was always listening; her gaze was always sharp and keen and curious, unlike Anna's. Where Anna grew rabbity with nerves at the sight of him, Marya—who was at least the same age, if not younger; barely a woman, still with a girl's narrow limbs—fixed her gaze on Lazar with such questioning intensity that he instinctively began to conceal himself from her. Unlike Antonov, who spoke freely of his dealings in front of his young wife, Lazar kept his secrets to himself.

Lazar and Anna lived separate lives, mostly, outside of the time it took for her to conceive a child. By then, Antonov had already had his firstborn—a girl named Marya. A fitting name, Lazar thought, though he didn't say so. A beautiful baby girl, Antonov's Marya. Like her mother, little Marya had sharp eyes from birth, and Lazar had the strangest feeling when he looked at her. She was her father's favorite ("Princess Marya," Antonov would coo to the baby in his arms, "my Masha, my little princess!") and while Lazar had no such connection to her, he had the sense that she would somehow be significant. That his life and hers, and the life of her too-quiet, too-clever mother, would forever be intertwined.

Then Dimitri was born.

Dimitri was born, and Lazar knew for the first time what it was to love something more than he had ever loved himself. From the very first cry that tore from his son's little lungs, the man called Koschei the Deathless had found his purpose. He had wanted an inheritor for everything he had built, but that day, he realized his calling was something much, much larger.

His life's purpose would be to create something that would be worthy of his eldest son.

Lazar found he had been right to befriend Antonov, not because the other man was in any way helpful, but because he was *useful*. Antonov seemed to have absolutely no concept of how valuable his skills were; he lacked any sort of drive, either, to be of any threat to Koschei's business, which meant that for once, rather than seeking a tool by which to destroy him (just in case), Lazar considered Antonov something of a pet. Lazar named his second son, Roman, after Antonov, knowing that such a gesture would mean considerably more to the younger man than it did to him. Antonov, a proud sort of man, aspired only to comfort, to camaraderie. But he was talented, and he doted on Lazar's son Dima, and it became obvious to Lazar that it would take very little effort at all to make sure Antonov was loyal to Koschei for all of his days.

"I'll name my own son after you," Antonov promised him, looking exuberant with the prospect, but Lazar watched Antonov's face fall in disappointment each time his wife Marya bore him a daughter. And another daughter. And another. Seven daughters in total, with little Masha, her mother's perfect miniature, at the helm. Each time, Antonov grew more deeply disappointed, and on the day his wife Marya told him she could bear him no more children, he succumbed to something of a listless melancholy, turning his attention to Lazar's sons.

By the time Anna died—a surprisingly crushing blow to Lazar, who had grown fond of his wife in the years since she'd become a mother to his sons—it had become clear that Antonov was not only a fool who'd misjudged his own talents, but also a fool who'd misjudged the army of beautiful young witches in his house. When Antonov began bringing his daughter Masha on his visits to Lazar's home, it struck Lazar that perhaps there was still more to gain from Antonov's friendship. Masha was an intensely capable witch, and what Antonov thought were little party tricks, Lazar could see were signs of magical prowess to rival her own father's. It occurred to Lazar that perhaps Masha had even been schooled not to let too much of her power show, and just as he thought it, he knew where that lesson must have come from.

"Your daughter," Lazar murmured to the elder Marya Antonova when her husband was busy playing with Dimitri. "She knows more than she lets on. I wonder where she learned to do that?"

Marya's dark eyes cut to his. "She's a clever girl, my Masha."

"Mm," Lazar agreed, watching a young Masha's cheeks flush as Dimitri turned, gallantly offering her something: a book, a toy, a trinket. Dimitri was never selfish, always bold. Masha turned her face away, made shy by the attention. "Well," Lazar said, "in my experience, the most precious jewels are usually hidden. Does her father know?"

"Know what?" Marya demurred, her voice carefully light.

"That she's as good a witch as you," Lazar said quietly, and Marya stiffened. "That, and what the two of you are up to."

He'd seen the potions passed quietly in his seedier circles and recognized instantly who had been behind them. Whose potions they were, firstly, but whose hand had rendered them far more desirable.

Hands, he corrected himself, because if Marya was involved, then Masha was certainly close by.

"Stay away from my husband," Marya warned in lieu of an answer. "I know who you are. I know you'll try to use him."

"Try?" Lazar echoed, laughing. "Is that what you think?"

He knew instantly he'd made a mistake; he'd said too much. He'd established himself as a threat, and the moment Marya turned away, he could feel a pulse of mistrust that forced itself between them. It would still be years before Marya struck, but Lazar knew he'd planted the seed of her displeasure as early as that little conversation, when he'd meant to impress her but miscalculated the degree to which she'd already known what he was.

It was obvious that the source of Marya's sudden break in patience with Antonov was the increasing closeness between her daughter and Lazar's son. Lazar himself had guessed as much already. He could smell the telling scent of rosewater in the air, lingering behind while Dimitri would stare out his window, smiling faintly into nothing. For all that Dimitri was softly foreign to Lazar—his golden son, who was braver and warmer and cleverer than anyone Lazar had ever known; charming and charismatic and yet loyal, dauntless, steadfast—it was clear enough: Dimitri was in love with Masha. Perhaps Masha even loved him back. If Antonov had lived, perhaps Dimitri would have proposed marriage to Masha, and probably she would have accepted. Then Masha would be a Fedorov daughter, a daughter of Koschei, as loyal to Lazar as his three capable

sons. Perhaps the joining of their families would have meant that
Antonov's clever witchery would then belong to Koschei—but as
the opportunity grew closer, more real, Lazar could see that Marya
had stood silently in the background for long enough.

"I think Marya's poisoning me," Antonov said to Lazar, coughing blood into a napkin. "I don't know why, Lazar—I don't know
what I'm supposed to have done—but . . . can I stay with you?"

Lazar grimaced, then sighed. "I'm sorry, my friend," he said.

Ten minutes later, he called Dimitri into the room.

"Dima," Lazar said, "you understand you will be Koschei one
day, don't you?"

Dimitri nodded numbly, staring at the body on the floor. Antonov
had been like an uncle to him, Lazar knew, but there was no time
like the present to learn that a doting Borough witch wasn't the same
thing as blood.

"As Koschei," Lazar continued, "you will have to do things that
are necessary from time to time. You will have to make choices.
Decisions are power," he said, and Dimitri looked up, golden brow
solemn with duty. "To be the one to make a decision is to hold true
power in your hands. But once a decision is made, sometimes you
will have to keep secrets."

"You don't want me to tell Masha," Dimitri interpreted correctly. He looked troubled at the thought, but only for a moment.
Perhaps he'd already judged for himself that Masha wouldn't want
to know.

Lazar nodded.

"Fetch Maksimov," Lazar instructed. "The Borough witch.
He owes me. Tell him he saw Antonov collapse during one of the
Borough meetings. When he has arranged it, have him summon
Masha's mother. Have him tell her to prepare herself."

"Prepare herself for what?" Dimitri asked.

"She'll know," Lazar said. "Do you understand?"

Dimitri nodded grimly. "Yes, Papa," he said, and turned on his
heel, leaving the room. No further questions. A loyal son and a

faultless heir, even at fifteen. He did everything precisely as he was told, and nobody suspected a thing of either Marya Antonova or Lazar. Roman Antonov died and was buried as the unremarkable Borough witch he was, and his family faded into obscurity until approximately three years later, when the Witches' Boroughs began to discuss the sudden prominence of a witch with questionable income, who was known only as Baba Yaga.

Lazar, who had expected such a thing to happen, knew precisely what Marya Antonova had done. After all, she'd hidden herself away for over two decades behind her husband, so why not do it again behind some other name? He chuckled to himself over the thought that perhaps she'd chosen it because of him. She knew he was Koschei the Deathless, so naturally she was Baba Yaga, and now, of course, they would be rivals.

Though, perhaps that wasn't precisely what he wanted.

"Marry me," he told Marya. He hadn't fully realized how he felt until the words came out. "You are in need of a husband, I am in need of a wife. We can be very useful to each other, don't you think?"

She told him she could not bear him children. He said he had no need of them, but failed to mention her children were already so valuable he could never imagine a need for any others.

She told him she didn't need his help. He said she could always use more help, but failed to confess that actually, he needed hers. He was aging, getting on in years. He was lonely since Anna died. He wanted a companion, a friend. *You do not need my help, but I need yours,* he didn't say, and perhaps that was what had done it.

He was a man more accustomed to threats than to promises. He said everything wrong, and when he called Dimitri to him that night to tell his son what had happened, he was sure he could already feel the consequences of his mistake tremoring in the air.

"I asked for Yaga's hand in marriage," he told his son, whose golden brow furrowed.

"Why?" Dimitri asked. Lazar hesitated.

Because she's strong. Stronger than me.

"I want her business" was all Lazar said. "She's positioning herself as my rival. I want to stop her before she succeeds."

"But I love her daughter," Dimitri said, frowning. "Are you asking me to put that aside?"

"No," Lazar said. "I'm not asking you anything, Dima. I'm telling you I've made the decision. I've done what is necessary."

Dimitri blinked. "But it will cost me Masha."

"Why?" Lazar asked, impatient. "It's just an arrangement, Dima."

"An arrangement which Masha will hate," Dimitri said. "You're trying to swallow her up, Papa, and she will know it. She'll know."

"It isn't Masha's decision," Lazar said.

"It is," Dimitri argued. "She and her mother are as good as one woman. Believe me, if Baba Yaga refuses you, it will be because Masha refused," he prophesied darkly, "and then I will lose her, Papa. I will lose her."

"She won't give you up," Lazar insisted. He had never refused his son—how could she, the girl who was so enamored with him? Even Lazar could see that little Masha had been in love with his eldest son for all of her youth. "She won't."

But she did.

And for exactly one day, Dimitri looked like a ghost, shell-shocked and frozen.

The following morning, however, Dimitri woke up renewed.

"She'll come back to me," Dimitri said. "Someday, she'll come back. I know she will."

"And until then?" Lazar asked.

"Until then," Dimitri said slowly, "we will build something for her to come back to."

Dimitri channeled his pain into progress. Lazar, who had suffered a loss of control for the first time since he'd been a boy, took a less active role. He continued to give instructions as Koschei, but withdrew from the activities of the Borough witches. He sent Dimitri on his errands. Within a year or two, very few could reach

Koschei directly anymore. He was said to have retreated to the basement of one of his buildings, where he oversaw his illegal creature trades.

In truth, the man called Koschei was waiting to be impressed by something; to feel something other than numbness in his veins. He waited and waited to be moved but, for years, he felt nothing.

The rest of the story has been told. How Lazar nearly lost his eldest son to Marya Antonova, the daughter of a useless Borough witch who grew up to hold Koschei's most precious treasure hostage. How Lazar nearly lost his second son Roman to Roman's own folly, and the unwise deal he'd made for selfishness's sake. How Lazar finally gave up his youngest, the son from whom he'd intentionally detached, just to make peace with Baba Yaga. How he'd finally drawn to an end the series of misfortunes that had cost him little bits of everything, only to find that the decision he'd made to undo the others had been the most excruciating blow of all.

What *hasn't* been told is that everything Lazar could see he was losing—his influence over the Borough witches, the unexplained silence from clients who had regularly sought him, his waning income with its corresponding lack of explanation—was almost nothing compared to the vacant look on Dimitri's face, or the frustration in Roman's brow. What so few knew of Koschei, no one knew of Lazar Fedorov, always the shadow of a man. He was withering away to nothing, slowly losing everything he'd built.

"Yaga," he said when he finally came to her, swallowing twelve years of pride. "Marya."

She looked up from where she sat. "I wondered when you'd come to find me, Lazar."

He sank into the chair opposite hers, shaking his head.

"Is it you?" he asked. The money. The Boroughs. Everything that was going wrong.

She fixed her solemn gaze on his. "If it was, you would deserve it."

He sighed.

"That's not an answer," he said.

"Well, you set the terms yourself, Lazar," she reminded him wearily. "You told me you would come for me if I crossed you, didn't you?"

Touch me and all the Boroughs will come for you, he'd said, and at the time, it had been true. It wasn't now.

"So, since I am sitting here, very much alive," Yaga said drily, gesturing to herself, "surely you must not be able to prove that I've done anything."

"I will always suspect you first, Marya, proof or not," he told her. "You're the only one strong enough to come against me. The only one to outwit me, or to beat me."

She blinked, internalizing this unprecedented candor.

Then she said gruffly, "What do you want, Lazar?"

He hesitated.

"I miss my son," Lazar confessed.

Dima. He was different.

Romik. He was troubled.

Lyovushka. He was gone.

"And I miss my daughter," Baba Yaga replied.

Lazar thought it best he didn't ask which one.

"I asked for too steep a price."

"You always did," she reminded him. "You've always wanted too much from me."

He gave a bitter laugh. "Yes, but Antonov wanted nothing from you," he reminded her, "and look what that got him."

"Nothing?" Yaga echoed. "You think it was nothing? You think my silence, my subservience, came at no considerable cost?"

He stiffened, registering his misstep yet again. "Marya—"

"You and I both know that my husband was a fool, but you're the one who would have taken what didn't belong to you," Yaga accused him. "You would have stolen what I and my daughters deserved. If I have stood against you, Lazar, it's only because you're a selfish man who believes he has a right to the universe itself."

"That's not true," Lazar insisted staunchly. "And it's because of me you had the freedom to become what you were, Marya."

"Oh, don't bother," Yaga snapped. "You know Antonov died at my hands. You threatened me with it before. So why pretend now?"

"Because you didn't," Lazar said, and she balked. "You didn't kill Antonov, Marya. I did."

Yaga stared at him. "You don't know what you're saying."

"I do. You needed it to look real, didn't you?" he reminded her. "You needed to do it slowly, carefully, because you lacked the ability to cover your tracks, but I didn't. He knew you were poisoning him and he came to me for help. He came to me, so I killed him," Lazar finally confessed, throat dry. "I killed him, Marya, for you. So that you could be free."

She paused, unable to speak.

"You didn't," she managed eventually. "You killed him so that you could have me yourself, didn't you?"

Lazar let out a growl of impatience. "Marya, you and your pride—"

"Oh, don't pretend at selflessness, Lazar," she spat. "You are only a shadow. You linger in the darkness and you wait, don't you? For your chance to strike. You have just been sitting with this truth, biding your time until you could use it as a weapon. You think you can sit there and tell me now, after all this time, that it is only because of you that I have any of this, which I built with my own two hands? With my own daughter, who had the audacity to love me more than she loved your son?"

Lazar flinched. "I did it for you, Marya, whether you believe me or not. If I had told you, you would feel indebted to me, and I never wanted that. I never wanted you to owe me."

"You want it from everyone else," Yaga scoffed. "Why not me?"

"Because," Lazar said angrily. "Because you are more like me than anyone, Marya Antonova. Because you built all this from nothing, as I did! Because—" he began, and sputtered. "Because we could have had everything, you and I."

She waited a moment.

Pressed her lips together.

"I am capable of having everything without you, Lazar," Yaga said coldly. "Haven't you figured that out by now? I don't need you."

"No, you don't, but look what being against me has cost you! What it has cost me, as well," he pressed, leaning toward her. "We have paid far more than we ever wished to simply by standing apart—so should we not, perhaps, bury our differences? I remember you, Marya, as you once were," he said, hearing the touch of pleading to his voice, the softness he'd kept to himself for decades. "You thought I never saw you, or that I saw you as something to be owned, or to be used, but I saw you precisely. I saw a woman unloved and unvalued; I saw a witch capable of far more than her husband ever was. I saw a partner, Marya. I knew you could be Baba Yaga before you did, and I was ready, and waiting—"

He stumbled to a halt, and she shook her head, finally sparing him a look of sympathy.

"Lazar," Yaga said softly. "Don't you think I would have been relieved to have you by my side?"

At last, a fragile moment of understanding. At last, some tender peace.

"What fools we were," Lazar lamented, shaking his head. "Could we not bury our differences, now that we have both lost so much?"

"Make amends, you mean?" Yaga asked him, and sighed. "It would be easier, Lazar. Much easier, to work with you instead of against you."

"We have only suffered for our differences," Lazar said, reaching out to rest his hands on Yaga's knuckles. "I only told you this to prove to you I have always been on your side. Always, Marya, I swear to you," he said, and looked up at her, swallowing hard. "Always."

She considered him.

He had first met the witch called Baba Yaga when she was a girl of eighteen, newly married. Now she was close to fifty and age had burrowed itself into the lines around her eyes, but she was just as lovely as she had always been. As lovely, and as calculating.

"Lazar," she eventually said, "there is no reversing the pain we have caused each other. Our losses cannot be undone."

Marya Antonova is not in the realm of the dead, Lazar heard The Bridge telling him, with that teasing gleam of pleasure in his eye at the havoc he could cause. Who was likely lying? Was it the fae who had nothing to gain but mayhem?

Or was it the witch who already knew what it was to play everyone else for fools?

"Yesterday is as it was," he told her, gambling on the hope she could be trusted. "We have already paid, Marya, blood for blood. But what will tomorrow bring?"

What more, after all, could he stand to lose?

Around him, the shadows danced with warning. They flickered and waned, restless. They were subtle creatures, always coming and going. Like Lazar himself, they were creatures of darkness who could not exist without light; without some promise, at least, of light.

But where he was a shadow, Baba Yaga was stone.

"I suppose, Lazar Fedorov," said Marya Antonova, "we will both have to wait and find out."

V. 2

(Poisoned Wells.)

"If you want my help taking down Koschei," Dimitri said to Sasha Antonova, "I'm going to need to know what you have in mind."

"Koschei's business may have suffered over time, but he still has too many friends among the Borough witches," Sasha said, which wasn't quite an answer. "He's too protected, he has too much influence, and as long as the others continue to revere him or fear him, there will be consequences to my family for his loss. I don't just want to kill him," she clarified. "That would be too easy, or at least easier than I'd like."

True. The trouble was always in the consequences, not the doing.

"Then what do you want?"

"I want to destroy him. I want to watch him lose everything the way I lost everything." She paused, testing him with a glance. "How firm is your loyalty to your father, Dima?"

He bristled at the informality. "It's Dimitri."

Doubtfully, she remarked, "Surely you don't prefer it."

He didn't, but that changed nothing. "This isn't a friendship," he reminded her. "This is a negotiation, and your price is still too high."

"Fine," she sighed facetiously, "have it your way. The question still requires an answer."

"How firm is his loyalty?" Bryn murmured, interrupting their conversation for the first time to look up at Dimitri from his drink. "Flaccid, I suspect."

Dimitri cut him a glare before turning back to Sasha. "It can be tested," he clarified, "but only if you have a plan. A sound one."

She seemed to find that reasonable. "My sister is in the process of growing our mother's empire beyond the scope of witches," she said. "I assume you know as much?"

Dimitri nodded.

"Standing against Koschei outright is costly," Sasha explained. "He controls too much. He can pull too many strings. I want him banished from the Boroughs. Excommunicated."

"Banished," Dimitri echoed. "An uncommon practice. And very few are even privileged enough to know who Koschei is."

"He'd have to commit a terrible crime," Sasha agreed. "Something the other Borough witches couldn't turn their heads from, even the ones he's already bought."

It was impressive under the circumstances that Dimitri restrained a laugh. "He's already notorious for exactly those crimes," Dimitri informed her. "And perhaps you've noticed? Any Borough witch who speaks against him is quick to lose their seat, or worse."

He didn't feel it necessary to add he was usually the reason for that. How many of Koschei's messes had Dimitri dutifully tidied, leaving no trace of wrongdoing behind? He knew better than anyone that no evidence of his father's indiscretions existed for anyone to find.

"Well," Sasha said, "what could the Boroughs not accept, then?"

"Wrong," The Bridge cut in when Dimitri opened his mouth, startling them both to silence. He crossed one leg spiritedly over the other, admonishing Sasha from his seat opposite hers. "You can't think to blow through a brick wall with one shot, Rusalka, no matter how powerful the weapon."

Dimitri slid Bryn an impatient glance. "I was about to say the same."

"Should've had the quicker draw, then," Bryn advised, half smiling, and Dimitri rolled his eyes, turning back to Sasha.

"The Bridge is right—you don't need a heavy blow. What you need is someone who can dismantle Koschei slowly, brick by brick. Some Borough witches can be intimidated away from his side to yours," he clarified, "while some can be persuaded or bought. I suppose it's possible that some may stand against him purely for the sake of truth," he conceded, grimacing, "or for righteousness. There's a few honorable ones in the bunch."

"Detestably," Bryn agreed, eyeing his nails.

"Well," Sasha said, shrugging. "I'm dead, so. It'll have to be you, Your Highness," she informed Dimitri, who reserved his ample doubts.

"What exactly is your role in this?" Dimitri asked her. "You want me to be the one to turn the Borough witches against my father, fine, but then what will you do?"

"Oh, I have some idea," Sasha said, exchanging a highly discomfiting glance with The Bridge. "After all, what is Koschei without his resources?"

"Still a man with an empire," Dimitri warned.

Another shrug. "Empires have toppled for less. And what is an emperor without heirs? Just a man in a worthless crown, I suspect."

Dimitri paused, considering her response. Namely, the mathematical significance of having no heirs when a son yet remained.

"Are you saying you plan to kill my brother?"

"Would you like me to?" Sasha replied sweetly.

Dimitri allowed himself the luxury of hesitation, though nothing beyond a single beat.

"No. Don't touch Roma," Dimitri warned. "You cross my brother and we're done here. More than done."

Sasha seemed unsurprised; she looked as if she'd expected him to say as much. "No need for threats, Dimitri. Just find a way to poison the well at the Boroughs."

"I'm the only reason the well isn't plenty toxic already," he informed her, stifling a scoff. "I prevented most of the poisoning myself."

"Well, then nobody knows better than you how to undo it," Sasha advised, slate eyes luminous against the dark.

V. 3

(Mourning.)

Roman was sitting in the dark when Dimitri came home late that night. He said nothing when Dimitri entered, merely watching him pause in the doorway. Dimitri, meanwhile, let his gaze travel over the outline of Roman's silhouette beside the open window, folding his arms neutrally over his chest.

"What are you doing here?" Dimitri asked, irritated. "I thought I made it clear to you that your presence was unwanted."

Roman swallowed heavily. "I can't sleep."

"Not my problem."

Dimitri turned to leave, but Roman leaned forward to rest his face in his hands.

"Dima," Roman said, his pleading muffled within the lines of his palms. "Dima, please, I can't sleep there. His room, it's . . ." A swallow, and then again, softer, "Dima, please."

Dimitri went stiff, pausing in place. Even he, in his anger, must have understood why Roman couldn't be alone in the place Lev had once lived.

"Fine," Dimitri said after a moment. "I need to discuss something with you anyway."

Roman lifted his head, instantly guarded. "What is it?"

"Stas Maksimov's vacant seat on the Witches' Boroughs. I'm going to run for it."

It was said entirely without expression, matter-of-factly and with no hesitation, and Roman blinked, taken by surprise.

"Have you spoken with Papa?" he asked.

"No," Dimitri replied.

"But—"

"I'm not asking his permission, or yours. I'm just informing you."

"But Dima, why—"

"My reasoning is none of your business," Dimitri cut in, entirely dispassionate. "I have an interest in being a Borough witch. I've already declared my intent to run. That's all you need to know."

"But—" Roman stared at him. "Papa already has connections with the Boroughs."

"Yes. I know."

"So why would you—"

"Because I want my own," Dimitri said. "Is that so hard to believe?"

"I—"

Yes, Roman wanted to say. Yes, of course it was. Why would Dimitri Fedorov, son of Koschei the Deathless, deign to take on the role of inconsequential Borough witch? Perhaps it would be worth it to be an Elder, to sway votes, but Stas Maksimov's position with the Boroughs had been limited at best. He'd had a vote, but no committee appointments, no substantial influence.

"I would like you to stay out of it," Dimitri said, as Roman took a deep breath, unable to draw meaning from anything his brother was saying. "You've taken very little care to keep your hands clean, Roma, and I prefer not to be viewed as a tool of Koschei's enterprise."

"Surely the Borough witches who know of you will suspect you of ulterior motives either way," Roman said, frowning. "You can't possibly think they'd *want* you to have that seat, do you?"

Dimitri shrugged. "Why should I care what the Borough witches want?"

"You should care what Papa wants."

"Oh, should I?" Dimitri mocked, with a hardened laugh. "Interesting assessment, Roma. And why should I care what *you* want, for that matter?"

"Dima. Please, I know you're . . ." Roman took care not to use the word *angry,* knowing it hadn't gone particularly well the last time. "I know I'm not who you wanted me to be, I know," he determined as a course of action, cautiously moving forward. "I know I've let you down in ways I may never be able to resolve. But you're still my brother," he insisted, rising to his feet, "and—"

"And perhaps if you'd spent more time caring about your brothers than you did yourself," Dimitri cut in, "you'd be asleep in your own bed now, Roma, instead of running to me."

Roman grimaced, letting his nails bite into his palm.

"Do you think I can take even *one breath* without the pain of his loss?" he asked Dimitri, letting them both suffer the unspoken weight of Lev's name. "Do you really believe I'm not drowning, Dima, in my own remorse?"

It took a moment for Dimitri to respond. For a second, Roman almost thought he saw his brother's face soften.

"I believe it." But then, once again, Dimitri Fedorov became a man of stone. "You want my forgiveness to help you breathe, is that it?" he asked, and to that, Roman said nothing. "I have no interest in providing you relief. If you suffocate for what you've done, so be it. You'll have done it well enough without my help."

Roman flinched. "Lev wouldn't want us to be like this with each other, Dima—"

"No, Roma." Dimitri's voice was hard and grim. "Don't delude yourself. Lev wouldn't want to be *dead*. Just because he would die for you, or I would, doesn't mean that either of us ever wished to. You don't get to speak for Lyova's ghost."

There was nothing to say to that, as Dimitri already knew. Roman merely stood in his brother's darkened living room and suffered in silence, forced again to bear the weight of what he'd done.

"Sleep on the couch," Dimitri muttered eventually. "You know where the blankets are."

Roman shook his head. "No. I should go. I shouldn't have come."

Dimitri looked for a moment like he might argue, but then he shrugged, impassive.

"We both have to adjust to life after Lev. Do what you must, Roma, and I'll do what I have to. You aren't nothing to me, you're just . . ." Dimitri trailed off. "We're different people than we were."

Roman nodded numbly, barely registering a sound as Dimitri took the corridor to his bedroom. Dimitri was right, after all. They had never really been close; Koschei had united them and Lev had softened them, but now—without Lev, and with Dimitri's newfound aggravation with their father—there was nothing but blood to keep them in the same room. By the time Dimitri's door fell shut, the sound echoing through the halls of his apartment, Roman finally managed the certainty to leave, making his way down to the street.

He shivered in the cold night air. It would be getting warm again soon, but that was unlikely to improve the chill in his bones. He turned, briskly making his way down the street, and stopped short at the sight of something.

The moonlight glowed on the long, dark hair of a shimmering figure, her grey gaze cold.

"Sasha," Roman said, and swallowed.

She didn't move. Didn't breathe. She was deathly still.

"Sasha," Roman said again, blinking. "Please, I never wanted this to happen—"

She stepped toward him and his hand shot out, crackling unsteadily. Whatever magic it would take to keep a ghost at bay, he no longer possessed it.

How had everything gone so wrong?

"Sasha, please—"

"Who did this to me?" she whispered, her voice as solemn and incorporeal as the icy breeze. "Was it you, Roman?"

"No, Sasha, I wouldn't—"

"Or was it Koschei," she said, her eyes flickering in the dark. "Tell me, son of Koschei, would I be dead if not for him?"

Roman stared at her, and stared.

Slowly, she tilted her head, smiling eerily at him.

"Will Koschei even mourn your loss, Roma Fedorov?" she asked, taking a step toward him, and immediately, Roman stumbled backward, tearing through the night without another glance.

V. 4

(Undead.)

Sasha waited until Roman was out of sight before reaching for her cheek, shaking her head.

"What do we need a 'moonlight glow' body butter for?" she'd asked her sister once when she was a teenager, skeptically eyeing the tub of skin cream. "Why would anyone want to look like this?"

Marya had shrugged. "You never know, Sashenka," she'd replied. "Perhaps some people have a very great wish to look like the undead."

Perhaps they do, Sasha thought now, wiping a small glob of it from her hairline.

She might have overdone it. Possibly. Then again, probably not.

Where would you begin if you wanted to rid a man of everything? Masha had asked her, and the answer had been simple enough.

Wipe out his army. His other two sons.

Dimitri had been easy. He'd needed almost no convincing to turn on his father.

As for the other Fedorov son . . .

Sasha smiled to herself, watching Roman disappear from view.

Then she turned and ventured out into the night, satisfied.

V. 5

(Indisposed.)

There was a polite knock at the door as Lev was counting bills, prompting him to glance up with displeasure. He tensed, shoving aside the tablets, and rose to his feet, pulling the door open.

"Yes?" he asked.

A man in a black suit frowned at him. "Where's Mr. Taylor?"

"Indisposed," Lev replied. "May I take a message?"

The man glanced suspiciously over Lev's shoulder, reaching inside the breast pocket of his suit jacket, and Lev paused the man's hand with a quick motion of his fingers.

"Better not," Lev advised, as the man frowned.

"Who are you?"

"I'm really not any of your business. But I'm very busy, so if you wouldn't mind—"

"I'm Mr. Taylor's security," the man said.

"He doesn't have security," Lev replied, attempting to shut the door, but the man threw out an arm to keep him from succeeding, giving Lev a glare.

"He does," the man corrected. "And unless you'd like to have a problem . . ."

He trailed off pointedly.

"Fine," Lev sighed, rolling his eyes and taking a step back from the threshold. "Come in." He beckoned, gesturing behind him to the living room. "Eric will be right with you."

The man cocked a brow warily. "You expect me to wait out here?"

"Well, it's not your house, is it?"

"It's not yours either."

"It's mine-adjacent," Lev said blandly, adding, "Just have a seat, would you? Take a load off. Answer some emails. Check your stock portfolio, or—" On second thought. "Your crypto account."

The man replied with a scowl.

"It's called hospitality," Lev said. "Just give me five minutes."

"Five minutes," the man warned, "and then I'm coming after you."

"Well, knock first. That's just polite."

Another gloomy stare.

"All right then," Lev muttered to himself, turning on his heel and heading back to Eric's bedroom, which was coincidentally where he'd stashed Eric himself. He slid inside, closing the door behind him, and knelt beside Eric on the floor, grimacing preemptively at the unpleasant chore ahead.

"Hey," he said, flicking Eric's temple. "Wake up."

Eric shot upright with a gasp, lurching forward and choking on the sudden influx of oxygen.

"You," he attempted, struggling. "You—"

"Yes," Lev said. "Me, I know. I was also there."

"You—you fucking *killed* me—"

"Oh, please," Lev said. "Spare me the melodramatics. You're clearly not dead, and even if you were, so what?" He shrugged. "I've died before."

"You're—"

Eric was clutching his chest. If Lev could have conjured the sympathy, he might have bothered lamenting that Eric's lungs were swelling now from temporary atrophy, which probably meant he was in a great deal of discomfort. Unfortunately for Eric Taylor, he wasn't exactly one of Lev's favorite people, so there was little Lev planned to do to ease his pain.

"You . . . Is this—" Eric choked, coughing up, "What is this . . . did Sasha—"

"Don't talk about Sasha."

"But did she—"

"I *said*," Lev snapped, launching forward, "don't talk about her."

Eric froze, eyes wide as he caught the threat of Lev's outstretched hand.

"What are you doing here?" Eric croaked, clutching his throat.

"Taking over," Lev said. "You've been replaced."

"Who says?"

"Marya."

"But I thought—"

"Do you want to take it up with her?" Lev prompted, and Eric blinked.

"No."

"I thought not." Lev paused, then added gruffly, "You have a visitor."

Eric frowned. "Who?"

"Grouchy guy in a suit. I didn't ask for his name."

"Oh. Baron."

Lev arched a brow. "Baron?"

"Security," Eric explained, rubbing his neck. "Hired some recently, considering the types of people I'm working with now." He gave Lev a pointed look, adding, "When I don't answer for a couple hours, Baron pays a visit."

"Well, I'm sure you'll be happy to know he's very devoted to the cause," Lev said drily. "Hence me temporarily waking you."

"*Temporarily?*" Eric echoed, balking. "Does that mean you're going to—"

"Leave you here until such time, when and if it ever occurs, that I need you? Yes."

"But—"

"No security you could hire is going to protect you from me," Lev warned. "Or from Marya."

To his credit, Eric sensed the threat sufficiently enough to suppress a shudder. "Worked, though, didn't it?"

"It did," Lev confirmed, "only because I don't feel like mopping up blood today. Call it self-care, if you will. But believe me," he cautioned again, "I have no interest in interacting with you outside of what's necessary."

"What are you planning to do with me, then?" Eric demanded.

"Handle your business for you." Lev shrugged. "You take too large a cut. A little less greed might have gone a long way."

"I have tuition to pay."

Lev scoffed. "Right. Sure. And this penthouse?"

"Takes money to make money," Eric said. "Besides, this apartment has a doorman. Top-of-the-line security. People come here to do business, they feel safe."

"Noted," Lev said. "But I don't need you. Just your contacts."

Unfortunately, Eric's mouth twitched with something Lev wasn't thrilled to see—disagreement. A spark of mutiny.

"Not true," Eric noted. "You *do* need me. You don't really know what it's like to work with criminals, do you?"

No, he didn't. His brothers did (correction: his brothers *were*, in fact, criminals, depending on who was asked), but for the most part, they'd deliberately kept him out of it. Lev had never actually met with any of his father's dealers or clients on his own; he had done very little, in fact, without oversight from Roman or Dimitri or both.

"You need me," Eric deduced from Lev's silence, and paused a moment before adding, "We could be partners."

"No," Lev said. "Rejected. I don't respect you. Or like you."

"Well, you can't kill me," Eric pointed out. "You need my help."

"I need your cooperation," Lev corrected, "but that I could get however I wanted."

"Maybe you could," said Eric, the cunning little weasel, "but voluntarily would be easiest, don't you think?"

Lev opened his mouth to answer but caught the sound of the door opening behind him, the man named Baron appearing in the doorframe.

"Everything all right in here?" Baron asked, doubtful.

Eric glanced pointedly at Lev, who grimaced.

"Fine," Lev muttered. "Not partners. But something reasonably close."

Eric leaned in, dropping his voice. "I want more money."

"No."

"Then I'm not doing it."

"Fine. You're just as much use to me dead."

Eric hissed his frustration. "What do you need the money for? Are you really that loyal to Baba Yaga?"

There was no possible way Eric Taylor could have known how much Lev Fedorov hated to consider the answer to that question, and yet he seemed satisfied by having hit a pressure point.

"Fine. You can keep the penthouse," Lev said after a beat. "I'm moving in."

Eric made a face. "Really?"

"Mr. Taylor?" Baron cut in, glancing irritably at Lev. "Is everything okay in here?"

Lev gave Eric a warning glance.

"I don't need you alive," he warned under his breath, "but I also don't need you on my conscience. I'm here to serve a purpose. When I'm done, you can have your life back."

"And when will you be done?"

"When I'm fucking done."

"Mr. Taylor?" Baron asked again.

A pause.

Eric pursed his lips, scowling briefly at Lev. "You can have the smaller bedroom."

"Fine," said Lev, who'd been in a tomb until not very long ago.

Eric rose to his feet, satisfied.

"Everything's fine, Baron," he said, flashing Lev a sidelong glare. "We're fine."

Lev clapped a hand on Eric's shoulder, prompting him to flinch.

"Good choice," he said in Eric's ear. "Now smile, look pretty, and tell your little friend to run along."

"You're dismissed, Baron," Eric said, gritting his teeth with annoyance.

Baron hesitated. "Sir, are you—"

Lev conjured a surge of power, letting it dance over his knuckles as he dug his hand into Eric's shoulder.

"*Go,*" Eric gritted out, and Baron nodded.

"Yes, sir," he said, glancing at Lev. "Should I add this gentleman to your approved list, then?"

"Why, thank you, Baron," Lev supplied on their mutual behalf. "That would be *much* appreciated."

V. 6

(Solnyshko.)

"I see you're considerably less dead," Marya noted, taking in Lev Fedorov's glowing look of health as he dropped into the seat opposite hers.

"You really have a way with flattery," Lev informed her drily, and Marya shrugged.

"It's what I'm known for."

Lev's mouth twisted with half a laugh as he pulled a black leather satchel from the pocket of his coat. "Here's the money from the latest sale," he offered, sliding the thick stack of bills across the desk without ceremony. The position suited him, Marya thought; he had an ease with money that was essential to business, in her opinion. He didn't worship it, nor did he fear it. Money was neither torment nor idol. It simply was what it was: a means to an end. "Though, while I'm here—any idea how long I'll have to do this for?"

"Not long," Marya assured him, accepting the pile of cash. "I take it you don't care for the dealer?"

"Who, Eric?" Lev said, making a face. "He's detestable. But not a threat."

"I don't typically go into business with threats," Marya agreed, and for a moment, Lev's mouth quirked slightly, something lingering on his tongue.

"You know," he ventured, "I used to think you were terrifying, but now I think you remind me quite a bit of my brother Dima."

"Oh?" Marya asked, careful not to betray any particular expression. "Well, I'm disappointed to hear I've lost my intrigue."

"No, it's not that. It's just . . . I understand you better now," Lev said. "How you think, I mean."

Marya arched a brow in warning.

"No, I just mean—" Lev chuckled to himself. "You know how in fairy tales, in stories, you never quite understand why a villain is a villain? They're cruel and coarse and ugly, of course, but impossible to understand. But you and Dima, you're the same. You're meticulous, calculating. You're ruthless, but it isn't . . . it isn't who you are. It's just how you work. Easier, I think," he determined with a long glance at her, "for both of you, to simply remove your feelings from the equation."

"Trying to get familiar, Fedorov?" Marya said, confirming nothing.

"No," he assured her with a low laugh. "But now that I know you're like my brother, I know you must have a plan you're not telling me. No one is more careful than Dima," he explained, a point on which Marya wanted, fruitlessly, to disagree. "With him things always seem distant and meaningless at first, and then, in retrospect, they make sense. Things come together."

"Your point?"

Lev shrugged. "You have a plan, but you've only told me the most superficial parts of it. If you were Dima, though," he suggested, leaning forward with a beatific smile on his face, "you'd have told me the rest of it by now."

She gauged him for a second, then rolled her eyes.

"You're a clever little idiot, Lev Fedorov," she told him, and he grinned.

"Might have worked," he said. "Besides, made you like me a bit more, didn't it?"

Internally, Marya sighed. If anyone was like Dimitri Fedorov, she thought silently, it was his youngest brother.

"The plan is very simple," she reminded him. "It's not a secret. We're going to make as much money as we can."

"Yes, but why?" Lev asked.

"Because money talks, Fedorov. It's really not clandestine in the slightest."

"Oh, come on, Marya. You're the woman who nearly killed my brother," he reminded her, "only to die bringing him back to life. Don't tell me your motives are something as uncomplicated as greed."

She did like him, she decided.

Which was deeply unfortunate.

"Not everything is a plot, Solnyshko," she said, and Lev tilted his head.

"Little sun," he translated. "Funny. I always think of my brother as the sun."

Marya paused.

"Do you?" she asked.

"Yes," Lev said, eyeing her expectantly.

She sighed.

"What is it, Fedorov?" she demanded, and his smile broadened.

"You're not telling me something."

"Yes," she agreed, rising to her feet. "I'm not telling you many things. Now, if that's all—"

"You were with my brother when you died," he said, musing it aloud, and she paused in place, hands tightening furtively around the pile of bills. "Now that I know you, I know you would never have done so unless you were . . . distracted. More than distracted."

"Get to the point, Lev," she murmured, not looking at him, and he folded his arms over his chest.

"You know the point, Marya," he said. "You're in love with my brother."

All that irreverent certainty, she thought, recognizing it with a maddening fondness. Clearly it was a Fedorov trait. "You think you know quite a lot, don't you?"

"Actually, I *know* quite a lot," Lev corrected, half smiling, and she was about to grumble her impatience with him when the door opened, revealing Ivan's head in the frame.

"Marya," he said. "A word?"

She nodded. It was as good a time as any.

"Wait here," she said to Lev.

"No 'Wait here, Solnyshko'?" he prompted. "I thought we were friends now."

"Don't push it, Fedorov."

"*Fine,*" he sighed, sliding down in his chair as Marya turned to Ivan, pulling the door shut behind her.

"Yes?" she asked, and Ivan hesitated, eyes darting to the door.

"Are you sure you don't want to tell—"

"She can't know," Marya warned in a low voice. "Not yet. Not until I know he can be trusted."

"Trusted with what?"

As she had with Lev, Marya arched a cautioning brow, and Ivan sighed.

"I just think—"

"I know what you think, Ivan, and truly, I value your thoughts. Always." She closed a hand around his shoulder. "But please. Keep this between us for now, and do not tell my sister."

Ivan nodded slowly, then cleared his throat.

"I just heard something very interesting from Raphael Santos," he said, obediently leaving the issue of Lev Fedorov aside. He would do as she asked; he always did. "Someone is running for Stas's seat on the Witches' Boroughs."

Marya shrugged. "Well, that was bound to happen. Whoever it is, we'll win them over."

"That's the thing," Ivan said. "I think you already have."

Interesting, Marya thought, and then, *Good interesting or bad interesting?* It seemed, by the look on his face, that even Ivan wasn't sure.

"Dimitri Fedorov," Ivan supplied, and Marya, who was almost never surprised, certainly was then.

"Dima?" she echoed, dropping her voice and pulling Ivan away from the room containing the youngest Fedorov son. "But the Fedorovs have never bothered with the Witches' Boroughs before. Why would he need a seat when he could just buy or leverage anything he needed?"

"Right. Hence my informing you as soon as I heard."

Marya permitted a slow nod, still thinking.

"See what you can find out, then," she told him, and gestured him out the door. "I won't be leaving for the night. I'll be fine alone."

"Are you sure?" Ivan asked, and she nodded.

"Go talk to Santos. I'll deal with Lev."

"Solnyshko, you mean?" Ivan said knowingly, and Marya sighed.

"It slipped out," she muttered.

Ivan chuckled, and then, briefly, his humor faltered. He hesitated, then asked her gently, "Could you wish someone better for Sasha?"

An unfair question, to which the answer was obvious.

"We have things to do right now, Ivan," Marya reminded him. "I swear, I'll tell them both eventually, but not yet. Not now. I have things to do." Lev was right, after all. Marya Antonova knew what she was doing, and the money was just the beginning.

Ivan nodded. "I trust you, Marya," he said, and inclined his head, taking his leave as she turned back toward her office.

"Lev," she called, opening the door to find him staring vacantly out the window. "You said your brother always has a plan, right?"

"Yes," he confirmed, turning to look at her. "Though none as good as yours, of course," he purred, sparing her a teasing look of impertinence. "If you ever cared to share your plans with me, I'd be happy to tell you just how much superior they are."

Marya sighed, shaking her head.

"You're impossible, Solnyshko," she told him.

For a moment, his smile flickered and waned.

"So I've heard," he agreed, looking a little lost once more.

V. 7

(Keen Observation.)

"Why would Dima want the Borough seat?"

"Holy hell," Bryn sputtered, promptly knocking over his mug of coffee as Marya sighed, pausing the motion of the liquid before returning it to the cup. "Thanks," he muttered under his breath, and she shrugged.

"Think of time as a series of threads," she said. "Strings to be plucked at will. A few seconds here and there isn't difficult—time has its own rules. The way it goes slowly when you're waiting for something," she explained, "or how it speeds up when you're running behind. It's all very easy to toy with when you know how it works."

Bryn stared at her for a second, his fingers twitching apprehensively. She could see him discreetly feeling around for them, though she figured he was too proud to chance making a mistake in front of her.

"Try it," she invited. "You have witch magic now. You should be able to feel them."

He eyed her warily, then stroked his thumb over something in the air, sending a small, barely noticeable ripple between them.

"Oh," said The Bridge.

"You're welcome," Marya said, falling into the seat across his desk. "Though, I can smell that," she said with a gesture to his mug, "and frankly, it's a little early in the day. Which isn't magic, by the way," she assured him wryly. "Just keen observation."

Bryn made a face.

"What do you want?" he said gruffly, looking as if he didn't particularly want to be helpful. She knew him, though. He couldn't be entirely useless—she'd already offered him something without a price, and his fae blood would ultimately sway him to her favor.

"Why is Dimitri Fedorov running for a seat with the Borough witches?" Marya asked again. "I told you to encourage him to turn on his father, not to take up some progressive new politics and waste both our time."

"I've done nothing of the sort," Bryn scoffed. "Whatever the Fedorov prince is up to is entirely his making."

"I doubt that," Marya said, and eyed him. "You're keeping something from me."

"Yes," Bryn said. "Though, a small thing, I'm sure."

"I'm sure," Marya sighed doubtfully, shaking her head. "Bridge, you exhaust me."

"I could," he offered. "If you wanted."

"Brynmor." A brief glance skyward. "There isn't a world in existence where you'd know what to do with me."

"Are you saying Dimitri Fedorov would?" he asked neutrally.

"I imagine I'll have to find out, considering you're no help at all."

She rose to her feet, letting her gaze flick knowingly to what he kept in his desk drawer.

"Time can be frozen, too," she informed him. "Temporarily slowed. It's one method of preservation."

She watched him sigh, concealed a smile to herself, and turned to the door.

"Wait," Bryn groaned unwillingly after her, grumbling it at her back. "You're doing this on purpose, Antonova."

She spun, the portrait of innocence. "Doing what, Bridge?"

"You know I can't let a favor go unpaid." His mouth was a grim line. "Though, at present I'm having difficulty finding reasons to take your side."

"Has Dimitri given you any reason to take his?"

"Who says there are only two sides?" Bryn countered, and Marya narrowed her eyes, somewhere between concerned and annoyed.

"Ask Fedorov about your sister," Bryn advised, with a bit too much confidence, in Marya's opinion. That could only mean trouble.

"Which sister?" Not that she had to ask.

Bryn shrugged. "See what Dimitri says," he offered. "If he says nothing, then you know he can't be trusted."

She bristled. "That's hardly a helpful answer."

"Isn't it, though? If I tell you what I know, that's easy. But this way, you get two answers. Whose side Dimitri Fedorov's on," he said, lifting a vacant palm to weigh the options, "and also, who's on *your* side."

"I could do without the games, Bridge." She paused. "But fine."

"You love the games, Marya," Bryn reminded her. "Otherwise you'd find a better place for your secrets than my office, don't you think?"

"You don't have my secrets. You're just a very useful set of eyes."

"True. Though I have other useful parts."

She rolled her eyes, dismissive. "If Dimitri comes to see you again, tell me."

"And if I don't?"

"I worry about your masochism, Bridge. Don't you have anything better to do than suffer my threats?"

His smile twitched. "No. You know that."

"Well," she determined, leaning over his desk. "How fast do you think time goes when you're suffocating?"

"Enlighten me," he drawled, inching lasciviously toward her, and in response she slid a perfunctory thumb over his larynx, pulling the strands of time further and further, notch by notch. She watched his eyes widen, chest stilling with lack of motion.

Then, gradually, she released him, letting him take a gasping breath.

"Why do you like witches so much?" she asked as he lurched forward, bracing his palms on the desk. "Surely you can't enjoy being surrounded by power you can't possibly possess."

"I don't," he confirmed with a rasp, clearing his throat. "But I learn more about you every time you use yours. Who's gotten you so tense?" he croaked, tilting his head. "Someone close to you, I imagine, or you wouldn't have bothered coming to me first before Dimitri." He paused, observing her like he could read his answer in the whites of her eyes. "Your mother, perhaps?"

Marya felt her mouth tighten. "Of course not."

"Have I struck a nerve? Everyone's got mommy problems," Bryn assured her, shrugging. "Which isn't magic. Just an easy guess."

Marya sighed. "Bridge, have I mentioned you exhaust me?"

"Once again, Marya, I could—"

"Stop." She slid a finger through the air, lacing his lips together. "I hate to miss my parting witticism, but truly. My patience is thin."

He smiled at her suggestively. She rolled her eyes.

"I heard that," she said, but walked away, leaving him behind.

She had questions to be answered. Fae lawyers and their games would have to wait.

V. 8

(Détente.)

Dimitri wasn't surprised to find Marya Antonova waiting in his bedroom once again, perched at the edge of his mattress when he walked in.

"Masha," he said neutrally. "Have you decided to help me, then?"

Today, her dress was structured and navy, her hair twisted up in an elegant knot. This was Marya Antonova, businesswoman. Witch of Significance. She rose to her feet, her stiletto heels tapping over the floor as she approached him.

"Dima," she said. "What are you plotting?"

He stepped inside the room, closing the door behind him.

"Why would I be plotting?" he asked, and her mouth pursed slightly with disapproval.

"Don't fuck with me, Dima. Why are you trying to take Stas's place?"

Her expression was stiff, suspicious. He stepped closer.

"I'm not," he said, and leaned toward her, feeling her pulse race from the vial resting against his chest. "You know perfectly well it's Stas who took *my* place," he reminded her, glorying in the way her breath stuck sharply in her throat.

"You know what I mean, Dima," she warned, and though he hadn't meant to be coy, he shrugged.

"I thought you decided there was no need to discuss our secrets? By that logic, my business with the Witches' Boroughs is none of yours."

She scrutinized him openly, puzzling him out without any attempt at discretion. One of these days, he thought with a surge of unexpected hurt, perhaps they might actually talk.

"You're doing this without your father's knowledge, aren't you?" she guessed. "Certainly without his permission."

Dimitri said nothing, and her tongue slipped carefully between her berry lips.

"Are you no longer a loyal son of Koschei, Dimitri Fedorov?"

A thud of silence.

A pulse.

Then his arm shot out, snaking around her waist and pulling her closer.

"I told you, Marya Antonova," he said in a low voice, observing with some triumph her struggle not to soften at his touch. "I told you I was my own man. I told you I would have gone to you if you'd asked me. I told you I would love you until my dying day. Did you think I was a liar?"

Her gaze gentled on his mouth. She was always too immovable to be startled.

"No," she said. "No, Dima, you've never been a liar."

"Then believe this, Masha: I choose you. I will always choose you." He tightened his grip on her, letting his fingers spread across her waist. Taking her space and making it his. "This, with the Witches' Boroughs, it's for you," he said quietly, with the weight of all their secrets gone unshared.

"It's obviously a plot, Dima," she sighed, though she rested her hands flat against his chest, contemplating him beneath her palms. "Who are you conspiring with?"

"Your sister. Sasha." Marya blinked; clearly, she hadn't actually expected him to confess. "She wants to take my father down," Dimitri clarified, "and I said I would help her. I'll discredit him, one Borough witch at a time, and gain my own empire. My own life. One that, one day, might be worthy of you." He bent his head, touching his lips to her forehead. "Someday, Masha," he murmured, "I will have done enough to give you everything you deserve, and perhaps then it will be enough to bring you back to me."

He felt her breath falter, her frame falling still in his arms.

Then she turned her head, resting her lips near the side of his neck.

"Dima," she said softly. "You know Stas never took your place."

He swallowed, saying nothing.

"How could he?" she pressed him. "You were all I ever wanted. From the day you told me you loved me, there has never been anyone else."

It wasn't simply a confession; he understood that much.

It was an offering.

"What are you saying?" he asked, and she pulled away, looking up at him.

"That Koschei wasn't the only one who did this to us," she said. "My mother is hardly innocent."

There was a strange note in her voice. New. Troubling. "Masha."

"I thought my mother would never lie to me. Not to me. I thought we were one in all things." There was a hardness to her expression, a shadow beneath her eyes, something that had been weighing on her. "Now, it seems everything has always been a lie. A lie that I was stupid enough to believe. To give up everything for."

She paused.

"This life," she said slowly, "this world, it's a curse. You were right, Dima. What they want from us, it's a sickness. A burden."

For a moment, Dimitri considered the wisdom of saying nothing.

But he couldn't help himself from murmuring, "My brother is gone."

Perhaps in saying so he hadn't really confessed to much, but she looked up at him with sympathy. Then she stiffened again to purpose.

"If you're going to use your position in the Boroughs to discredit your father, I'll help you. I have resources just as you do, connections of my own. But," she said, fixing her gaze on his, "on one condition."

He waited.

"When you win," she said slowly, "we burn it down. We set the match and light it." At his questioning glance, she clarified, "We leave behind the kingdoms we kept for Koschei and Baba Yaga, and together, we build something new."

He stared down at her, stunned. "You mean that?"

"Yes." Her expression was cold. "We didn't suffer purely for your father's errors, Dima. We both suffered, because both our parents are selfish fools. So," she ventured, tracing her fingertips over the column of his throat, "no more. We'll build something together, Dima." Her hand stopped just shy of the vial at his neck, pressing into the cavern of his sternum. "My mother would be nothing without me, just as your father is nothing without you. Together, we could be everything."

It wasn't remotely the outcome he'd expected. "Are you sure?"

She nodded. "Don't tell Sasha," she warned, and he frowned, but nodded slowly. "Let this be between us for now, but let me help you." She slid her arms around his neck, pulling him closer. Drawing him into her. "Let me love you, Dima," she told him softly, "the way I should have done twelve years ago. With nothing in my way."

It was an offer he'd never hoped to receive; one he'd never dream of refusing. Dimitri took a ragged, capitulating breath, bending toward her with unseemly, unequivocal devotion. "I should have fought for you then, Masha," he said. "We shouldn't have wasted so much time—"

"The past is nothing. We are everything." Her hand curled securely around the back of his neck, anchoring him. He felt a spark beneath his fingertips, a flood of his own magic that had been dormant since he'd suffered at her hands. He marveled that for him, she could be crime and punishment both; vice and virtue all at once. "Dimitri Fedorov, I already gave you my useless heart. Now, have everything else that matters. Have my loyalty, my right hand. Have everything that was once my mother's," Marya offered fiercely, "and give me everything you once swore to Koschei. Give me all of you, take everything of me, and let's see who stands against us then."

She was soft and unbending, delicate and impossible in his hands. She was power, and powerful, and full of little intricacies that he felt with a sudden thrill of fear he'd never fully know because it would be like counting the stars, like naming grains of sand, and there could never possibly be enough time for any of it. He could feel all her little fissures, the cracklings of fury and desperation underneath, and he reached up to tug her hair loose, letting it fall gently around her shoulders with a rose-scented sigh, her lips parting slowly. How many nights would it take to know her again, to know her at all? At least another, and another, and another. And then forever after that.

"I've loved you through so much distance it seems strange to hold you now," he said quietly. "Like something could so easily take you from me."

"Never again, Dima." Her fingers toyed with the buttons of his shirt while his found the zipper of her dress. "I thought I was weak for you, Dima, but I was wrong. I'm Marya Antonova," she told him, meeting his eye, "and I am loved by Dimitri Fedorov, and for that, I could never be weak."

"And I'm the man who possesses Marya Antonova's heart." His breath quickened as Marya's hands traversed his chest. "Nothing will ever stop me."

The kiss between them was another promise, the swearing of an oath. Her lips were sure and supple against his as he traced the iron notches of her spine, hands fitted around the perilous blades of her shoulders.

"I have money," she told him, murmuring it as his lips wandered to her neck. "However much you need."

"I know which men will turn on my father," Dimitri said, sliding her dress down her arms to let the fabric pool at her feet. "Which ones we can use."

"Good," she gasped, pulling him with her as they tumbled back against his bed. "And," she said, and paused, a little hint of guilt rising in her cheeks, "I also know which ones I've already turned against you."

Dimitri stopped, pulling back to frown at her. "What?"

She shrugged.

"I'm Marya Antonova," she said. "I'm terrifying. Some things just *are*."

He rolled his eyes, rolling onto his back and pulling her with him.

"How long have you been working against me?" he asked as she slid her hands over his bare torso, tracing the crevices of him.

"Too long," she confessed, and kissed him defiantly as proof, tasting like wild euphoria and the sweetness of disaster as he tightened his fingers in her hair.

"Does this mean you'll help me with Lev?" he asked her, and she paused, lips bitten and cheeks flushed, painted brilliantly from a palette of incandescence.

"One thing at a time, Dima," she said. "Do you trust me?"

His hands curled around her arms as he considered her question. He'd slept for twelve years with the memory of her face, observing his reels of memories of the girl she'd once been and projecting the woman she might become, and to look at her now, it was strange to realize how much he'd been mistaken. He'd misremembered her—not the color of her eyes or the shape of her mouth, but the heat of being close to her. The details of her had been accurate, but his memories of her were softer, filled with longing. Now that he held her, though, he remembered the truth: that Marya Antonova was as mighty as a strike of lightning, and as difficult to hold. She was as captivating as fear, as undeniable as hunger, and he had loved her then—and loved her now—for all the tremor and the fury that she was.

He slid her onto her back, shifting down the length of the bed to settle himself below her hips.

"Do I trust you, Masha?" he echoed, fighting a bitter laugh. "More than I should."

His hands dug into her thighs and she let out a gasp, fingers twisting in the roots of his hair.

"Good," she said, and shivered, closing her eyes.

V. 9

(A Koschei Problem.)

Roman had been seeing Sasha Antonova's ghost all over Manhattan.

In the wake of Dimitri's rejection and his father's request for him to lie low, his magic still functionally unrecovered, Roman had been doing very little in the vein of business operations or even witchery itself. He'd mostly occupied himself by going for walks around the city, trying to keep out of trouble. Unfortunately, it seemed trouble was continuously finding him.

Roman saw Sasha's face in reflections of buildings, always turning to find nobody was there. He avoided pools of water after seeing her once in a fountain installation in Central Park, discovering her grey gaze peering over his shoulder with a jolt. Each time he saw her she had a ghastly pallor, a rueful little smile on her face, and she always said variations of the same thing.

Who did this to me, Roma?

After a few weeks of it, Roman was determined to do something.

He stormed over to Brynmor Attaway's office, bursting through the doors.

"She's haunting me," he announced without preamble, and Bryn looked up with obvious irritation.

"I'm with a client, Roman," Bryn said, gesturing to the suited pair sitting opposite him. "You can wait. My apologies," he added to the others. "Some of my other clients are, as you can see, seriously disturbed."

"Ah," said one of the men, visibly uncomfortable, and Roman chewed a grimace, backing out of the office and pacing irritably beside the door.

Ten minutes later, the two suits walked out, eyeing Roman with conspiratorial interest—difficult to tell these days if he might be the CEO of some new tech disruptor, a leverageable product of corporate nepotism, the latest pitiable victim of a retaliatory #MeToo investigation (and therefore a cautionary tale that could easily happen to anyone!), or just clinically deranged—as he shoved past them into the office.

"How do you people always know where to find me?" Bryn demanded before Roman could speak. "I *do* have a day job, you know—"

"Sasha Antonova," Roman said, mumbling with a furtive glance over his shoulder for fear it might unintentionally summon her from the void. "She's haunting me."

"Sounds wild," Bryn said, leaning back to prop his feet on the edge of his desk. "Any particular reason why?"

"Because I—" Roman swallowed. "I killed her."

"*No,*" Bryn gasped. "You, Fedorov? *Killing* someone? That just doesn't sound like you *at all*—"

"That's—Stop it. It's my fault she's dead," Roman muttered, pacing again, this time in front of Bryn's desk. "If I hadn't . . . if this hadn't happened, if I'd never—" He broke off, gritting his teeth. "If my father hadn't—"

"Your father," Bryn plucked out from Roman's unintelligible

rant with interest, drolly tapping his mouth. "He's responsible for quite a lot, isn't he?"

Roman grimaced. "He's . . . It's not important. The point is—"

"The point is," Bryn cut in, tucking his hands behind his head with a sense of leisurely detachment, "that Koschei is the one who made the deal with Baba Yaga, isn't he? Not you. Certainly not me."

In Roman's bristled silence, Bryn pondered aloud, "I simply wonder what *he's* doing about your little demon problem, considering that last I checked, I'm simply a handsome third-party observer." He dropped his arms, leaning forward to brace them expectantly on his desk. "You're hardly innocent, Roman, we both know that, but if anyone has Sasha Antonova's blood on his hands, I think we can agree it's Koschei the Deathless."

"He's—" Roman flinched at the finality of the deduction he'd already tried several times not to make. That way, he felt certain, lay madness. Whatever madness he didn't already possess. "I can't bring this to him right now."

"And why not?"

"He's . . . busy." Roman scratched at his arms, suddenly itchy and uncomfortable, as if the air itself had turned on him. "You wouldn't understand, Bridge."

"You keep saying that," Bryn remarked, "and yet you're still here seeking my counsel, aren't you?"

"Yes, but only because I just—"

Then Roman looked up, catching a blur of iridescence from his periphery, and reeled backward in alarm.

"There!" His heart thudded in warning—a drastic *fuckfuck-fuck*—as he pointed to the ghost of Sasha Antonova. She stood behind Bryn, just over his shoulder, materialized from nothing with that same chilling smile on her face. "Bridge, do you see her?"

"Hm?" Bryn asked, turning over his shoulder. "See who?"

"Roma," Sasha's ghost whispered mournfully, "son of Koschei, who did this to me?"

"Jesus, Bridge, don't fuck with me." Roman shrank back and felt behind him for the wall, wondering how Bryn could sit there so unaffected, so insidiously nonplussed despite the dead girl breathing down his neck. "Do you really not see her? She's *right there*—"

"Mm, yes, hello Sasha," Bryn said with a roll of his eyes, waving slightly to the right of where she was standing. "Should I fetch the three of us some tea, or—?"

"Roman Fedorov," Sasha's ghost whispered, her dark hair falling into her bloodshot eyes as she stepped toward him, lifting one hand, one malevolent finger. "Help me, I can't rest. Who did this?" Her voice had an echo, like the room had swallowed him up. "Who did this to me, Roma?"

Roman forced his eyes shut. "Stop, stop, *stop*—"

"Roman," Bryn said, "if you're going to have a meltdown, I'd prefer you not do it on the carpet."

"BRIDGE," Roman shouted. "She's, she's going to kill me, she's—"

Sasha stretched her hand out, stroking the air to reach for him, and Roman felt a primal buzzing in his ears, in his limbs, dissonance in crescendo. All his senses, in unison: *run.*

"I have to go," he choked out, fumbling for the door handle behind him.

"Well, bye, then," Bryn called after him. "Though, again, this really does seem like a Koschei problem, doesn't it?"

Roman let the door slam in his wake as he hurried out of the office, hands shaking as he went.

V. 10

(Happy Haunting.)

"You're very terrifying," Bryn commented to Sasha after the door had fallen shut, savoring the midday diversion of Roman sprinting doggedly away. "Look at him, he's totally unhinged."

"Hm? Oh yes, I know," Sasha agreed, touching up her makeup in the reflection of her compact mirror before promptly snapping it shut, replacing it in her pocket. "Thanks for agreeing to do this, Bridge."

"My pleasure," Bryn assured her, passing her an ironic salute as he returned his attention to his files. "Happy haunting, Rusalka."

"Always," Sasha replied, lips twitching with placation as she disappeared.

V. 11

(The Brooklyn Witch.)

Of all the Borough witches, Dimitri and Marya agreed that Jonathan Moronoe, head of the Brooklyn Borough, posed the best candidacy for their own most valuable pawn. A parasocially inspiring marvel, Jonathan Moronoe had managed, somehow, to be untainted by either Baba Yaga or Koschei the Deathless, and had run a routinely successful campaign based almost exclusively on the basis of his integrity.

It was a sad fact of life, in the opinions of both Dimitri Fedorov and Marya Antonova, that men of morals were astoundingly easy to manipulate.

"Let me get this straight," Jonathan said, glancing between Dimitri and Marya. "You're running for the Borough seat in order to . . ." (Understandable pause for bemusement.) "Discredit Koschei and Yaga both? I don't—" He broke off, frowning. "What exactly is the platform for your campaign?"

"Criminal reform, of course," Marya supplied, smiling. She slid a thin leather book across the desk to the Borough Elder. "This book contains a log of every illegally obtained creature Koschei the Deathless has ever trafficked in. Surely this defies a number of Borough laws, doesn't it?"

"Who's your source?" Jonathan asked, frowning.

"An honest man," Marya said simply. "Like you. And Dimitri."

"Yaga is also selling magical drugs to the non-magical community," Dimitri contributed, passing Jonathan a ledger of sales. "Which she does not have Borough permission to do."

"Well, of course she doesn't, as Koschei would make certain to stop her," Jonathan said, looking somewhere between frustrated and puzzled by having to say so aloud. "You two know better than anyone the reasons both Yaga and Koschei get away with defying Borough laws."

"Yes. And isn't it time that came to an end?" Marya posed, with a neutral glance at Dimitri.

"With us involved in the Boroughs' decisions," Dimitri explained on their mutual behalf, "we can end Koschei's influence over the other witches. Thus, we're precisely what you need in order to address magical crime across all the Boroughs."

"But—" Jonathan stared at them. "But everyone knows who you are. You're Baba Yaga's enforcer," he said to Marya, becoming uneasy the moment she failed to deny it. "There isn't a witch on this council that hasn't encountered you at one time or another. Unfavorably, I might add."

"Well, I'm not the one taking the seat, am I?" Marya said, shrugging. "The seat belongs to Dimitri—or, at least, it will with your support. And once he holds it, we can give you ample evidence against both Koschei and Yaga. Enough to bring them down several times over."

"And all I have to do is . . ." Jonathan stared at the ledger. The book. The ledger. The book. Then he glanced between them, presumably dismayed by his own failing to see the punch line, or else the other shoe. "What *exactly* do you want me to do?"

"Vote your conscience," Dimitri assured him easily.

"Your conscience *does* tell you corruption in the Witches' Boroughs is wrong, doesn't it?" Marya prompted. "And only one candidate can help you end it."

"And you can really do this," Jonathan said slowly, "*together,* with no . . . guilt? No remorse, even? I thought you both hated each other."

Dimitri and Marya exchanged a glance.

"*Hate* is a strong word," Dimitri said to her. "Don't you think, Masha?"

"Oh, of course, Dima," Marya agreed, "though *vengeance* is somewhat stronger."

They smiled at each other.

Then they turned back to Jonathan.

"We'll bring down Koschei and Yaga," Dimitri concluded. "Don't worry about our consciences, Moronoe, only your own. All you have to do is vote for me," he explained again, "and convince the rest of your Borough's witches to do the same. That's all we ask."

"No strings?" Jonathan asked tentatively.

"What strings?" Marya said. "Move as you wish. We all want the same things."

"Safety," Dimitri contributed. "Sustainability."

"Peace," Marya suggested emphatically, and Jonathan sighed, relenting.

"Fine. Then I'll see to it you have Brooklyn."

"Excellent," Marya said, sweeping up the ledger and the log in one smooth motion before tucking them both into the pocket of her coat. "We'll reconvene when Dimitri's won, then."

Jonathan gave a guarded nod, and with another wave of her hand, Marya and Dimitri were back in Dimitri's loft, facing each other in the living room.

"Did you hear him, Dima?" Marya asked, slowly undoing the buttons of her coat. "You have Brooklyn."

"Oh, I heard, Masha," Dimitri replied, casually undoing his tie before discarding it. "I wonder, how should I spend the rest of my day, hm?"

She let her coat fall to the floor with a smile, letting her dress slide down after it.

"Perhaps you'd like to explore your dominion in Manhattan," she murmured, and he took her in his arms, kissing her until the vial of her heart sang *yesyesyes* against his chest.

"Perhaps I would," he agreed, and tugged her down to the sofa, his hands searing-hot on her hips.

V. 12

(Loss.)

After a few weeks, Sasha had picked up a habit of taking a little time out of each day to plague Roman Fedorov to festering hysteria. Before long, it was as compulsory an act as brushing her teeth or washing her face: breakfast, lunch, scaring Roman half out of his wits, dinner. All regularly scheduled activities. All equally contributing to the improvement of Sasha's health and well-being.

As with most habits, she didn't expect to see results immediately. She anticipated months of haunting, even beginning to daydream in her free time about how to traumatize him in ways most befitting the atmospheric advantages of particular holidays or inclement weather, e.g., on Ash Wednesday and/or thunderstorms. Thus, she was surprised, and perhaps a bit disappointed, to find that Roman was in the midst of full psychological disintegration well before she'd expected to see her plans bear fruit.

She'd been waiting to alarm Roman in his living room one day when Koschei suddenly entered the apartment without warning, prompting Sasha to remain concealed in the corner. It was the first time she could remember having seen Koschei in the flesh, though there was no question who else he could be.

"What is Dima doing running for the Witches' Boroughs?" Koschei demanded of his middle son, who'd been in the midst of twitchily pacing his living room. (The choicest opportunity for weeping, Sasha's current goal, had not yet arrived.) "Has he spoken of his plans to you?"

"What? No," Roman said, though Sasha had been watching him long enough to know that was an utterance of total, irredeemable falsehood. He'd recently begun muttering about it to himself in his sleep. "I knew he was considering a campaign," Roman amended, apparently realizing his father could sense the flimsy edges of a lie, "but I don't know why he's doing it. He's as angry with me as he is with you, Papa, and he tells me nothing." That, however, was true. Even if Sasha had no knowledge of Dimitri's plans, she would know he had not spoken to Roman in weeks. Aside from The Bridge, Roman's only company was Sasha—very depressing news considering she was driving him into an early grave.

"My sources tell me nothing either," Koschei growled, looking almost as unsettled as Roman. "Santos is all but missing; someone's hiding him, I'm sure of it. Moronoe must know something, he's bolder than ever—he had one of my dealers publicly removed from his Borough just yesterday. And I swear, that bodyguard of Marya Antonova's has been hovering like a fly for weeks—"

"What do you want from me, then?" Roman suddenly snapped, startling both Sasha and his father with the outburst. "You told me to stay out of your way and I *am*, am I not?"

"Well, I need you now, Romik. I need you to find out what's going on with Dima," Koschei said, and Roman looked up, eyes wild, to face his father with the full extent of madness Sasha had been so optimistic he'd one day achieve.

"I have my own problems, Papa!" Roman shouted, voice rattling the walls as his knuckles sparked, a mix of uncontrollable rage and unreliable magic. "I'm not here to . . . to *spy* on your favorite son—"

"Roma, you're hysterical," Koschei noted, to which Sasha stifled a snort of laughter. "What's wrong with you?"

"What's wrong with *me*?" Roman demanded. "This is your fault, Papa! *You* killed her, not me! You," he muttered to himself, "and your deal with that demon Baba Yaga—"

"Romik—"

"Just *go*," Roman snarled, nails biting briefly into his jaw as he dragged a hand over his face. "If Dima's failed you, then perhaps it's what you deserve."

Koschei stood dumbly, staring at his son amid a heavy, loaded silence. Even Sasha was struck by it, the tone of disrespect and incisive bitterness that none of them, not for a second, would ever have used against their mother. Not without fear, or staggering remorse.

"Romik," Koschei said eventually. "You've never spoken to me this way."

"Well, then perhaps it's been a long time coming," Roman said, and shoved past his father for the front door, letting it slam behind him.

Koschei stood in silence, contemplating his losses, and mentally, Sasha made a note of self-congratulations. She was, after all, well ahead of schedule.

Wipe out his army.

Dimitri was gone. Roman was all but useless.

Sasha nearly smiled to herself, watching Koschei the Deathless begin to cradle his own head in his hands, until suddenly, an uninvited thought slid into the back of her mind: None of it would do her any good. Her mind whispered to her in Lev's voice, laughing as only he could laugh. No sliver of Roman's sanity would repair the gaping holes in her heart. No weary sigh from Koschei would return the air to her lungs. *None of it,* Lev's memory murmured to her, *will ever bring me back.*

Still, she thought firmly, Koschei's loss was one step closer to matching the depths of her own.

Someday, she thought, *you will know I had a hand in this.*

But not today.

Not yet.

Not until there's no coming back for you.

Then she slid silently out of the air, moving on to the next of her compulsory tasks as the shadows shifted mournfully around her.

V. 13

(Darkness.)

The witch called Baba Yaga was beginning to wonder if she had made a terrible mistake when she allowed her daughter to come back to the land of the living without first making her whole. She had once known her eldest daughter's heart as well as she knew her own, but now, for the first time, Marya was secretive; distracted.

Marya had only been that way once before, and the same person who held her heart now had possessed it then, too.

"You've been seeing Dima, haven't you?" Yaga said to her daughter's back one night while Marya was working, bent once again over the tablets they'd both worked so hard to design.

Marya didn't answer, and Yaga sighed, taking the seat beside her daughter.

Implied: *What else are you keeping from me?*

Unspoken: *For the first time since you were born, Masha, I feel terribly alone.*

Aloud: "What is happening to us, Mashenka?" Yaga asked, watching Marya flinch as Yaga reached out to touch her cheek, hand faltering in the air. "Are you angry with me?"

For a moment, it looked like Marya still might not answer.

But then she said, voice low, "I'm beginning to wonder, Mama, if you still have the stomach for this."

Yaga frowned. "For our business?"

"Not just our business." Marya's gaze didn't rise from her work. "I notice you've made no effort to put Koschei in his place."

Yaga paused, surprised. "Masha, the best revenge we have against Koschei is our success. And we are succeeding," she reminded her, referencing the tablets beneath Marya's fingers. "Every day that our business grows is another we rise above Koschei."

"Yes, but is that enough?" Marya asked, and looked up sharply, her dark eyes fixed on Yaga's. "What about retribution, Mama? What about making him pay for what his enmity has cost us?"

Seeing her daughter's anger, Yaga softened and sighed, reaching out to pull her eldest child into her arms.

"Hatred is a curse, Mashenka," she said to Marya's dark hair, breathing in the familiar rosewater scent of her. "At my age, you gain a little wisdom. In my experience," she murmured soothingly, "holding on to hatred only comes back to haunt you."

She waited for Marya to sigh a little; to make a joke, to say *Mama, you're not so old,* and take comfort from her arms, as she usually did. Instead, Marya grew stiff and detached, her voice like a cold wind from a distance.

"I'm glad your wisdom gives you peace, Mama," Marya said. "Even if it came at the price of my pain."

Yaga blinked, feeling her daughter pull away from her, and stared with paralyzing disquietude as Marya's eyes flashed in the light of their workshop.

"You know, you forget the sort of darkness this business requires," Marya said, casting an eye over the tablets in front of them. "You haven't had to run it yourself in quite a long time."

"No, I haven't," Yaga warily agreed. "I've always had you, Masha. I do not forget that."

"Yes," Marya said. "You do forget. You forget that while I have always been on your side, you have never truly been on mine." She glanced up stiffly. "We have both only ever worked for you, haven't we, Mama?"

"Masha," Yaga said, troubled by her daughter's tone, but Marya shook her head.

"I kept your hands clean for twelve years, Baba Yaga," said Marya Antonova. "But now, these filthy hands are taking what's theirs."

She rose to her feet, and oddly, only one thought occurred to Yaga then. Her own words coming back to her, sharp and bitter and full of slashes, stinging her chest with the irony.

My daughters are diamonds. Nothing is more beautiful. Nothing shines brighter.

Nothing will break them, and then, with a twist of the knife: *Because I am the one who taught them how to be this cold.*

"I hope your peace serves you well," Marya said, "because I am no longer willing."

And then, with a wave of her hand, she gathered the tablets from the workshop, taking them with her as she went.

V. 14

(Do Not Call Her.)

As far as roommates went, there were worse ones than Eric Taylor. Largely because he spent most of his time in pseudo-forced captivity, of course, but still—Lev figured plenty of hostages would be happy to make a fuss if given the opportunity. Not Eric. He seemed to be enjoying his role, for whatever reason. It only occurred to Lev much later that perhaps Eric hadn't had enough friends in his life to recognize that Lev technically wasn't one.

"How was the meeting?" Eric would ask when Lev arrived back at the penthouse, laden down with dirty money he would eventually pass over to Marya. What she was doing with it, he had no idea. She was intensely secretive, but it made no difference to him. If there was one thing Lev Fedorov trusted, it was that Marya Antonova knew how to get what she wanted, whatever that was.

"Fine," Lev would say, because it always was. There wasn't a lot of sophistication in magical drug dealing; certainly not any more than any errand he'd run for his father. The product, as far as Lev could see, was flawless. The buyers were addicts. Complexities were slim. "Another day, another client."

That, and another visit to Marya.

"You're good at this," Marya noted, dark gaze watching Lev slide the money across the desk, as he usually did. "Why do you think that is?"

"People seem to like me," Lev said, as Marya's mouth quirked.

"Not as universal a trait as you might think," she informed him.

"Maybe not," he agreed, "but then again, I've never cursed anyone half to death, so why shouldn't they like me?"

She laughed. She was the sort of person who could laugh at history; discard it, throw it away, never at its mercy. "True."

He didn't ask when he could see his brothers. It wasn't Marya who was preventing him from doing so, truth be told. He didn't ask about his father, either. Lev, unlike Marya Antonova, wasn't so quick to part with the truth. Falsity had never been his strength, and he doubted he could lie to them, successfully or not.

He did, however, ask her frequently about The Plan.

"What are you doing?" he would press her. "With the money. Why work so hard to grow this business when you don't even seem to care what it brings you?"

"Don't be ridiculous, Solnyshko," Marya would say. "In this world, money is a far more compelling magic than witchcraft. The more of it you have, the more untouchable you are—it doesn't need to be *for* something, it just is."

"Maybe so," Lev would say, "but not for you."

And she would shake her head and send him back to Eric, adding only the promise that he would understand everything clearly soon enough.

"Consider it a favor," she would say. "Someday, you will know why I have done all of this, and you will know it was worth it, worth everything. Someday, when you replay all your little questions knowing what you know, you'll feel silly for even asking. But for now, I think having all the answers would simply weigh you down."

She wasn't unkind about it, but she was firm. Not unlike Sasha, who would have had to learn it from somewhere. When the thought of Sasha's origins would inevitably occur to Lev, he would think longer of her, of the future she'd said they were supposed to have, and then to claw himself out of his misery he would take careful stock of his assets and think: Well, at least Eric Taylor wasn't the worst roommate in the world.

Most of the time, actually, Eric was stoned.

"You witches," Eric said deliriously, setting a tablet onto his tongue like an after-dinner mint or lozenge. "You're all totally fucked."

"Funny, coming from you," Lev said over his pad thai, taking a sip of his beer. He'd tried the Yaga tablets once himself out of curiosity and relived his night with Sasha, moment by moment, over and over for what felt like a thousand crushing days. He later discovered it had only been about two hours. "You think your parents are proud of what you've accomplished?"

"Mine don't give a shit." Eric smiled faintly. "Nobody does."

"A tragic backstory doesn't make you sympathetic," Lev said.

"Nope," Eric agreed. "Some people are just shitty, don't you think?"

"Yes," Lev agreed, thinking that at least there were shitty people who still did the dishes and didn't eat his leftovers, and then Eric turned his head slowly, eyeing the bright white face of his phone.

"Got a caller," he said, gesturing to it. "Want to take that?"

"I thought you were opposed to me handling your business," Lev said through another sip of Sapporo, and Eric shrugged.

"Whatever," he said, which about summed it up. Lev reached over, eyeing the face of it.

DO NOT CALL HER, the screen said. He hit answer.

"Hello?" he said.

A hitch on the other end. "Eric?"

He froze.

"No," Lev managed. "But close enough."

A pause.

"Who is this?" The voice was hard and mean. "This isn't funny."

Lev sat up slowly, noodles and assets forgotten.

"No," he agreed. "This isn't funny at all."

Silence.

"You're supposed to be dead," she said.

His mouth felt cottony. Dry.

"Yes," he confirmed. "As are you."

He heard the sound of a throat clearing.

"I suppose this is what I get for fucking with Roma," she said flatly. "Now I'm being haunted, too."

"Too?" he echoed.

"Never mind." A pause. "I think I'm dreaming."

"Yeah," Lev said. "Yeah, probably."

"I'm . . ." Hesitation. "I'm going to hang up now. And maybe . . ." A swallow. "I'm going to call back in the morning, I think. To prove this was a dream."

Lev's hand tightened around the phone.

"Don't you want to prove it now?" he asked.

"No." He heard a motion, a rustle, soft fabric, like she was rolling over in bed. "No, not yet. If it's not real, then I don't want to end it too soon."

"And if it's real?" he asked.

A long pause.

"It isn't."

"Right." He exhaled. "Right."

"Yes." He could hear something tapping quietly on the other end. "Okay, so. Bye."

"Wait," he cut in, a little breathless. "Did you need something from Eric?"

"Oh. Yeah. I just wanted to tell him—" A shaky laugh. "My plan's working."

Lev reached over to pick at the label of his beer, shifting the phone from one ear to the other.

"Is it?" he asked.

Her tone didn't change. "Yeah."

"Well—" Lev glanced at Eric, who was blandly observing his thumbs. "He's here, if you want to speak to him."

"No, I . . . I should sleep." Another pause. "I'm clearly starting to hallucinate."

"Right," Lev said, clearing his throat. "Well, sleep well, Sasha."

He thought he heard her breath falter, like maybe she was crying.

"You're not real," she said, voice muffled. "You can't be."

After a moment, the line disconnected, and Lev gradually let his hand fall.

"Who was it?" Eric asked him, eyes closed.

"'Do not call her,'" Lev told him.

"Ah," Eric said, making a face. "Yeah. She fucks me up, man. I don't . . . I don't get her."

Lev exhaled slowly.

"Why didn't you say anything?" he asked after a moment, staring down at the phone in his hands.

Eric shrugged. "You said not to."

Strange, Lev thought.

That was the sort of answer a friend might give.

"I thought she was dead," Lev eventually told him.

"Yikes," Eric replied. "Bummer."

Lev picked up his beer again, sliding his thumb over the bottle. It was slick with condensation. Had the phone call lasted for hours, or merely breaths?

"So," he said. "Sasha Antonova's alive."

"Uh, yeah," Eric confirmed. "Very much so."

Lev grimaced, realization tightening his chest. "And Marya knows that, doesn't she?"

"Hm? Yeah. Fuck, Marya knows everything." Eric tipped his head back. "Sometimes I think she can read my mind."

"It's not that complex in there; even I can read it. You want to fuck Sasha. You want to fuck Marya." A shrug. "Easy."

Eric's mouth twitched into a smile.

"I'm also hungry," he added. "So joke's on you."

Lev glanced down at his half-eaten pad thai.

Then he slid it over on the coffee table.

"If you just found out the love of your life was alive," Lev ventured slowly, "what would you do?"

Eric picked up the Thai food, squinting at it.

"Depends," he said. "Why'd she die?"

"Because your parents made a deal," Lev said. "You died. She died. That was supposed to be the price of peace."

"Fuck, man," Eric said, lazily picking up a piece of shrimp with his fingers. "I'd kill my parents first, I bet. Then I'd probably bring her flowers or some shit."

Oddly, it was Marya's voice that rang through Lev's mind.

Someday, when you replay all your little questions knowing what you know, you'll feel silly for even asking.

Consider it a favor.

"Yeah," Lev said. "That makes sense."

He paused for a second, considering his options. Running the numbers, projecting the simulations only to find they wound up in the same place, like constants of inevitability. Like doom, or fate.

"I have to go," he said, and Eric waved a pair of chopsticks at him.

"Do it, bro," Eric said, which wasn't necessarily the pep talk Lev had wanted, but wasn't totally unwelcome. "Good luck."

Lev rose to his feet, shaking his head.

Then he slid through the air, pulling back the space between them.

V. 15

(Long Story.)

Sasha had been lying sleepless in her bed when she dialed Eric's number, which was in her phone under *Douche-Tool Moneybags*. She stared at the call log for several minutes, wondering how it was possible that a call made in a moment of extreme loneliness on the vast, empty tides of insecurity and grief could have possibly resulted in something so . . .

She couldn't actually decide what it was.

She sat upright, still holding her phone, and stared into nothing.

Then it rang suddenly in her hand, an unknown number lighting up the blackened room, and she raised it warily to her ear.

"Hello?" she said.

"Hi. Sasha. So listen, here's the thing."

Oh, fuck. Oh fuck oh fuck. Oh fuck.

"You're not real," she reminded him, and he made a sound, a little scoff of *that's not important right now, Sasha, pay attention,* before carrying on as if she'd said nothing.

"Listen, I always knew we were a long story," he told her neutrally, "but I think I underestimated it. Can you imagine, love after death? Even I couldn't have guessed that. And I really am an optimist."

She didn't know whether to laugh or cry.

"Lev—"

"I need to see you. Now, actually."

She blinked, walking over to her window, and took a deep breath before glancing down.

Her stomach twisted. Nothing.

"You're not here," she said with quiet, overpowering bereavement.

"Of course not, Sasha, I don't know where you are."

Oh. True. "Then what do you mean—"

"Tell me where to meet you. Tell me where you are."

"Lev, I—"

What if it was a trick? She was tricking Roman. Karmically speaking this would be exactly what she deserved.

"Meet me where we first met," she decided. "That first night, when you—"

"When I kissed you, yeah." She could hear him grinning on the other side of the phone. "You're testing me, aren't you? You think I won't remember, but I remember everything. Every detail. Test me all you want, Sasha Antonova," he said with a laugh. "Believe me, I'll pass."

She shut her eyes. Inhaled.

Exhaled.

"Two minutes," she said, and hung up.

When she opened her eyes again, she was standing on the sidewalk outside the bar, The Misfit. Had it always been an omen? A sign? If any two things had never fit together, it was them. She hesitated, staring at the bar's tinted windows and the dubious emptiness of the sidewalk, and then moved to open the door, only to feel a hand closing around her right shoulder.

She whipped around with a blind left hook and whoever it was promptly doubled over, staggering backward with a string of profanity only Galina could have said aloud without blushing.

"This," her assailant sputtered, "is *not* what happened, at least not to me—"

"Lev?"

The name slipped from Sasha's lips without her permission as she slowly registered the components of his presence, cataloguing him piece by piece. Same dark hair, same lanky build, same look of restrained exasperation. She recognized him by his knuckles; by the motion of his fingers; by the way his gaze settled on hers with that look of *Sasha*.

Sasha, really?

He straightened with one hand pressed to his eye.

"But it can't be you," she said, gaping at him, her sense of rationality suddenly at war with her eyes, with her desperation to believe them. "Is this . . . Did Bryn put you up to this?"

She was breathing hard, blatantly staring, and he slowly lowered his hand.

"Sasha," said Lev, but it couldn't be Lev.

Lev was gone.

Lev was *dead*.

Wasn't he?

"You can't be," she said again, but that time, even she heard her own voice falter.

He took a step, and she didn't move.

Another, and she couldn't look away.

"Tell me what I said to you." He reached out to brush her hair back from her face, fingers soft and inconceivably corporeal. "What was the last thing I said to you, Sasha?"

She shivered. His palm kissed her cheek fleetingly, gently, while he savored her with a glance, scouring her face like something precious, lost and found.

"You said," she began, and swallowed. "You said, 'I'll find you, Sasha.'"

"Yes. I said I would find you."

She felt a little hitch in time, a hiccup, a tiny faltering of reality, and like a record scratch, a CD skip, the movie hit fast-forward. When had she stepped this close? She couldn't remember ever moving, ever breathing at all, but she was near enough now that her parted lips rose up for his—just to convince herself that he was real, that both of them were real, that he was alive and she was here and he was hers and they and this moment, this feeling, existed.

"I keep my word," he rasped against her mouth, and his kiss was a pulse of strange familiarity; a strike of dull impossibility; a moment that folded over itself in time to bring her a glimpse of perfect synchronicity, newness and repetition all at once.

"How," she gasped, the word falling from her lips unbidden, and he shook his head.

"Let tomorrow come tomorrow," he told her. "Tonight, I want tonight."

If it was a dream, he seemed to say, then let it end in the morning. Let the sun do its worst.

So she pulled Lev back into her and kissed him again, firmly this time, with all the conviction she thought she'd lost. The world had looked so different without Lev Fedorov in it—with him, it was suddenly brighter and fuller. The air itself was thick with anticipation, crowded with possibility, the night an inky shade of rapture and relief.

"Is it too late to love you, Lev Fedorov?" she asked him, her hands finding his, and he laughed, pulling her with him.

"Sasha, it's never too late for us," he promised hoarsely, and with a brush of his thumb to her cheek, they both vanished into the dark.

V. 16

(Populism.)

For the Boroughs, the lack of Stas Maksimov was a vacancy in more than just a missing vote. It was the loss of someone who had already been accepted, who possessed a subtle, unteachable understanding of their customs, their secrets and their lives. As a result, they were in something of a hurry to fill the hollow absence with stability, and specifically, with someone they could either grudgingly trust or easily lie to, depending on what was more convenient as the slate of candidates arose.

Stas had been more of the former: a quiet sort of man, well trained by his father not to stand too aggressively against the political status quo. For all that Stas Maksimov was considered one of the good ones, he was also notably one of the smart ones. He knew the important things, like who to avoid crossing and with whom to make an appeal if he were ever truly in need, and he knew how to keep his mouth shut, which was a particular virtue that had gone both ways. He kept his suspicions to himself; likewise, those who suspected him of undue influence by his wife (her, and her questionable misdeeds) followed suit.

Ideally, the Boroughs would have replaced Stas with another version of himself—some young twenty-something who would know to keep his head down if he wanted to climb, which he might do over the course of the next several decades if he made no mistakes and didn't step on the toes of anyone more important. The best-case scenario, in most of the Borough witches' minds, was a blank canvas, new blood. Someone they could mold, or break, with an underlying implication of circuitry: someone who could be built up from nothing who would, as a result, owe his every success (and the entirety of his loyalty) back to the Borough witches themselves.

Dimitri Fedorov, a witch already possessing a man's reputation, was exactly nothing the Boroughs had in mind. Fortunately, Dimitri and Marya had already understood this, and they had played their respective cards well. Marya in particular had been right that Jonathan Moronoe was a most valuable pawn. Once Brooklyn had leaned Fedorov—the result of Moronoe's subtlest political work, with little more than glimpses of furtively shaken hands—then Queens, Staten Island, and the Bronx were unanimously in agreement as well.

The last Borough, Manhattan, was wary. Some had resented Koschei's influence for generations and regarded Dimitri, a known Koschei associate, with concern, or even fear. Others had been friends of Stas Maksimov and his father and, unable to stomach the idea of someone like Dimitri Fedorov in a Maksimov seat, argued against him relentlessly. Dimitri couldn't be broken, they pointed out, and he wouldn't be used, so doubtlessly, he couldn't be swayed. To give Dimitri Fedorov Stas Maksimov's vote was to take something that had belonged to a fox and give it to a snake. One was safe, they argued, and manageable, once you knew where its claws were. The other could only be counted on to strike.

Ultimately, though, decisions had to be made, and discord had little choice but to settle. With the four other Boroughs in agreement, Manhattan's vote rapidly became a fight not worth having. While the end result wasn't unanimous (even to call it resigned would be excessively polite), Manhattan ultimately selected Dimitri Fedorov to fill the vacancy left by Stas Maksimov's untimely death.

Within a matter of hours, Dimitri had won all five Boroughs.

"Congratulations," offered a satisfied Jonathan Moronoe, who believed he'd done nothing wrong. Of course, perhaps he hadn't— what did it matter his intent? Power was power, as Koschei often said, and Koschei was a lot of things, but not wrong. Decisions (and those who made them) always had power, and choosing to use it, unduly or not, was still a choice. "What will you do now, Dimitri?"

"Exactly as I promised," Dimitri assured him. "The Boroughs have been under the thumb of one criminal or another for too long," he announced to the room, peering expectantly around it. "That's about to change."

There was a ripple of both excitement and, of course, panic.

"Do you plan to take down Baba Yaga?" one Borough witch prompted. He'd voted Fedorov without hesitation—not everyone had been a friend of Stas Maksimov. Many had disliked the woman whose interests Stas had quietly stood to protect, for reasons varying from valid to not.

"Yes," Dimitri said, and immediately, several witches turned to each other with apprehension, expressions contorting with concern. This was what they'd been afraid of, they muttered and groaned. Baba Yaga was mostly harmless, they whispered; there were worse criminals, and at least she stayed out of the Boroughs' way. Without Yaga, what new threat would rise to fill the role of Koschei's rival?

"*And* Koschei?" Jonathan prompted warily, addressing the cause for outburst.

"Yes," Dimitri confirmed.

Another ripple of whispers, tension rumbling like thunderclouds.

Dimitri waited, and after another moment of growing unease—a brimming silence set to overfill—a Queens witch got to his feet.

"How?" the Borough witch demanded.

"An excellent question," Dimitri said from behind the mask of a cordial smile as he glanced tiredly around the room. Marya would be here soon, he reminded himself. It was almost over, and that was relief enough. "I'm so pleased you thought to ask."

V. 17

(Deliverance.)

Barely a word passed between Sasha and Lev in the moments they stood alone in the dark, reaching silently for each other and transmuting the afflictions of *I missed you, only you, always you* into tiny, penitent experiments. She touched the features of his face, one by one, to prove they were his, to prove she hadn't dreamt him, and he tangled his fingers in her hair, holding himself captive by the sanctity of each blessed strand. She seemed unsure of him, as if he might slip through her fingers at any moment, so he undressed her with care, with patience, pausing to remind her of her existence, the actuality of her, the cravings of her appetites and the physicality of her needs, and his. To remind her of this, *here,* with his hands digging into her waist so she'd suck in a breath, to prove her lungs could fill. *Here,* with his lips near her ear, to remember her blood could rush. It was a silence that spoke volumes, that made promises; a rush of urgency they both knew would have no patience for the luxury of a mattress, of permanence and sheets. When the blades of her scapulae hit the wall behind her, Lev thought only *here, now, this.*

They reminded each other of the little carnalities of existence— sweat that glistened in sheens, first, then in slow beads of it; the rawness of contact, not an inch left untouched; the gentle quaking of limbs, oppression of breaths that could not come fast enough; all their mundane limitations. With barely a sound, they both caught a sigh of relief, of release, of captivation, before being delivered to a different sort of silence, this one heavy with things yet to come.

Lucky the city never slept. Disruptive bleats of banality called up to them from the street, binding them to the rigidity of the present. Gradually, they lay together in his bed, Sasha's head on Lev's chest, her fingers resting like puzzle pieces in the slats of his ribs. She'd placed them there deliberately, he suspected, to root him to this world, to fix him at her side. He, likewise, had rested the tips of his fingers along the notches of her vertebrae, floating tenderly atop her spine.

"Why did you come back?" she whispered.

"To save you," he replied.

"From what?"

He shrugged, sliding one hand behind his head. "From everything."

She closed her eyes, saying nothing.

"I expected you to tell me you don't need saving," Lev commented, shifting to look at her, and felt Sasha's lashes fluttering against his chest as her eyes floated open.

"I think I did, this time," she confessed. "This time, I do. Not from the world, though." She paused, letting him toy with her hair. "From myself."

He waited, saying nothing.

"I was . . . angry," she admitted, fingers digging shamefully into his torso as she spoke. "But now that you're here, none of it seems worth it. I just want to stay here, to be with you. Everything else can continue as it was." She closed her eyes again. "I no longer care whether Roman ruins himself or not. Your father seems to be doing plenty to destroy his sons without my help."

"What?" Lev asked, startled.

She seemed surprised, lifting her head to look at him. "Did you not . . . know that?"

He wasn't sure how to explain to her the volumes he clearly hadn't known, which she must have seen on his face.

"Dimitri isn't speaking to Koschei," Sasha told him, looking uneasy at being the one to deliver the news. "He won't forgive him for letting you die, or forgive Roman, either. It's a mess." She held him tighter. "Whatever happens next, though, I no longer want any part of it."

Understandable, Lev thought.

But still.

"Sasha," he said, frowning. "What's your sister Marya's role in this?"

He felt her stiffen. "Masha?"

"Yes." Abruptly, Sasha pulled back to look at him, visibly as surprised to hear her sister's name on his lips as he'd been to hear his brothers' on hers. "Why do you think I was answering Eric's phone?" Lev reminded her, and she balked, clearly not having had the opportunity to question it. "I've been working for your sister."

"What?" Sasha asked, gaping at him. "But—"

"She brought me back," Lev explained, and then amended quickly, "No, actually. Marya didn't, technically, but she was the one who, I don't know. Made me. *Fixed* me. I was just awake, but not alive," he clarified uncertainly, "until Marya."

Sasha grew increasingly uneasy. "So Masha knew? This whole time, she knew you were alive?"

"Yes, of course," Lev said, frowning down at her. "Which is why I'm asking. What exactly is her plan, Sasha?"

The Plan. There must have been one. There must still be one.

"I . . . I don't know." Sasha looked dizzied with dismay, nearly swaying as she sat upright. "She wants to destroy Koschei, that I know, but—"

"Whatever she's doing, it's more than that," Lev said, and Sasha pulled out of his reach, staring down at him.

"You've just told me my sister lied to me," she said hoarsely. "She lied to me. She *betrayed* me. She let me carry on with a broken heart, but *you*—" She broke off, sputtering. "You only care what her plan was?"

"Well, I'm not overjoyed with her, Sasha, believe me," Lev said, shifting upright. "But still, you know your sister, don't you? You can't really think she did any of this to hurt you."

Sasha blinked.

"No," Sasha said. "No, she didn't do it to hurt me." Her expression stiffened. "She did it to *use* me."

"I—" Lev hesitated. "Sasha," he murmured, reaching for her. "Sasha, let's just—"

But she was already on her feet, picking up her clothes from where they'd been discarded across his floor and hastily yanking them back on.

"I'm going to talk to her," Sasha announced, stumbling to pull on her shoes and then whipping around to glare at him. "Are you coming?"

On the one hand, it was probably unwise.

On the other, it was *spectacularly* unwise.

Still, he'd followed Sasha back from the dead. How could he not follow her to her sister's house?

"Fine," Lev said, rising to his feet after her and taking her arm gently, coaxing her into his chest. "But Sasha—"

"What?" she sighed impatiently, glaring up at him. A nightmare.

He paused, taking a moment to tuck a loose curl behind her ear.

"I'll never spend another night without you," he said.

If she softened, it was only for a moment. Only enough to return his touch with certainty, and then she was back to her usual self. To the version of her, Lev thought, that came as much from Marya Antonova as it did from the witch Baba Yaga.

Then, "Shut *up,* Lev" was all Sasha said, though she touched his mouth with sweetness.

V. 18

(Formalwear.)

"Did he win then, Ivan?"

"Yes, Marya," Ivan confirmed. "He won. He's waiting for you now."

She nodded, distracted.

"I'll be there shortly," she said, eyeing the outfits she'd set out on the bed. What did one wear to such a victory? She hated to make an improper expression of her triumph, particularly after the years she'd spent cultivating a talent for dressing for the occasion. The first time she'd loved Dimitri Fedorov she'd been a girl—naïve, blind, trusting. Now she was a woman who understood more about the world, like which silhouettes were best suited to her figure and how to bring the Boroughs to their knees. "In the meantime, give him that, would you?" she said, gesturing to the package she'd left out on her vanity. "Go on without me, Ivan. I'll be right there."

He seemed hesitant to leave her, per usual, but he eventually conceded with a slight nod.

"Yes, Marya," he said, tucking the package into the lining of his jacket and heading into the corridor, leaving her to continue eyeing her choices. To define herself, somehow, by the constraints of colors and shapes.

The red dress always fit so well, she thought idly. It conformed to her curves and edges easily, no matter what shape she took. It was a statement, a direct one, and a forceful one, at that. The grey one, on the other hand, spoke more quietly, but power didn't need to shout. Red was a color of ostentatiousness, of opulence, where the grey was evidence of her will. It was all strident lines, harsh edges. It was the meagerness of necessity, the coldness of steel.

As she stood contemplating her choices, Marya heard the door slam. She recognized the footsteps as they approached and comfortably matched the sound of urgency with a sense of recognition, piecing together what must have happened.

"MASHA," she heard her sister shout, and Marya closed her eyes, the door to her bedroom swinging open behind her.

"Masha, *how could you—*"

"Finally." Marya exhaled, opening her eyes and turning over her shoulder. She let her gaze fix slowly on the figures before her—first on her sister Sasha, who was furious and glinting with rage, and then on Lev, who stood stoically by Sasha's side. "Sashenka," Marya noted. "Solnyshko. A bit late, don't you think?"

Sasha stared at her. "Is that actually what you're going to say to me, Masha?"

"Yes, Sasha, it is. I figured you'd find him sooner or later." She shrugged. "I suppose this timing is as good as any."

"Masha." Sasha stared at her. "I told you. I *told* you my pain. I told you everything, and you said . . ." She trailed off, knuckles tensing at her side. "You said you'd felt it, too. You said you *understood it*—was that a lie?"

"Of course not," Marya said, glancing briefly at Lev, who looked uncertain of his place in the conflict between sisters. "I understand it far better than you think, Sashenka."

"Masha, Lev is—" Sasha broke off, her gaze darting quickly to his face and then lingering, falling briefly on each of the details, on every strand and freckle and line. "He's not just anyone, he's—he's *more,* and he's—"

"I know very well what he is to you, Sasha." Marya glanced back down at her dresses, still indecisive. "Do you like the grey or the red?"

"*Masha.*" Sasha's voice was hard and disbelieving. "Are you serious?"

Marya turned over her shoulder. "Is there something specific you want from me, Sashenka?"

"I—" Sasha was gaping at her. "Of *course* there is—"

"An apology?" Marya mused, wondering now if she shouldn't contemplate her navy dress. That one was unremarkable, but at least she wouldn't chance any spills. "I was never given any apologies either, you know." She ran her fingers along the lines of the grey sheath. "This world, Sasha, it will never apologize to you. It doesn't serve either of us well to behave any differently, I expect."

"When exactly were you going to tell me?" Sasha demanded.

Lev, Marya observed, still hadn't spoken. She didn't bother turning around to glance at his expression. She could guess it by now. He always bore traces of curiosity, of searching, his fingers tapping at his thigh. He was in constant motion, or more accurately, the space between motions. The lurch between action and inaction was Lev Fedorov's sweet spot.

"Tomorrow," Marya said, and heard Sasha scoff.

"Really," Sasha sardonically retorted. "Tomorrow, honestly, you were just going to what, announce that Lev was alive?"

Without hesitation: "Yes."

Clearly Sasha had her doubts. *Good,* Marya thought. *I trained you well.*

"Masha," Sasha ground out again, sounding pained this time. "How can you be so . . ."

Marya waited, schooling her shoulders not to flinch.

"Heartless," Sasha finally said, and Marya, who was precisely that, was relieved to find the remark predictably acceptable to stomach. "How could you stand there and watch me suffer, Masha, when this whole time you knew he was *alive?"*

"I had things to finish," Marya said.

"But if you knew, then Ivan must have known!"

"Ivan works for me, not you," Marya reminded her plainly, and Sasha cast her gaze askance in obvious rage. "It pained him. It pained me. But some things must be done, Sashenka. You know that."

"But you had Lev *working* for you," Sasha began, clearly venturing another helpless rant, and Marya turned to look at the Lev in question.

"Does that anger you, Solnyshko?" she asked him.

He waited a moment, then gave her a thin smile. "It doesn't thrill me, Marya."

"Well," Marya determined after a moment. "I suppose not everything goes the way we'd like, does it?"

He said nothing. So Marya turned back to Sasha, who was still gawking at her, unsatisfied.

"I have told you many lies," Marya informed her sister, glancing at her watch. She was running late. "Is that what's upsetting you?" she pressed, unfazed. "Did you come here to shame me for my omissions, my untruths? Because if so, you should know that I've been lying to you forever, Sashenka, since practically the day you opened your eyes, by letting you think this life could ever fulfill you, or satisfy you. It does not." She paused, and then said placidly, "It will not."

But Sasha seemed determined to miss the truth of the statement.

"I just want to know *why*," she shot at Marya. "Why, Masha?"

Maybe she wasn't ready yet, Marya thought.

Maybe she couldn't yet understand.

So Marya simply shrugged. "Perhaps I just wanted chaos."

"No."

Lev's voice startled both of them. In the subsequent beat of silence, he stepped toward Marya.

"No," he said again, "you did this for a reason. All of it. Didn't you?"

She sighed. His insistence on her plan was so resolute it was almost like faith, which she would never have personally recommended as a lifestyle choice. Faith was an unwise extension of hope, which was nearly always dashed, destroyed, burned on a pyre of routine and almost unvarying disappointment. Expectations, at least, like Sasha's, faced a more meager consequence of being raised or lowered. Whatever Lev had in her, it was in constant danger of being irreparably shattered. Nobody knew better than Marya Antonova that such blindness was to risk damage from which he could never return.

"You want so badly for me to have a purpose, Solnyshko," she remarked. "Why is that?"

"Because you do. You have to. Why bring me back at all?" he pressed while Sasha looked on, condemning her in silence. "If you really wanted it to be a secret, you could have left me dead. You must have known this would happen," he pointed out. "You put me in a position to find Sasha eventually, didn't you?"

Another shrug. "I still arranged for it to be a secret. I couldn't have your father coming for my mother."

"Not before you were ready, you mean," Sasha accused. "So you *did* use me, Masha. You used my anger, my hatred. And you kept Lev away from me so that I would help you destroy Koschei, didn't you?"

"Yes," Marya said. "Of course. If you were thinking clearly, you would see it was the obvious thing to do."

"But I—" Sasha looked hurt, and furious. "Why?" she demanded again, though Marya could see that the question wasn't about anything in particular. It was merely a reflex, a muscle spasm in response to everything Marya had done. "Why any of this?"

"That is simply what this life is, Sashenka," Marya reminded her. "Sacrifice and loss. So long as you remain a part of it, that's all you'll be capable of feeling. It's all you'll be able to do. Your only gifts will be what you can take, what you can break, and what you can ruin." She glanced at Lev, then back at her sister. "This life is a thief, Sasha. It takes and takes, and then maybe you die or maybe you don't. But either way, this life will try to leave you empty-handed unless you learn to strike first."

Lev glanced down at his own hands, but said nothing.

"I love you, Sashenka," Marya said, and Sasha opened her mouth to contradict her, but Marya cut her off with a shake of her head. "I love you, whether you see it or not. Whether you choose to believe it today or not. But don't cross me, Sasha."

She stepped forward, swapping her robe for a dress with a wave of a hand, and stepped into her shoes, one by one. In her bare feet, without her usual armor—her high heels, her berry-red lips, her constricting shapes and textured fabrics—she'd been just below her sister's eyeline, but still there had been no mistaking who was in control then. There certainly wasn't now.

Marya straightened her dress, eyeing herself in the mirror.

Grey. Immobility, subtlety. A little beckon of *underestimate me, I dare you, just try.*

"Run if you like, Sasha," Marya suggested, picking up her earrings from her vanity and putting them on, eyeing the final effect. "Turn your back on me if you want, but do not get in my way."

From the mirror, Marya watched Sasha stare at her back, disbelieving. Mistrusting.

"Do you belong to anyone, Masha?" Sasha asked hoarsely. "Do you even belong to me?"

Marya turned around to glance first at Lev, and then at Sasha.

Someday, she thought to say, *when you replay all your little questions knowing what you know, you'll feel silly for even asking.*

Instead, she said nothing. She merely slid a glance that said *let me go,* and Sasha, like everyone who'd ever stood in Marya's way, gradually stepped aside.

Then Marya Antonova slipped into the corridor, leaving her sister behind her, and ventured out into the night.

V. 19

(Disruption.)

It had been a Manhattan witch who finally put the Boroughs' disbelief into words.

"How can you possibly bring us Koschei and Baba Yaga?" Translation: *How can you bring us them?*

That wasn't the real question, Dimitri thought idly, wanting to admonish them for the inefficiency of not simply saying what they'd meant. The real question, in his mind, was: *How is it possible that we have been fools with our hands tied for so many years, and yet after five minutes in this room you can promise unfathomable reward?*

And to that, he wasn't sure he even knew the answer.

Dimitri opened his mouth, then paused, scanning the room again for Marya. She was supposed to be here by now, and though Marya Antonova was many things, late was never one of them. He saw the figure of her bodyguard Ivan slipping into the room and frowned, registering a sudden sense of unease.

"One moment," he called over the heads of the bickering Borough witches, then stepped directly toward Ivan, gesturing him to the corner away from the murmurs of dissatisfaction at his back.

"Where is she?" he asked, and Ivan shook his head.

"She said she'd be here. She's just running a bit late."

"Marya's never late," Dimitri said in a low voice, impatient, and read in Ivan's face the obvious unspoken agreement. "Try calling her?"

Ivan nodded, sliding his phone from his pocket.

From where he was standing, Dimitri could hear the phone ring.

And ring.

And ring.

With each subsequent ring he felt a thud against his chest; a bleakness. A weary malcontent that festered, growing firmer with each pulse. Dimitri, who'd grown accustomed to the patterns of Marya Antonova's heart, grew increasingly agitated as he and Ivan waited. In sequence: a ring, a pulse, a pang. The wait was thunderous with warning. The ache tucked invisibly under his shirt only seemed to grow, and it felt like fear, or distress, or excitement. It felt like all those things at once, with the added cacophony of suspension, as if she'd suddenly held her breath.

Marya Antonova was never late, and everything she did had a purpose.

Dimitri's mind flashed to the evening, to the afternoon, to the morning, playing itself out in reverse. Had her rhythms changed? Had he missed something, some subtle sign? Could she have lied to his face without him knowing the difference, even with the core of what she was strung around his neck?

What disruption might have happened? Dimitri thought selfishly of himself first. Had he done something? Said something? Had he touched her less reverently? Had she?

No. To his knowledge, nothing between them had changed.

Or—?

The chattering behind him yanked him back to reality, his

attention snagging on the inscrutable glances from elsewhere in the room. *Of course,* he thought abruptly, feeling a lurch. Of course. He'd been a fool. *One* thing had changed. Something—*one little thing*—was new and stark and different. Because for the first time, Dimitri wasn't simply a Fedorov, a son of Koschei. He was Dimitri Fedorov, a Borough witch. A representative of the Manhattan Witches' Borough, and a man who stood alone.

He'd changed, but he wasn't the part that mattered. He was a much smaller piece than he'd thought.

"I know where she is," Dimitri said as the call eventually went to voicemail, and Ivan frowned.

"Where?" Ivan asked, but Dimitri didn't have time to explain himself.

"I have to go" was all he said, shoving Ivan aside and ignoring the rising shouts of protest behind him.

V. 20

(History.)

Marya's departure left Sasha feeling numb for reasons she wasn't entirely sure she could define. She supposed a more honest part of her had expected Marya to break down in tears, in apology, to beg forgiveness, despite never having seen Marya do anything like that before. In reality, Sasha had never seen Marya Antonova react with anything but precisely the degree of certainty she'd had then, and perhaps that was what was so upsetting. That now, Sasha was just like anyone else in the world, which was something her sister Marya had never made her feel before.

"What do we do now?" she asked Lev, mumbling it. It was difficult to calculate her gains and her losses. Yesterday, no Lev. Today, no Masha. Was she only ever meant to have one or the other? Was she now supposed to choose?

"I don't know." Lev's lips pressed into her hair, comforting her. "But I do think we have to stop your sister before she's too far gone."

"What can she possibly *want,* though?" Sasha asked, pained. "Your father's been brought low already. Roman's half mad as we speak. And Dimitri . . ."

She trailed off, uncertain.

And then Lev spoke.

"I think I always knew my brother loved someone," he admitted slowly. "It's strange, saying that in the past tense and never having known my brother while he was *in* love. He just always had an air of heartbreak to him, and I think it's what made him so . . . vast. So untouchable." He paused. "He always had this grace about him, like a man who had lost everything and still refused to be hollowed out."

The words echoed in the vacancies of Sasha's recognition. The holes in a history she'd never known but tacitly understood were always meant to be filled.

"My sister was the same," she eventually said. "I always thought she was what she was because of something that had happened before I was even born. Like she'd been suffering a loss for centuries. For lifetimes."

"Can you imagine?" Lev asked her, shaking his head. "Feeling that way." He slid his arms around her, almost by necessity. As if the words were absent any meaning without tactility, without proof. "I can't imagine having found you only to let you go now. I couldn't do it." She felt his grip tighten. "Not for anything. I'd learn to hate every shred of everything, of every person who'd kept me from you."

Sasha slowly relaxed in his hold, leaning her cheek against his chest.

She took a breath for certainty. In, slowly, and out.

Another for cleansing.

Then a third, for understanding.

"I think we have to find out where she's going," Sasha said, the realization dawning slowly, tendrils of it creeping through her bones. "Don't we?"

Lev's voice was uncharacteristically grim. "Yes. I really think we do."

V. 21

(Dead Girls.)

"Bridge," Roman said, begging from the moment he appeared in Bryn's office, "please. I need your help. You know the dead, don't you? If you could just intercede on my behalf, if you could tell her that I'm sorry—"

"Roman," Bryn said, rising to his feet, "when I said to meet me here, it was so that you could help me, for once. Not the other way around."

Roman blinked, still wild-eyed. "And why would I do you any favors, Bridge?"

"Oh, you aren't *doing* the favor," Bryn assured him with a laugh. "You *are* the favor."

He stepped aside, revealing Marya Antonova seated in the chair behind him, as Roman turned slowly to stare at her.

"So you're alive, then." His voice was hoarse, uncertain, and she chuckled.

"Yes, despite your best attempts," she confirmed, eyeing him for a moment. "You look afraid, Roma," she noted, and turned to Bryn. "Doesn't he look afraid, Bridge?"

"He does," Bryn agreed, leaning against his bookcase. "Rightfully, don't you think?"

"I do," Marya said, turning back to Roman. "I hear my sister is haunting you," she remarked dispassionately, and at his silence, a smile pulled at her lips. "Good. Personally, I had plans to do the same."

"What do you want from me?" came from Roman's apprehensive mouth. "I'm trying to repent."

"You're not trying very hard," Marya said. "I'm not very impressed. Are you, Bridge?"

"No," Bryn gamely confirmed, before letting his gaze flick to hers with obvious expectancy. "My payment, Marya?" he prompted, having waited long enough.

She waved a hand over his desk drawer, levitating the kidney from it. She passed a hand over it, pausing a moment, and then beckoned to him.

"Come here," she said, crooking a finger, and with a mostly feigned reluctance, Bryn went, Roman's eyes following their movements warily. "Now, Roma," Marya said, "tell me more about what ails you. You worry my dead sister will kill you, is that it?"

She placed a cool hand on Bryn's back, pulling his shirt loose from where it had been tucked into his trousers. Slowly, her fingers crept under the fabric, running comfortingly over his spine as he shivered, unsure what was to come.

"I can talk to her for you," Marya continued to Roman, "if you'll do something for me."

Abruptly, her nails dug into Bryn's back, leaving him to bite down on a hiss of pain. He twisted around, staring down at her with a look of betrayal, and she shook her head with a long-suffering sigh.

"Quiet, please," she warned him. "I'm making a deal with Roma."

Bryn had the distinct sensation her witchy little fingers had dug in under his skin.

"I just want Sasha to know it wasn't my fault she's dead," Roman was saying, voice toneless and dull. "I just need someone to show her it wasn't my fault."

"You know, it's your fault *I'm* dead," Marya said. From the light of his study, Bryn was certain the scar over her heart was showing; he was positive Roman could see the carved-out edge of what he'd caused. "So, whose fault is Sasha's death, Roma, if not yours?"

Something twisted in Bryn's internal organs. He bit down on a yell.

"It's my father's fault," Roman whispered, and then Marya wrenched open Bryn's flesh, scalding him from the inside out as he let out a terrible shout, bracing himself with his palms flat on his desk. Sweat from his forehead met the grains of the wood below like the sound of a ticking clock.

"Yes, it is," Marya confirmed, and then, all at once, the pain had stopped. Vanished. She withdrew her hand, giving Bryn a brief pat on the back. "All done," she told him. "Now it's yours to use."

He stared at her, unsure what to say, but she had already turned back to Roman.

"A knife, Bridge?" Marya requested. "No, wait. A sword." She turned to face him. "Do you know what a spatha is?"

Bryn blinked. "The gladiator sword?"

"Yes, that," she said, as from a distance, Roman's waxy pallor went increasingly pale. "Do you know it?"

"I know what it is," Bryn said with a sudden thrill of impatience, "but witchcraft or not, I don't have a fucking spatha sitting around my office, Marya—"

"Summon it." She slid him a sidelong glance. "Put your hand out," she said with an uncharacteristic gentleness, gesturing for him to mimic her, "and call it forth. I know where there's one you can use," she added with another fleeting glance at Roman. "Koschei has one in his warehouse."

Bryn gritted his teeth. "But that's impossible, I can't just—"

"You can now," Marya said, beckoning again. "So, get to it, Bridge."

Brynmor Attaway thought, as he often did, how dearly he had always hated witches. He hated anyone for whom things came easily. Sure, things came to him easily enough *now,* but the title *Esquire* after one's name tended to take care of that matter for him. People were free to dislike him as they pleased, even mock him or belittle him, because every minute they spent talking to him still had an exorbitant dollar amount attached whether they liked it or not. He had value, even if he lacked worth. Witches, on the other hand, were worthy in any context. A little twitch of a finger could alter the physicalities of the universe. For an entire shitty lifetime, Bryn had pressed and pressed and pressed against the laws and customs of reality and still risen up empty-handed every time.

But today, a witch asked him to fetch an outrageous sword from probably miles away and he held out his hand as if that request were reasonable, curling his fingers up as if it were possible. He imagined closing his fingers around it, shutting his eyes, still only half convinced. Could this really be how simple, how easy it all was? Had he never actually overestimated the gift of witchery and, in fact, *underestimated* it? He crooked a finger, then another. Imagined the girth of the spatha's pommel in his hand—the heft of it, the weight.

Something in his body jerked to life—stretched out, yawned, and said, *Finally.*

Then Bryn opened his eyes to find the spatha in his grip, and slowly, Marya Antonova smiled.

"Give it to Roma," she said.

Bryn didn't want to. *I did this,* he thought. He was the sort of person who hung evidence of his value around his office. Surely it should go somewhere for other people to see. *Look, look what I've done.*

"You can make another one," Marya said impatiently. "Give that one to Roma."

Already, Roman looked seven types of dead. Bryn, who'd seen countless more types of that, was certain of it. Still, a deal was a deal. Witch organs, fae blood. The blood won out. He handed the spatha to Roman, who took it numbly.

"What are you doing?" forced itself blankly through Roman's lips.

"Playing a game," Marya said. "Running an experiment. How badly did you want me dead, Roma Fedorov?"

"Badly enough to do it myself," he answered.

"Yes, true. I admire that sort of initiative," she said. "Maybe in another life we might have been friends."

Bryn watched Roman's jaw tighten. "And in this one?"

Marya's lips twitched.

Then she angled the desk lamp, adjusting her shadow.

"We agreed," she said to her shadow. "Didn't we?"

The shadow nodded. Bryn, startled, blinked.

"Tell Koschei the Deathless that his son Roma is in trouble," Marya said, and then glanced up at Roman to drive the point home. "Tell him that Romik is at home, losing himself in his darkened thoughts."

Roman frowned. "But—"

"Then tell Koschei the Deathless that his son Dimitri is about to make a deal," she went on, "in the office of a fae called The Bridge." The shadows had now gathered reverently around her, awaiting instruction like small children at her knee. "Let's see where he goes, shall we?"

Roman's hand tightened around the spatha, and Marya lifted her gaze to his in warning.

"When all of this is over, you will know that I never lifted a hand against you, Roma, even though you failed to offer the same courtesy to me," Marya warned as the shadows melted from the walls, dripping through the cracks in the floors and disappearing gradually from sight.

"Oh, and Bridge?"

Bryn glanced at her. "Yes, witch?"

"Stay out of it."

His brow twitched. "I have no business with the affairs of Koschei the Deathless."

"Nonsense. You have his magic. You lured his son." Marya's eyes were dark and unreadable. "You'll feel the consequences of that someday, if not today."

Bryn swallowed. She smiled.

"A pity you could never love me, Bridge," Marya said.

He hesitated. "I could."

Roman gave him a wounded look.

She lifted a brow. "Sit down."

Bryn sat.

"Don't interfere," she said again.

"I have no plans to—"

"Don't make me lose my temper," she cautioned, and he sighed, closing his lips.

The clock on the wall tapped out thirty beats of future history. There was a buzzing from the pocket of Marya's coat, someone trying to reach her. Her attention, however, failed to shift.

"I could just leave," Roman told her. "Escape your little trap. Maybe I don't need this answer."

Inwardly, Bryn stifled a laugh. Roman Fedorov, leave?

Never had anyone been more desperate to stay.

"You could, but you won't," Marya assured him, unfazed. "You have to know what he chooses, don't you? You or Dima."

Roman said nothing.

"What will you do, Romik," Marya asked softly, "when you finally learn the truth of your father's heart?"

The second hand on the clock neared midnight.

Three, two, one.

Then there was a rip in time, and Koschei the Deathless appeared.

V. 22

(A Reckoning.)

Dima.

Koschei's heart raced.

Dima, my son—

"Where is he?"

Only it wasn't Dimitri who sat waiting for him in the office of The Bridge.

"You," Koschei said to Marya Antonova.

She sat motionless, more dead than alive, but he didn't find that surprising. She'd been a quiet girl, introspective, but like her mother, there was more than met the eye.

Since Marya Antonova had been small, others had always feared her. She'd had a bodyguard, that hulking Ivan, but nobody had ever shrank from him. If anything, Ivan was like the cloak of the grim reaper. Just a decoration to indicate that Death Herself was on her way.

"Yes, me," Marya confirmed, leaning back against the desk chair. "You're already familiar with The Bridge, I presume?"

Koschei let his narrow gaze travel to Bryn, who sat neutrally to the side. His hands gripped the arms of his chair, his eyes fixed elsewhere in the room.

"And, of course, you know your son," Marya commented lazily, and Koschei turned slowly, finding Roman's dark eyes fixed on his back.

"Roma," Koschei said, frowning. "I thought you were—"

"I know what you thought," Roman said flatly.

Koschei noticed his son gripped a thin sword in his hand. Koschei, a collector of objects, knew more about the spatha in Roman's hand than about any of the tension floating in the room. It had a history longer than anyone else's. It was made of stronger materials. It would outlast them all.

"What is this?" Koschei asked Marya, turning to her. "Yaga and I have a deal."

"Yes," Marya said. "And I don't care for it."

"Are you here to renegotiate?" Koschei said.

"No," Marya said. "I already have everything I need from you, Koschei."

Her gaze fell weightily from him to Roman.

"Do you know why your father gave his kidney to The Bridge?" she asked, and Koschei shot a glance at Bryn, who said nothing.

"To save me," Roman said, warily.

"Mm, yes," Marya permitted. "But how did he know you needed it?"

"I—" Roman hesitated. "He's my father."

"He has you followed," Marya corrected, and Koschei blinked.

"How did you—"

"You should treat your creatures better, Koschei," Marya advised, the shadows flickering on the walls behind her. They coiled around her chair to crowd it like a throne, and he turned, stomach lurching, to his son.

"I watch all of you," Koschei told Roman carefully. "Of course. Of course I watch over you."

"No, actually," Marya said, rising to her feet. "He doesn't watch Dimitri. He didn't watch Lev. He only watched you. And do you know why, Roma?"

Confusion flitted over Roman's brow.

"Because you're the weak one," Marya said, lips curling up in a triumphant smile.

Roman's eyes darted accusingly to his father.

"Don't listen to her," Koschei sighed. "Romik, please. What have I always told you about the Antonova witches?"

"Oh, are you against them now?" Roman asked blankly. "Because when I tried to do something about it—"

"You made a mess of it," Koschei said. "We wouldn't be here now if not for you, and now, if there's nothing left to say, we're leaving. We're done here," he said, turning to Marya. "Whatever you hoped to accomplish by this, Marya, you will not gain from me or my sons."

"Oh, won't I?" she asked doubtfully. "As of a few hours ago, Dimitri turned over your paperwork to the Boroughs. All of your receipts," she clarified, as Koschei felt his face drain of color. "Your creatures. Your illegal rents. Every favor you have ever owed or fulfilled, Dimitri has record of it, and the Boroughs have it now."

"You're lying," Koschei said instantly.

She smiled. "Dead girls don't lie, Koschei." Her attention slipped back to Roman. "Do they, Roma?"

Whatever Koschei had expected to see from his son, fear had not been it.

"Such a pity you fight so hard to protect your father, Roma,"

Marya was murmuring to him. "Haven't you realized by now which son he will always choose?"

Koschei grimaced. Forget what kind of witch Marya Antonova was—she was, and would always be, a dastardly clever woman, dragging her claws through the entrails of all their insecurities and flaws. "Romik, listen to me—"

"You chose Dima." Koschei could see his middle son piecing together the little doubts he had always clung to, the toxicity of his inadequacies festering once again. "Papa, once again, you choose Dima over me, even while he betrays you!"

"Dima would never betray me," Koschei said firmly. "She's lying, Romik, and look, it's working—"

"No. She isn't." Roman's voice was hard and brittle, falling like rubble from his lips. "Dima hasn't been loyal to you for months now. He left your side the moment you abandoned Lev. *My god,*" Roman spat, his hand tightening around the spatha in his hand. "I can't believe it. I cannot believe it. All this time, Papa, I was fighting for a cause that didn't even exist—"

"You're being dramatic, Roma, and irrational. Of course I love all my sons."

"No," Roman said, shaking his head. "No, you don't. You threw Lev away. Even Dima, who you claim to love most of all—"

Koschei stiffened. "Do not question that."

"—you caused him the worst pain of his life!"

"Roma, you forget yourself—"

"I thought it was the Antonovas who would destroy us! I thought *they* were the dangerous ones, the vipers—I thought *she*," Roman hissed, aiming the tip of the spatha at the scar on Marya's chest, "would be the one to tear us apart. But it isn't, is it? It's you," he spat at Koschei. "*You're* the poison in this family!"

Koschei's mouth tightened. "Roma, please—"

"What if you had let Dima have his life with her, hm?" Roman demanded. "All those years ago, if you had just let them be, she'd be nothing. The Antonovas would be nothing. You *created* Baba Yaga," he shouted at his father, "and if you hadn't done such a thoughtless, selfish thing, all three of your sons would still be at your side!"

"Roma, listen to me—"

"But you had to have *your heir,* didn't you?" Roman continued, gravelly with rage. "If I am the weaker son, Papa, then it's because of you. Because we are not equal in your eyes. Because you were so afraid Dima might love something else more than he loved you. That's the worst thing you can imagine, isn't it? Having me, your least worthy son, inherit your precious kingdom in Dima's place!"

Roman's chest rose and fell with anguish, the sword in his hand still aimed at an impassive Marya. "Dima would have chosen Masha," Roman said bitterly. "He would have always chosen Masha—and was that really so bleak a prophecy you preferred to destroy all your sons just to keep one at your side?"

The words left Koschei's mouth without permission. "You are selfish," he said to Roman. "You are like me, Roma. You're too desperate, too starved. You will never be enough. Just like me," he said, swallowing hard, "Just like me, Romik, my son—you are not enough."

Roman stared at him.

Then, slowly, the blade in his hand traveled away from Marya's throat, aiming itself at his father's chest instead.

"Because of you, I am haunted," Roman said hoarsely. "Because of you, Sasha Antonova haunts me, and Lev, too. Because of all I've done for you, and now you say I'm not enough?"

Koschei said nothing.

"I could have been enough if you had ever let me," Roman said, taking a lunging step forward, and for the first time, Koschei saw that his son's dark eyes were bloodshot and wide. Shadows crept under them, luminous and black. Roman had not been sleeping well, Koschei realized. Something had kept his middle son awake at night. Demons had danced on his skull. He was owed a reckoning.

It was Marya's voice that jolted them.

"If you kill him," she said, taking a few steps to stand beside Koschei as Roman hurriedly re-aimed the spatha at her throat, "I'll bring Lev back. After all, the deal will be broken and there will be no further need for enmity. My mother has no need for a rival," she said with a shrug, "and your family won't stay powerful for long. Your empire will fall to me, to my mother, to my sisters. Already, you have nothing left to fight for. Nothing left to lose."

Roman blinked.

Koschei opened his mouth, but made no sound.

"I don't want what's yours, Roma," Marya continued to say to him, her voice a disconcerting tone of comfort. "Perhaps you wanted to take from me, but I have no claim to what's yours. You're trapped by your father's animosity?" she posed to him, beguiling as she always was. "Break the chains, then, Roma. Free yourself."

Roman didn't fight it when Marya held up a hand, guiding the spatha's edge to place it just beneath Koschei's jaw. Koschei stiffened, hardly blinking. A careless breath would be enough to cut his throat.

"What do you think your father would choose?" Marya whispered to Roman, whose mouth tightened.

"He never chooses me."

"No, Romik," she said sadly, "he doesn't."

Koschei held his breath, waiting.

Life doesn't flash, he realized abruptly. At the end, it's a sticky sort of glue, lining the back of a single image. It seemed foolish to bother with regrets. Now, here? Koschei remembered only one thing from his life, a single sensation, and it was the precise feeling of Dimitri's hair under his fingers. *Looks like gold, feels like silk,* he'd always thought proudly. *This,* he had thought with a smile, *is luxury.* This is opulence. This is treasure itself: the wealth of the perfect son.

Now, the vision of Roman before him dimmed.

Marya was telling the truth about Dimitri, Koschei realized, letting recognition wash over him in a wave. He wasn't a fool; he knew the pitch and timbre of his children, down to every bone and pulse and thought. Dimitri had surely betrayed him, because of course he had. Dimitri was a good man, not a good son. His father had wronged him, had cost him everything he loved, and Dimitri was not so weak as to continue on his knees. Dimitri would make a life for himself. Dimitri would be fine.

Roman, on the other hand, would not.

Roman needed redemption. He needed a reckoning.

And whatever anyone else believed, Koschei treasured his middle son enough to give him that.

"Do it," he said, hazarding a swallow against the sword's edge. "She's right, Romik. I do love Dima more."

Roman's mouth became a broken arch of loss. It twisted to the corpse of a smile.

"This is your fault," Roman said.

Yes, thought Lazar Fedorov, closing his eyes.

This was his fault, the work of his hands.

This was the consequence of his lifetime, and in his final moments, he knew it to be true.

This was the empire Koschei the Deathless had built.

V. 23

(Strikes.)

Sasha and Lev met Ivan outside the meeting hall of the Witches' Boroughs, hurrying toward him. He stood away from the dull clamor from inside, scrapes of chairs and argumentative voices stretching unintelligibly toward the street.

"What's going on?" Sasha asked, Lev half a step behind her, and Ivan shook his head, angling himself in her direction.

"Nothing. It's only some excitement, it will—" Abruptly, Ivan blinked, registering Lev's appearance. "Pass," he finished with confusion, and then, somewhat guiltily, "Oh." A pause. "You both, you're—"

"My sister's planning something," Sasha said urgently, drawing Ivan's attention back to her. "Do you know where she is?"

"No," Ivan confessed, looking grimly apprehensive. "But Dimitri just said something about going to find her, and—" He paused, digging into his pocket. "She gave me this, if it helps. I don't know what it contains."

Ivan handed Sasha an envelope from inside his coat, which she could see hadn't been opened. Leave it to a man like Ivan to carry a mysterious package for her sister without ever asking why.

"Who was it meant for?" Lev asked, and Ivan gave a small gesture over his shoulder as Sasha pulled out a handwritten letter, beginning to read.

"The Boroughs," he said. "They're up in arms about Dimitri's abscosion at the moment, so I haven't had a chance to hand it over, but—"

"Lev," Sasha said, nudging him after she'd finished scanning the letter. "Look at this."

Lev skimmed the page, then frowned.

"Did I—" He blinked. "Did I read that wrong?"

Sasha shook her head, tracing the lines of her sister's handwriting under her thumb.

This life will try to leave you empty-handed, she heard her sister say, *unless you learn to strike first.*

"No," Sasha said, and looked up. "We have to find her. Now."

V. 24

(Choices.)

Roman stepped forward, the tip of the spatha pressing the imprint of a thin white line into his father's throat. A flick of his wrist would do it. Barely an inch. Marya watched him, waiting, and the moment Koschei relented, his shoulders falling in resignation—the moment the Deathless accepted his death—she caught the edge of the blade in her hand, letting the metal bite into her palm.

"Very good, Koschei," she murmured to him, and his lungs abruptly filled, launching him unsteadily back a step. "Drop it," she said to Roman, who seemed to wake from a trance the moment she spoke, hastily letting the sword fall. He stared at his own shaking hands as if he could hardly believe they belonged to him, and Marya swung the spatha up in the air, catching the pommel deftly.

"I thought," Roman said, swallowing. "I thought you wanted me to—"

"To kill him? No, Roma. This is much better," Marya said, smiling at him in approval. "Death is so easy, isn't it? Hardly anything at all, compared with other things—like the necessity of choices. You chose yourself over your father," she clarified, aiming the blade at Roman before swinging it pointedly to Koschei, "and *you* chose one son over the other. You both chose, as I once chose, and now you've both known loss as I have known it, because neither of you can ever forget what you've done."

She could see on Koschei's face that he understood as much; already, his skin was ragged and sallow with grief. He'd seen his own death and done nothing to prevent it. He'd confessed to his own son that he loved another more, and seeing as Roman would never understand what Marya had observed from watching—Roman, after all, would not have noticed the lie Koschei had told to secure his own fate—he would always remember the words: *I love Dima more.*

"Still," Marya said, and stepped forward with the sword in her hand, transforming it quickly to a knife. Easier to maneuver, and she was no gruesome Fedorov assassin. She had an Antonova's delicate hands. "I have vendettas to resolve, Koschei. You understand," she said, pressing the side of the blade to his neck herself. "I couldn't leave the satisfaction of your death to Roma."

"No," Roman said, stepping forward. "No, don't—"

Marya's hand shot out, slamming him against the wall.

"Stay there," she told him. "You made your choice. Live with it." She slid the edge of the knife higher, nicking a bit of Koschei's silver hair. "My turn," she murmured, and Koschei gave her a bitter smile.

"You've really taken everything from me, Marya," he murmured.

"Yes. Like you once did." The metal of the blade was kissing his neck, slithering up to his jaw. "And now you can't stop me, Koschei. You can't hurt me. Your own son has ensured that you can do nothing to touch me or my family, and now you have no choice but to lie at my feet and rot to nothing if that's the fate I choose for you."

She leaned forward, speaking in his ear.

"You destroyed all three of your sons," she whispered to him. "One by one, Koschei the Deathless, you broke them, and now none of them will mourn you. They'll only mourn themselves and what they might have been without you, without your greed. Without your darkness."

She didn't mention what had become of her sisters. What *would* become of them, corrupted by the world in which they lived. She didn't mention that the path Koschei had given his sons wasn't the only one responsible for damage, as she'd made her own arrangements to deal with the rest. Koschei's death would only solve half a problem. Marya Antonova, ruthlessly effective as she was, had made arrangements for what remained.

Still, she wasn't so cruel as to rob him of his moment. Let him think her life revolved around the end of his. Let death bring him peace, if it wished to.

"You are your mother's daughter, Marya Antonova," Koschei rasped under his breath. By now, she was no longer surprised to hear him say it with faint traces of awe.

She didn't bother replying. They both knew it was true.

Instead she tightened her hand around the knife, taking the breath that would drag them both to the feet of a lifetime's inevitability.

V. 25

(Inevitability.)

When had Dimitri Fedorov known he loved Marya Antonova?

He had known it like the voice of his soul, the sanctity of every prayer. With certainty equal to the changing of the seasons, borne on devotion as relentless as the tide. He had known he loved her like he knew he would rise each day, like knowing his lungs would fill with each breath, like knowing he could bleed with every puncture. With motions as practiced as each step he took. He had loved her with the whole of his being, as if he'd been made to do it; as if he'd been crafted that way by some divine hand. She was in his blood, beating in his chest, racing against it. He felt the ache of her now, pressed flat against the bone of his sternum. With each moment since he'd begun racing to reach her, a fraction of her heart had shattered more, each sliver of shrapnel as much his doing as hers. As much his pain as it was hers.

Why had he loved her? Not for her strength, though she had plenty of it. For that, he'd admired her. She was untouchable for it, for her courage, for her unyielding surety. It was easy to love. It was why anyone would be drawn to her. Still, it wasn't why Dimitri had loved her.

No. That had been for her goodness. For her loyalty.

For her heart.

Dimitri Fedorov had loved Marya Antonova with his entire being for his entire life, which was how he'd somehow come to miss the now-obvious signs that his plans and hers weren't entirely the same.

Burn the world down.

She hadn't meant the whole world.

Just the world she'd been forced to live in.

Dimitri raced into The Bridge's office, bursting through the doors. "Masha, no," he gasped, seeing her with her knife to his father's throat, and she looked up, confusion flickering briefly on her brow. He summoned the knife from her hand, ripping it from her fingers as his father lurched backward and nearly fell, Roman staggering forward from across the room to catch him.

Dimitri caught the blade of Marya's knife in his palm, waiting as she turned to face him.

This was only part of her plan. Ridding the world of Koschei was only half. For twelve years, it had been a rivalry, a two-part equation. Koschei and Baba Yaga, two halves of a symbiotic whole.

Koschei was only the beginning of something Dimitri hadn't managed to see at first.

"Masha," he said with a faint overtone of pleading, and at the sight of him, she smiled grimly.

"Everything's different now," she told him. "You did it, Dima. You won."

"We won," he told her with a creak of anguish, and she shook her head.

"*You* won," she corrected. "I've lost. Well, that's not quite true," she said with a hollow laugh. "Is it a loss if it's a forfeit?"

He'd known she'd never give up her mother. Marya Antonova was a witch, but before that she was a daughter. A sister. A woman with countless regrets. Her family would be fine. He was positive that she'd made sure of it somehow.

But tonight, for the first time, Dimitri Fedorov had stood alone, his own man—and now, like him, she was doing the same.

For once, Marya Antonova was taking her fate into her own hands.

"You don't have to," he told her, voice breaking with the sorrow she couldn't feel.

Her mouth quirked.

"No," she agreed. "But you would, if you were me. I know you understand it."

Her gaze dropped to the heart he wore around his neck, and the pulse of it he knew by now, memorized for every fit and start that it possessed. *If I ever decide to give my heart to you, Dima,* she'd said once, holding his hand palm up, *then cut it out of my chest and keep it somewhere safe, where no one else can get to it. Keep it locked somewhere, Dima, where no one will ever find it.*

"I can't keep it," he told her painfully. "It isn't mine."

"So don't," she said with a shrug. "It's a good plan, you know." Her smile broadened slightly. "With Koschei gone and you installed in the Boroughs, my family can be safe. Sasha can choose another life. They all can."

"Baba Yaga can't simply walk away from her crimes," Dimitri said, and she shook her head.

"No, she can't," she agreed, though it was hollow-sounding. False-sounding. As if she knew something he didn't, which he understood now that she always had. "But still, someone can fall, Dima," she murmured, meeting his eye. "Can't they?"

He curled his hand tightly around the knife.

"It can't be you," he said flatly.

She looked amused. "Why not?"

"Because." He swallowed hard, thrusting around for an answer. "Because you can't die."

"Oh, but I can," she reminded him, dark gaze falling again to the vial around his neck as he shivered, registering what she meant. "It should be relatively easy for you, shouldn't it?" she asked him. "Look what I might have done to your father. To your brother. Can you say you wouldn't have done it yourself, if I'd succeeded?"

Dimitri pictured his father's bloodied corpse on the floor, as it might have been if he'd been even a second too late. The flash of it in his mind was filled with gore, grotesque and unreal. Impossibly so.

Her pulse, amid his hesitation, was calm, expectant, knowing. His, by contrast, raced.

"You wouldn't have," he forced himself to say, though he only half believed it.

"I would have," she assured him. "For my family, Dima? I would."

"But you said you were angry with them," he argued. "You said—"

"I know what I said," Marya permitted tightly, "but I told you." She lifted her chin, watching his thumb slide along the knife's handle. "I wanted a new kingdom. I never said it had to be mine."

He wondered if he shouldn't have guessed it sooner, decades ago, that it would eventually come to this. Time seemed to run in circles, chasing its tail. *If I ever decide to give my heart to you, Dima, then cut it out of my chest and keep it somewhere safe.*

Many people in love have failed to kill each other before.

Dima, this love I have for you will be the death of me.

"You're asking me to do the impossible," Dimitri managed hoarsely.

"Well," Marya said, "only because you're so very capable."

Her intent was grossly clear. Behind her, Bryn twitched forward, apprehensive. Sensing it, she held out a hand.

"You said you wouldn't interfere, Bridge," Marya warned.

He sat back unwillingly, waiting, as Dimitri eyed the knife in his hand, still resistant.

"You don't have to," he said again.

"I know." Her gaze fell to his chest, to the vial beating against it. "For the record, you could have at least let me finish the job," she said, her gaze flicking to Koschei and Roman.

Dimitri wanted to laugh, but couldn't. The effort would overtax his fragile constitution to the point of helpless collapse. "It won't heal you, Masha," he told her sincerely. "It won't make you whole."

She set her jaw. "Then what will?" she asked knowingly.

A pause. A swallow. A confession.

He'd felt the pain in her heart where it lay against his as fully as if it had been conjured from within his own chest. He'd felt it alternately race and throb, skipping beats, shattering itself in anguish. He'd felt it respond to things he'd never known about her before, leaving him to wonder now what he had missed while he'd only been looking. Had she left pieces of herself with him, or had he taken them himself? Had anyone ever given Marya Antonova as much as she had given them? He suspected the answer was no.

Now, though, the pain in her heart was his alone to bear. None of it registered on her face—only he could feel it. He figured he had two choices: He could stop her. Put it back in her chest. Make her see what she'd done. Make sure she knew the pain that echoed now against him, see how it would change her mind. He could remind her who she was; make her see she was a consequence of secrets, a tower built on deceit. He could take the heart from around his neck, press it into her palm, and remind her of who she'd been, of what she'd done. He could let her feel the consequences of her grief, the madness of her pain. The destruction of her love.

Or, he thought quietly, he could carry it for her. Help her carry on.

He stood a little straighter, convinced of that much. How many times can you fail a woman before you redeem yourself for her? Let her burden be his now, he thought, and glanced down at the knife in his hand, and then back up at her face.

His father's death would not have made her whole.

Then what will?

"I will," he promised her, and Bryn let out a muted sound of disbelief as Dimitri raised the knife and drove it into the vial around his neck, into the heart he carried there. It sank in through enchanted glass, the metal blooming crimson and dripping in slender rivulets down his wrists, and from afar Marya stumbled forward, dazed.

It wouldn't pain her. Not at this distance. She'd merely fade away if she didn't come closer, but of course she did, reaching out for Dimitri until she caught herself on his outstretched arm, one hand still wrapped around the knife. By then The Bridge's face had gone pale, Roman's expression more haunted than ever, but Dimitri was focused on Marya, on his Marya. On the agony spreading across her lips the closer she came to the heart in his hand.

"Masha," he whispered, enveloping her with one arm as she staggered into him, hands outstretched. He buried his nose in her hair, in her sweetness, one hand on her still-bleeding heart. "Masha, my Masha."

"I always knew you would be the death of me, Dima," she managed to say, her voice delirious with gratification as she dragged the tips of her fingers to his mouth. "But still, didn't you promise me forever?"

Dimitri looked up at his father. His brother.

Then Dimitri Fedorov looked down at Marya Antonova, watching her eyes flutter shut.

Don't you know we belong together, Masha?

It's inevitable.

You might as well give in.

"Don't worry, Masha," he said quietly, pulling her close, his hand still tight around the handle of the knife. "I would never make you go alone."

Dimitri took the blade, driving it through the scar on his chest until he felt it slice and puncture and burst, numbness flooding his limbs only to be swallowed up by a monstrous, quaking pain. It was incomprehensible discomfort, to say the least. His every bone and organ opposed it, and Dimitri already knew from experience that blood was never as beautiful as sacrifice prescribed. In reality it was carnal and human and real, and for that, it was everything he'd always sworn he'd give up for her. It was life itself, and death; it was forever, and so were they—and briefly, with the last of her strength, Marya managed to smile.

The last sound was a whimper from his father. It wouldn't end with a bang, Dimitri thought, but at least it would end, and for that, he was comfortably satisfied.

Dimitri brought Marya's lips up to his, letting himself grow drowsy with inconsequential aching from his chest, the roaring rush of silence gradually filling the channels of his ears. It was nothing, he thought wearily, nothing at all compared to her, and his last thought was peaceful, because it was *Masha*. Because it was her, finally—at last—and then they tumbled together into nothing, her final breath of relief the very last thing to fill his lungs.

V. 26

(Inheritance.)

Some miles away, the witch called Baba Yaga sat upright, feeling for all her vitals. Pulse, breath, limbs. She counted her fingers and toes. She counted her daughters, listing them off in her head. *Irina, who hears the dead. Ekaterina, who sees them. Yelena, my girl of stars. Liliya, my dreamer. Galina, my pretty one. Sasha, my little one.*

Marya, my soul.

It struck her with a pang, and as the knob turned at her bedroom door, she knew. Even before she saw that a tearstained Irina stood behind it, she knew.

"She's staying this time," Yaga said, swallowing. "Isn't she?"

Irina nodded silently.

"Did she say anything?" Yaga asked, bitterly hopeful.

Another nod. "She says you'll understand."

No, Yaga thought gently, *this time, Mashenka, I do not think so.*

She rose to her feet slowly, feeling blindly for the floor. Her limbs would not give out. She was Baba Yaga. She was the curator of an enterprise. She had risen up from nothing. She would rise again tonight.

Yaga rested a hand on Irina's shoulder, saying nothing, and headed down the hall. Galina's room was shut. Sasha's was empty. At the end of the hall would be Liliya, who would be sleeping, as she often was; she was fondest of sleep and of quiet.

Yaga opened the door, slipping inside, and shut it behind her with only the ghost of a sound.

"Liliya," she whispered, perching at the side of her fifth daughter's bed. "Lilenka, are you dreaming?"

Liliya's eyes fluttered open.

"Hi, Mama," she said sleepily, as Yaga brushed her forehead, smoothing her thumb over the crease of concern. "What is it?"

"Shh, nothing," Yaga told her. Nothing that couldn't wait until morning. "I just wanted to hear about your dreams, Lilenka. You know I always like the things you see."

Liliya nodded, lying on her back and considering the request. Her hair, dark like her sisters', spread out in waves across the silky lightness of her pillowcase.

"I did have a dream," Liliya said eventually, frowning into the darkened space of her bedroom to recall it. "I dreamt just now of our inheritance. But it was the strangest thing," she said, turning on her side to face her mother. "I could see nothing, because it was locked inside a box." She paused, chewing lightly at her lip. "What would I have found, Mama, if I had opened it?"

At once, Yaga's chest tightened, and then released.

She says you'll understand.

Oh, Mashenka, Yaga thought sadly. *You always understood too much.*

"Mama?" Liliya asked, watching her expression change. "Is everything okay?"

Yaga took a breath and bent her head, brushing her lips against Liliya's forehead.

"Of course, Lilenka," she said. "Go back to sleep. Everything will be fine in the morning."

V. 27

(Heaven Finds Means.)

When Lev and Sasha arrived, it was too late. By the time they'd pieced together enough of her mind to know what she must have done, Marya Antonova already lay with her long dark hair across the unmoving chest of Dimitri Fedorov, and all was said and done.

More was said, in fact, than anyone but Lev and Sasha had any knowledge of, because Marya Antonova had put it in a letter.

On the evening Marya Antonova and Dimitri Fedorov died, the

Borough witches received two important envelopes. One, as Marya
had truthfully informed Roman and his father, was from Dimitri
Fedorov, which included a lengthy series of records in Dimitri's
own hand detailing the crimes of Koschei the Deathless. At the
bottom of a letter urging the Borough witches to act on their consciences, he stipulated firmly that his brothers were blameless. He
detailed the location of every creature Koschei the Deathless had
ever bought or sold or traded, and signed ownership of Koschei's
rents over to the Boroughs themselves. Then he'd said, *It's over.
This is all there is. Let his kingdom fall.*

The other, from Marya Antonova, was something so similar as
to be a mirror image. Even her handwriting was strangely reflec-
tive of Dimitri Fedorov's, leaning slightly left to the same degree
his had leaned right. Hers was a similar confession of evidence, and
included a signature at the bottom: *Baba Yaga.*

She had shrugged on her mother's title and worn it comfortably
for the first and last time.

There is money, Marya Antonova wrote. *A lot of money, in fact, and
in anticipation of my own reparations, I have seen fit to distribute it among
the Boroughs. Consider it a gift. You will notice, I imagine, that there is
still a reasonable sum unaccounted for. This is intentional. I warn you
not to be greedy. Do not look for it. I am gone now and so is Koschei, so let
this be the end.*

"Well?" the Borough witches asked Jonathan Moronoe. "What
will we do?"

"You read the letters," he said, shrugging.

In Jonathan Moronoe's mind, Dimitri Fedorov and Marya
Antonova had kept to their ends of the deal. Evidence had been
compiled. Sins had been confessed. Wrongs had been righted. Reparations had been paid. Life would go on unhindered. Life, in the
end, would go on.

The Borough Elders arrived to arrest Lazar Fedorov, a witch
long suspected of his alter ego, but the warehouse belonging to

Koschei the Deathless had been emptied, with nothing left in its place. He'd been there, of course, waiting for them, and had been vacantly surprised when they turned away empty-handed. Unbeknownst to him, the shadow creatures he'd employed had hidden him from sight, briefly, as the first of their unrestricted acts.

After the Borough witches left, Koschei went downtown for a much-needed drink, where he ran into a man named Ivan.

"I need a favor," Koschei said, and Ivan turned his head, considering him.

"Depends," Ivan said. "What is it?"

"Let's discuss it over a drink," Koschei suggested.

Later that night, two men parted ways. One would be known in whispers for the rest of his life as Koschei the Deathless, though he had taken on a new enterprise drastically different from what he had done before. He protected the small, a purveyor of aid to the underprivileged, and offered counsel to those in need. Later, people would remark that he had something of a mild-mannered air to him. He had, as many people noted, a soldier's presence.

The other man left as Lazar Fedorov, who never appeared in the Manhattan Borough again.

Many of the later bits, everything aside from Marya's letter, were relayed to Lev Fedorov in retrospect by the man who introduced himself as Brynmor Attaway, an attorney apparently nicknamed The Bridge.

"I was Marya Antonova's attorney at the time of her death," Bryn explained to Lev, adding, "She stipulated in her will to leave you this."

This was an envelope full of cash, to which a note had been pinned.

Solnyshko, the note said. *The plan was always that the sun would rise.*

"Thank you," Lev said to The Bridge, a bit perplexed. He noted that beside him, however, Sasha was pretending not to know their unexpected visitor. It seemed to be a performance acted out by both parties until Bryn turned to her.

"Rusalka," he said, nodding in departure. "I think maybe we won't be seeing each other again."

"Don't be stupid, Bridge," Sasha replied. "We're friends."

"I don't have friends," said The Bridge.

"Seems unlikely," Lev remarked.

"Where'd you find this guy?" The Bridge asked Sasha, gesturing skeptically to Lev, and she shrugged.

"Picked him up in a bar," she said.

The Bridge smiled. "Well, see you," he said. "Or not. We'll see." Then he tipped his hat, disappearing into the air.

"Oh," Lev said, startled. "I didn't know he was a witch."

"He's . . . a long story," Sasha demurred, rising to her feet and joining Lev, pausing to brush her lips against his cheek. "So," she said. "How are you holding up?"

"Fairly well, I think," Lev said. "Your sister repaired me nicely. Almost no odd creaks."

"Not what I meant, Lev," Sasha sighed, to which he smiled faintly.

"With the fact that my brother is gone, you mean?" he asked. "The world feels different. A little less bright. But I think I understand what he chose."

She said nothing. He cleared his throat, tilting his head down to look at her.

"So," Lev said. "Don't you have a shift at the store in a few minutes?"

"Yes," she said. "As do you."

"Actually, I can't tonight. I mean, for one thing, I'm independently wealthy and don't need to work," he informed her playfully, holding up the envelope from Marya as Sasha swatted it away with a roll of her eyes, "but for another, I thought I'd pay a visit to the Witches' Boroughs. See what they're doing about my brother's vacant seat."

"Ah. Okay, then." Sasha kissed him again lightly, with the distraction of ordinary life, before stepping back to grab her keys. "I'll see you tonight after work. Bye, Eric," she called over her shoulder, and in answer, Eric raised a fork, not looking up from the television.

"Later, Sasha," he said.

"Hey," Lev said, catching her arm just before she left. "Maybe I can come by for fifteen minutes? When I'm done with the Boroughs."

Her lips quirked. "Sure. Fifteen. No more, no less."

"Ouch, Sasha," he whispered, sliding an arm around her waist and kissing her swiftly. "Text me if you get bored?"

"Yes." She bit lightly on his lip. "Now let me go, Fedorov. I've got things to do."

He grudgingly released her, watching her slip out the front door.

For a while, Lev had been disappointed that his brother hadn't left anything for him. No message, no final words. According to Roman, Dimitri hadn't said anything to any of them before he died, and for a while, Lev had been consumed by the idea that perhaps their brother had left something behind. A meaningful token, possibly. Maybe a letter. He had searched and searched through all his brothers' things, and he knew Sasha had done the same for her sister. In the end, though, they'd overturned their siblings' homes for nothing. Neither Marya nor Dimitri had been particularly sentimental, or so it seemed.

But then Lev had fallen onto the sofa, exhausted and wrung out with loss, and as Sasha had curled into his side, he'd realized why his brother hadn't said anything. After all, the gift was obvious, wasn't it? Marya and Dimitri had given Sasha and Lev the simplicity—the beautiful normality—that they themselves had been denied. Dimitri had given Lev freedom from a life he'd never wanted. He'd given him choices. Last words would have been paltry in comparison to this: the Antonova witch who kissed him goodbye with the words *let me go*, because she would be back. She would be back, and she would be his.

He pulled his cell phone out of his pocket, selecting her name from his contacts.

> LEV: *miss you already*
> SASHA: *lev you are the absolute corniest*
> SASHA: *don't forget we're having dinner with galya tomorrow*
> SASHA: *also, make sure eric looks for a job today. remind him that drug dealing is not a marketable skill and neither is overusing bath bombs*
> SASHA: *if he gives you any lip tell him I'll punch him again*

Lev chuckled.

> LEV: *sasha*
> SASHA: *yes lev what is it*
> LEV: *this is my favorite book*
> SASHA: *GROAN*
> SASHA: *but yeah*
> SASHA: *ok fine*
> SASHA: *me too*

A pause. He watched her typing.

> SASHA: *I love you*

This, he thought with certainty.

This was why Dimitri hadn't left him a note.

He would have known Lev would have precisely what he wanted him to hear, even if it came from someone else.

> LEV: *I love you too*
> SASHA: *come see me tonight ok? I mean it*

LEV: don't read into this too much alexandra
LEV: but I was definitely going to even if you told me not to
SASHA: ok cool
LEV: see you then

He slid his phone back in his pocket.

"Sometimes death is peace," Roman had said, after all of it. "Then again," he mused, pointedly eyeing Lev, "I suppose sometimes death is only temporary, isn't it?"

Lev smiled at the thought.

"Sometimes an end is just a cleverly disguised beginning," he'd replied, seeing that he was someone who would know.

He glanced down at his watch; time to get going. The nights were growing longer now, hot and muggy and restless without sleep. Still, there was a moment, Lev knew, as he stepped out onto the sidewalk, when he could see the blend of night and day—the sun, the moon, and the stars. There was a moment when all of it aligned, and he didn't want to miss it.

"Be well, Dima," he said to his brother, wherever he was. "Keep him in line, Masha."

He either imagined a nod, or felt it.

Then Lev Fedorov turned, half smiling, and let his feet carry him down the sidewalk, traveling the newness of his path.

THE EPILOGUE

It was a strange thing, having a witch's magic. For a time, Brynmor Attaway really thought it wouldn't take. Surgeries, after all, went wrong all the time. Transplants (which typically involved far more precision than a vaguely suicidal witch blindly digging around with her bare hands) had consequences. Bryn waited to become ill, or for the electric buzz in his veins to eventually fizzle out, crackling like power failure and static. It would have been enough, Bryn reasoned, to have made the effort, even if it couldn't last. Which, of course, it wouldn't—couldn't possibly.

He waited for failure, but oddly, it never came.

"Well, that's rather a nice thing, don't you think?" asked his mother. She wore her hair in a crown of braids around her head, like usual.

She still looked sweetly eighteen, like she had his entire life, which was becoming more and more hilarious to Bryn the longer he came to visit. The older he got, the stranger their dynamic.

"I'm not opposed," he said. She lifted the kettle from where she stood barefoot in her kitchen, and he paused her, lifting a finger. Fairies were attuned to subtle gestures—he was glad to be here with her rather than with someone for whom he'd have to clear his throat, or put on an act of exhausting human normalcy. "Let me," he offered, and levitated the kettle over to the table, depositing her hyacinth tea into their respective cups.

"Show-off," she groused, flouncing into her chair. She seemed secretly pleased in the way young women were usually pleased—as if they enjoyed being in on the joke, but were loath to admit it. "How are the others, then? Your witch friends."

"My witch friends?" Bryn echoed doubtfully, raising the teacup to his lips.

"They're witches. They're your friends. Don't be difficult, Brynmor."

"My alleged 'witch friends' seem to enjoy my difficulty, Mother."

"Don't call me that. It makes me feel old."

"Mum. Mama."

"Stop."

He sipped his tea, smiling into the cup.

"How's your father?" she asked after a moment, and then brightened. "Dead yet?"

"Not yet, Mom." Senator Attaway, like most of his kind (i.e., white male politicians), would live to see a decent age. Bryn set the tea down, adding, "I'm sure you'll see him soon."

She sighed dreamily. "I can't wait. He was such an utter delight."

Bryn shrugged. "Well, he's human. He's clinging to life, as they tend to do."

"Hm, unfortunate. And the others?" she asked, abruptly remembering her question. "How's the young one?"

"Lev?" Bryn guessed, and she nodded. "He holds the cursed Borough position now. The one previously held by Dimitri Fedorov," he clarified, "and by Marya's husband before that."

She lifted a brow. "Curse? Was that your doing?"

"No, not an actual curse." Who had the time? "Just magicless superstition." Bryn rolled his eyes, annoyed all over again. "Imagine thinking something is cursed simply because others would die for it. What's love, then?"

His mother fixed him with her brightest smile.

"Idiocy," she said, "in its loveliest form."

Before he could argue, she gave a pleasant shrug. "How's the other one?"

"Roma?" Another nod. "He's been working as a paralegal in my firm the last few months, actually. Keeping his head down, staying away from witches." Bryn paused for a moment. "But I think he'll leave soon."

His mother tilted her head, waiting.

"Sometimes he looks down at his hands, you know, and I see it. Static. A spark." Bryn briskly sipped his tea, aiming for impassivity. "His magic is coming back. I don't think he'll be able to deny it for much longer."

"You said he was trying to escape it, didn't you?"

"Yes," Bryn said slowly, "but . . ." He glanced down at his own hands. The lines in them looked different now, changed. There was something in the crevices of his palms that hadn't been there before, and he doubted that anyone born with that sort of remarkability had the restraint to deny what they were for long, grieving or not. Remorseful or not. Punishment, or not.

"I don't think he'll be able to," Bryn repeated, and his mother gave him a quizzical glance. Then she rose lightly to her feet, rummaging through a cabinet full of decanters and pulling out a dusty amber bottle of something syrupy and viscous.

"Here," she said, handing it to him. "Try this."

Bryn grimaced. "I'm not going to drug him, Mother."

"Who said anything about drugging him?" she asked innocently, and he took the bottle from her with a sigh.

"You don't have to say it for me to know perfectly well what you mean," he informed her, and she gave him another dazzling smile.

"It's just something I played around with. Meant to be shared."

He arched a brow. She blew him a kiss.

"Fine," he relented, and she smiled, pleased. "I'll take the gift, but just so you know, I'm not going to stop him if he wants to leave. He isn't beholden to me, and we certainly aren't friends." He sipped the last of his tea. "We never made a deal that he would stay."

"Oh, Brynmor," she sighed. "You have such a terribly human way of looking at things sometimes."

"Do I?"

"Yes, of course. But anyway, take the bottle," she urged him. "For your friend."

"He's not my friend," he repeated, exasperated, but she wasn't listening. It was very hard to keep her attention. She was young yet, as far as fairies went.

Eventually Bryn rose to his feet, the neck of the bottle clutched tightly in his hand. He leaned over to kiss her cheek as he went.

"Do you think your father will die soon?" his mother asked again absently, looking out the window.

Just as he hadn't before, Bryn didn't tell her that the boy she'd known was a man now, covered with grey hair and lines and with no sense of wonder, far less interesting to her now than he was all those years ago. She would probably consider it a detestably mortal thing to have done, if not a total betrayal.

"I'll kill him myself if he doesn't," Bryn offered fondly instead, and she smiled at him, waving him away as she turned back to her reverie. He strode to the front door, pulling it open, and behind him, the house disappeared. She'd have taken a new and more interesting form by then, surely. Meanwhile, it might take him all day to leave this realm if he didn't start walking now.

Bryn wandered the pathway in silence, pondering each step. In this realm, things weren't quite so permanent. Time moved in whatever direction it felt it should, turning and retracting in on itself in invisible currents and tides. He reached a hand out, feeling it warp pleasantly under his fingers, darting and preening and slithering. He might have been here an hour, maybe a whole day. By now, though, he knew well enough when to leave, to avoid missing the deposition in the morning.

Bryn was nearly back to the bridge for which he'd been named when he paused, catching something from afar. A young man with golden hair sat beneath a green oak tree, lazing in the shade with a dark-haired girl in his arms. He was conjuring something, a little flutter of wings for her amusement, and she looked up with an unburdened laugh, fingers outstretched to reach for it.

It took a moment for Bryn to realize he was staring. At a certain point, though, the girl looked over, lifting her chin. She sat up slightly, letting her long hair cascade in waves down her back, and gave him a small wave, the boy beside her turning to follow her gaze.

Bryn raised a hand, returning the gesture. Marya Antonova smiled, soft and slow, and then blinked, as if she'd forgotten what she was looking at. She turned back to Dimitri Fedorov, looking momentarily lost, and he pressed his lips to her temple, soothing her. They curled into each other, retreating back into their private little world, and Bryn took a last, long look at them.

The scar on her chest was gone.

Bryn nodded, satisfied.

He crossed back into the land of the living sometime in the dead hours, the not-quite-morning ticks of the clock, and shook his head as he set the bottle from his mother on the corner of his desk. He hadn't been totally honest with her, though that wasn't quite the insult to fae that it was to humans. There was no point sharing truth with fae; they didn't know what to do with it. They liked their own imaginations more.

Bryn glanced down at the envelope he still hadn't opened, eyeing the script on the front.

Bridge.

He didn't need to know what parting words Roman Fedorov had left for him when he'd gone; not yet. Instead, Bryn tucked the letter away, pulling a knife from his desk drawer and cracking the seal on his mother's bottle of brandy, taking a moment to let it breathe. From where the bottle sat, it smelled like sentiment and too much time in the sun. She thought herself clever, and she was.

Bryn poured the brandy into his WORLD'S BEST LAWYER mug and settled himself in his chair, propping his feet on the desk. He raised the beverage to his lips, closing his eyes, and let his mother's brandy do its work. Letting it bring him an old oak tree, eternal summer, and a pair of tender arms.

He took a second sip, and then another.

On a whim, he reached out, waving away the glow from his desk lamp. He smiled to himself, oddly sated by the stillness of the hour, and watched the shadows fade to nothing.

"What fools these witches be," he mused, to no one in particular.

Tendrils of sun would creep over the edges of his desk well before he moved again.

ACKNOWLEDGMENTS

January 2019

Thank you to *Witch Way Magazine,* the original home to the first half of this story, back when it was titled *Fume of Sighs* and ended with unrepentant disaster. (It still does, kind of, but differently.) Thank you to Tonya Brown, as always, for allowing me to write whatever devastating and sometimes very strange stories I see fit.

Many thanks to this story's editors, all three of whom saw it in different forms. Aurora, please insert a *Princess Diaries* GIF here, along with an emoji of a ball of string. I don't know if you actually *like* receiving world-building texts at 4 A.M., or, for that matter, if you enjoy reading drafts of the same things multiple times because I've decided to wail into the void and start over, but the fact that you do it anyway is really very nice. Thank u, I like u. Cynthia, your enthusiasm for my work and the way you always seem happy to come to my aid (much to my disbelief) is positively astounding to me, and I will always be grateful to you. I'm sure I'll never be able to properly repay you, but I look forward to the process of trying. Stacie, pursuing this insane dream is much, much better with you on my side. Thank you for loving this story, and for believing in me. I look forward to our future martinis (exclusively for the aesthetic).

Chmura, my pierogi princess, my favorite artist, my one-woman squad: Truly, I have yet to dream up a story you couldn't bring to life, and at this point I don't think it's possible. Thank you for everything you do for me, and even more than being my illustrator, thank you for being my friend. You are . . . SIMPLY THE BEST.

To my parents. Especially my mother: Thank you for being the strong woman who (hopefully) raised one, too. Grandma, there is too much sex in this story for you to have liked it, but I hope you see how you were part of it all the same. To my family and friends, who are supportive of my work in so many inconceivable ways (most astoundingly, by reading it): Allie, Cara, Carrie, David, Elena, Garrett, Kayla, Lauren, Mackenzie, Tom. To the Boxing Book Club, Lex and Nacho. To Mr. Blake: I should kill thee with such cherishing. (That's a quote from *Romeo and Juliet,* not a threat. I love you and your life is not in danger. Though, you *would* make the face of heaven so fine that all the world would be in love with night . . . and yes, that's also a quote. You're still fine.)

And, of course, to you, for being here. Shortly after I write this, I will be turning another year older, perhaps a little wiser, but certainly another year luckier, especially now that you've willingly spent some hours sharing a world with me. It continues to be the greatest thing you could possibly do for me, and I am endlessly grateful that you're here.

As always, it has been an honor to put these words down for you, and I sincerely hope you've enjoyed the story.

September 2022

As my books continue to be blessed with a second chance at life, I have ever more gratitude to bestow. Enormous thanks to my beloved agent Amelia Appel as well as Dr. Uwe Stender of Triada US. To my incredible team at Tor—my gift of an editor Lindsey Hall and Aislyn Fredsall; my publicists Desirae Friesen and Sarah Reidy; my marketing team Eileen Lawrence, Andrew King, and Emily Mlynek; my production team Dakota Griffin, Rafal Gibek, Jim Kapp, and Michelle Foytek; my interior designer Greg Collins; my publishers Devi Pillai and Lucille Rettino; foreign rights agent Chris Scheina; Christine Jaeger and sales team; audio producer Steve Wagner. On the UK side, thanks to my editor Bella Pagan; to

Lucy Hale and Georgia Summers; to my marketing team Ellie Bailey, Claire Evans, Jamie Forrest, Becky Lushey, Lucy Grainger, and Andy Joannou; to my publicity team Hannah Corbett and Jamie-Lee Nadone and Stephen Haskins of Black Crow PR; to my production and editorial team Holly Sheldrake, Sian Chilvers, and Rebecca Needes; to sales team Stuart Dwyer, Richard Green, Rory O'Brien, Leanne Williams, Joanna Dawkins, Beth Wentworth, and Kadie McGinley; the audiobook team Rebecca Lloyd and Molly Robinson.

On the art side of things, huge thanks to cover designer Jamie Stafford-Hill and UK designer Neil Lang, and of course to Little Chmura (@littlechmura) for breathtaking new interior illustrations and to Laura (@WcLasq) for gorgeous endpapers.

To Garrett and Henry, forever, as many times as I can say it, as profoundly as I can.

And finally, to the bookish social media communities whose love of these books has given me the shot of a lifetime. I won't waste a breath of it. Thank you for letting me tell you a story, and I hope you're enjoying the ride.

xx, Olivie

Turn the page for a sneak peek
of more from Olivie Blake

Forever is a gift...
and a curse.

MASTERS OF DEATH

NEW YORK TIMES BESTSELLING AUTHOR
OF *The Atlas Six*

OLIVIE BLAKE

Available Summer 2023 from Tor

PRELUDE

Even after centuries of practice, it never grew less unsettling when it happened this way—sloppily. Gorily. Murder had never been his favorite method of disposal.

"What's this?" he asked impatiently, staring down at the bloodied mess on the floor.

"Oh good," remarked a figure concealed by shadows, only a familiar glint of malice appearing from the darkness of the room. "You're here. Finally, I might add."

Worrying. Very worrying.

"This," he remarked in lieu of jumping to hysterical conclusions, "is quite an escalation. Are you responsible for this?"

"Depends on how you look at it, doesn't it?" replied the figure, with the faint suggestion of a shrug. "You could very well be *responsible,* couldn't you? If that's the verbiage you're going with."

Sequentially speaking that wasn't untrue, and he supposed he had played fast and loose with the literal.

Still—"I'm not the one holding the knife," he placidly observed.

"Fair enough." An arm sluiced through shadow as the figure tossed the blade, still gruesomely slick, onto the floor between them. "Though that doesn't really matter, does it? Now that we have you here, I mean."

That flickering, primeval sense of concern flared again, unhelpfully. Best to stick to the assets, like what was or wasn't true. "*Have* me? I assure you," he said, "you don't *have* me."

"Well, then," a second figure suggested, stepping pointedly into the light. "Try to escape."

No.

No, no, no.

This was all wrong. Very wrong.

"But *you're* not—"

"But I am," the second figure confirmed, nodding once.

"But surely the two of you aren't—"

"Oh, only by necessity, of course," the first figure said, another beam of motion splitting the shadows as the two figures exchanged a complicit nod. The effect of it was uncanny, as if shared between two separate planes of existence.

The prick of danger—of the past catching up with him at last—finally set in.

"Don't worry, you'll understand soon," the first figure assured him.

Two thoughts flashed epiphanically before him like a promise fulfilled: A face. A memory.

No, three thoughts. The dizzying lightness of being irrevocably fucked.

No, four thoughts. "Is this supposed to be a game?"

In unison—like a slithering ouroboros, darkness consuming light—the two figures laughed.

"Everything's a game if you play it right," the second figure said.

"But no, strictly speaking, this is no longer a game," said the first figure. "Now it's a war."

And then everything went dark.

TALES OF QLD

Hello, children. It's time for Death.

Oh, you didn't think I spoke? I do. I'm fantastically verbose, and transcendently literate, and quite frankly, I'm disappointed you would think otherwise. I've seen all the greats, you know, and learned from them—taken bits and pieces here and there—and everything that humanity has known, I have known, too. In fact, I'm responsible for most of history's adoration—nothing defines a career quite like an untimely visit from me. You'd think I'd be more widely beloved for my part in humanity's reverence, but again, you'd be mistaken. I'm rather an unpopular party guest.

Popularity aside, though, I have to confess that humanity's fixation with me is astonishing. Flattering, to be sure, but alarming, and relentless, and generally diabolical, and if it did not manifest so often in spectacular failure I would make more of an effort to combat it—but, as it is, people spend the duration of their time on earth trying to skirt me only to end up chasing me instead.

The funny thing is how simple it all actually is. Do you know what it really takes to make someone immortal? Rid them of fear. If they no longer fear pain, they no longer fear death, and before long they fear nothing, and in their minds they live eternal—but I'm told my philosophizing does little to ease the mind.

Not many who meet me are given the privilege to tell about it. There are some exceptions, of course, yourself included—though this is an anomaly. In general, as your kind would have it, there are two things a person can be: human (and thus, susceptible to the pitfalls of my profession), or deity (and thus, entirely a thorn in my side).

This is, however, not entirely accurate, as there are actually *three* things a person can be, as far as I'm concerned.

There are those I can take (the mortals);

Those I *can't* take (the immortals);

And those who cheat (everyone else).

Let me explain.

The job is fairly straightforward. In essence, I'm like a bike messenger without a bicycle. There's a time and a place for pickup and delivery, but the route I take to get there is deliciously up to me. (I suppose I *could* employ a bicycle if I wanted, and I certainly have in the past, but let's not dip our toes into the swampy details of my variants of execution quite yet, shall we?)

First of all, it is important to grasp that there is such a thing as to be not dead, but not alive; an in-between. (Requisite terminology takes countless incarnations, all of which may vary as widely from culture to culture as do colors of eyes and hair and skin, but the term *un*-dead seems to serve as an acceptable catchall.) These are the cheaters, the ones with shoddy timing, who cling to life so ferociously that I—by some sliver of an initial flaw that widens like the birth of the universe itself to a gaping, logic-defying chasm of supernatural mutation—simply commune with them. I exist beside them, but I can neither aid nor destroy them.

In truth, I find they often destroy themselves; but that story, like many others, is not the story at hand.

Before you say anything, I should be certain we're both clear that this is not a vanity project. Are we in agreement? This is not my story. This is *a* story, and a worthy one, but it doesn't belong to me.

For one thing, you should know that this all starts with another story entirely, and one that people tell about me. It's stupid (and quite frankly libelous), but it's important—so here it is, with as little disdain as I can manage.

Once upon a time, there was a couple in poor health, cursed

by poverty, who were fool enough to have a child. Now, knowing that neither husband nor wife had much time on earth left to
spare, and rather than simply enjoy it—whatever enjoyment is to
be taken from mortality, that is—I've never been totally clear on
the details—the husband took the baby from his ailing wife's arms
and began to travel the nearby path through the woods, searching
for someone who might care for his child.

A boy, by the way. A total snot of one, too, but we'll get to that
later.

After walking several miles, the man encountered an angel. He
thought at first to ask her to care for his child, but upon remembering that she, as a messenger of God, condoned the poverty with
which the poor man and his wife had been stricken, he ultimately
declined.

Then he encountered a reaper, a foot soldier of Lucifer, and considered it again, but found himself discouraged by the knowledge
that the devil might lead his son astray—

(—which he most certainly *would* have, by the way, and he'd
have laughed doing it. Frankly, I could go on at length about God,
too, but I won't, as it's quite rude to gossip.)

(Where was I?)

(Ah, yes.)

(Me.)

So then the man found me, or so the stories say. That's actually
not at all what happened, and it also makes it sound like I have the
sort of freedom with which to wander about *being* found, which I
don't have and don't appreciate. In reality, the situation was this:
The man was dying, so for obvious reasons and no paternal moti-
vations, there I was, unexpectedly burdened with a baby. They say
the man asked me to be the child's godfather; more accurately, he
gargled up some incoherent nonsense (dehydration, it's murder on
the vocal cords) and then, before I knew it, I was holding a baby,
and when I went to take it back home (as any responsible courier
would do), the mother had died, too.

Okay, again, I was there to take her, but let's not get caught up in semantics.

This is the story mortals tell about a man who was the godson of Death, who they say eventually learned my secrets and came to control me, and who still walks the earth today, eternally youthful, as he keeps Death close at his side, a golden lasso tied around my neck with which to prevent me, cunningly and valiantly, from taking ownership of his soul.

Which is *so* very rude, and I'm still deeply unhappy with Fox for not putting a stop to it ("Never complain, never explain" he chants to me in the voice of someone I presume to be the queen). Fond as I am of him, he does chronically suffer from a touch of motherfucker (a general loucheness, or rakery, if you will) so I suppose I'll just have all of eternity to deal with it.

And anyway, this is my *point,* isn't it? That this isn't my story— not at all, really.

It's Fox's story. I just happen to be the one who raised him.

Why did I name him Fox? Well, I'm slightly out of touch with popular culture, but I've always liked a good fairy tale, and out of all the things he might have been (like dutiful or attentive, or polite or principled or even the slightest bit punctual), like an idiot I merely wanted him to be clever. Foxes are clever, after all, and he had the tiniest nose; and so he was Fox, and just as clever as I'd hoped, though not nearly as industrious as I ought to have requested. He's spent the last two hundred years or so doing . . . Well, again, that's not my story, so I'll not go into detail, but suffice it to say Fox is . . .

Well, he's a mortal, put it that way. And not one I would recommend as a friend, or a counselor, or a lover, or basically anything of consequence unless you wish to rob a bank, or commit a heist.

I love him, but he's a right little shit, and unfortunately, this is the story of how he bested me.

The *real* story.

Unfortunately.